12-12-15

Annie Clark Cole

LEGEND OF

PANTHER HOLLER

A Masterful Tale of the Old West

To Janie & Becky
Great friends!

Annie Clark Cole

ISBN: 1516963180
ISBN 13: 9781516963188

Acknowledgement

S pecial thanks to:

James Carpenter Editor

Lori Mixson, Bea Rouse, Kathleen Rottweiller, Ralph Holliday, Rope Spinks (model for my book cover) John Castellanos, family and friends. Your experience and encouragement was greatly appreciated.

Forword

I have known Annie a number of years and never knew the lioness that lives within her until recently.

Those who know Annie describe her as a gentle and lovely person, but when she sits at her computer and delves into the world of the characters she has created, she takes on a determination and resiliency that's to be admired.

As she told me her idea for this story, her enthusiasm was infectious. She had a great idea...and a deep knowledge that her story was going somewhere. Her resolve that the story was going to be wonderful was unshakeable. My place in this project was to inspire and encourage and also be a sounding board for the angles, corners, twist and turns, of the story structure that were tumbling out of her on a daily basis. Step-by-step, they rapidly enriched and deepened her plot and saga.

Soon the encourager became the encouraged, the inspirer, became the inspired. I couldn't wait for those calls from Annie where she described a new twist, a new link in the chain, and a new strand in the web.

I watched her story bloom before my eyes. Annie had a passion and focus that was daunting to watch. And pretty soon she became a writer. You'll see..

I know you'll enjoy this book. It is a great ride.

John Castellanos
Actor/Producer/Writer

ACCLAIM

As a Director, I receive many books from Authors who would like to make their book a feature film. " Legend of Panther Holler" is at the top of my list for consideration. This book takes us on a journey throughout the old west. There are many twist and turns and just when you think you know where it's going, think again! Author Annie Cole has written what I believe to be one of the greatest novels I have read to date! Enjoy your experience as I have! Now.. "Let's Ride!!"

Tino Luciano
Executive Producer/Director
Law Dog Productions LLC

Designer and Photographer

I have worked with writer Annie Clark Cole, on a few feature film projects and got to know her. When she approached me to create the book cover of Legend of Panther Holler, I was thrilled. Finally the picture I had for her cover had become a reality.

I am always pleased to have full creative control of a project and this is what Annie gave me.

I will always be thankful to work with Annie who gave me the opportunity to work on a story so close to her heart.

SANJAY N. PATEL PHOTOGRAPHER.
TWELVE YEARS A SLAVE

Dedication

To my loving husband Jim Cole who has provided encouragement to me and made it possible to have time to write. His ideas, suggestions, sacrifice and love have been paramount in this process. Jim is my greatest supporter. For this I am very grateful.

About the Author

Annie Clark Cole and her husband Jim Cole live north of Houston, Texas. Jim, is a retired Military pilot, American Airlines Captain and FAA Training Center Program Manger.

Prior to discovering her love for writing, Annie had a successful career in wholesale/retail business. She was also a Flight Attendant with American Airlines, and the owner of a popular Antique and Gift Store in Montgomery, Texas called Simply Divine.

Annie has one daughter and Jim has two daughters living in the Houston and Austin, area. There are also 3 grandchildren and 3 great grandchildren.

The Cole's two poodles are a writer and pilot's greatest companions.

OTHER WORKS:

GHOST OF PANTHER HOLLER
Sequel to Legend of Panther Holler- COMING 2015

CAJUN FIRE
To be announced.

ANNIE CLARK COLE

Legend of
Panther Holler

Chapter 1

BEING WANTED FOR MURDER CAN MAKE YOU EDGY.

Being wanted for seven murders will really keep you on your toes. An outlaw wanted in Arkansas might be safe in West Texas, at least for a few days. Perhaps he could stay out of trouble long enough to find Buck Dupree, the Australian who had framed him for murder.

Vick Porter had been on the run for five years when he finally arrived in Odessa, Texas on a cold and windy morning in November of 1898. Stepping off the stagecoach with his saddle and saddlebags slung over his shoulder, a well-chewed cigar between his teeth, and his pearl handled six-shooter in full view, he drew plenty of unwanted attention.

The ruggedly handsome cowboy with a prominent scar hidden beneath a full beard, was approaching the age of twenty-five and stood a little over six feet. His black hair and blue eyes accentuated the intensity of his good looks. Walking into any saloon Vick carried himself with importance, often being mistaken for a Mississippi gambler. His swagger and air of sophistication, along with his confidence, caught the eye of the ladies. No one would guess he was a man on the run with a troubled past and whose days just might be numbered.

Vick was sure Buck would not recognize him since he had matured and grown about a foot taller. He imagined his former mentor would be remembering a young boy with a spider scar on his face rather than a grown man with a full beard concealing his identity.

His only hope to save his neck was to find Buck and force him to confess; to make him admit that he was lying when he accused him of killing that family at Panther Holler.

Vick had traveled to Odessa to find the scumbag sitting at a poker table. He imagined himself plopping down across from Buck, completely unrecognizable — baiting and working him, drawing out the game, then tightening the screws and ultimately closing the trap. He figured he'd put the squeeze on him near the end when he had almost all of Buck's money and had beaten him at his own game.

He'd play him like a fiddle, talking about "his little cabin" in the Arkansas woods. He could almost feel the moment when Buck began to realize who Vick was. In a flash Vick would shove his pistol in Buck's face and the lying bastard would either confess or eat a bullet, whichever came first. Vick found great comfort in his thoughts.

Odessa was a disappointment to him, in no way was it a thriving town like Buck had said. Vick laughed when it turned out to be nothing more than a few dusty buildings. The town was desolate and looked like any other dust bowl. There was virtually no landscape, just a flat, barren horizon that could hardly be compared to the beautiful green landscape of Arkansas.

He had just stepped down from the stagecoach onto a platform and stopped for a moment to light his cigar when a gust of West Texas wind hit him full in the face, blowing out the match. The stagecoach driver noticed Vick's hesitation.

"Mister, don't waste your time lightin' that thing," the jolly feller, laughed. You better hang on to your hat. Do you need directions to where you're goin'?"

"Directions? Ain't much here! Is it always this windy?" Vick queried.

"You're in the plains of West Texas son, just a bunch of dust, and wind storms brewing this time of the year and cold as hell. Anything west of Fort Worth, well, you're lookin' at it!"

Vick shuddered from the cold as he walked in the direction of town, looking for the Coldwater Saloon that Buck had talked about.

As he made his way he was hunched over and shivering, pushing himself through the cold as a few tumbleweeds rolled past. His lips were numb and his cheeks stung from the wind lashing against his face. "What could possibly be the lure that brought gamblers to this God forsaken place?" he wondered. "And what if Buck were nowhere to be found after making this long trip to this dusty hell of a town?" That was a disappointment he wouldn't allow himself to even consider.

When he finally reached the center of town, he found the saloon, bustling with activity. No surprise there. "What else would anyone do in this wasteland?" Vick smirked when he saw the jail directly across the street from the Coldwater.

"I guess the sheriff is not as stupid as I'd hoped," he muttered. Knowing exactly where the jail is located was always useful information, just in case he had to make a run for it.

He stood in front of the saloon looking up and down the street, seeing there were only three other buildings: a blacksmith shop, a mercantile and a boarding house. "Buck Dupree was nothing but a liar. he said under his breath. Thinking back over the time he'd spent with Buck, he wondered why he hadn't seen that from the beginning.

The saloon in Odessa was typical in every way, with a door hitting your head going in and your ass going out. As he entered the dark room from the bright light outside, Vick couldn't see much.

"Haven't seen you around these parts," said the bartender from somewhere in the murk as Vick found the bar.

"Don't reckon you have," Vick answered back. "How about a whiskey." As his eyes adjusted to the light, he took a quick look for exits. Sitting there waiting for his drink, Vick noticed some cowboys playing cards in the far corner. To his disappointment, Buck was not among them.

Before long, he was puffing on a cigar and sipping whiskey.

The bartender continued to study the stranger curiously. Finally he asked, "Mister, are you a poker player, or are you just here to drink?"

Buck always used to say, "The poker game begins the second you step into the saloon. You have to figure out what's going to make the dupes want to play cards with you. Should you act like the fool who will be an easy mark? Or should you play the arrogant upstart who needs to be taken down a peg? Or out? Or are you clever enough to play all three at once and let the chips fall where they may?"

Vick looked at the bartender like he resented the questions. "I'll let you know when I've made up my mind."

The bartender turned and went about his business, trying to determine if this stranger was trouble or just a man of few words. The exchange gave Vick exactly what he was after, as the men at the poker table were now staring at him.

Vick just made as though he was enjoying his whiskey, never letting on that he was surveying the room, considering his options. It was apparent to him that one of the poker players was the town bully because of his obnoxious loud voice and the spell he seemed to have over the other gamblers. One of the men called that man "Marlin." When the game was over, only Marlin remained at the card table, the others headed to the bar to drink away the sting of losing.

One of the losers looked Vick up and down. "Mister, did you just come in off the stagecoach?"

"Just passing through," Vick answered without looking at him.

The insolent Marlin Winfrey a rich rancher, finally joined the men and began to razz Vick. "Don't reckon you heard the man's question! He didn't ask you if you were passing through. He asked if you just came in off the stagecoach!"

Buck used to say with a big grin, "Poker is like fightin' a dog over a bone. The harder you pull, the harder he pulls back, and that's what makes it fun!"

Vick, cool as a cucumber, took a sip of his drink, and slowly turned to Marlin, looking him dead in the eye. "I ain't lookin for trouble. I see you won your poker game, and I congratulate you. But I'm here enjoying my drink, and if that offends you, I suggest you walk away."

"Kind of cocky, ain't you mister? So, why don't you finish your drink and get the hell out of here?" Marlin snarled.

Keeping his cool, remembering the jail was just across the street, Vick started to think of how satisfying it would be to take this blowhard down a peg or two.

"When's your next game?" Vick asked the bartender.

"We got one tomorrow night, but it's high stakes."

Vick turned back to Marlin, "Care to put your money where your mouth is, or are you just a lot of hot air?" he challenged.

Marlin's look could have killed, but he kept himself under control, when perhaps he had a chance to win some serious money. He noticed Vick's expensive saddlebags and assumed he might be wealthy. "I'm going to whip your ass one way or the other, so you better be here," Marlin gloated and gritted his teeth; a terrible habit he had that he was oblivious too. As he stared at Vick's profile, Vick was watching him in the bar mirror behind the bartender.

After finishing his drink, Vick picked up his saddle and bags, then started toward the swinging doors. Before he left, he turned and faced Marlin, "By the way, you never introduced yourself, but I did hear somebody call you Marlin. Well, Marlin, I want you to take a good look at my saddle bags here because the next time you see them walk out this door, they're gonna to be full of your money." He turned and was barely out the door as he said, "Just so you know."

Marlin's temper flared and he flung himself toward Vick, violently throwing off two men who tried to hold him back.

"Don't you ever touch me!" The other men gave way, and Marlin watched intently as the saloon doors swung back and forth.

After this encounter, he had three things on his mind: First, get a goodnight's sleep, next take Marlin's money and finally, hightail it out of town. To Vick, Marlin was a minor distraction. Once he'd fleeced the blowhard, he would get back to his real reason for coming to West Texas, and that was to find Buck Dupree.

Word got around that Marlin Winfrey was going head to head with an unknown gambler. What they didn't know was that Vick was already five steps ahead of Marlin in tonight's game, even though it had yet to begin. The locals also didn't know that Vick was one of the fastest guns around and had walked away from many a poker table after holstering a smoking pistol. Unlike Buck, however, Vick was basically honest, as con men go, except when he ran into men like Marlin. In those cases, it gave him great pleasure to take 'em down ... at the card table that is.

The next day, shortly after sundown, Vick headed back to the saloon. He wanted to get there early so he could get a good feel for the crowd and pick up a bit of extra cash. The bar was packed with boisterous cowboys who were all pretty loose from drinking. The room fell hushed when the tall lean cowboy walked in carrying his saddlebags.

One man standing at the bar yelled out, "I'm taking bets on the gambler, just step right over here."

A few men lined up to bet on Vick, but the majority was backing Marlin, mostly because they were afraid not to. They'd seen him destroy many a stranger in the past, but he was always far more vicious toward any local folk bold enough or stupid enough to cross him.

Vick stood at the bar, his foot on the brass footrest, his back to the poker parlor, appearing nonchalant while clandestinely watching the people through the mirror behind the bar. There was excitement in the air. The more they drank, the louder they became.

As Vick continued to study the room he heard a voice holler, "When are the painted ladies gonna be here?

"Tickets are five cents apiece if you want to dance." Cowboys immediately began crowding up to buy tickets from the bartender, producing money from hidden pockets, boots, hat liners and other secret personal hiding places.

As the clock struck seven, the piano player sat down and began pounding out familiar songs. As if on cue, all the balcony doors upstairs swung open and painted ladies, all dolled up in frilly dresses and colorful shoes, strutted into view. In single file, as though they'd rehearsed it a thousand times, they descended the stairs to the main floor. The men went wild, yelling, and waving their hats. The ladies threw kisses and swung their hips as they paraded onto the dance floor.

The cowboy's yelled, "Pop those can-cans!" and "Show us them stockings!"

One very innocent looking young cowpoke who clearly had never seen women like these before just stared, with his mouth agape, at a particularly worldly looking lady. "I got a dance saved for you cowboy," she said saucily as she went by. He looked like he was about to pass out as he watched her prance.

One flashy lady came up to Vick, "Win the jackpot honey, and I'm yours for the night. Mmmm, ya' got fine clothes on ... yeah, real fine," as she rubbed Vick's suit jacket. Vick thought she was probably the prettiest thing he'd ever seen, but dancehall girls were not his type.

The men really let loose when the fiddler joined the piano player. They whooped and hollered as they drank their whiskey and frolicked with the women. Vick remembered that this was what Buck liked, wild women and plenty of whiskey.

He took in the whole picture, learning people's names, where they were from, what they did, and tidbits about their families, as he listened to the rumblings of the crowd. Never spoke a word — just listened. One stout, woolly man talked about how his puritanical great aunt had kept a tight leash on him as a boy. Another mourned woefully about the recent death of a horse he'd had since childhood. Others talked about what they'd made, what they'd lost ... a sea of humanity, doing what humans do. Yes, this was the perfect place for Buck Dupree.

He noticed the sheriff step inside the door, look around for a moment and leave. Clearly he had heard of what was about to take place. Vick had no doubt he'd be back. "Well, at least now I know what he looks like," he mused. This gave him a huge advantage.

Some sheriffs liked to stand right in front of him while he played, hands on their hips just glaring at him. Others would stand way off in a corner or try to hide around the far end of the bar. Some would try to cover their badge to avoid recognition. But Vick could always tell a sheriff by that, "I'm gonna getcha" look in his eye. Dealing with local sheriffs was just part of the job. The trick was to stay one step ahead of them.

"Small town sheriffs are my specialty," Buck once said. "They always think they're in charge, blustering about like pantomime puppets. Frankly mate, I just find them funny." Vick would never forget how Buck would then lean in, look him straight in the eye, and say with great importance, "Remember this, mate: Never see the authorities … or your opponents, for that matter, as enemies. You've got to work the situation to make them your allies. In other words, find a way to make them work for you." Buck had then leaned back and gazed off with a faraway look in his eye before saying, "If the cat-and-mouse game with a local sheriff doesn't make your job more fun … then you're not doing it right."

Vick scanned the room periodically, but Marlin was nowhere to be seen. He wasn't surprised. Fellows like Marlin always wanted to make a big entrance with fanfare. Not that he was in a hurry. The longer Marlin wanted to draw this out, the more satisfying it would be for Vick when he took him down.

At eight o'clock, the men began clearing the dance floor to make room for the poker and Faro tables. Some men gathered at tables to drink, while a few couples headed upstairs for some intimate, but costly, entertainment. There was a mad rush for the few poker seats, and although Vick moved as quickly as he could, he didn't make it in time. Just as he'd reached the table, the rough scuffling concluded and the woolly man who had been near him at the bar took the last chair.

Still compressed in the tight crowd wanting to watch the game, Vick moved in, put his hand on the man's shoulder, leaned down and whispered into his ear. "Now, Walter, you know how Auntie Evelyn would feel about you 'shuffling the symbols and suits of the devil." The man's eyes went wide, the color instantly drained from his face. Vick took hold of the chair back edging closer, "Walk away young Walter; turn ye back and walk away!"

The woolly man grabbed his money and stumbled away from the chair as if he'd heard a ghost. Vick quickly slid into the seat and scooted the chair to the table as the cards were being dealt. Vick never saw Walter back away through the crowd, muttering, "I'm sorry Auntie. I'm sorry! How did she know? ... How did she know?" He looked around as if he was being watched then hurried toward the door, mumbling, "Turn ye back on sin boy, walk ye away."

Vick dumped the first three hands as he drank in every bit of information from his table mates. Buck had always coached, "A man at cards is an open book ... you just have to read him." He took a hand here and there, but made one of Buck's other rules of thumb his main objective: "In cards, you're always playing two separate games at once — One on the table and the one in the hearts and minds of your opponents, and you must be equally superior at both." Vick was a firm believer that, win or lose, every hand is a victory to the attentive man.

Great poker is a game of hunger, as Buck would say: "Feed the wolves, Vick, feed the wolves." Another of his sayings was, "A player who's winning hungers for more victory, and a player who's losing, hungers for his money back." Hunger's a weakness. Buck had taught him well on how to exploit it. "First you make him hungry, then you feed his hunger — until it's time to make him starve."

As is the case in most poker games, the players take turns dealing, moving in a clockwise direction. Vick made a point of losing the first two hands he dealt. The pots were big, but money was moving evenly around the table.

He helped feed the excitement until the pitch was ripe and blooming. About then, the crowd began to whisper. Vick didn't need to look up to know that Marlin had just arrived. Marlin looked right at Vick as if he already knew where he'd be sitting, then sauntered over to the Faro table. One cowboy made a point of stepping aside, as if making way for the "King." Marlin had dressed for the occasion, wearing a flashy winter jacket with his hair thickly oiled and slicked back. The hairdressing had a reddish tint to it, accentuating the part in his tonic-saturated hair.

Vick had been waiting for this moment. He calmly took two big hands in a row. They went so fast they were over before anyone took any real notice. Everyone except Marlin, that is. His eyes were on his Faro game but every fiber of his being was fixed on Vick's table. The players and onlookers moaned as Vick dragged the second large pot in and made a point of carefully stacking his bills and coins. The other players were staring at the substantial pile of cash in front of Vick, comparing his pile to the suddenly puny ones in front of each of the rest of them.

Marlin appeared, standing over the table looking down on Vick in particular. "Why don't you rustlers step over to the Faro table and play a real man's game. That is, if you know how."

Vick knew exactly what Marlin was doing. He saw that Vick had started a good run and wanted to kill it. He smiled kindly at Marlin, then addressed his fellow players, "Boys, as you can see, this fine gentleman and I have an appointment, so I only have time for one more hand."

"We done lost most of our money, you gotta' give us a chance to win it back," said one of the men.

"And sir, that's exactly what I'm going to do, if each of you will agree to go all in." Vick slid his entire pot into the center of the table, as the room suddenly fell silent. … "then so will I."

Marlin's face was like stone. He wasn't about to let Vick know what he was thinking. But he already did. Vick knew what everyone was thinking. There was over one thousand dollars in the center of the table, and not one of the other players had more than a hundred bucks in front of him. Anyone who passed up those odds was a fool. Each player readily agreed, sliding every dime they had into the center.

Oh, could Vick smell the hunger! But he knew exactly what he was doing. This was a crazy, stupid bet, risking over a thousand dollars to win just a few hundred. But the way he saw it, he couldn't lose.

Whether he won or lost the pot, Marlin would see Vick as a careless, reckless fool. But more specifically, if he lost the pot, Marlin would feel that his own presence had intimidated Vick into making an arrogant bet like that. This would make him feel even cockier than he already was. After all, everyone loves playing poker with an idiot. But if Vick won the hand, Marlin would see him as an even bigger threat to his exalted position in town. If Marlin felt challenged, he would become even more bitterly competitive. Finally, if all the men in the room congratulated Vick for his boldness, that would make Marlin even more livid. Vick knew just how to make each of these outcomes work in his favor.

Marlin didn't miss the fact that it was now Vick's turn to deal. A man who attempts to deal from the bottom while every eye in the house is watching has nerves of steel. Any man who can do it without being detected, has got you by the throat.

Vick never took his eyes off Marlin as he deftly, masterfully, slid the cards out to the other players. But Marlin never took his eyes off Vick's hands. That is, until he was dealing the last round of cards when he smiled broadly at Marlin and said, "I'm feeling lucky, Marlin."

Just for an instant, Marlin's eyes snapped to Vicks. Every other eye around the table darted to Marlin to see his reaction. By the time Marlin looked back, the cards were all dealt.

The room was deathly silent as the hand played out. Finally after all the other players had turned over their cards, Vick slowly turned over a "hand of many colors." When the room saw his hand of all face cards, they burst into cheers and applause. Vick reached out with both hands and scooped in all the money.

"So, Marlin. How about some Faro?" Vick asked, smiling broadly.

Red faced, Marlin watched Vick gather his winnings, then sat at the Faro table with a thud. Marlin had no choice but to act as though he was unaffected by the events and try to appear cheerful. The crowd moved to gather around the Faro table now. Most offered encouraging words to Marlin, many of those with empty pockets.

It was time for him to have a little fun out of Marlin, Vick thought. Since he was bragging about how well seasoned he was as a gambler, now was the time for him to be duped. Knowing that Faro had two other names that the novice gambler would probably not know, Vick decided to take a chance and see if Marlin knew as much as he thought he did.

"Marlin, if you'd rather play another game, perhaps we could play 'Twisting the Tiger's Tail' or perhaps 'Bucking the Tiger.'"

Exasperated, Marlin barked, "I think we should stick to Faro."

Vick was laughing inside, seeing Marlin never showed a sign of knowing the two games he suggested were just slang names for Faro.

This game of Marlin's was a slightly different version, since Vick and Marlin were squaring off head to head. It was determined that whoever won the most of their bets would win the accumulated losses of each opponent, which could end up being a hefty pot.

"Take him down, Marlin!" voices rang out from the crowd.

"I'd rather you have my money than him, sir," someone jeered.

Vick acted unsure of himself. "I ain't played Faro that much, but I'm not about to walk away from a challenge. It's been a long time since I've tried."

"What's the matter, you need a little brush up?" Marlin chided.

Vick pretended to study the board. "Oh yes, now that I see the 13 Spades, I remember. I just place my bet beside the cards.

"That's right! And you can place as many bets as you want, right by each one of the Spades. After he had explained the game he smirked convinced that he was about to empty Vick's saddlebags.

Marlin gritted his teeth as he waited for Vick to answer, the most annoying habit Vick had ever heard.

"Yeah, yeah. I think I've got it now. It's like roulette, but instead of betting on numbers you can bet on any of the 13 Spades," Vick said.

A voice rang out from the crowd, "Marlin, for goodness sakes, if the man knows how to play roulette he dang sure oughta' know how to play Faro." Everyone applauded. "Yeah, get on with it," someone else shouted.

Although Marlin was sure he had the game in the bag he had beads of sweat pouring off his forehead. Vick, the apparent under-dog, was cool as he could be. Now, he was certain that the Faro game was rigged in Marlin's favor. Vick was making bad bets intending to lose, feeding the hunger in his opponent. He could see Marlin feeling more and more arrogant as he continued winning.

When the Dealer got to the last three cards, he made an announcement. "All right men, we have only three cards left, so place your bets." Marlin was quiet knowing that after this last bet he would be the winner of the pot.

Vick could see how eager his greedy opponent was to end the game but not before he proposed his one last bet.

"Marlin, since you're ahead, how about us making it a little more interesting."

"Marlin gloated. And what would that be, when it appears you've had the most losses?"

"Well then, since I'm down, how about one last bet?"

"Sure, I'll take your money," Marlin said, with a smug confidence covering his face.

"Winner takes all if I can guess the last three cards the Dealer is holding," Vick announced loud for all to hear.

"You must be crazy! Nobody makes a bet like that! Now, let me get this right: Are you just guessing the last three cards or are you betting that you can name the three cards in sequence as the Dealer deals them?"

A hush came over the crowd as they strained to hear the conversation.

"No, Marlin, I'm betting winner take all that I can name the last three cards the Dealer has in his hand ... Here's my two hundred and all you have to do is match it and we have a bet.

"You're stupid to make a bet like that." His eyes were darting back and forth from Vick to the money, which was a sizable pot. Marlin studied him more closely and felt sure he was not being hustled.

Vick continued to prod him. "If you're afraid to bet, I'll understand."

Marlin looked around the room as the onlookers nodded their heads, urging him to go for it. He hesitated and studied Vick's face intently. This would give him a chance to win a couple hundred bucks, plus the pot, a substantial win for Odessa, Texas. The crowd's urging helped him to finally yell, "You got a bet!" Everyone knew that Marlin was a wealthy rancher and had the money to go along with such a rich bet.

Marlin pushed in all of his money in and matched Vicks. The cheers were deafening.

Card counters like Vick could make a killing against gamblers like Marlin who thought they were far better than what they were.

"Okay cowboy, I don't have all night," Marlin said in a loud voice, glancing around the room to make sure everyone was going to witness his victory. The saloon was the quietest it had been all night, heads straining to see the Faro table.

Vick leaned forward in his chair with a studied look on his face and stared Marlin square in the eyes and said, "The Dealer is holding the 10 of Diamonds, the 4 of Clubs and the Jack of Hearts!"

The Dealer's expression did not change as he heard Marlin say, "What a sucker."

Most of the men had started in support of Marlin, but now, sentiments had shifted a bit, many side bets going on. They wanted to see if the bold stranger could pull this off. Even the painted ladies seemed spellbound. The Dealer was very deliberate when he laid the first card down. It was the 4 of Clubs.

Marlin almost jerked a crick in his neck, gritting his teeth and a "Oooooh" went through the crowd. He looked at Vick with raging intensity, the blood draining from his face. The Dealer quickly laid down the 10 of Diamonds, followed by the predicted Jack of Hearts.

Without warning, Marlin threw the table over on its side, sending money and cards flying everywhere. The women and cowboys alike were diving for the money, scrambling furiously at Marlin and Vick's feet.

Some men ran for the door with handfuls of cash, while others backed away to take cover, as if they knew what was coming next.

Before the table had even landed, Marlin's gun was drawn and pointed at Vick. "You ... you no better than a horse thief."

"No one twisted your arm! You placed your bet, you took a chance and you lost," Vick's voice was calm and rational.

"I'd rather see you rot than take my money," Marlin shouted.

Despite the ominous rhetoric, those on their hands and knees furiously continued grabbing for cash, oblivious to the threat of gunfire over their heads.

Vick knew there was likely going to be trouble, but this wasn't what he expected. "Turning over the table after losing all your money was a pretty good ploy," he thought. "After all, what have you got to lose?" It did give Marlin a chance to get the drop on him.

Vick was impressed. "Well played," he thought. But he could see the desperation in Marlin's face, and knew this man was ready to kill him.

When Marlin cocked his gun, Vick dove sideways to the floor and drew his pistol. Marlin fired, his bullet hitting the floor. Vick was too fast for him. Instinctively, Marlin tried to turn away from the line of fire, but caught a bullet in his side, almost in his back. The bartender ducked behind the bar, peering out only after Marlin was down on the floor.

The sheriff, heard the gunfire and ran across the street to the saloon, his gun drawn. The crowd parted to let him through. He checked Marlin but there was no sign of life. Marlin's eyes were wide open in a shocked expression, blood began running from the corner of his mouth. The sheriff looked at the entrance wound, closed Marlin's eyes, and pronounced him dead. He turned to the bartender, asking, "Did you see who shot first?"

The bartender was badly shaken, hardly able to speak. "Everyone scattered as soon as Marlin turned over the table, and money went flying everywhere. I heard Marlin hollerin' and then I heard gunfire. That's all I know,"

The sheriff asked the crowd, "Any of you see who shot first?" But, they acted like they hadn't seen a thing or even heard the sheriff's question.

"With no witnesses, and the way the bullet went in, it appears you shot Marlin in the back," the sheriff said.

"I didn't shoot him in the back!" Vick protested. "He had his gun on me, and he went to cock the hammer. Everybody in here heard him say he was gonna kill me!" Vick looked around, pleading with his eyes for someone to tell what had happened. "They're just not admitting it!"

The sheriff shook his head, "I'm gonna have to take you in before they start talking about lynching. The Circuit Judge will decide your fate. You know, Marlin was a hometown boy who grew up here. Gimme' your gun, son." Vick turned over his weapon without another word and the sheriff led him the short distance to the jail.

Chapter 2

Waiting for first light, Vick tossed and turned while lying in his jail cell, wondering how shooting Marlin in self-defense was going to play out. It was cold with nothing to cover him but a blanket. This was a first for him. He marveled after all this time of being a wanted man, that he had never spent a full night in jail. He hated being locked up. It reminded him of his childhood and the abuses he and his little brother suffered.

"Jail's a pretty safe place when you've just killed a man," he tried to rationalize. "Except for those that want to avenge my death. The man was mean as a snake but Marlin was also a powerful local man." But it wasn't so much that, but something else that made him feel oddly unsettled, something that he couldn't quite put his finger on.

Was it just that he was now finally in some serious trouble? After all, he'd just shot a man, seemingly, in the back. "This is going to be tough to beat without witnesses to step forward and tell the truth: That Marlin shot first, and he was only defending himself, that everyone was stampeding for the spilled cash."

After wrestling with his predicament, he finally drifted off to sleep.

Vick immediately had several short dreams, just images really, that woke him. He fell asleep again and the images returned and expanded. Soon he was dreaming of times when he and his brother were young boys living at home with their Pa in Arkansas. He dreamt of how he had convinced his brother, Sam, to run away to escape what he thought was their apparent doom.

The boys had been constant companions due to the brutality of their youth that caused them to form an inseparable bond of "my brother's keeper." They were so tight that they could feel each other's pain, and knew exactly what each was thinking. Bonds like that never go away, no matter what.

Shortly after Sam died, he dreamed about his brother coming to visit him. In these dreams he was never able to express how he missed him and how sorry he was that he couldn't protect him.

He would wake up, drift off, and then begin dreaming again, when suddenly he was caught up in an apparition of sorts that had often appeared to him as a young boy: The scene of his Pa punishing Sam. Vick was frightened, but as he dreamed the image of Buck appeared, watching him struggle with the mountain man who cut his face. He again felt the pain of the knife. He saw the image of Buck laughing at him, gloating in an effort to punish Vick for reasons he did not understand.

As the dreams continued, they became more surreal. He was carried down a very dark road that led him to a mirror with distorted images. He was frightened as he stood before the reflections until they became more focused. It was Mattie, reaching out to him, trying to tell him something, and he knew she was in trouble.

As her image diminished, it was replaced by another woman's face. She was beautiful but very angry. "Who was this woman?" he wondered.

When Vick awoke, he was unnerved by the dream. It was so vivid, and he thought it was a sign that Mattie needed him. Confused by the dream, he kept asking himself, "Who was the other woman?"

The more he thought, the more he felt it was Elizabeth Barkin, the daughter of the man who killed himself after Vick won their family fortune in a card game.

That night, those worries mixed with his thoughts about his brother Sam and his own questionable future continued to haunt his dreams.

Chapter 3

BEING LOCKED UP BROUGHT BACK THE DISTURBING MEMORIES OF **when Vick's Pa abused him and his brother Sam.** Those were some bad times, but despite the years of abuse, there was one person who tried to save them: an Indian boy named Hawk. "Where is Hawk now, when I need him?" he whispered in his despair.

He remembered his Indian friend saying he had been summoned by the Great Spirit to free them from their bondage, and he believed him.

Vick's Pa, Percy Porter, was a hopeless alcoholic, leaving his boys home alone, attached to a twenty foot rope, while he drank and played card games all day in the local saloon. Vick and Sam thought being tied onto the end of a rope was normal, since they were very young and had no other friends to learn otherwise.

Their Pa justified his actions by convincing himself, and them, that he did not want them running away while he was in town, or even on those rare occasions when he was lucky enough to find work or work found him. Most nights, in the wee hours of the morning Percy would arrive home, stumbling drunk, to find his boys huddled together sleeping on a dirty old blanket in the exact spot he left them that morning. He'd stand gazing down on them with a sense of contentment. Comforting as it was for him, it was also tinged with a foreboding he didn't quite understand. As for the boys, they would fade off into a daze of boredom almost every night. Other times, they would cry themselves to sleep with mouths of dirt-caked drool and mud on their cheeks, defined by the tracks of their tears. This didn't seem to bother Percy, because as long as he had his boys that was all that mattered. If you don't tie down what's yours, it will run away, Percy had learned — like his mother had, then his Pa a year later and the death of his wife when Sam was born.

Over the years, all that pain, from sense of loss and self-loathing was washed away by whiskey. This was one of the great lessons of his life: whiskey and a good rope can solve just about anything. Seemingly, all of his "great revelations" came from the bottom of a whiskey bottle.

Percy never had much money, just the little bit he could steal, finagle, or eke out when he did work. What he made gave him just enough for his pleasures, with very little left for food and clothing for his two children. So it was ropes, sorrow, pain, and the lacking of life's essentials, both physical and emotional, that taught Vick to fend for himself while watching out for little Sam.

Whenever the boys fought, they were locked away for however long it took Percy to sober up, so they were careful not to argue in front of their Pa. If he thought one of the boys had misbehaved, he would whip them both mercilessly with a strap.

A bond of partnership formed between the boys, as well as a strong sense of teamwork. Spawned as mere self-preservation, it quickly grew into their greatest comfort. Thus, the brothers learned to coexist, and found ways to entertain themselves, playing marbles and other games they created to pass the time.

Vick was ten years old when a young Sioux Indian boy, Chaytan, happened upon their cabin. It wasn't long before he announced his real name was "Hawk!" Proud and arrogant, he believed his fierce spirit made him master of his world.

When he saw the boys tied up, he thought it was cruel punishment and quickly freed them — imagining himself a large hawk that was their protector.

Once freed to play, Vick imagined that he, too, was a wise bird with special powers to fly far away with Sam. Each day, as Percy was on his way to town, the young Indian would come to free them, and seeing how thin they were, he brought food from his village.

One day, Hawk surprised them with spears and then led them to a place where they could run and swing on vines, something they had never done before.

The boys listened intently, while Hawk showed them there were edible berries and roots all around the woods and then pointed out the ones they should never eat. At first they were concerned they had drifted so far away from home, but their adventures were too tempting.

"What about Pa? Will he be mad?" Sam would sometimes ask.

"Don't worry, Sammy, we'll hide our spears under the house, before he get's home."

"You promise? 'Cause I don't want him mad at us."

Soon, their worries were forgotten, and they ran like little warriors through the woods, throwing their spears, having the time of their lives. Even when Sam struggled, he was determined to keep up with Vick and Hawk.

～

Vick's fitful dreams that night were full of thoughts of his young Indian friend who had saved him and Sam from many miserable days. The memory of the day he had saved Hawk's life played through his mind.

It was a perfect day, with bright sunshine and clear blue sky, near perfect weather. They were exploring areas of the woods that they had never ventured into before and took turns swinging on vines across the stream, from one dirt mound to another.

The day before, Hawk had taken a small pistol his Pa had given him out of his bag and showed Vick and Sam how to cock it and spent some time showing Vick how to shoot safely. Vick was fascinated and loved this new experience.

On one such day, Vick asked to carry the pistol. Hawk gave him the gun as they headed upstream into a more densely wooded area, hoping to find bigger streams, climbing trees and vines to swing on.

Soon they came to a small waterfall that looked enticing. They were about to undress for a swim when a panther suddenly appeared from the woods. The animal crept slowly toward them, stalking; the sound of his breathing a deep, raspy roar.

The brothers froze, but Hawk felt it was important that he showed how brave he was. He lifted his spear and began charging the big cat. With the speed of lightning, the panther swatted Hawk with his paw, sending him sailing over a ledge. As he was falling, he grabbed a small bush protruding from the hill. Hawk looked down at the rocks below and held on with all his might.

Frustrated at having lost a meal, the monstrous cat turned his attention toward Vick and Sam. Vick feared the limb would not hold Hawk very long. As the hungry predator leapt toward him, Vick drew the gun with such ease that it seemed natural in his hand — a hand that was destined for legendary prowess. Without hesitation he had drawn the gun, cocked it, aimed and fired, wounding the cat in the shoulder. Vick watched the animal fall, then get up and limp into the woods.

When Vick ran to help Hawk, he saw the roots of the bush loosening from the hill. Vick reached for his hand before Hawk fell to certain death.

"Hawk! Take my hand — don't look down."

With adrenalin kicking in, Vick bent down grabbing his hand and hoisted him to safety with a single swoop. Laying him flat on the ground, he could see that his young friend's chest was badly clawed. Vick tore off part of Hawk's shirt and wrapped around his wounds to stop the bleeding.

Although in pain, Hawk noticed the fierce determination and tender concern in Vick's eyes as he worked to tend his wounds. This is when Hawk realized he was in the presence of a great warrior.

"You shot the panther and saved my life," the young Indian whispered. "Now, as my friend, I will watch over you and be your protector all your days!"

While Vick appreciated Hawk's wanting to protect him in the future, he felt that if he didn't get him home soon, he might not live long enough to protect anyone.

"You're going to be all right, but we've got to get you home. You're bleeding a lot." Vick looked at Sam, who was still frightened and practically in a state of shock. "Sammy, you're going to have to help me get Hawk back to the village."

"Okay, but I ain't strong like you."

Working together, as they had become accustomed to doing, Vick and Sam struggled to get Hawk to his feet and back to the village. When the boys arrived, Hawk's mother immediately set about cleaning and dressing her son's injuries. When he was strong enough to talk, Hawk told his parents what had happened, how Vick had saved his life. The entire village was amazed at the young boy's bravery.

Hawk's father took a beautifully beaded knife and sheath from his side and ceremoniously presented it to Vick. He then turned to Sam and, taking a bear tooth strung on a length of leather from his neck, handed it to Sam. The boys were amazed at these gifts honoring them as brave warriors. The boys rushed home, beaming and chattering about the day, proud of their gifts.

They searched until they found a wooden box to hide the gifts under the house, fearing their Pa would take them away. They then rushed to tie each other up. Fortunately, Percy was too drunk to realize that they weren't tied up very well.

~

Vick lay in his cell thinking of the promise Hawk made to him when they were kids. The thought came to him again: "Where are you Hawk, when I need you?"

He recalled how thankful the Indian tribe was for Vick's actions and thought, "If it wasn't for Hawk and his family, I don't know how me and Sam could have survived those years."

The Indians were industrious people, helping each other, working hard and growing their own crops. They shared their food to help a family they saw in need.

Percy never figured out why the Indians started coming around with gifts. He would find they would leave baskets they had woven filled with food and sometimes handmade blankets for the boys to keep warm. He wasn't interested in having them around so naturally, he resented their charity. "Tell them damn Indians to stay off my property, you hear?" He had no idea how indebted they were to Vick. If his mother had lived he felt sure things would have been different.

When Vick began to mature he became frustrated, hearing how his Pa hated his Indian friends who did more for him and Sam than Percy had ever done. Nothing his Pa could do would stop the good will of the Indian people. The more the old man ranted at them when he would see them coming or going, the more they did for Vick and Sam after Percy was gone.

They knew the kids father was a drunk and sensed he was a bit crazy, so they just ignored all of his rants and mocked him in private. Percy would mutter, "Gonna kill me some Injuns." At least he had refocused his anger toward them instead of his sons for a while.

After a few years the Indian village moved for some unknown reason. When Hawk unexpectedly came by one morning to tell the boys goodbye, he really didn't have an answer about why. He said that they moved whenever the Elders felt it was time. Vick thought it was because they had become uneasy with how much Percy hated them, and that the Elders thought they should leave before things got out of hand. Both Vick and Sam were devastated to see Hawk leave without a trace. They were convinced that he was, indeed, their great protector!

Meanwhile, Percy's rage continued until Vick was almost four-teen. He could see Vick maturing and his resentment was out of control. He wasn't that concerned with Sam, since he was a couple years younger, an small for his age. But, Vick was showing signs of being strong and rebellious. Percy watched the tension building in his eldest son and decided to ease up on him. Even though Percy freed the boys from their restraint, the resentment was there.

Even so, they knew their Pa, and were wise to never provoke him. The boys were given chores to do during the day. They had to chop wood, haul water, and most importantly, they learned to hunt.

Back when they were younger, Vick had realized that they could crawl under the porch to get out of the heat. Sam was wary because it was dark. He couldn't see what was under there, but Vick enjoyed the adventure of it, the thrill of the unknown. Vick would crawl under first, and feel ahead in the blackness as he went. The first day he tried it, he patted his way deep into the darkness and his hand landed on a large snake. It tried to scurry away, but Vick kept a grip as he dragged it out into the light.

He killed it, skinned it, and cooked it without batting an eye. Sam was amazed and impressed by what his big brother had done. That fearless feat gave Vick a sense of accomplishment.

The next day, Vick got Percy's old rifle and told Sam he was going to shoot them some supper. He remembered the excitement of shooting the big panther when he had saved Hawk.

He loved to lure his prey up to the house, but his aim had to be nearly perfect to drop an animal in its tracks and kill it within their boundary. Sam threw out corn, some pinecones, and a few fresh vegetables right in front of their house since they were forbidden to stray from their yard. The boys would then hide around the side of the porch, waiting for their unsuspecting prey.

"Sammy, it's real important that you don't make a sound. You can't even move, alright?" Vick whispered.

Sam thought for a moment, and then whispered back. "I'm not very good at that."

"Well you have to get good at it right now!" Vick hissed.

Sam considered all his options, and then whispered as softly as he could. "Can I whisper?"

"No!" Vick shot back. "Well how come you get to whisper and I don't?" Sam whispered as loud as possible.

"Shhhh!"

They lost quite a few kills, thanks to Sam's boredom and at times, excitement. In fact, it took three days for him to learn to be still and just about as long for Vick to gain patience, control his frustration, and to perfect his aim.

Vick didn't know it then, but these three days gave him some of the most valuable lessons of his life.

On the third day, just after dark, the boys had squirrel for supper. Rabbit, squirrel and deer gradually followed in the months to come. Vick proudly used his Indian knife to dress his kill.

The brothers never went to school, and had very little knowledge of the outside world. Their only excitement was going to town with their Pa to purchase feed for their meager livestock. Percy took them so they could carry the heavy feedbags and spare his back. They didn't mind the heavy lifting, since this was the only time they were permitted to leave the house.

On one such day his Pa pointed out Mr. Thomas Barkin and his little girl. Percy told the boys that the girl was Mr. Barkin's daughter and he was the richest man in town. While the boys were loading the wagon the man and his daughter passed by the boys. Vick looked at the girl and she smiled at him. This was the first time he had seen a girl smile at him. He had no idea of why he had such feelings but her smile excited him. Her father quickly pulled her arm as if to warn her that she was better than them.

"That's old man Barkin," Percy said. "He thinks he's better than the town folk cause he's got money."

"Pa, do we got money?" Sam asked. That earned him a quick cuff to his head, and a sharp word.

"No, boy— we what ya call po' folks."

But, something about riding into town had started a fire inside Vick — a yearning for something more, for some kind of adventure. They had explored the immediate surroundings with Hawk, but now that he was gone, Vick wanted to see even more of the world and what it might be like free from his Pa's clutches.

He decided it was time to stand up to and voice his opinion about how Sam was treated. When Percy came stumbling up to the cabin that night with a half empty jug, Vick spoke up. He knew immediately by the look on his Pa's face that he had greatly misjudged his reaction to his outburst.

Sensing the best way to keep Vick controlled, his Pa took it out on Sam, beating him mercilessly, and telling Sam that from now on he would be responsible to make sure his brother never back-talked — if Vick ever did that again, they would both pay the price.

Despite his Pa's cruelty to Sam, Vick wished for a better life for him and his brother, plotting to run away. The more he thought about it, the more enticing it became to finally be free. He didn't even stop to think about what difficulties he and his brother might face in the outside world, a world that he was sure couldn't be as unfair and evil as their Pa's. And even if it was, he was willing to meet with any danger as long as it was away from home!

He finally got up enough courage to leave when Percy came home drunk and began slapping them around for no reason. For the first time, Vick tried to stand up for his younger brother. He was tired of seeing him beaten when there was no call for it.

"So ya think there ain't no reason?" Percy bellowed, "Alright, you just gave me a reason! Now I'm gonna beat him because of your mouth! And I'm gonna give him the beating of his life!"

And he did. Percy struck Sam harder than he ever had before. He would stop occasionally, dripping in sweat and panting for breath. He would ask Vick, "Did you want to say something else?" He'd wait for an answer but Vick would only shake his head "no." Percy would continue his beating, then stop again and ask, "Are you sure?" Vick would lower his head and slowly shake it "no" again. The only thing that kept Vick from attacking his Pa to stop the beating was the fear that he wasn't strong enough, and Sam would be beaten even worse.

Percy was so drunk and out of breath, he could barely stand. When Sam finally fell unconscious, Percy, now exhausted and wheezing, used that as an excuse to quit. He left Sam where he lay, then stumbled into the house, passing out on his bed.

Vick quickly and gently gathered up the limp and battered Sam and carried him around to the side of the house, as far as his 20 feet of rope would allow since his Pa had restrained them again. He lay Sam across his lap and held him with both arms. Sam's breathing was fitful and erratic. Vick never took his eyes off his little brother. He watched every breath, as if witnessing each one would ensure the next. A couple times Sam would begin to jerk and whimper as if warding off an imaginary attacker in his dream. Vick would just hold him tighter and whisper to him until the flailing subsided. "It's all right Sammy, it's all right. It's over now. It's all over."

Not for a second did Vick feel like sleeping, and that was the night he finally decided that they would run away.

The next morning Percy stumbled onto the front porch in a familiar daze. His eyes went immediately to the porch posts that secured the boys' ropes. Then, like every other morning of his life, he followed the rope to his sons. When he saw Sam, now barely conscious, glassy-eyed, swollen and bruised, he asked, "What happened to him?"

Vick never looked up. He knew better than to answer.

Slowly, sparks of memory flickered though Percy's mind. His face showed just a hint of shock and horror — but just a hint. There was no way he'd show any sign of remorse. Quick as a flash, he buried the images in that special corner of his mind, like he had done so many mornings of his life. He walked away.

"Do your chores," was all he could manage in a lost, hollow tone. Soon he was gone on down the road. Percy drank all that day. He drank with a vengeance. When he stumbled back to the cabin just before dawn, he was drunker than Vick had ever seen him.

It took almost two weeks for Sammy to recover, and Percy was hardly sober the entire time. He hadn't spoken a word to the boys since Sam's beating, and refused to even look at them. Sammy didn't say much for those two weeks. He was different now, more aware, more focused. Vick was glad about that, actually. He knew that would work in their favor in the future.

One night, as they were getting ready for bed, Sam stared into his brother's eyes and said, "I don't want to live here — anymore." Sam didn't even hear himself say those words. But Vick knew it meant that it was time to put his plan in motion.

Chapter 4

V<small>ICK LAY AWAKE THINKING OF THE NIGHT HE AND</small> S<small>AM HAD RUN AWAY</small>
from home and how their lives were changed.

The night before the boys left, Percy had virtually crawled into the house, and Vick had to help him get to bed.

"You're a good boy … a good boy," Percy mumbled just before he passed out. Vick stood over him and stared in wonder. How ironic that tonight he finally heard the first and only kind words from his Pa.

It was the perfect night, he thought. Percy had passed out drunk, the whiskey jug was placed next to his Pa's bed so that as soon as he awoke, he'd drink some more. All Vick had to do was to wake Sam and run.

Vick lay awake on the floor next to his Pa and waited. As expected, Percy stirred awake, fumbled for his jug and drained it dry. In seconds he was out again.

Vick nudged Sam awake. "Sammy, wake up; we got to go," he whispered.

"Where we going?" he asked, still half asleep.

"Shhhhh, we got to be real quiet. Follow me."

After the boys dressed, Vick slipped out of the house with his brother, his plan was to never see his Pa again. The boys left with no food and only the clothing on their backs. They didn't dare take anything. They knew how Percy felt about his possessions.

As they ran into the night they were suddenly wide-awake. It was exhilarating, knowing they were free to wander wherever they wanted and without their Pa breathing down their neck. No more punishment by a drunk who did not care a thing about them. It was a warm humid night and their excitement was overwhelming with suspense of not knowing or caring where they were going.

Occasionally, they would feel a damp coolness that would later form the early morning dew. Every strange sound and sensation from the night was intense to these brothers who had experienced so little of life. They ran and skipped until their feet began to hurt from pounding against the hard dirt. But they kept going; knowing that unimaginable wonders were probably just ahead; glad to be leaving this place behind.

They stopped short when they heard the haunting whistle of a distant train. Vick didn't know why, but a sad eerie feeling came over him, a longing to be riding the rails and be carried miles away. He started in the direction of the train but decided it was too far to walk and there was no trail in that direction.

Eventually they began to tire, and settled into a very slow walking pace. Now they could hear the strange, creepy sounds of the night. They heard small animals rushing through the brush and owls' mating calls. Sam would grab Vick's arm or the tail of his shirt for security. Vick tried to comfort him. "It's just owls and squirrels."

"But it's not our owls and squirrels!" Sam said.

That's when it fully sunk in that they actually were in a whole different world — a world they had no knowledge of whatsoever. Everything from this day forward was going to be wildly new.

When they made it to the nearest town, uncertainty set in with a thud. They wondered if they should never have run away. After all, where were they going? And what would they do when they got there? But more importantly, how would they live? That was something neither had thought much about, and now found themselves contemplating if they should go back home before their hotheaded Pa sobered up completely and found them gone.

As hunger set in, even the thought of punishment didn't seem so bad. The horrible life at home almost seemed a comfort up against the utter unknown. After all, home was all they knew. And now they belonged nowhere. They had nothing and had no place to go.

Sam was slowing down and looking scared; Vick knew both of them needed to have something to eat.

He began to think how difficult it would be to take on the responsibility of his brother. Sammy was so young and depended on him for everything. And, he thought again that the idea of running away was not such a good idea at all. He blamed himself for making a stupid decision.

"What was done, was done," he thought, and now, he decided, it was up to him to figure their way out of this dilemma and get back home. What a whippin' they would both get if their Pa learned they had left.

It wasn't light yet and the town was deadly quiet as they walked down the main street looking for food but unable to find any. They didn't dare stay till daylight for fear of attracting attention, so, against Sam's famished objections, they passed through the town and headed back toward their home, determined to get back before Percy awoke, which should be possible, since he always slept late.

Soon after heading out of town, Vick could see a man in a wagon in the distance behind them. Vick pulled Sam to the side of the road behind some brush and told him he had an idea. They hid until the wagon passed, and then followed it.

Vick was sure they were going back in the direction of their home. Sam's eyes went wide when Vick insisted that they catch up to the wagon and hop on the back. He was shaking with fright, sure that they would be seen — not to mention his fear of when they would get home. Vick encouraged him, "You can do it Sammy! But you have to be real quiet, just like when we're hunting."

That's something Sam understood. He didn't want to disappoint his big brother. Now more than ever before, his whole life depended on Vick. Sam grabbed Vick's hand as they raced up behind the wagon. They quietly jumped onto the back of the slow moving wagon and stowed themselves in between two big crates where they couldn't be seen. The plan was to jump off as they got near the trail that led back home.

Vick assured Sam they would be home before their Pa woke up, hoping against hope that he was right.

The tired boys quietly stretched out between the crates to rest until the time was right to jump off the wagon. As the wagon moved down the road, the gentle swaying put both of them into a deep sleep. When Vick and Sam awoke, they were still wedged between the crates.

Not only had they slept through sunrise, but most of the day. They did not recognize any of their surroundings. They had slept well past their jumping off place, and had no idea where they were or how long they had been traveling. It seemed the man had taken them in an entirely different direction. Now their concern was who they were traveling with, and where exactly they were going. Every thing looked so different, Vick thought.

Vick could see the hunger in Sam's eyes, they were both famished. He punched Sam when his stomach growled because he was afraid the driver might hear. Inching himself past the crates Vick found scraps of biscuits on the wagon floor, and the boys devoured them.

The man rode till almost sunset, his only stop being in a wooded area near a pond to water his horses and make coffee.

Vick knew they were now definitely on their own. All he could think about was getting off the wagon. It was late in the day, and they both had to relieve themselves.

When the man got back on the wagon, and the wagon was again on the move, Vick whispered into Sam's ear. "When I tell you to jump, don't be a baby." Sam gave him a startled look and nodded.

Vick peeked around the crate at the man driving the wagon, wondering where he was taking them. He became alarmed when he caught a glimpse of the man's mean looking profile. As they approached a town, Vick nudged Sam as a cue to be ready to make their move. Vick pointed to the man's knapsack resting beside the man, Sam nodded in agreement. *That's probably food*, Vick thought.

The driver stopped the wagon unexpectedly and climbed to the back of the wagon, walking right toward their hiding place, forcing the boys to move and move fast. He yelled, "Hey, what's with this?" the driver bellowed when he saw his stowaways.

Vick and Sam jumped and as they ran past the driver's side of the wagon, Vick grabbed the man's knapsack.

"Hey, come back with that!" the man shouted.

They ran as fast as their feet would carry them into the nearby woods. They kept running, never looking back to see if he was behind them.

Vick had never seen Sam run that fast. Finally, Vick saw that they were not being pursued. As he found a place to catch their breaths they looked at each other panting and smiled. With all the excitement, they forgot their hunger.

When they could breathe normally, they looked at each other and began laughing unable to stop. They ended up rolling on the ground with laughter until it hurt. It had been a long time since Vick had seen Sam laugh, and for a moment he looked healthy and alive.

Vick carried the heavy knapsack, which was now their prized possession. They couldn't wait to be far enough away so they could examine the contents of the bag in hopes of finding food.

They had no choice but to follow a path that led them deeper into the woods with thick vines slowing their progress, as they kept going in and out of deep hollers picking berries that helped with the hunger.

"I didn't know there were gonna be all these hills, did you?" asked Sam.

"Don't go getting tired on me Sammy!" Vick snapped.

They realized they were off the trail, and had no idea how long they might be trapped in the deep underbrush before finding their way out. Poor Sam looked like a whipped pup. "Whew, when we gonna stop? I'm sure tired." but Vick kept walking, trying to ignore Sam's whining.

"I know you're dying to look in the sack, but we ain't got time."

The boys fought their way through the jungle-like landscape for hours before they finally found an opening that led them onto a path.

The sun's rays were flickering in and out of the tall trees as they continued to walk. Vick knew there was little time left before darkness set in, and he desperately wanted to find a safe place to sleep before dark. It was apparent they were lost; he now had no hope of finding their way back home.

"No need to backtrack," he thought. Vick was never one to give up, but for the first time, he felt like giving up and crying. *A kid my age ain't supposed to be crying, especially when I'm the one that got us into this mess. What would Sam do if he saw me cry?* Vick thought as he fought back tears.

He knew he had no sense of direction, and they could easily be going in circles, which frightened him. Everything around them looked the same. Vick began to fear that they might die before they found their way out.

Young Sam was slowing down again and complaining, while Vick knew he had to keep pushing to find a suitable place to camp. They were approaching a very high hill.

Vick could see how tired Sam was. "Sam, you think you can make it to the top of the hill?"

"I don't know ... I'll try."

Vick thought regardless of what lies ahead, once they get over the hill, they would have to break for the night. As the boys struggled to top the hill, Vick had to help Sam. "Look Sam, there's something down there."

"I don't see nothing but a big open field."

"I know we're gonna find something. Let's hurry." Vick kept pushing.

"It's a lot faster going down the hill, ain't it, Vick?"

"Yeah, it sure is, buddy. You're doing great. Sam. When they got to the bottom Vick said, "it looks like a battlefield."

"I don't know what a battlefield is supposed to look like," Sam whispered. "This is what Hawk told us about. Remember when we had the spears?"

"Hawk told us all about the soldiers during the war. And, look at that broken down cannon." Vick could tell Sam was not interested.

"Yeah, but I still didn't know what he was talking about."

"Don't you remember Pa cussing about the war?"

"I was always too scared to know what he was yelling about."

Vick ignored Sam as he saw evidence of a military campsite. There were shells from the weapons that had evidently been fired there. As he walked on ahead, Sam was left sitting in the field while Vick looked for shelter.

It was exciting knowing he had saved the day, finding a place to safely camp for the night.

He walked past a grove of trees, and in the midst of the trees was a small military camp shelter. Next to the cabin was a pile of rusty old rifle parts. He finally hollered to Sam, "You got to hurry, I found a place to stay!"

Vick found the door unlocked and entered. He threw the knapsack on the floor of the cabin, then began looking around to see if he could find anything that could make their night more comfortable. When his brother finally caught up with him, Vick could see that Sam was not impressed.

"This place ain't got nothing on the windows."

"So? ... it's a place for us to sleep ... I don't care that we got flying bugs! Sammy, look at this old place. I wonder if the soldiers stayed here during the war?"

As Sam eyed the knapsack, Vick sensed he was not at all interested in the war. "Okay, I can see you're not gonna be happy until we open the knapsack."

Sammy's eyes got big as Vick opened the sack to see what the wagon master had left for them. "Now I know why the knapsack was so heavy. It's a damn iron skillet," complained Vick as he threw the skillet aside.

Sammy snapped back at Vick, "You know Pa don't like us to cuss."

"Pa ain't here, and I can say what I want to. That's what it means to be free, we can do what we want."

"Well, I want to eat and it don't look like the man left us anything."

"We got some jerky, and look, he left us some playing cards,"

"Just some old pieces of dried jerky, that's all. Besides, I don't know how to play cards," Sammy whined.

"I got to make us a fire. Do you think you could help find some wood, so we can get the fire going before dark?"

Sam only looked at him, not wanting to be bothered.

"Never mind. I'll get the wood. You can get the jerky ready if you want to help."

When Vick came back, Sam was still sitting in the encasement where the windows used to be.

"I didn't get the jerky out. That stuff is too hard to eat."

"So, you just sat there and let me do all the work? Sammy, you got to pull your weight." Vick felt sorry for his little brother. "We ran out of berries, and I couldn't find any more around here. You have to eat to be strong enough to walk the trail tomorrow. Jerky is all we got."

Vick put the wood down just outside the door so it would be handy. "I'm going to get this fire started, just in case varmints come snooping around during the night."

"You don't think some big panther like the one that almost got Hawk is gonna come around, do you?"

Vick was feeling a little mischievous and said, "No, but we may see a couple of bears. Don't tell me you're afraid of a bear."

"I ain't no more afraid than you are. I seen how you acted when that big panther had us cornered."

"Yeah, you seen me shoot him too!." Vick pointed his finger at Sam like it was a gun cocked, ready to shoot.

"You didn't kill him. If I had the gun I would have killed that panther just like I would if a bear came after me," Sam chided continuing their bickering.

"I'm the one that found this camp" Vick said.

"I don't care if you did find this camp, because if it wasn't for you, I would still be home with Pa."

"You'd rather be home with a Pa that whips you every time he comes home? I got you outta' there before he killed us! So don't say how I took you away from Pa. Besides, you said you didn't want to live there anymore, remember?"

Sam sat quietly for a moment, looking down at the floor. "You still want me to get the jerky?" Sam asked by way of a weak apology.

The boys needed to get their frustrations out after their stressful day, aggravated by their hunger. They were both beat, so Vick let Sam think he won the argument.

During the night the clouds moved in, the weather changed to cold. Before dawn the two were huddled together, trying to stay dry. Heavy sheets of rain had washed right through the leaks in the roof of the old camp house and drenched the two in spite of their efforts to protect themselves.

The next morning they went through the knapsack, keeping the things they needed for their journey and discarding the things they didn't. "Now you can help me carry the sack," Vick said.

"Why?" Sam asked.

"Because I threw away the heavy iron skillet, knot head."

"Oh! … and don't be calling me no knot head," Sam retorted.

The kid made a face at Vick; then took the sack, and once again the boys began their journey.

~

Vick continued to ponder over the bond he had with Sam as he grew more concerned with the worst to come. Again the memories continued as he wrestled for sleep.

~

The boys had no idea how many miles of hills they would crest before they found people that might take them in. Vick thought surely if they stayed on the trail it would lead them someplace where they could find help. He tried to keep Sam talking so he wouldn't think about being tired.

"Sam, when we find someone to take us in, we have to help them work. They ain't going to want no slouches."

"Are you talking to me?" Sam asked.

"Who else? There ain't nobody else to talk to, unless I'm talking to a bear."

"I'll do my part, don't worry," Sam replied. Vick laughed to himself seeing how Sam was getting into his role as a runaway.

Vick noticed something different about his little brother — his sudden air of confidence. Maybe being away from an abusive Pa was helping his brother, who had always been unsure of his abilities.

The Arkansas thicket was lush and beautiful; anyone lost may never get out. Without a map it was nearly impossible. The terrain got more rugged as they traveled, pushing themselves through heavy brush. Vick was concerned as hope began to wane cresting hill after hill, seeing nothing but more forest.

The good thing about the thicket is there were so many delicious berries and wild turnips along the way that they could eat and put in the knapsack for later. They sure wished, though, that they had a gun to shoot a squirrel or rabbit. Berries and turnips were good, but meat would have been a blessing.

The hills were becoming more like small mountains, and the trail changed from dirt to rock. Some rocks were very jagged and could do serious injury if they weren't careful. Vick was frightened when they came upon a very deep holler near the side of a mountain. They decided they had to go around it. One slip and they would go off the ledge. Vick had to do some big talking to get Sam around it. When they finally made it, Vick praised Sam for not giving up.

"See, you don't know what you can do, till you do it," Vick praised.

"Is that what I'm supposed to do? Prove that I can do something?"

"Well, you did it didn't you?"

Sam proudly said, "Yeah, I reckon I did. But that don't mean nothin'… if I don't like it."

"So what you're saying is, you have to like something before you try something new," Vick said, getting peeved.

"Well, maybe I could be the leader for awhile?"

Vick looked down at his younger brother and shook his head "no."

"I figured you wouldn't go for me being the leader," Sam complained. "You always have to be the one telling me what to do. Look where you've led me!"

"Sam, you're about to make me mad. Why don't you lead us back home then? How about that?"

Sam didn't respond.

"I knew that would shut your mouth, 'cause you don't know the way back home, that's why."

As they walked, arguing most of the day, they came to another deep holler and then started up another mountain. When he had had enough, Vick stopped and turned to Sam. "Okay, it's your turn to lead. Go on," he demanded, motioning to Sam to get in front, "I'm going to be right behind you."

Seeing that this mountain looked more treacherous than the one before, Sam had a change of heart.

"That's okay! You're doing a good job. I'm a much better follower."

"Okay, I'll lead, but I don't want to hear anything more about me not letting you lead."

Vick knew it was either go forward around the mountain or travel into possible deeper terrain. They decided to go around. It was becoming more dangerous, the hollers deeper, so they traveled by day and camped at night. They feared slipping off the trail and never being heard from or seen again.

They continued to walk until they heard what sounded like water flowing down the mountain. As they walked around the edge, they saw a small trickling stream, which led to a beautiful blue lake. "Wow, look at that," Sam said.

The boys were thirsty and had not seen fresh water to drink since they jumped from the wagon. They ran to the edge of the lake and fell to the ground, splashing the cold water on their faces as they gulped the water from the stream.

They were really dirty from their travels, so Vick told Sam they should strip off their clothing and wash them, while they were bathing. The clear blue water was inviting to the brothers, who had never experienced swimming before.

As they entered the water, Sam glanced up at a nearby tree and pointed saying, "Look, there's a hawk! He's the biggest one I've ever seen," Sam said excitedly.

"Yeah, I see him, but you better watch where you're going. There's probably a lot of hawks in these woods."

Before they entered the lake, the hawk swooped down and nearly hit Vick in the head. He flinched but kept walking slowly, edging his way into the water. They held their clothing out in front of them.

Vick didn't see Sam step off into a deep crevice, disappearing out of sight. His clothing surfaced, catching Vick's attention. He grabbed them but Sam was nowhere to be seen. He threw their clothes toward the shore and began feeling around for Sam. He didn't see where he had gone under, so he began reaching in front of him, trying to feel Sam's body. He kept turning in the water, frantically looking in all directions, then the hawk began to squawk over and over. Vick glanced at the noisy hawk, then noticed bubbles at the water's surface.

He held his breath and went beneath the water, forcing his eyes to open to see if he could find him. He kept turning under the water until he saw Sam's motionless body, floating beneath the surface. He grabbed him and splashed his way back to shore, then placed Sam on his stomach.

He was frantic as he pounded Sam's back with no response. At first, Vick didn't know what he was doing, but instinct had taken over. "Sammy, wake up! You have to be okay!"

Finally, Sam began spitting up water, and after a few seconds, Sam coughed and opened his eyes. Vick showed the emotion of a frightened brother, as tears welled up in his eyes, knowing that he almost lost him.

"What you crying for?" Sam asked.

Vick was so happy to see his brother open his eyes that he hugged him, ignoring the question.

The full impact of what had happened to him had not registered with Sam until he saw Vick actually crying. He placed his arm on Vick's shoulder all that was needed for Vick to know his brother was grateful. After they rested and Sam was okay, they dressed themselves in their wet clothes, then rested by a fire Vick made for them to dry off. This was the first time the knapsack came in handy.

They sat speechless by the fire until Vick broke the silence. "You scared me when you went under the water. You know, you almost drowned."

Sam looked at his brother tenderly and said, "I think I did drown, but you brought me back to life."

That night the sounds of the waterfall put the boys to sleep, and it was by far their best night's rest since they left home.

The next morning, Vick was glad to see his brother open his eyes. Sam did not know how to thank his older brother for saving him, but somehow they understood each other's feelings without uttering a word.

When they got ready to leave, Vick punched Sam and told him to look across the lake.

"That's the same hawk; guess he's been there all night."

They were several days into their journey and had already faced danger. Vick hated to leave the beauty of the lake, but knew it was important to find people that would open their home to them, and give them food.

As they traveled, they noticed a drastic change in the temperature again. The wind started to pick up, the sky was turning dark, a storm brewing. They had not found food in awhile, and Sam began complaining again.

"Stop whining Sam, please! I can't do no better," Vick said.

The boys were desperate to find shelter of some kind. After they rounded the last bend there in the distance was a cabin. What a welcome sight, the boys thought as they ran to the cabin door. There was a sign on the porch that read Panther Holler but the boys could not read.

Vick knocked politely, hoping to be greeted by friendly people who would invite them in. They were tired and so very hungry and desperate for relief. After waiting, knocking harder and waiting again, they decided no one was home and Vick peeked inside, then entered the empty cabin.

After making sure no one was there, they pilfered around trying to find something to eat. They didn't notice that the house had been ransacked.

The owners appeared to have left in a hurry: there were plates on the table with dried food and more vegetables in the cabinets. The boys didn't worry much that the food was several days old. It was food, and they would have eaten almost anything. The jerky and few berries they came upon had long since gone, and any semblance of food was what they needed.

The house was cold, but at least they were out of the storm.

"Sam, you try to warm up while I go find some wood."

When he went outside, he saw the storm getting worse. The wind was howling and he had to strain to stand upright, but he kept searching for firewood.

Vick got the fire going while Sam found scraps of food for them to eat. Afterwards, the boys crawled into bed and fell asleep as soon as their heads hit the mattress.

The next morning, the storm was even worse. They thought surely the owners would be returning to their cabin to shield themselves from the storm. This concerned them, knowing the owners may be angry they were there and put them out in the storm. They decided they should hide in the storm shelter, across from the cabin. "At least we'll keep dry if they don't know we're here," Vick explained, grabbing their knapsack.

"Sam, when I open the door, let's run for the shelter." Sam nodded "yes."

They finally made it across the yard to the shelter where Vick had to struggle to open the door against the wind's pressure. When it did open, the pressure pushed Vick and Sam inside with the door slamming behind them. Everything went pitch-black.

"Vick, what is this smell? We can't stay here. I'll be sick."

Vick thought it must be a dead animal. The smell reminded him of when he had killed and dressed a deer back home. That smell had to be blood, Vick decided.

"Sam, something is dead in here. We gotta get out!"

The boys couldn't stand the vile odor, and since they could not see, they began feeling around until Vick stumbled over something. He again felt around on the floor, trying to find what he had tripped over. This was when the harsh reality set in, as a bolt of lightning shone through a broken board disclosing the object, it was a dead man.

Vick jumped back and let out a scream so loud that it startled Sam over the sound of the storm up above. The scream told his brother that something horrible was there and they needed to get out and fast.

"Somebody's dead in here!" Vick was finally able to say. Sam ran to the door, and with strength he did not know he possessed, flung it open and ran out into the storm. Vick was running behind him trying to keep up. All they knew was they had to get as far away from the shelter and cabin as possible. Sam was completely out of control, running straight into the woods, rain beating down on them. Vick followed him, trying to catch up and yelling for him to come back to the cabin. The path had large trees on both sides, all swaying with the tremendous force of the wind when a lightning bolt lit everything up striking a nearby tree, causing a limb to snap, pinning Sam to the ground.

"Noooooo! Sam!" Vick yelled out. But the boy was trapped by the huge limb and appeared to be unconscious.

Vick knelt down, yelling into Sam's ear, "I have to go back to the storm shelter and find something to help you. Hold on, Sam."

Vick's only choice was to run back to the shelter and feel around until he came across an axe or something else to free Sam.

There was no time for tears, as raw emotion began to control his instincts. Vick found a small log he used to prop open the shelter door just enough to have light, as he frantically searched for an axe. He faced his fears, walking through the shelter looking for anything that could free Sam, holding his nose from the smell. Flashes of lightening allowed Vick to see not one body, but the bodies of a whole family. There was a young girl, a boy about the age of Sam who appeared to have had their throats cut and their parents who had wounds all over their bodies. It was a gruesome sight for a young boy to see, but Vick had to stifle the urge to throw up, and to stick to his one thought: find an axe and save Sam!

He finally found what he needed, ran back to save his brother, but could see that he had died. He started hacking at the limb.

"I brought you back to life when you drowned, I'll bring you back again," Vick yelled to Sam's lifeless body. "Hang in there Sam; don't give up! I need you with me!"

He continued hacking at the huge limb, wielding the ax like a grown man. All the memories and frustration Vick had endured as a boy were now released with each thrust. He could hear his own sounds of panic come from him as he repeatedly struck the limb. Vick finally cut through the limb enough to free Sam, but it was too late. He fell down beside him and pulled his limp body onto his lap, crying and rocking him, as the rain beat against his face. He kept willing Sam to open his eyes. He called on the Great Spirits for help, but they did not work their magic. He continued to cradle Sam as if he could somehow comfort his lifeless body as the winds continued to blow and rain washed away his tears.

"I wasn't with you when you died," he said, "and you died because of me." The adrenaline was still pumping, as he picked up Sam and carried his body back to the cabin, where so much evil had taken place.

He thought about his Pa. He knew he could never face him and tell him he was responsible for his brother's death. Vick laid Sam on a child's bed and wrapped him with the sheet, trying to shield his body from the cold.

"I need to keep him warm," he whispered to himself. The enormity of what had happened, hit Vick again. But by this time, there were no more tears left to shed, as he fell asleep next to Sam, just like he had done so many times before.

The next morning's light brought a beautiful sunny but saddest day of his life. It was easier for him to bury the family that had died at the hands of a killer, than it was for him to lay his brother to rest.

Vick dug five graves in the wet ground, thankful he had found the owners work gloves, making it possible to wrap the family's bodies one by one in a sheet to drag them to their graves. His intense sadness and the condition of the four bodies caused him to throw up what was left in his stomach. "Everyone needs a decent burial," he thought. He shoveled dirt over their bodies and stood quietly in reverence. The thunderstorm had made the dirt easier to dig, but the burial of all five victims took all that day.

The only religion Vick knew was what he had learned from the Indians. He remembered Hawk explaining how the Great Spirit watched over his people. Vick stood by Sam's grave and looked up to the sky and muttered, "Why didn't the Great Spirit save Sam?"

As he hammered a crude cross at Sam's grave like he and Sam had seen in a small cemetery near their home, he knew something was supposed to be written on the board, but his lack of schooling left him unable to mark his brother's grave were one would know whose body was there.

Vick bent down and ran his hand across the grave as he pondered what life will be like without his brother.

Chapter 5

It seemed to Vick that this night in jail would never end. He had already awakened three or four times from the dreams of his past only to find that he was still in the cold, dark cell.

Lying awake, he recalled his last night at Panther Holler after burying his brother, his constant companion. He thought about the events that had taken place from the time they ran away until Sam died. He remembered that he had determined that night to make some decisions in order to survive. The mere thought of returning home to face his Pa was out of the question.

He saw himself lying alone in the cabin, and remembered the very moment he knew he had to grow up and become a man. He vowed to make the best of his situation, although he knew a murderer was on the loose and could possibly return to the cabin and kill him. Vick wasn't ready to die. If some madman was running around killing people, he didn't want to be next on the casualty list. He had to have protection, the kind that only a gun could afford him.

Vick began a frantic search, looking through drawers and other places he thought a gun might be. He went through the house until there was no place left to look. "Surely, the dead man had a gun to protect his family."

He began thinking about where he would hide a gun if his family were in danger. The only place he had not looked was under the mattress of the bed! He went to the bedroom and pulled back the mattress. There, lying before his eyes was a beautiful, shiny, pearl-handled .45, in its holster, fully loaded, and ready to shoot.

Vick remembered how his Pa handled a pistol, and how often he and Sam had seen him load and unload his weapon. He put the gun holster on his hip, synching it as tight as he could over his thin hips and then tested his quick draw. He was pleased at how natural it felt, as he clutched the gun and quickly pulled it out of the holster. He was almost as good as his Pa, he thought.

He slept with the gun by his side, within reach.

The next morning, Vick was charged up, determined to survive. He got up and cooked himself breakfast of just vegetables he scrounged up from the dead families little garden. He had forgotten what it was like to have a full stomach.

He thought, "This is the day I need to move on, because the murderer may be coming back." Besides, the memories of the murdered family and Sam's violent death would be far easier to forget if he could find his way to the next town, and get on with his life.

Vick had immediately gotten used to the warm bed in the cabin, but there was no way he was going to stay around and wait for the murderer or murderers to come back. In preparing for his trip, he found enough clothing to take with him, along with more jerky for nourishment. He had to pack lightly since there was no horse on the place. Whoever killed that family must have taken their livestock or turned them loose, Vick reasoned. He dreaded the trip, but knew he could not continue to live in a cabin where such evil had taken place and more could possibly happen there. Besides, he had no ammunition except what was in the gun. He had to make each bullet count.

He picked up his gear to leave, but had to take some time to visit Sam's grave before he left. "It's going to be lonely without you brother," Vick said. "All our years of being together are gone now, but I will remember them all the days of my life." He still blamed himself for Sam's untimely death and it was difficult to leave his burial place.

Vick stood there a moment pondering their lives together, when a sparrow lit on Sam's grave. He watched the bird as it pecked around, unafraid of Vick standing nearby. He thought of himself in relation to the bird that showed no signs of fear. "I have to show the same kind of courage, no matter what."

Vick followed the bird with his eyes as it perched on a limb in a nest of nearby trees. Somehow the bird reminded him of Hawk.

Perhaps it was Vick's connection to his Indian friend that gave him the courage to move on.

He remembered the promise Hawk made to him when Vick saved his life; that he would be his protector. "Okay Hawk," he said aloud, looking up at the bird, "you watch over my brother's grave and keep it safe."

Vick walked all that day on a trail that led deep into the woods. At dusk, he stopped to gather wood for a campfire, but before he lit the fire, he had an eerie feeling that he was not alone. He heard movement and quickly raked his foot over the kindling, scattering it about so that whoever was approaching would not know someone was close by.

His stomach was in knots from the fear that this could be the same murderer that had killed the family he found in the storm shelter. As the footsteps grew closer, he peered from behind a tree and saw a giant mountain man clothed in a grizzly bear skin coat. He had dirty brown hair hanging around his face, a long bushy beard, and made a distinctive sound when he breathed that was more like an animal than a human. Vick remained frozen, scared to move, as the man came closer to him.

Vick could tell he was getting closer from the crackle of the branches under the big man's feet, so he continued to edge himself around the tree, not to be seen, afraid that with one slip he might be heard. "This has to be the killer," he thought. As the man passed, Vick saw he was carrying one heavy large burlap sack he assumed was filled with whatever he had stolen from the people he had killed.

He could hear some metal items clinking together as the man lumbered by.

Terrified as he was, he felt that his only hope to find his way was to follow this creature of a man. So he had to take the risk, no matter what. Continuing to press after him, as the man maneuvered in strange patterns on and off the trail, Vick followed along until he stopped, put down the sacks and began to collect small branches for a fire. Ravenously hungry, Vick recognized the aroma of cooked squirrel, just like his Pa used to make. He would have given anything for the leftovers. In fact, he would have given anything to be back home with his Pa.

It was cold that night. Vick wrapped himself in a blanket he had packed, then crawled inside a hollow tree trunk that offered just enough protection to shield him from the dew. Vick was restless during the night, thinking about the murderer who lay just a stone's throw away!

"This is crazy, laying here in a log on the cold ground when I could be back in the cabin sleeping in a warm bed," he begrudged.

The next morning, Vick awoke with a shock, awakened by the man's loud coughing as he gathered his things to break camp and move out. Careful not to make any sudden move that might alert the man that someone was on his tail, the frightened boy lay frozen, breathing as quietly as he could, eager for the man to clear his campsite and move on. Finally, the man picked up his walking stick and gear to resume his journey. Vick dared not walk past the campsite until he knew there was no danger of being seen. When the coast was clear he hoped to find something left over from the mountain man's supper, but there were only bare bones. Vick followed him again all day and into the late evening, when a small cabin appeared in the distant waning light. Vick had hoped that they would be in a town by now, so he was discouraged, thinking that he might never find his way out of the dense forest and get back home. The frightened boy stayed far behind, covered in the brush while the man stopped short of his cabin and looked around. Vick froze, thinking perhaps he had been seen … the very thought sending cold chills up and down his spine.

After making sure that no one was nearby, the man began digging a big hole that Vick imagined could be his grave. It was certainly big enough to be a grave. He placed the one large sack in the hole then stamped it down level with the ground, finally spreading the excess dirt around the area.

"Sure enough, it must be a treasure," Vick, thought.

After the man finished disguising the hole, he instinctively looked around. Vick questioned to himself, "Why would he look around? Is he setting me up in order to capture me? I will have to be very careful."

Vick remained frozen several minutes after the shovel was leaned against the shack and the man went in. Unable to tell if anyone else was in the cabin, to be extra safe, he waited for several hours before daring to make a move. Again Vick knew he had to find safe shelter for the night but he first wanted to take back what belonged to the family the man had murdered.

It took every ounce of courage he could muster, but after he made his decision, Vick eased out of hiding, slipped up to the cabin to re-trieve the shovel, then began furiously digging. The shovel finally hit something. He could feel the soil beneath his fingernails as he clawed at the dirt, soon finding cloth and pulling the bag out before he had to remove much of the loose dirt.

He was elated as he lifted the heavy sack then ran back to his hid-ing place and decided to leave his knapsack hidden so no one would find it. Vick ran in the direction of the cabin but avoided the trail the man had taken. He had to get as far away as he could and as fast as he could. He didn't know how long it would take before the huge man realized that his treasure was missing. He felt the only safe place was the cabin where he buried his brother Sam, so he backtracked toward the cabin as fast as he could with the burden of the sack.

Unbeknownst to Vick, the man discovered the theft only a short time later. When his shovel was missing he knew something sinister had taken place. He ran to the open hole, and the bag gone, it was like a blast of shock sending a cold rush throughout his body. He let out a roar that echoed through the forest like that of a wounded beast, but Vick was so far away, he did not hear the echo. The man could not believe how fast this had happened and correctly figured that someone had been spying on him.

Crazed with anger, he ran back into the cabin, snatched up his gear and began tracking down whoever stole his sack. He moved through the brush like a giant warrior going to war, not letting any grass grow under his feet in the process, using his tracking abilities to find the man who stole his sack.

Meanwhile, Vick was running and stumbling up ahead, and had moved onto the trail to now make better time. There was only a sliver of a moon, making it difficult for him to stay on the trail. He had run for a long time, powered by his adrenalin but was really getting tired now. Vick had no idea that the huge, powerful man was hot on his trail, filled with rage and swearing that the man who stole from him would die by his hand. When Vick could no longer see the trail, he found a place to hide the treasure to wait for daylight.

"No sense taking chances, just in case the man jumps me during the night," he thought. He kept his pistol handy for the possibility.

Vick lay down behind a clump of brush, thinking about all he had gone through. Before he had a chance to drift off to sleep, the mountain man sprung out of nowhere! He grabbed the boy, pulled him up off his feet in midair, choking him with his own shirt. Vick did not have time to feel frightened. In fact, he was still too numb from the mental distress of dealing with Sam's death, plus the horror of burying the family he found dead at the cabin, to feel anything except the instinct to survive.

With the killer holding Vick with one hand and about to wield his knife with the other, His only defense was to bite the man's hand as hard as he could. It worked. The man released his hold and dropped him but was on top of Vick before he could scramble to his feet and escape. He was no competition for this powerful, angry man who now had him on the ground with his entire massive body weight pressed against him, his huge hands going toward Vick's neck. Vick looked into the beady eyes flashing down at him and blurted out, "I hid your treasure. If you kill me now, you'll never find it."

The man abruptly stopped, pulling Vick to his feet as he pulled a huge knife out of his belt, held it to Vick's throat as he stared in his eyes. "You stole from me, boy! Where is it?" he demanded in that deep, raspy voice.

"Put your knife away, and I will get it for you," Vick said somehow demanding. All the man could think about was finding his stolen property, so he let go of Vick, allowing the boy an instant to scrabble and reach for his .45 pistol he had near his quilt.

Before it registered with the man that Vick had a pistol, the boy aimed and squeezed the trigger. Hit directly in the chest at close range, the gigantic mountain man fell with the knife-thrusting forward toward Vick's throat. Vick turned sideways, barely deflecting the blade from a lethal slice through his neck, but it slashed his left cheek deeply as the two hit the ground.

With blood gushing from his cheek, Vick momentarily stood up, then fell on the dying man. "Why did you kill those people?" he demanded. The man could hardly speak as he moved his mouth, struggling to get the words out. "Watch out," whispered the man, staring incredulously into Vick's eyes.

Vick thought someone must be watching them. He looked around in a panic, holding his face, as blood poured through his fingers and down his cheek, but also ready to shoot who he was to "watch out" for.

He was thankful to be alive, but knew he needed to stop the bleeding as his eyes searched his surroundings for another threat. Vick was scrambling around, looking for anything that could absorb the blood. He opened one of the sacks and found a book he thought might be useful. He ripped out some of the pages, and used them to pack the wound. When that did not work, he remembered how his Pa used tobacco whenever the boys cut themselves or stuck nails in their feet. No tobacco here.

Vick realized that he had to stop the bleeding to survive, and that meant going back to the mountain man's cabin. He ran through the woods, finally finding the cabin, wondering how he managed to find his way. He was exhausted from running, the loss of blood creating symptoms of shock, plus trauma of having killed the huge man.

His wound was so severe that it took every ounce of strength he had left to look for medicine that could relieve the pain. He could now barely move as despair began to creep in. He began to wonder why he should go on, when he had already lost Sam. Finally that something inside him that had marked Vick as a man of determination finally kicked in, telling him that no matter what, he had to keep fighting to survive.

He found an old shirt and held it to his face to close the wound and stop the bleeding. He began walking the floor, holding the side of his swollen and throbbing face. His eye on that side was now swollen closed. A dirty broken mirror showed him that the knife had almost reached his eye.

Vick searched the cabin and finally found a keg of bootleg whiskey. He remembered his Pa saying he drank to relieve pain, so Vick drank some, hoping it would make him feel better. He braced himself and painfully poured some whiskey over the shirt on his cheek to cleanse the wound. He yelped as that momentarily intensified the pain.

The whiskey was thankfully very strong. Within a few swallows, he began to feel sleepy. It did not take much before Vick was feeling no pain. He barely made it to the bed before he fell into a deep sleep. Throughout the night Vick would awake suddenly sitting straight up, gasping for air as he began hyperventilating. When he drank more whiskey he slept the night and most of the next day.

"It must have been the whiskey," he thought. And there was plenty of it.

Vick was too weak to move and remained in bed another full day before he began to feel better. He tried to eat, but it caused tremendous pain in his wound.

He worried about the bag of treasure he had hidden in the forest, but did not have the strength to retrieve it yet. He had to just hope no one would discover them until he could go back. Even if someone found the big man's body, they shouldn't find the hidden bag.

After two more days of bed rest, he was able to move around and was starving. He could eat with minimal pain in his cheek, so he ate until he couldn't hold another bite. He looked around the cabin for things he may need to take with him, such as food, farming supplies … and whiskey.

There was a young horse behind the cabin that Vick saddled and packed with items needed to take back to Panther Holler. He headed back toward where he had hidden his knapsack and the treasure, still wondering what all was in the bag.

Vick knew he was approaching the area where he hid the treasure when the wind changed and he caught the scent of a foul order. That smell had to be the man's body, so he knew he was near his hiding place. After finding the corpse it was difficult to take time to bury the body but Hawk had taught him about sacred burials. "The Great Spirit requires every death the sanctity of a burial," his young friend would say although the white man's burial was different than the Indians.

He added the one bag to the horse's load, which meant he would have to walk the horse to the cabin that would turn out to be his home for the next few years.

It seemed to take Vick forever traveling with his wound. He was still weak and had to travel slower than usual. When he finally did arrive, he spent three more days nursing his injury, eating the mountain man's food, his only relief coming from the whiskey he brought with him.

Vick had examined the contents of the burlap sack as soon as he unpacked. He found the treasure was more precious than he thought. It was filled with gold nuggets, rubies, diamonds, many pieces of gold and silver, along with thousands of silver certificates, but he had no idea what they were or their value, but figured they wouldn't have been in the bag if they hadn't been valuable.

Vick didn't know anything about wealth, but even he knew the treasure was worth a lot. It took several hours to divide the jewelry and certificates into separate sacks. He kept what he thought was the best of the treasure separate from the broken jewelry and items he didn't think were valuable.

Even though he couldn't read, Vick decided to keep the little book, along with the ripped out pages, for it was part of the treasure, something important since it belonged to the murdered family. Vick decided that the family must have brought these things with them when they settled in the thicket.

He felt a bit uncomfortable establishing himself as the owner of the treasure, but at this point he felt the family would want the treasure in the company of someone who cared for it. Common sense told him to hide the treasure in two different places, in case someone came looking or even just happened to stumble upon one of his hiding places. He hid the less valuable part under the loose plank in the kitchen and the more desirable treasured items he hid in the shelter.

As days turned into weeks, Vick discovered many things around the cabin that helped him survive. He found where the murdered man had hidden his ammunition, which he used to hunt for his meat, but was careful not to waste any. It took months for the stench to air out of the storm shelter. Vick found more seeds and farming tools in there, which he used to cultivate a garden.

Vick became quite comfortable with his new found freedom, working when he wanted and having no one to answer to. He was never bored, and spent a lot of time practicing his fast draw perfecting his skill that surpassed his own expectations. Before he realized it, he had been in the wilderness for over two years. As he aged, he was turning into a strong and handsome young man, despite the scar on his face.

~

After the restless night in jail filled with these memories of his life and survival as a youth, Vick woke up yet again to face the stark reality that he might be lynched. The only thing he could see in his immediate future was to be taken aboard a wagon that would haul him on a bone-chilling trip to Abilene, Texas, to see the Circuit Judge.

"All this because of a man named Buck Dupree," Vick said to himself.

How could I have been so wrong about a man that I thought was a friend?

Restlessly waiting for daylight, he thought of Buck and their first meeting.

Chapter 6

BUCK WAS THE REASON VICK WAS IN ODESSA, AND BECAUSE OF BUCK Vick was in jail. In a few hours it would be first light and the sheriff would load him into the back of a wagon to be taken to Abilene to find out his fate for trying to defend himself.

His remaining hours in jail he recalled the first time he met Buck and what a disappointment he turned out to be.

Born in Australia, Buck spoke with a thick accent that lulled his listeners into a trusting comfort. He was a dramatic fella who seemed to be a loner. He sported a luxurious mustache with a brown and grey beard.

Widely traveled in the West, and moving from boom town the Australian gambler marveled in telling folks he rode with men that were well known gamblers. He was brilliant at his craft, and had traveled from California to North Dakota, through Dodge City where he met Virgil Earp, Wyatt's brother. After he left Dodge City he rode to Texas and then to Arkansas, playing along the way with professionals, including legendary characters like Wyatt Earp and Doc Holliday.

Small town gamblers didn't have a chance against a man with Buck's skill. He used his charm, cunning and experience to outwit and outplay the run-of-the-mill player, but poker wasn't where Buck made his big splash.

The years he traveled through the hinterlands, Faro was favored among gamblers over other table games. Saloons normally had Faro tables available during that time and cheating was rampant among both players and the casinos. The Dealers usually knew how to make the house win more than they lost.

Buck became a master at Faro and also counting cards. He had already cheated many of the big name casinos out of thousands of dollars. The operators of these casino's had all begun to wonder if he was really that lucky, just that good, or something else. They watched him intently trying to catch him in the act of cheating.

He would enter a Faro game, pretend to be drunk and then work his magic. Buck's game was always the same: he would lure his opponents into making wild side bets, the last of which being that he could guess the last three cards in the Dealer's hand. He loved relating to Vick these successes, and his student learned the process well. Buck became impressed with Vick who was a fast learner and also listened to Buck's tall tales, which included his mentor's charades that almost always succeeded in fleecing his opponents and the casinos. Sometimes, winning came with a price attached. The losers sought revenge by pulling a knife, a gun or challenging him to a duel. Those who had lost a month's earnings on the "last three cards," absolutely certain they would win, were the ones who reacted the worst. "They were the hungriest" Buck would say.

Once the gloves were off, Buck would have to rely on his quick draw with his shiny six-shooter. With time and age, however, he could tell his reactions were slower, and he had some close calls. Facing the fact that there would eventually be someone younger and faster who would make him a statistic; the obvious solution, to him, came in the form of a "metal breastplate." He had a blacksmith fabricate one just to be thick enough to stop a .45 slug, yet light enough to offer reasonable comfort and movement. He concealed the breastplate by wearing a heavy coat year round, giving him a rather ridiculous appearance that enhanced his charade, as most thought he was slightly off his rocker.

Gamblers would think him a bit touched when he showed up wearing a winter coat in the heat of summer, but he would capitalize on one basic rule that always remains the same: "if you're about to cheat someone at cards, get their attention on something other than the game." He was a multi-tiered operator, one might call him, as he scanned his victims well before he carefully conned them out of all their cash.

It was a number of years and many a scam before anyone realized that the famed Aussie's main strategy was card counting. Before long, Buck was banned from entering nearly all known casinos and gambling halls in the West and some in the East had heard of him.

Nevertheless, Buck tried to go back to familiar saloons wherever he could, but professional and recreational poker players alike would refuse to play with him. Soon, he had no choice but to leave the West, and travel eastward.

Buck's travel across the plains to Texas was significantly less profitable and dangerous, now that he was known as a cheat. He moved quickly through treacherous territory, trying to avoid being recognized, headed for Arkansas.

It was there, years before, in the rustic card rooms and gambling tents of the bustling town of Hot Springs, that Buck had begun his deceptions. As a very young bloke, he had tried his hand at cards, quickly realizing it was ludicrous to rely on knowledge of the game and luck — a great card player would need something more to make a living at it. Perfecting the skill he had learned from an uncle back in Australia on how to count cards; he honed his craft and practiced his trade for years, going along without a hitch. His confidence grew, and at times he even surprised himself with his ingenuity and inventiveness. Eventually he headed east for "the big time."

He was surprised at how much Hot Springs had grown over the years. In the hustle and bustle, he saw no faces he recognized, which in his line of work was a blessing. He wasted no time finding a card game with his favorites: small time gamblers.

Buck's luck was wearing thin after many towns and so many scams, his edge wasn't as keen as it once was. Things had begun to backfire on him. It should have been easy, a cakewalk, but it no longer was. Virtually nothing he tried worked; he suffered a quick succession of the closest calls he'd ever had.

Had the town grown up that much? Had the dupes gotten smarter? Or, had Buck Dupree lost his edge?

Vick had safely lived in Panther Holler for two years when the Australian was on the lamb again. Cheating a number of gambling halls, there was only one place left to go — a little cabin deep in a remote section of the woods. There he thought he would feel safe. There he could regroup and restructure, and there too, he had a bit of history — Panther Holler.

The Ozarks still looked so very familiar, as if he'd never left. He headed straight for the cabin he had once "visited," deep in the hollers. He had used it as a haven for hunting, which was his passion.

This area of the Ozarks was a hunter's paradise, covered with heavy terrain and unlimited wildlife. The ride took several days, but he had no trouble retracing his path, despite the thick growth, hollers and groundcover that now obscured the trail. The cabin was in a particularly densely forested area, nearly impossible to find unless you knew what you were looking for. Here, he always felt his privacy was secure; a place to get lost.

It was nearly midnight when Buck finally arrived at the cabin in Panther Holler. As he approached, he was surprised to see a light inside, and smoke coming from the chimney. He sneaked to a side window, and peering in, saw a figure sleeping on a makeshift pallet in front of a glowing fire. Gun drawn, Buck quietly entered the door and approached the sleeping figure. A teenage boy lay curled on the floor.

Buck silently pulled up and straddled a chair near the boy, sat down, and said, "Make yourself at home." The boy jolted awake.

"Easy, mate, easy." Buck said in a calm and dulcet tone.

The startled young man blinked away his shock, and tried to gather his wits, pushing himself back and away from the man. He saw the pistol resting in Buck's lap, but the older man's carefree ease gave Vick enough confidence to speak.

"I'm sorry, the cabin was empty and I was lost, and it didn't look like anyone … lived here."

Buck liked the way this was going. If the boy wanted to think Buck owned the cabin, well, that was just fine. Nothing like having the advantage, He thought.

"What's your name mate?" asked Buck.

"Vick. Vick Porter."

"Not to worry, Vick Porter." Buck said with a gentle smile, showing a bit of his tobacco-stained teeth, "There's always room for one more."

Buck stood, holstered his gun, removed his coat, and moved to hang it by the door. He then removed his gun belt and hung it up as well.

"Lost, eh?"

Vick noticed the man's heavy accent. Now feeling safer, Vick explained how he had lost his way in the thicket some couple of years back and had stumbled upon the abandoned cabin. He didn't want to bring up the family he had found murdered, and certainly not the treasures he had hidden.

Buck thought better of asking him what he was doing this deep in the Ozarks in the first place. He figured there were plenty of perfectly good explanations. Besides, he didn't particularly want to have to answer that same question himself. Buck noticed Vick's scar, but never questioned him about it. A man's scars should be left undisturbed by others. Every man knew that.

Vick was delighted to have the company. He'd been here by himself for some time now, and although he loved the cabin and the tremendous hunting, he had been a little lonely.

Vick was careful not to let on about what had happened when he met the mountain man. The least said the better. At any rate, he was glad to have someone to talk to.

Something about this young man put Buck at ease. He had spent many years having to keep his guard up around the clock, never allowing himself to relax. For the first time since he was an adult, Buck didn't need to watch his back, here at the cabin. Now he could actually talk without every word being part of a structured manipulation. He took full advantage of it. He started to talk to Vick about himself. He talked about where he'd been, all he'd done, and what he'd learned.

Vick hung on every word. Initially it was just because of Buck's strange, almost hypnotic accent, but soon it became more about the stories of adventure. Vick knew nothing of Buck's fast and exciting world. Yet he had no trouble imagining what it would be like to live it.

Even after all Vick had experienced, his own stories were only about pain and survival. He was mesmerized by Buck's tales, and was eager to learn more. He was most captivated by the explanations of the cons themselves, since Buck relished in bragging about how he used what he called the "Con's Creed" to his advantage. Vick was all ears when Buck ran down the elements of how to con. Somehow he sensed that it could be very important to him in the future. He hung on every word. "You have to gain the confidence of your mark and give him the idea you don't consider him a threat. Let him think he is controlling you. And if he, too, is trying to run a con, it makes everything a whole lot easier. Basically, you're beating him at his own game. But things don't always go like you plan, so you should be prepared to use your secret exit strategy, that nobody can detect, not even the House. That's when your true mastery comes into play."

Vick was young and didn't know anything about different lifestyles, like being a gambler, a con man, and living by standards that set people apart from what Buck called, "the garbage of the world" but Vick listened, learned, and became schooled.

Buck noticed that Vick seemed to have a mind for the building blocks and intricacies of the most complex con structures. This was exciting for Buck. After all, he had spent his life perfecting the art of the con, and for the first time, he'd met someone who was as fascinated with the concept as he was. At first he loved seeing Vick soak up everything from being a gentleman to owning the game but now, Buck thought he might have taken it to a different level.

Card counting became easy to Vick and Buck was sharing all his secrets of poker and Faro. Each day Buck grew more concerned with Vick's ability to out-draw and out-shoot him, killing twice as many squirrels as he did. "The kid was a stupid genius, and should have been in a sideshow; riding, roping and shooting like ole Wild Bill," Buck thought. What he observed was the kid had everything, good looks, a swagger about him and a powerful personality that caused Buck to have pangs of jealousy, however he did not want to admit it.

The two would hunt during the day and play cards at night. It seemed only right that he should teach Vick the trade, since he needed someone to keep him sharp. Vick challenged him, and kept him on his toes. This was something Buck never would have imagined, finding an illiterate kid living alone in a wilderness, who was smart as a whip.

Finally, gambling was fun again!

That's when Buck realized over the last few years why things had started to go wrong for him. Gambling, cons and scams of all kinds, used to be a thrill for him. Actually, it was the best fun he could imagine. He had loved every second of it. Recently, though, it had become more like a job, even drudgery at times. But now, teaching Vick brought new life into Buck.

There was something else Buck hadn't counted on: The best way to learn something is to teach it to someone else. Your understanding of the subject becomes much deeper and more refined. Vick's aptitude and enthusiasm was pushing Buck to be better at cards than he had ever been.

It wasn't long before Buck realized, no matter how he refined his own game, Vick's game seemed to be getting better than his. It troubled him, seeing the kid not having to struggle, and he realized he was sitting before a brilliant player. Buck had been so caught up in his own enjoyment and gratification of passing on his pearls of wisdom to Vick, that he had forgotten to consider the ramifications. Suddenly, he realized that maybe educating Vick wasn't such a good idea after all, and that really began to disturb him.

Not only was this young bloke a genius with cards, but he also was probably the most skillful gunman Buck had ever met in his travels. This made Vick a double threat.

One thing Buck didn't want was someone dipping into his game and sharing his secrets with someone else. Buck couldn't have other gamblers know about his breastplate, how he read cards, and how he manipulated the game. After all, Buck had been the only hustler with any substantial knowledge of the casino cons, and now he had allowed those secrets to slip out.

Buck knew he had to think of something before he left the cabin, and somehow, protect himself from his own indiscretion. Buck's nurturing, caring attitude had changed to resentment and fear of losing his own livelihood. The young bloke's very presence began to gnaw at him. The only way to protect himself from Vick, was to kill him.

Chapter 7

VICK HAD JUST TURNED EIGHTEEN, AND WAS READY TO MOVE ON WHEN **Buck began to resent how sophisticated and polished, that Vick had become.** His student was everything he wasn't and the jealousy began to eat away at him.

Buck had to make sure Vick never left Panther Holler. He felt he had wasted time giving Vick the trappings of a southern gentleman, teaching him the traits that were critical in selling himself as an established citizen, training him to be a con. Vick was smooth as silk and knew how to act and talk. But there was one thing missing, Vick wanted and needed to know how to act around women, but Buck would say, "Settle down, your time will come with the ladies."

Buck had already taught Vick to detect and ingratiate himself with the wealthy who had money. After all, a poker player wants to play against a man with plenty of cash so he can take it. Vick had to look the part and play the part of a well-heeled gentleman in order to capitalize on the ineptitude of his opponents. This is what Buck trained him to do, but he had now grown to resent Vick's expertise.

Vick who had expected to leave the holler with Buck was now being plotted against to never leave the Holler alive.

"I didn't know the kid would be so smart and become my competition," Buck thought.

The Aussie had created a world-class poker player and knew it. He now begrudged that creation, knowing that he could end up sitting on the opposite side of the table from this kid some day. Buck imagined he was renowned as one of the best … so he said. And, he wasn't about to let Vick take his notoriety away from him.

The more he thought about it, the more he knew that he had to get rid of him. He was itching to move on but needed to concoct a plan that would not draw suspicion. The bloke was no pushover; Buck had taught him well. And he had to be careful not to be conned himself or shot in self-defense.

Vick had asked him once "What kind of name is 'Buck'?

Buck then confessed that his real name was William Abberly and he had worked on a ship for five years before staying in America. He had become good friends with a Frenchman named "Buck Dupree." When the Frenchman died in an accident on the ship, Buck told Vick that he had been so despondent over the death that he took Buck's name when he got off the ship to honor his memory and start a new life for himself.

In truth, he and Buck Dupree didn't get along and it was William Abberly's mistake on the ship that caused the accident that killed Dupree. He wasn't about to tell Vick he took that name because he had stolen the captain's money when he jumped ship, that he needed a new identity, and that he chose that name because he knew Buck Dupree had a clean record. Another tidbit he left out was that William Abberly was wanted for murder in Australia. As "Buck Dupree," he only faced minor legal charges against him, all from gambling events.

The next morning, Buck was going to pretend to go hunting alone to come up with a plan as to how he would end Vick's life without bringing attention or charges against himself. "Committing a crime in Panther Holler who would know anyway," he surmised.

"Mate, hope you don't mind, but I'm taking the day by myself. Need some time to clear the webs."

Vick didn't care; he had noticed how restless Buck had become. Every man needed some time alone.

"Go ahead. I got things to do. What time will you be back?"

Vick's question annoyed Buck, but he tried not to show it.

"I'll be back before nightfall."

The ride did Buck good. He rode deep into the densest areas of the thicket and took pleasure thinking how he would orchestrate Vick's last breath.

"I'm going to miss this place," Buck thought, as his horse's hooves creaked across broken limbs and brush. He could relax without fear of anyone gunning for him in these woods. The squirrels were running up and down the trees, giving Buck the feeling for a split second that he should just stay on a while longer and deal with Vick later. It was a beautiful day, reminding him of his youth in Australia.

His mother and father were good people who had been killed by a group of Aborigines who came in from the Outback looking for trouble, ransacking homes, pilfering, and raping every woman they encountered along the way. It was in their own home where his father was murdered and then his mother and sister were savagely beaten and raped. Luckily, Buck was hunting with his cousin on that dreadful day his family was murdered.

He had a difficult time after that, being handed from pillar to post throughout the remainder of his early youth. He finally went to live with an uncle, who not only taught him to be ruthless, but also how to cheat at poker. Over time, Buck developed an edge, becoming quite good.

In his early twenties, he killed his first man in a card game and was sure to face jail if he stayed in Australia. He had no compelling reason to stay anyway, since the good part of him was dead. He had buried his family long ago, so stowing away on a ship bound for America to escape his probable doom was an easy decision. Of course, the captain of the ship eventually found Buck onboard and gave him the option of being thrown overboard or working as a hand on the ship for five years. Buck was still young and impressionable enough to believe him, readily signing the agreement.

Buck had nothing better to do anyway, so he stayed on, visiting different countries and learning the ways of the world. Over time,

Buck had made a pretty good but cantankerous hand, when at the end of his five years' work, he heard about the California gold rush. When they arrived in San Francisco Harbor, the Captain and his men got drunk. Seizing the opportunity, he broke into the Captain's quarters, stole over two thousand dollars, jumped ship, slipped around customs, and headed east to "gold country!"

Buck relished in thinking about the old times and what he had been through. "There's no place better than the Holler and there's no way I'm going to let this kid ruin it for me," Buck thought. He enjoyed being alone in the solitude of his thoughts.

He remembered the women in his life and wondered why they always left him? "Perhaps it was because I was never really there for them. Women! Bah," Buck said to himself.

"There ain't a woman around that understands my needs: my need for hunting, my need for gambling, and my need for other women." He laughed to himself, "I'm a needy bloke."

The sun had begun to dim, the day seemed short as he wandered the woods. It was time to stop and set up camp, since he had actually planned to stay overnight. It was turning cold by the time Buck stopped. He took his time scouring around until he had found enough wood for a fire and ate a bit of food from his saddlebag before he settled in for the evening. He was preparing his bedroll and was about to lie down when he heard a noise behind him. Buck didn't have time to turn around before a mountain man dressed in bearskin jumped from out of nowhere and attacked him with a knife.

Taken by surprise, but momentarily holding him off, Buck said, "Don't kill me, I'm unarmed!" Buck was horrified to be looking into the face of this creature.

"You're the one that killed my partner and stole our treasure! I been lookin' for you for two years. Where is it?"

Buck could hardly understand his mumblings. The beast kept rambling until Buck finally pieced together what he was trying to say was "treasure."

"I don't know what you're talking about. I haven't killed anybody and don't know anything about a treasure." Buck tried to free himself, but he was defenseless looking into the face of the man with big brown teeth and beady eyes. There was no sign of mercy or reason. Unable to even move, Buck could only watch in horror as the huge man lifted his knife to stab him. "This is it," he thought, lying underneath the huge, smelly man. No sooner than the man lifted his knife, a shot rang out and the mountain man abruptly stiffened then slumped down on Buck. He looked up, startled to see Vick standing there looking at him and the dead man.

"Damn, he came a hair of killing me. I saw my life flash before my eyes. Mate, where did you come from? And not a lick too soon!"

"You didn't show for supper, so I came looking. Who's your friend?"

Buck sat for a moment in shock, remembering what the man said, about a treasure.

"Come on let's get out of here!" Buck admonished.

"Don't worry, I got your back," Vick said, calmly.

"Come on mate, let's go before his friends come along."

"We can't go and leave the body?"

" I don't know about you, but I'm getting out of here! Forget the body!"

"Go on, I'll meet up with you later," Vick urged.

"You're not going to stay and bury him, are ya?"

"You go, I killed the man, so I'll bury him, I'll meet up with you later."

"You and your puritanical thoughts! That Indian stuff must have rubbed off on you. No worries mate. See you back at the cabin."

Vick never got on board with Buck's careless disregard for life. Even though burying the man was Buck's responsibility, the Indian culture had taught Vick about the preparation of the body for the departure of the spirit, and its sanctity. Unlike the Indians, white men buried their dead instead of placing them on a platform.

Buck knew the kid was private, and did not like sharing his business, but now was the time to get serious with the questions. He remembered the time Vick lost his temper when asked about his scar. He figured the scar had something to do with the mountain man's dead partner. Buck was now sure that the dead man's partner must have sliced Vick's face in a fight over a treasure! Suddenly things began to make sense. And the more he thought about it, the more certain he was that there was information he needed to find out about this treasure.

Buck couldn't have cared less about the man who tried to kill him. All he could think about was getting back to the cabin and look for the treasure.

Buck was now certain that he was right about Vick killing the man's partner over the treasure. All the time Buck had been in the holler, Vick was the only one he had seen, so it had to be him for they had ridden all over the holler together and there was no one else. The more Buck thought about it, the more betrayed he felt and the madder he got. "The kid never told me anything about a treasure."

"What else is he hiding he hasn't told me about?" These questions were looming in his head and he intended to find answers.

Riding back to the cabin, Buck kept trying to figure Vick out.

"Tonight I will loosen him up with some whiskey and cards. The kid has secrets, and by the end of the night I plan to know what they are." Buck planned.

Remembering how steady and cool Vick was when he shot the mountain man, he imagined Vick would have no hesitation killing in self-defense or perhaps for a treasure.

The more he put two and two together, the more he felt Vick was not only a liar, but a damn good one and up to no good.

By the time Vick got back to the cabin, Buck was ready for answers.

"Mate, how about a game and a little whiskey? You want to bring out the jug?"

"Sure, we both need a drink after what happened."

Vick had no idea Buck was setting him up.

Vick went to the cabinet where the whiskey was stored, and got two tin cups. He smiled inwardly as he shuffled the cards for their nightly showdown. The kid was not only good at reading cards, but also equally good at reading Buck. He knew there was something fishy about how he was acting.

The more they drank, the looser the Aussie got, but it didn't seem to affect Vick. It only made him better, which irritated Buck. Vick poured two more shots of the strong whiskey and gave it to Buck. Whiskey, as good as it was, as the old saying goes, "strong enough to kill a horse," did not seem to faze Vick.

Finally, Buck was drunk as a skunk.

"You know what that damn mountain man accused me of?" Buck asked, slurring his words.

"I'm sure you want to tell me." Vick said, cool as could be.

"Well mate, he accused me of killing his friend over some treasure, and since I didn't do it, who else but you could it be? You're damn good with that gun of yours!" Buck continued to slur.

Vick thought, "he's as good as accusing me— so this is what's eating Buck? Vick didn't know how to approach what happened with the mountain man, since he had lied about the family abandoning their home. He was still thinking like the boy he was, and felt sure Buck would not understand.

"You wouldn't understand," Vick said.

"Why don't you try me? Seems like you've been holding this in a long time. Tell me so I won't imagine the worse."

Vick thought for a few minutes, and decided to tell him part of the truth, reserving the rest until later. He would let Buck soak in a little at a time, and then it would be easier to fill him in on the details later, possibly even next time they played cards.

He started at the beginning, when he and his brother ran away from home, got lost, and then found Panther Holler. He went through the entire scenario of finding the family dead, his brother getting killed in the storm, and his having to bury all of them. Vick went on to explain how he had tracked the mountain man who had killed the family, but left out the part about the treasure.

Vick was afraid that Buck would think he'd shot the mountain man in cold blood over his treasure trove, especially since he had never mentioned it.

While he was explaining the details of how he arrived at the cabin, Buck was thinking, "What a lying bastard this kid is. He's deliberately holding back about the treasure." Buck felt he had to be careful and not allow Vick to know he was on to him, at least until he found the "loot." After that, he would have no problem riding to the next town and turning Vick in for killing seven people. "Let the law take care of him, and save me the trouble of killing him myself. No use risking my life trying to kill the bloke, when the law can hang him. It'll serve him right," he rationalized, "and I won't have to risk my life doing the dirty work."

Buck knew Vick was vulnerable, but it was in his own best interest not to test Vick by making threats. Buck went on with his charade, using the information Vick confided in him as a means to discourage the kid from leaving Panther Holler.

"Son, I'm worried about you leaving the holler. Don't know if the sheriff would ever believe your story about how all these people died around here. Now that you've told me what happened, I think the sheriff might think you had something to do with all these murders and possibly involve me."

Buck took every opportunity to frighten Vick. He described, in graphic detail, what it was like to see a man hang.

Vick was disappointed that Buck seemed suspicious of him. He thought, " Buck thinks I might have killed the family. Why wouldn't he defend me and tell the sheriff I was innocent of murder?" He had seen me kill without reservation to save him, so perhaps he thought I could have killed the family. The more Vick contemplated his plight, the more he began to distrust Buck.

Over the next few weeks, without Vick's knowledge Buck continued looking for the treasure. Finally, he noticed a loose plank in the kitchen and wondered if this could be where the treasure was hidden. He had to get Vick out of the cabin before he could do a proper search.

Vick's trusting nature, made it easy for Buck to conjure up a story about being sick. He asked Vick to kill a couple squirrels for stew that would settle his upset stomach.

After Vick left, Buck aggressively began his search. He lifted the loose plank, but to his disappointment, did not find what he imagined could be a fortune. He went through the cabin, working as fast as possible to find the treasure before Vick returned.

It was getting late and the cabin was a mess. He knew today had to be the day or move on without it.

After he ransacked the cabin, without finding anything, he went back to the loose plank. "Maybe I didn't look far enough under the floor," he thought. Buck lay on the floor again, and stretched his arm as far as possible under the floor. Much to his surprise, he touched a cloth bag, which he thought could be the treasure. He pulled it out without taking time to untie the string and examine it. Happy to have finally found it, he didn't waste time throwing his things together to leave.

Vick was smart to hide the more valuable part of the windfall elsewhere. Not even suspecting it existed; Buck grabbed his clothes, his bedroll, a little food, and was on his way. He was sure that after Vick returned to the cabin and saw it ransacked, he would come looking for him. His only hope was to make it out of the holler and back to town before Vick caught up with him. There he would weave his tale for the sheriff and leave Vick to fall into the web.

Returning to the cabin, Vick knew Buck had played him for a fool. The plank ripped from the floor confirmed that Buck had found what he was looking for. Hurrying to the other hiding place, Vick was relieved to find the more valuable treasure was still intact. His good friend Buck had made off with only the less valuable scraps, barely making a dent in the overall value of the other treasure.

"What next?" he wondered.

Chapter 8

Now, that Buck had run out on Vick, he knew the kid would be coming after him. And he was right.

Buck was a professional con and Vick knew he would scheme until he found a way to entrap Vick by convincing people he was a murderer. "It was only a matter of time, before the sheriff and his posse would be there to take him in for murder," Vick imagined.

He had planned the future leaving Panther Holler with Buck, but he never expected the sheriff would be coming to make the arrest for him killing seven people, — because Buck threw in the lie that Vick killed his own brother.

"That sidewinder!" hollered Vick, kicking the ground in disgust.

He remembered the scenario Buck had painted suggesting that the sheriff would have him hanged for killing the two mountain men and the defenseless family in Panther Holler. Buck had even described horrifying details: "Mate, it's going to be difficult to prove you didn't kill that family, especially since I saw you kill that mountain man."

The deck was stacked against him for not telling Buck about the treasure.

Just as Vick had suspected, the man he had most looked up to, had ridden to the nearest town and stumbled into the sheriff's office, telling his lying tale of Vick Porter, a young crazed cowboy who had murdered seven people.

"The kid's loco — capped it off by blowing his own brother's head off. The Australian gambler who was extremely unkempt and wearing a long bearskin coat told his story with such intensity that Sheriff Jenkins and his men believed there was a crazed killer on the loose.

One deputy, who was a bit overcome asked, "So is this how he ended his killing spree? Holy Lord Almighty! He's just a kid ... and he killed his own brother!"

It was such a compelling story with such graphic details that the sheriff thought no man could make up a tale like that.

"Where can we find this boy?" the sheriff finally asked.

"He's living about a two days' ride from here, deep in the backwoods at a place called Panther Holler. He's easy to recognize, with a big scar on the left side of his face."

"Ain't nothing but thickets in the Ozarks, how we goin' to find him?" the sheriff asked.

"I can draw you a map, but I have to warn you, he's hardly a kid. He's crazy, but smart like a fox. Get what I'm saying?"

By the time the news got out that a gun-slinging kid was on the rampage, a crowd began forming in front of the sheriff's office. People were bunched together, discussing the frightening details of a kid on a murderous rampage. Buck looked on with pride for causing such a stir. Seizing the moment, he stood on the porch continuing to frighten the people by explaining how Vick had murdered innocent children. A voice from the crowd cautioned, "That's quite a tale you're spinning there."

"It's pretty gruesome all right, but it ain't no tale!" Buck lashed out, resenting the man's doubting statement.

"I'm here to warn you that he could make his way to your town, and it's up to you to protect yourselves. So what are you going to do about it?" he shouted.

"We gotta stop him!" an overly distraught woman cried out. Buck could see he had single-handedly aroused the crowd to a panic state.

Urgency to find the killer overwhelmed the sheriff after he heard Buck's tale of an unbridled murderer on the loose. Only six volunteers stepped forward to stand by Sheriff Jenkins, willing to risk their lives, while many able-bodied men stayed behind, Buck included, declining to be deputized.

At midday the sheriff and his deputies left in pursuit of Vick, while Buck distanced himself by riding off in the opposite direction.

By the time the men stopped for the night, the sun had set, changing the bright bluish sky to indigo, mixed with shades of pinks and orange. The weary riders had found a good resting place near a mountain stream where their horses could have a good drink and graze a bit. The main party unpacked the supplies, set up camp, and made a fire, while two men rode off to shoot a mess of squirrels and rabbits.

Despite the idyllic setting, the sheriff was vigilant in ordering the men to take turns standing guard over the camp during the night. Their deliberations as to what order they would stand watch, and re-counting of the day's ride, were interrupted by occasional gunshots in the distance. "I reckon supper is on its way," a deputy noted.

After dinner, the men rekindled the fire and sat around camp listening to the sheriff's plan to capture Vick Porter. "We don't even know if that Buck feller is telling the truth?" one of the deputies chimed in. "Something about this ain't right. We ain't never heard of no place called Panther Holler."

"I spec' they got all kinds of places deep in the Ozarks you ain't heard of. If you ain't been there, then you don't know." said the sheriff, studying Buck's crude map as he talked.

"I heard tell of some mighty bad mountain men in them parts. I reckon we have to be on the lookout for them as much as that Vick feller. What if this ain't nothin' but the man's imagination?

He might be as crazy as the kid."

"Didn't you hear that feller say, when the kid kills a man, he scalps 'em, then offers 'em up in some kind of devil ceremony? I reckon he kills just 'cause he likes to. And that's why we got to get to him before he finds his way into our town. Paranoia was running rampant as their imaginations ran wild.

The deputies talk continued on until one by one they fell asleep, leaving the first man on watch alone, listening to the crackling fire and wondering to himself about what the next day might bring.

It was a short night and after a quick breakfast, the sheriff and his grim-faced posse mounted up and walked their horses across the stream in a misting rain, as they entered the thicket toward Panther Holler.

The six men followed the landmarks that kept them on course, and made camp before nightfall each day. They entered a jungle-like landscape and discovered they had no idea the thicket was made up of deep hollers and underbrush.

As the men traveled farther into the unknown, they began doubting Buck, thinking his story might well be nothing more than a figment of his imagination. The sheriff quickly dispelled any doubt by assuring them that no man could make up such a story. But he had not known the likes of Buck Dupree.

As they fought their way through the thick prickly brush, grabbing at their clothes and hands and even agitating the horses, they developed more desire to kill Vick when they caught him instead of bringing him in for a fair trial. The next day, it would be sundown before they reached a mountainous area that was even more brutal for the horses. This was where Buck told them they would find Vick, in a cabin with a sign on it called Panther Holler.

They continued to push their way relentlessly until they found a trail that helped them make better time. They enjoyed an easy trail in the cool morning as they rode in threesomes, with the sheriff in the lead.

Vick knew he had to be on the trail early in case Buck was able to convince a lawman that he was a murderer. He didn't want to be surprised and thrown in jail or worse. He packed the treasure and took limited supplies, in case he had to make a run for it, confident that he knew every inch of the wooded area around him. If there was to be no posse, he worried that Buck might come back after figuring he had been duped. There were too many issues that concerned him. He thought the best thing to do was stake out the cabin and wait.

As Vick rode through the forest, he knew he would miss the place. Traces of jasmine permeated the air and everything was lush and green. He didn't understand why, but he felt reverential until he began thinking about what Buck might do when he got to town. Vick knew the path well and had an escape route unknown to Buck plus he had a plan.

He would lead the posse into a rugged mountainside filled with holes and jagged rocks, bad enough to cause their horses to lose their footing and maybe plunge over into the deep holler. This was the only way Vick knew to avoid capture. At least his plan would keep them trapped long enough for him to get away.

He rode the entire day and just before dusk, it was as though an unseen hand had placed him directly in back of the sheriff and his posse. The sight of the riders shocked Vick, even though he was half-way expecting them.

As he inched his way closer behind them, he could hear parts of their conversations. Every now and then the sheriff would stop and look at their map, and then continue on.

Vick kept getting closer and closer to the group of riders.

Finally, one member of the posse asked Sheriff Jenkins something about the "outlaw Vick Porter," and the seven people he had killed.

A jolt went through Vick's body like a bolt of lightning. They were accusing him of killing seven people, including his brother! He was riled, hearing his name connected with seven murders because of Buck's lies. He had only killed the mountain men to keep them from killing him and Buck. So, his thanks for saving Buck's life was for Buck to say it was murder!

As for his good friend Buck, the sorry bastard had upped the ante by the unfathomable accusation he had killed his little brother, Sam. "How could he have turned me in for killing my own brother?" Vick fumed.

He began having doubts, wondering if the name they said was just similar to his, until he heard his name mentioned again. He kept edging closer, until he overheard talk of hanging him to stop his murdering rampage. "These people aren't here to arrest me; they're here to kill me!"

He knew he could never explain his way out of Buck's accusations. He had to get away and hunt down the sorry no good liar and make him tell the truth. Vick pulled his horse off the trail when the sheriff stopped suddenly to talk to his men. He suggested they enter Panther Holler from two different directions. Vick watched as they consulted the map and then split up leaving the sheriff with one deputy. They made their way into a small mountain pass, just as Vick had hoped. If they followed as he expected, the horses would trip and plunge into the holler. Vick followed, wishing he had their map.

He was paying too much attention to them and got too close behind the posse. They stopped again, hearing a noise and turned. Seeing Vick's facial scar, their eyes registered recognition.

"Aubrey, I think we have 'em." Look at that scar," said one. The deputized riders spun their horses and whipped their horses into a run, chasing Vick.

The sheriff and deputy continued toward the cabin, not knowing his other men had encountered Vick.

The riders were no competition for the young cowboy, as he darted in and out of places that the men did not know existed. When the deputies came to the mountain passage, they entered blindly, as Vick planned. It was sundown, which made it more difficult for them to see. One by one they were thrown head first off the ledge into the dense holler. The last man didn't quite make it to the ledge, but was thrown into the mountain, knocking him semi-conscious.

Vick watched as the men and horses fell about ten feet below, far enough to delay pursuit but not far enough of a fall to maim man or horse. He dismounted and quickly exchanged his jacket for the dazed deputy's jacket, then loaded the man on Sugar, Vick's horse.

He whispered in the horse's ear, "Do your job, Sugar," then turned toward the trail to the cabin, slapped her haunch, sending horse and rider on their way. Vick was sure the sheriff would see who he thought might be Vick since the deputy was in an unfamiliar jacket and on a horse he didn't recognize.

He then grabbed the deputy's horse, mounted, and raced off in the opposite direction.

The sun had just set, but still a little light in the sky when Sheriff Jenkins and his deputy arrived at the cabin. He saw the shadow of a rider coming out from the side of the mountain path. As he got closer, Sheriff Jenkins knew it had to be Vick Porter. The deputy and the sheriff rode aggressively toward who they thought was Vick firing their guns as they dug their spurs into their horse's flanks.

The deputy who was thought to be Vick, regained his senses, then yelled, "No, Sheriff! It's me, John!" waving frantically. The sheriff and deputy continued firing and rushing toward the rider, too excited to hear John's words.

Finally, the deputy had no choice but to turn and race back into the rugged mountainside, leading the sheriff and his deputy into the narrow trail to a sudden lunge into the holler. No one had a chance at the rate of speed the horses were going.

When Vick escaped unscathed, he knew going back to the cabin would be a mistake. He had little food, but he had the treasure and no matter what, he knew in order to survive he had to make his way to a town.

The night was setting in, but he had to keep moving. Finally, when it became pitch dark, he decided he had to take a chance and stop to rest. The lack of moonlight made traveling in the rough terrain too dangerous for his horse. Vick hated leaving Sugar behind but the deputy's horse was faster and more spirited.

He made camp away from the trail, but had a frightful night's sleep. He kept hearing sounds, thinking some of the men had found their way out of the holler and were catching up with him.

Ultimately, after having a number of wild dreams and very little sleep, he decided it must be a sign for him to continue on. At least he and his horse had some rest. It would be slow moving, but it was just a couple hours before first light.

Vick saddled the horse and continued on, hoping he was still going in the direction of a town. He was making real good time; he marveled at how much stronger and faster this horse was compared to Sugar.

As he rode, he discovered the map in the deputy's jacket he was wearing. He hadn't even seen a map before, but had seen the posse looking at a piece of paper and pointing here and there. For the first time in four years, Vick allowed himself to think this paper with familiar looking pattern of lines might help him find his way back home.

Chapter 9

VICK THOUGHT HE MIGHT BE TRAVELING IN CIRCLES UNTIL HIS HORSE **unexpectedly stepped out of the thicket and onto a trail.** After several days of fighting the heavy brush, he found a trail that encouraged him to think he might be heading back to civilization and possibly home. As he followed the trail, Vick began to imagine the worst. Surely there was a bounty on his head for whomever tracked him down. Now that he was a marked man, he would have to be looking over his shoulder for that unknown gun that could open fire at any time. The trail led him into a town. Ordinarily, he would have stopped there, but he no longer could chance being recognized and thrown in jail. He assumed this was the town the sheriff and his posse had come from. His heart pounded as he passed a mercantile store and finally the jail. He kept moving, even though it was doubtful any of the posse had made it back.

He rode virtually unnoticed through the town and was relieved to be in the clear again. Vick rode for another day before he saw anyone. When he came upon a group of logging men along the trail, he stopped to query them about the next town and where he could find a job.

"Right up ahead they're hiring," said one of the muleskinners. The men acted as if they felt he looked a tad young to be doing a grown man's job. He thanked them and rode on until he passed the foreman's shack. It was evident he was in logging country with all the timber.

Vick recalled Buck's admonition of the importance of being clean and well dressed in order to be taken seriously. When he arrived in the next town, he stopped at a boarding house and used some of the money from the treasure to rent a room. Buck had taught him well how to count money. It was a nice comfortable house, with a bathroom down the hall. This suited him just fine, since all he needed was a place to sleep and eat.

The room he rented was very comfortable and he immediately fell asleep and slept until late the next day. When he finally awoke, for a brief moment, he thought he was back in the little cabin at Panther Holler. His heart sank as he remembered he was now a fugitive on the run, all because of Buck Dupree the man he trusted.

"I'm no longer the young boy who ran away from home," he said to the ceiling. "I'm almost nineteen and a man who needs to find his way in this new world. I have to get a grip on things and clear my name so I can live a normal life."

Vick had never had the luxury of buying clothes or boots for himself, so when he entered the mercantile store, he was in awe of the fine clothing. He had no choice but to dip more into the treasure, the value of which he had not a clue except for the bills. In spite of being a hunted man, he liked the feeling of having enough money and seeing what all it could buy. Fortunately for him, the saleslady could guess his sizes. He returned to his room, loaded down with several sets of clothes that would last him awhile. He was finally glad to be out of the old boots and clothing Buck had given him.

The next morning, while enjoying a long soak in a tub of hot water, there was a knock on the door. He was startled to hear a woman's voice.

"Young man, is everything okay in there?" his landlady asked.

"Just fine, I'll be out in a minute," Vick answered, somewhat embarrassed.

"No rush. Just thought you might have gone to sleep." The woman had a jolly little laugh as she walked away. Vick hurried along until he was clean-shaven and fully dressed. Looking into the mirror seeing himself in his new shirt and pants, as a matured man for the first time, he thought, "Not bad." The nasty scar on his face would always be a reminder of his past, but he felt handsome in spite of it. Vick put tonic on his hair and combed it straight back, giving him the refined look Buck had taught him about. This was all very good for his ego.

When he came out of the bedroom, dressed and ready to go, the landlady hardly recognized him. Taken aback by his good looks.

"My, my, Mr. Porter, you do dress up well," she blurted out before she could stop herself, turning beet red. Vick smiled and tipped his hat, amused at her embarrassment over her reaction to his looks.

Saddling his horse, Vick rode back out to the logging camp, feeling like a million dollars and so did his horse he named "Shadow," a beautiful gray stallion, standing almost 17 hands high.

He was determined to get a muleskinner job, and walked right into the foreman's office. Stepping inside, he asked to speak to the foreman. "You're looking at him son," the big man answered.

"I heard you were hiring." Vick spoke with confidence.

"How old are you boy? What makes you think you can do a man's job?"

"Don't worry, I'm old enough to work! Age has nothing to do with a man's ability to do a man's job." He could tell he had the foreman's attention.

"You're young, but sure of yourself, I like that! I hope you're a morning riser, for we start things rolling around here early — six o'clock in the morning. I suggest you be on time and ready to work. No fancy clothes like those you're awearin', 'cause you gonna be plenty dirty and tired when I git through with you. By the way, what's your name?"

"My name's, uh, Vick Porter. What do I call you?"

"Just call me Boss."

Vick tipped his hat and walked out; excited to know he had his first job and not caring what it paid.

His boss wondered what the story was behind his scar.

After a few weeks, Vick was known as being more than a common laborer. He worked hard and was fast doin' more than his share of the work and was good with the mules.

Ole Boss liked him 'cause he did his job with no complaints and he had a good attitude, making him an easy selection when he needed someone to oversee a crew of loggers. Many of the men disliked a kid overseeing them but, after a few days seeing how he carried himself and treating them equal, he had earned their respect.

Vick couldn't believe, after being on the job less than a month he had already gotten a raise and a promotion, but what he really liked were the hours. He could now go into town to the local saloon and play poker. Knowing he had kept a low profile because of Buck's lies, he would dress in his best clothes after work, and go to the local saloon for a drink. For several weeks, he just watched the men deal and play, not yet ready to jump into the fire. Finally joining in when one of the loggers urged him on, Vick was soon known as "the man to beat."

He was classed as a good poker player, while the women thought of him as a dapper dresser. Regarded as a professional when he walked into the saloon, the painted ladies paid close attention, and made sure he was served before the crowd. There was one woman who paid a little too much attention to Vick; the other cowboys noticed the preferential treatment. They began making digs at Vick, which resulted in a fight, but only one time, as it did not go well for them!

The word was out that Vick was not only a good fighter, but also a lady's man who was getting sweet on Felicia. She was a pretty little thing and was known for her reputation with men. One man spoke favorably of Felicia carrying on with him, which gave Vick the idea he might have a chance with her. This excited him since he was curious about women he had never been with, but she lived with one of his workers.

One evening, Felicia began making physical contact, while serving Vick his whiskey. She had been flirting with him ever since his first visit to the saloon, making eyes and giving him sultry looks, but Vick had tried to play it down. Buck had told him that, "his day would come with the ladies," but Felicia wasn't the one since Vick was smart enough to know that it would be a mistake to go after a muleskinner's woman.

Any red-blooded man would have noticed the sexuality of a woman like Felicia Parsons, with her pretty face and voluptuous body. Her smile intrigued him and he wondered what it would be like to kiss her, since he had never kissed a woman. He imagined himself with her; and he was more vulnerable because he had a bit more than usual to drink.

She seemed to show even more interest that night, intriguing him even more. Examining her with his eyes as she walked across the floor carrying a tray of drinks, he tried to ignore his feelings, but her smile and flirting made it very difficult. Trying to dispel the rumor of their attraction with the gamblers sitting at the table, Vick used the flirting to his advantage, setting the distracted cowboys up and working them until he could win their money.

It was especially enticing when Felicia would rub her hand across his. The cat and mouse game went on until the end of the evening when the saloon was closing and Vick found himself the last to leave. Did he really intend to stay that long or was he hoping for something else?

Felicia came down the stairs, filling the hall with the fragrance of her perfume just as Vick was paying his bill and the bartender was blowing out the kerosene lamp. It was difficult to see her, but there she was in the night's shadows, slinking across the room. Her image literally took Vick's breath away. She stopped and stared at him, beckoning him to follow her. She slipped through the saloon doors and down a long narrow walkway that led into an alley.

It was a beautiful warm night with a bright moon. It seemed that every star in the sky was winking at him as Vick stepped outside, following Felicia into the inky darkness. He stopped momentarily, smoking his cigar, and then took a deep breath as his passion continued to direct him. This was the closest Vick had come to prayer, when he said underneath his breath, "help me, Lord," knowing he was entering a gravity of no return.

They quickly slipped out of sight between two buildings, where she was sure no one could hear or see them. Now in the shadows, Vick stopped and stared for a moment, before walking slowly toward her. Getting closer, he knew she was the prettiest creature he had ever seen! With passion rising within him he had to concentrate to be gentle.

He threw his cigar on the ground and took her in his arms, kissing her softly as he had often imagined. He kissed her again, pulling back after what seemed like forever, but it was only a few seconds. The scent of her perfume captivated him, as she had known it would when she dabbed it on before leaving her room. He was spellbound.

"Felicia, not here. Follow me." They walked hurriedly to the back entrance to the rooming house, and Vick slipped his key into the lock.

"We must be quiet," he said, as they both put their finger on their lips and walked quietly into Vick's room. He had dreamt of his first time with a woman and knew he would remember it all his life. He also knew it wouldn't be his last. For these few moments of ecstasy, transcended his thoughts of being a hunted man. The beauty standing before him was like watching an exotic cat, as she weaved and twisted slipping out of her clothing. She was mesmerizing to watch, as if she was hypnotizing her prey, before her kill. "So this is what it's like to be with a woman?" Vick thought. Felicia started walking toward him as he explored this beautiful work of art. When she got to the edge of the bed he was completely animated as he took her hand and laid her down beside him. She could see the excitement in his eyes as she wantonly summoned him into a private sanctuary that no one could otherwise enter, unless invited. The night was beautiful and nothing else seemed to matter but him and Felicia.

The next morning, Vick was in a state of denial that he had allowed himself to lose control and sleep with his workers woman. He knew he was in trouble and couldn't believe how stupid he had been the night before, although he enjoyed every second he spent with Felicia. In a few hours, the word would be out and a fight, possibly to the death, would ensue, if he did not leave town first. With there likely being a price on his head, he could not afford the attention. He had already heard vague rumors about a crazed madman wandering around in the woods near a not too distant town, and any more attention might trigger his discovery.

"Of all the luck, I've found someone I really like, and now I have to leave." These thoughts kept ringing in his mind as he lay beside her, conflicting sharply with the realities of his past. Felicia awoke as Vick was dressing.

"Much as I hate to, I've got to go," he said, as he reached down to kiss her. The sunlight was leaking in around the heavy window curtain.

"We must have fallen asleep. Vick, you know what this means. I can never see you again."

He sat on the side of the bed and slipped on his boots.

"Are you going to be all right?" he asked.

"Why? Where are you going?"

"Don't worry about me. I meant to tell you last night, but today is my last day in town."

"Because of me? It's probably best; you know what could happen," Felicia said, sadly.

Vick listened without talking and began packing. He knew the trouble he would be in if he stayed, and if Felicia's lover found out she had spent the night with Vick, well it would be dangerous for both of them.

He helped her steal away out the back door, then packed his gear and clothing along with the treasure he had brought with him.

On the way out of town, Vick stopped by the logging office to resign, but was met head on by Boss. The news had already circulated that Vick had moved in on one of Vick's fellow worker's girl, something not to be tolerated. Consequently, he was fired on the spot. The last words he heard were, "Why don't you grow a beard, Scarface!"

Vick left and never looked back. Felicia would become a special memory, and one that he would often think about, as he kept one step ahead of the law. "Growing a beard sounded like a good idea," he thought, and decided to give it a try. Even after a day of growth, Vick realized that it would be the best thing he could do for himself. Soon he would be able to hide behind the beard and move about without being known for the scar. After the day's ride, he stopped in the next town. He stayed there for two days before riding on. Now, with nearly three day's growth, his beard was beginning to hide his scar.

When he arrived in Jonesboro, one of the first things he did was visit the local barber and had his beard trimmed with a haircut stylish of the day. When he looked at his clear blue eyes and black hair in the mirror, he realized he looked different: like quite a gentleman. One could still see his scar but his beard was growing fast and not too long he would have a full beard.

After leaving the barber, he rode through town where everything became vaguely familiar. It wasn't until he passed the mercantile store that he recognized it as the store he and his brother Sam had visited with his Pa!

The store looked smaller than he remembered, but he was sure it was the same one. Strangely enough, he had found his way back to the town and the home he and his little brother Sam had run away from. Passing the blacksmith shop and the jail, he kept riding in the familiar direction.

He hadn't thought about returning home in a long time. But having been away for almost five years, his heart told him he should go by and see the old place. Vick didn't know if he was excited, or if it was a case of jittery nerves, but something was pulling him in the direction of his Pa.

"My ol' man, may have drank himself to death by now," he thought. He was still not sure he wanted to see him, but he decided to take it one step at a time and make his mind up when he got there. He was sure he wanted to see the old home place, since it now seemed like only something from a dream.

He turned around and rode back to the blacksmith shop, seeking directions after seeing changes he did not recognize. Getting off his horse, Vick walked over to the colored man who was working there. The man stopped his work and looked at Vick as if he was trying to recognize him.

"Howdy, what can I do fer you? Name's, Johnny Earl."

"Nice to know you Johnny. Maybe you can help me. I used to know how to get to the old Porter place, but everything has changed around here," Vick said.

"Yo' lookin' fer' tuh' ole Porter place? I ain't seen ole man Porter fer' a long time. Don't know if he's still ah living."

"I'd appreciate it if you could tell me how to get there?" asked Vick.

"It used to be way out in dem' woods, but it don't seem so far no more, since the logging company come to town."

"Is the place still there?" asked Vick.

"Yep, I reckon it is, but I ain't been that way in a long time. Why don't you follow that road till it ends, then go left about two mile out. You can't miss it. You gonna be surprised to see a big logging company out there. Yep, like I said, things sho' has changed. You sho' yo' horse don't need shoein'?"

"Not this time, maybe when I have more time."

"Happy to help. Sho' hope ya find that ol' place."

Vick followed Johnny's directions, trying to recognize anything familiar. All he could think about was how he would break the news to his Pa about Sam. That is, if Percy was still living. His emotions were running high, remembering all the times he wished he were back home after he had taken his brother and run away. Now, he was back, and didn't know how he was going to face the man that had severely abused him.

"How on earth am I going to explain Sam's death?" he asked himself. Vick felt like he had been gone a lifetime, but he couldn't help but revert back to the image he had of himself as a little boy who would be reprimanded for doing something his Pa thought was bad.

Indeed, he noticed all the changes the blacksmith had warned him about. The old trail to his home had turned into a freshly graded road, the small trees were now stately pines, standing tall on both sides of the road. Everything was familiar, barely recognizable.

As he rounded the bend, he came to a huge long white building, apparently the logging office. Compared to what he had seen in his travels, it looked very modern. But there, about three hundred feet away, and a distance from the road, was a small house, which was made out of raw timber. He had to look twice at the house before he fully recognized it as his home. It had ceased to be the home he remembered for there were thick vines growing all around the log blocks the house rested on, and it was much smaller than he imagined.

It looked abandoned. Vick thought it might be a blessing if his Pa had died, as the man would be spared the news of Sam's death, and Vick would not have to lie about why he ran away.

He got off his horse and walked through the yard, populated with nothing but vines and tall weeds. It was not at all like he remembered, when he and Sam were playing marbles in the dirt, and looking under the foundation.

The house had never seen a drop of paint and vines now covered some of the trim boards and windows, much unlike the flashbacks

Vick had of what it looked like. He didn't remember the raw timber with no paint. In his mind, he thought the place was painted. His most vivid memory was being able to see underneath the house from the front to the back. What he saw now was a run-down old structure badly in need of repair.

Chapter 10

Vᴠɪᴄᴋ sᴀᴛ ᴏɴ ʜɪs ʜᴏʀsᴇ, ʟᴏᴏᴋɪɴɢ ᴀᴛ ᴛʜᴇ ᴏʟᴅ ᴘʟᴀᴄᴇ, ᴘᴜꜰꜰɪɴɢ ᴏɴ ᴀ **cigar, wondering if it was wise to revisit his past.** He had not seen his Pa in nearly five years and now the only thing separating them was the door to his childhood home. Since his Pa hadn't been seen in town in awhile, he could likely be dead and buried.

After an agonizing few minutes, he dropped his cigar and walked to the small barn to hitch his horse and hide the treasure. When he walked up the steps to the door, his boots were as loud as the echo in a canyon. His heart skipped a beat from not knowing what to expect and for a moment, he felt the urge to turn and walk away. He really did not know what he would say when he faced his Pa, but he felt compelled to see the face of the man that had so severely abused him and his brother when they were growing up.

Vick knocked softly, and then was startled when he heard a raspy weak voice from within, "Who's there? I want you off my property right now!" the voice yelled from within the house.

He thought he would recognize his Pa's voice, but this did not sound like the man who used to scream profanities at him. He thought perhaps someone was poaching in his Pa's house. He replied in a soft voice, "I'm looking for Percy Porter who used to live here."

"Are you in cahoots with that logging company next door?"

"No, I'm Vick, Percy's son." There was a pause and then Vick heard the man's voice crack.

"You're trying to trick me. My sons are dead! I want you off my property. I got a gun right here ready to use, so ya best git' goin'."

"That's my Pa, but with the voice of a much older man," Vick thought, as he reached for the door to walk in. As he walked in, the old man cautioned,

"You ain't got no right coming in my house. Who are you?"

Vick was shocked to see the frailty of his Pa. He was now skinny and much older looking than his age, standing there in old baggy overalls with only one strap holding them up. He was apparently blind and had lost most of his hair.

Percy stood staring into space with the help of a cane, near a single bed. Vick walked over to his Pa, for whom he now felt sorry, and said, "No Pa, I'm your son, Vick, and I'm very much alive."

Percy, unsteady on his feet sat down on the bed. "My mind's playing tricks on me. I'm not a well man. My boys are dead."

"No, your mind is just fine. I'm Vick, and I've come home."

The old man gasped for air, as the realization that this really was his son, began to sink in.

"Are you sure you're Vick? 'Cause Vick and Sam were kidnapped five years ago. Sam was twelve and Vick was fourteen. Are you sure you're alive and I'm not dead? With that beard and my eyesight, it's hard to recognize you. "

Vick couldn't help but smile at his Pa, who seemed altogether different now that he was old and sick. "Maybe it would be better to have him think Sam was away and would be returning home soon," he thought, wanting to save his Pa the pain.

"I heard you were sick, and I wanted to come and take care of you."

"Where is Sam?" Percy asked. The old man's mouth quivered and his eyes began to water. He kept rubbing them, trying not to show he was touched that his son was home.

"Sam … is going to be coming as soon as he can. He don't want you worrying.

"You think I'll get to talk to him soon? I don't know how much longer I can hold on, and I have lots to tell him."

"What do you mean, hold on? You're just fine," Vick said.

"I could have died a couple times, but I knew I had to keep it together in case you and your brother came home. Something told me if you boys were kidnapped you would grow up … and let me hear from ya."

"Well, I'm here now, and I'm not leaving," Vick reassured his Pa. Vick had not cried since Sam had died. But seeing his Pa in this condition was more than he could stand, as he fought hard to hold back the tears.

"Pa, how have you been getting along here by yourself?"

"I've been making it alright, I got a little gal by the name of Mattie lives not too fer' down the road and she's been lookin' in on me. Her mama died a while back and she brings me food once a week. Little good it does though, 'cause I can't eat much anymore; but it sure smells good. I reckon I still have my smeller."

"Can you drink coffee?"

"Son, I ain't had coffee in so long I don't remember how it tastes … six months, I reckon. It was giving me heartburn, but I sho' like the way it smells."

"What about whiskey?" Vick asked.

"When you boys was kidnapped, I quit drinking 'cause I had to go lookin' fer ya. I'm blind as a bat now and couldn't look no more. There was all kinds of tales about what happened to ya. I knew I was being punished 'cause I let yo mama down, didn't do right by you boys, either. That whiskey made me a mean sonavobitch, but I don't reckon I knew wha' it was doin' to me."

Percy tried to laugh, but got strangled and began to cough uncontrollably. Vick ran over to the sink and found a cloth to wipe his Percy's face.

"Your face is red as a beet. Do you have something you can take to get your fever down?"

"No, don't take nothing no more. I use to drink myself silly but I quit, 'cause my boys needed me to find 'em." Percy began repeating himself. "When did ya say your brother was comin' home? I ain't long for this world."

Percy laid down on his little bed shivering even though it was midsummer.

"I'm proud you quit drinking, but you need something to get your fever down," Vick urged. "Maybe I need to go fetch a doctor."

Vick leaned closer to hear his Pa, who was now talking in a whisper. "Pa, please don't try and talk. Why don't you close your eyes and rest for a while?"

"I gotta tell you about that damn logging company next door. They been tryin' to take my land away from me. I got over two hundred acres of timber. It's prime timber mind ya, and they want to steal it. It's the best timber around... the best, and I need you to stop em' from stealing it. That ol' man Barkin has stole the whole town. He's nothing but a thief! Ain't nobody in this town can trust 'em."

Percy lifted his shaking hand and pointed to a corner of the room. "You remember Thomas Barkin don't ya?"

"I reckon you pointed him out to me when I was a kid."

"All my papers are in that black saddlebag over in that corner. You take 'em to the judge and show them bastards that this is my property! Well, I mean yours and Sam's, when I die. Barkin's been tryin' to take it away from me."

Vick could tell his Pa was visibly upset and needed to talk, but he did not remember his Pa having anything but the small frame house. His Pa had never let on that he owned two hundred acres.

"Pa, are you sure you own two hundred acres?"

"Yeah, that's what I'm sayin'! I homesteaded all two hundred acres and I have the papers. I want you to go get that black leather bag fer me. My land is up and down this road on both sides and goes fer miles."

Vick looked at where his Pa was pointing, and saw an old leather saddlebag, bulging at the seams with old papers.

"I just want to visit with you right now. I'll look through the bag later."

"Are you sure you're my boy? You don't sound like Vick. Tell me something I'll remember so I'll know it's really you?"

"Well, when me and Sam were little, we used to wait for you to get home every night. Sometimes, you'd take us to town and we'd help you load feed in the wagon. You remember that, don't you, Pa?"

"I reckon I do son ... I tied you boys when you were little 'cause I was afraid you and Sam would run off while I was in town working."

Vick knew his Pa was trying to rationalize what he did to them when he and Sam were young. He got the feeling Percy was sorry and thought, "Why relive the last moments of my father's life rehashing the past wrongs done to me and my brother." He patted his Pa on the shoulder, and assured him he understood.

"You rest Pa; I know you did the best you could."

"Thanks son, I never told you, but you take after ya mama. She was a good wife and mother, but she never had no chance. Them Indians gave her the cholera. That's why I tried to keep 'em away from you boys. They took ya mama away from me and I dang sure weren't gonna let 'em take you boys away from me, too. Ya mama was good as they come and she made me happy."

How strange it was to hear his Pa talk about his mother, because he never spoke of her when he and Sam were little.

"She must have been special," Vick said. He could see his Pa tear up at the mention of her, and watched as he tried to conceal his feelings by changing the subject.

"I reckon it was too painful to talk about your mama back then ... and still is. Son, about that logging, ya can't let them steal this place and land from under ya. Old man Barkin has stole property all around me, but he ain't taking mine. Don't cut no deals 'cause we got prime timber." Vick could see his Pa slipping away.

"Pa, don't worry, I'll take care of things. Why don't you lay back and try to rest. You've talked long enough and I'll be right here when you wake up."

"I may not wake up. There' a lot to say. This place is all I got to leave you boys. I've been saving it fer ya." Percy grabbed Vick's shirt and Vick let him pull him closer.

"Son, if I go, tell Sammy I'm sorry." Percy fought to stay awake as his hollow eyes stared at the ceiling. Finally, he closed his eyes.

Indeed, Percy's fears about not waking up were well founded, as he fell asleep right after telling Vick about the property. The moment he closed his eyes, he slipped into a coma. Vick's efforts to find a doctor were in vain, and the old man died three days later. He was surprised at how much he loved his Pa, even after hearing his flimsy reasons for treating him and Sam the way he did. He still loved him.

Vick had learned more about his Pa than he realized before Percy went into a coma. Many of those revelations came to Vick as he sat by his Pa's side those three days before his death. It helped ease his mind knowing that Percy's love for his wife was the real reason for his fear and hatred toward the Indians. All the years of pain and hate left Vick. There was no more regret or desire for revenge, just the normal peace and love a son would have for his Pa.

He wished he had come a few weeks or days earlier to spend more time with him. Percy having said emphatically, he had been holding on, refusing to die until his sons came home, eased Vick's guilt. His heart ached for more time with his father.

He was thrilled to find old pictures of the early days when his Ma and Pa were content and happy. "How different his and Sam's life would have been if she had lived," he thought. Vick decided that Percy must have lost his will to live when she died, and turned to the bottle to drown his pain. "Why else would his Pa have been so mean?" If only he had been old enough to understand what was really happening, he could have helped him.

It took a few days for Vick to come to grips with the passing of Percy; then he sought to take care of business.

Within a few days Vick was eager to restore the old place to the way he remembered. He also wanted to stay and settle his Pa's affairs before he moved on. After he cut the vines around the house and barn, he bent down and looked under the house from front to back, just as he and Sam did as kids. While Vick was down on all fours, he heard a snicker. He looked up to see a beautiful young woman smiling. He imagined it was because he was looking under the house. Vick tried not to show his embarrassment when he stood, but his face turned bright red.

"I noticed you cleaned the yard for Mr. Percy; is he okay?" the girl asked.

Vick thought, "This must be Mattie, the one who was taking care of his Pa."

"I'm Vick, Percy's son. Pa passed away several days ago."

She was visibly shaken and immediately started to cry. She had taken care of Percy for over a year and knew only the new Percy Porter. "I am so sorry. Mr. Percy was like family to me; such a kind man."

"You must be Mattie," he said as he helped her from her horse. This was only the second time he'd been this close to a woman.

"I'm so sorry, I wish I would have known Mr. Percy died. I would have paid my respects. I brought soup for him, but you may as well enjoy it now," she offered, lifting the jar from her saddlebag.

"Where did you bury your Pa?"

"We got a place out back close to where my Ma is buried."

Mattie was looking Vick up and down.

"I'm so sorry," she said.

"Thank you for asking and coming by. I haven't had soup in a long time. I feel I owe you for taking care of my Pa."

He could tell she was a real person and sensed she liked him. He accepted the soup, sat it on the porch and motioned for her to sit by him on the steps. "Have a seat?"

She sat down and Vick sat as close as he dared, smitten by her beauty.

"I suppose I should introduce myself. I'm Vick, ah, Vick Porter."

"Oh, I'm sorry. My names Mattie Lea Hodge," she said nervously, affected by Vick's good looks.

"It's good to meet you. I'm staying here until I get the work done around the place and then I aim to settle the property. You can see this place needs a lot of work."

"I guess your Pa told you about the lumber company." Her face registering concern.

"Oh, you know about that?"

"All I know is what Mr. Percy told me. He talked and I listened, but I didn't know much about what he was talking about. My mama was ill awhile and recently died, too, and we never knew what was going on in town. The conversation began to lull…Vick it was nice meeting you but I need to be on my way. Are you sure you're going to be all right?" she asked as she rose.

Vick walked beside her in silence, trying to think of something to say. He felt the blood rush to his head as she shook his hand and helped her onto her horse. For the first time, he felt he had met someone who was like him. He could see why his Pa liked her.

"I can't tell you how sorry I am about Mr. Percy," Mattie said.

"Yeah, I was lucky I made it home in time." She could see the tears well up in his eyes. Mattie's eyes did the same.

He hated to see her leave but he did not want her to know that he had feelings for her.

As bad as he hated to ask for help, he knew he had to have someone trustworthy look over his Pa's papers. The next day he headed for town to have the Will and other papers read to him. As he passed the logging company, he saw a young woman and an older man he presumed to be her Pa enter the office to the logging company. She was impeccably dressed and, although strikingly beautiful, seemed very proper with long strawberry red hair. "A little too stiff for me," he thought. When she glanced at him, he tipped his hat and kept riding.

"I bet that's Mr. Barkin and his daughter," he thought.

Vick arrived at the courthouse and was referred to the man in charge of homesteading and census records. The transfer went easier than he thought, and before he left, he had a clear deed to his Pa's property. Percy had been right. The two hundred acres he had told Vick about were indeed his property, with all the paperwork to prove it. The clerk also informed Vick that he owned one of the best parcels of land he knew of and that the timber alone was worth a sizable amount.

On the way back home, he checked out his property and found stakes with the Porter name on it, which verified where the land started and ended. Interestingly enough, the land passed right in front of old man Barkin's lumber company.

Several weeks passed, when early one morning, Vick was awakened by a knock at the door. He thought perhaps it was Mattie. He quickly dressed and got to the door just in time to see a young lady walking away. It was the beautiful red-haired lady he had seen walking into the lumber company's office. She was embarrassed to have awakened Vick, who was surprisingly handsome. As he stood looking at her, there was something about his gentlemanly mannerisms that intrigued her. She developed an instant spark for him.

Vick was annoyed, knowing this woman and her Pa planned to steal his property. He noticed the difficulty she had conversing and wondered why she was flustered.

"Oh, I uh … I'm sorry to wake you, but I heard the owner of this property passed away. Is the property for sale?" asked the young woman.

Vick thought, "Old man Barkin had sent his daughter to do his dirty work, and I ain't buying it." He was not eager to warm up to this pretty young thing, knowing they had planned to take advantage of his Pa.

"And who are you?" Vick asked.

"I'm sorry; I meant to introduce myself. I'm Elizabeth Barkin."

"Lady, I'm in no frame of mind to deal with you," Vick chided. The woman was annoyed with Vick's response.

"May I ask who you are?"

"I don't know what business it is of yours, but my name is Vick Porter. I'm the son of the man that just died. He warned me of your Pa's intentions." Miss Barkin was confused by the harsh attitude of his accusations.

"Oh, so this is your property?" she asked, standing her ground.

"Not that it's any of your business, but you are trespassing," Vick fervently reasserted. "I don't think I made myself clear: you are not welcome on my property."

She stood motionless, unable to move, until she recovered her wits, then turned and walked away without looking back. When she got to the gate, she hesitated and then turned, walking back toward Vick.

"It is my business to find out if this land is for sale! I'm sure there is a misunderstanding. Do you mind taking a moment to clear it up?" Elizabeth asked.

Again, Vick noticed how pretty and proper she seemed to be; so perfectly groomed and polite, as if she were on her way to a tea party instead of out doing business. He could see that Miss Barkin would do anything to have me sign away my property.

"My father filled me in on your Pa before he died, and that's all I need to know. You don't seem to understand that I know your logging company is out to steal my land. I'm on to you, so take your purse and leave. In other words, get the heck off my property!" Vick could not believe the words and tone that came out of his mouth. This was a beautiful woman he was speaking indignantly to, much like the old Percy would have done!

She was stunned as well as frustrated with his rudeness, but was not about to let him get the best of her.

"We contacted Mr. Percy about purchasing his property, but that was as far as it got. I don't know the condition your father was in before he died, but I can assure you, we never pressured your Pa. Would you be willing to talk to my father about this? What you've said is simply not true, and if you're at all fair, you will agree to a meeting."

Vick thought for a minute, and wondered if Percy had misunderstood. Suppose she was right? The logging company was a big business, and he knew at some point he may need a job, and perhaps he should hear her out.

"I assure you Mr. Porter, that we never tried to steal your father's property. We are honorable, and our company does not enter into the practices of which you have accused us! I understand your father was sick and may have misunderstood our intentions. We always addressed him through mail, and he must have misinterpreted our letters."

Vick thought, "It would be reasonable to at least hear them out. I don't even know if Pa could read, and if he couldn't, it could be he was ill advised."

"What time would you like to meet?" Vick asked.

"I'm sorry but I can't remember if you introduced yourself?"

"Just call me Vick," he replied.

"It's nice to meet you. My name is Elizabeth…

"Yes I know," Vick said.

She remembered a boy who smiled at her when she was a child. *This must be the boy I remember.* Finally she spoke, "how about seven o'clock this evening." In case you don't know, we have a place about five miles down the road, close to the old Indian Village. We purchased the land from the Indians before they left."

"I think I can find my way." Vick couldn't help but wonder if they beat the Indians out of their land too.

That evening, Vick was getting properly dressed for the meeting when he heard a knock on his door. He opened the door to find Mattie crying. She had a brown wrap draped loosely over her lovely white blouse and light blue skirt, looking wonderful despite the tears. Her long brown hair reached halfway down her back and flowed over her shoulders, completing a lovely effect. She threw her arms around Vick.

He was stunned since he hardly knew her. He helped her inside as she commenced telling him, through her sobs, about her Aunt Rose who had just died. She was talking fast and making little sense, but it was clear that he was the one she needed to talk to. Especially since he knew her mother had also recently passed. Mattie's appearance was making Vick late for his meeting with the Barkins, but he felt Mattie came first, no matter what.

She finally said, "Aunt Rose was the last of my family. What am I to do?"

Vick thought about the treasure, and how he could give her money if she needed it. "Here, let me take your wrap. Now, we need to wipe those tears."

He slid Mattie's wrap off her delicate white shoulders, and draped it over the back of a chair next to her. He got up and went to the kitchen for a cloth to wipe her eyes. The time for his appointment had passed, but he was unable to ask Mattie to leave. Vick knew it would not set well with Elizabeth and her Pa, who were waiting for him, but Mattie needed attention, and Vick was the only one who could give it to her. It was the least he could do for someone who had taken care of his ailing Pa for over a year, he thought.

He came back into the room and looked at Mattie sitting demurely there on the settee. He was thinking how sweet she was, and how glad he was to be able to be there for her, not worried about the Barkins who wanted to steal his land. When he sat down next to her and began wiping her face, she looked at him with the eyes of an angel.

"I'm so upset because I know I should be at my aunt's funeral, but I cannot get there."

"Mattie, if you need money, I can get it. It may take me a trip into town, but I am sure I can get enough money for you, if you will allow me to help you?"

"You're too kind. I couldn't let you do that. I shouldn't have come. I'll leave," Mattie said, starting to rise.

"You'll do no such thing." He urged her to sit. "I'm happy to be here for you." Vick slid closer to Mattie and began dabbing her damp eyes again.

He also liked the feeling of a woman leaning on him for support. Being near her brought back some of the feelings he had for Felicia. If it wasn't for the circumstances surrounding his encounter with Felicia and his necessity to leave, he'd surely have spent a lot more time enjoying her company. Survival always comes first. He learned that long before he became a man.

Too many emotional forces were at work on Vick. His natural need for intimacy, combined with the tenderness of this beautiful woman he was trying to console, made them both vulnerable to the moment. With one kiss, they were both swept away with desire. Afterwards, he felt ashamed that he had allowed his passion to get the best of him.

As they lay in each other's arms, Vick looked into her eyes. "Mattie, I want you to understand something. I loved this, but it should never have happened. I'm not in a position to offer you the security and stability a girl like you needs. You need to know, though, that it has nothing to do with you … it's me. I wish I could explain better, but I can't."

Mattie was embarrassed as she reached for her clothing. "Vick, this is as much my doing as yours, but if you regret this, I'll try and stay away."

"No, I don't want you to stay away. It's just that I have something going on in my life that I need to settle before I can get serious about a girl."

"If that's the case, then you needed me as much as I needed you." Not looking at him, she said, "Shall we just forget what happened and continue being friends?"

"That's not what I'm saying. I guess what I mean is … I like you a lot, but I'm not free to offer you any more than what I can give right now. I hope you understand."

"Are you married? Is this what you are trying to tell me?"

"No, you can rest assured, I'm not married. I wish I could tell you, but now is not the time. Perhaps one day." His words told her that Vick had something important in his past, and hoped it was not serious.

He took her in his arms and whispered in her ear, "I think we are a little more than friends." She looked into Vick's eyes and gave him the most beautiful smile.

Hearing Vick say they were more than friends was all she needed to give her hope for a relationship with him. She stayed with him through the night then left early the next morning.

Vick fell hard for Mattie and she was all he could think about in the days to come. He did not want to spend one day apart from her. The evening of passion with Mattie came with a price, however. Mr. Barkin was set on destroying Vick for his insolence in standing up his daughter and him.

"No one treats a Barkin that way, especially not a peon like Vick Porter," he bellowed. The wealthy businessman was cocked and primed to reek havoc on Vick. His plan had been to steal old man Porter's land when he got sick enough to be taken advantage of. The timber was just waiting to be cut and sent to the mill, as he saw it. Having Percy Porter's son, Vick, come out of nowhere at the last minute, was not at all what Barkin expected, and had ruined his plans.

The next day, Vick saw Elizabeth from afar, but she turned her head quickly to show her disgust for his having disappointed her and her father. Vick was not happy to have stood them up either, but how was he going to explain what happened? There was no way he could tell them he was too busy seducing a young innocent girl to make it to their scheduled meeting. He felt like he was in a trap with no way to explain his way out.

Thomas Barkin was known throughout the county as a heavy drinker and could be found many nights in the local saloon playing poker. Vick now avoided those nights in the saloon when Barkin and his friends were there. He was well aware what whiskey could do when a man gets hot around the collar.

Other nights, Vick would hear all the stories about how ruthless the old man was, and how he had set up many of the local property owners so he could take their land. He wondered if Elizabeth knew this about her father.

Months passed, and he and Mattie would periodically ride over his property, finding some of his choice timber cut and stolen. When Vick would see this bold move on the part of the Barkin Lumber Company, it made him furious. He knew it had to be dealt with.

The first time this happened, he rode out passed the old Indian village to confront Mr. Barkin but thought better of it when he saw their surprisingly large estate. He had heard people speak of the manor, but when Vick rounded the bend, coming upon the breathtaking mansion, he had a difficult time visualizing how people lived with such wealth. "These people are indeed rich," he thought. As a boy Vick had never seen the manor and when he had come home he was too busy to ride that far out.

He supposed Mr. Barkin didn't like the Indians living near him, and had them run out of town. He thought of his young Indian friend Hawk, wondering where they had relocated.

Mattie later told Vick she heard Hawk had been bitten by a rattlesnake, but did not know where he was or if he was still living. He always had the intention of repaying the young Indian for the many times he came to his and Sam's rescue, during the days and nights his Pa was in town drinking. Again, it crossed his mind what Hawk had told him about always being "his protector."

As Vick and Mattie rode the two hundred acres, they saw many trees cut. The damage was considerable, but Vick knew there was little he could do without proof, unless they could somehow turn the tables on Barkin and beat him at his own game. "Let's see him try to beat me out of my land," Vick thought. He carefully considered his options, and decided to have a meeting with Mr. Barkin, to demand that he quit trespassing and cutting his trees.

In the meantime, Vick learned the rumors were all true, that Thomas Barkin had manipulated the people in town, accumulating his wealth by deception. This knowledge made Vick's blood boil. He contemplated the only way he knew to stop him: turn the tables on Thomas Barkin in a card game. "How about I beat him out of his land?" he mused. Vick knew that if Barkin wanted the Porter land bad enough, he was sure he could challenge Barkin into risking his lumber company to win Vick's property, especially if he could bring Barkin's pride into the picture. "What goes around, comes around," Buck would say.

The more Vick thought about his two hundred acres up against the Barkin Lumber Company, the more he believed he could do just that. It seemed a pretty good way to solve the lumber theft, although a good chance that Barkin wouldn't accept. The plan would either be ingenious or irresponsible, he decided.

To challenge one of the best poker players around would be the last things Barkin would expect from a young man he had dismissed as an ill-mannered misfit. Mattie tried to talk Vick out of the challenge, but Vick knew this was something he had to do. He would end up either rich or as poor as he was before he came home, but he would regret it if he lost the acreage his Pa had held onto for so long just so he could leave it to him and Sam.

Chapter 11

VICK'S EYES OPENED AGAIN TO STARE AT A JAIL WALL ON THIS NIGHT **that would never end.** He continued thinking about Thomas Barkin, Elizabeth's father who had stolen money and land from everyone he could.

Slowly he replayed how he turned the tables on old man Barkin.

At first, Vick had thought he could settle their issue in a business-like manner, but when he learned of the tactics Barkin used to settle his conflicts, it had become even more appealing to settle this over a game of poker and maybe a little Faro since everyone loved the game.

Vick knew that he could convince Barkin to jump at a chance to win his land. Surely the old man would accept his challenge to win such a prize from a young inexperienced cowboy. After all, Thomas Barkin won most of his fortune by ripping off unsuspecting gamblers who had no way of paying their gambling debt other than turning over their land deeds to him.

His only dread was running into Elizabeth when he called on her father to issue the challenge. Sure enough, as luck would have it, he ran head on into the beauty as she was leaving the office, her smug nose stuck properly in the air.

Stunned and at a loss for words, Vick managed to say, "Nice to see you," as he tipped his hat.

"Good day, Mr. Porter," Elizabeth replied, as she forced a faint smile on her face and kept walking.

"I'm here to see your father." She ignored Vick without giving him the time of day. He nervously tipped his hat again, watching Elizabeth hurry out the door. "She's a strange one, he thought."

Elizabeth was dumbfounded at why she was drawn to this "nobody" whom she convinced was beneath her! This rude, cocky stranger with his superior attitude stirred something inside her that made her doubt her sanity. "I hope father runs him off," she thought, trying to ignore her feelings.

Vick stood in the doorway of the Barkin office waiting to be invited in, when the old man peered over his spectacles; he was surprised to see him.

He instinctively reached for a bottle of whiskey, thinking Vick was there to make a deal concerning his property.

"Well, well, you've finally come to your senses. Come on in boy, have a seat, while I pour you a drink." Mr. Barkin continued to talk as he filled the drink glass to the brim. "Glad to see you, son. Are you enjoying being back home?"

"The superficial sonavobitch is trying to butter me up," Vick thought, as the two men shook hands. As he sat, studying Barkin's gestures, he wondered how he would be around a poker table. "A little too arrogant and overly confident, just like his daughter."

Of course, Barkin had already drawn conclusions about Vick. "A stupid kid who does not know the value of what he has." Vick was ahead of him, as he studied the self-assured man, just like Buck had taught him.

"Since you're pouring, I'm drinking," said Vick who was becoming somewhat of a surprise.

"He's an easy mark," Barkin surmised. "Wait til the kid has a couple of drinks in 'em." As the two men talked idly about their peripheral interests, Vick could see that Barkin was beginning to feel his liquor. He waited until just the right moment before mentioning, "I've heard you're a pretty good poker player."

"I reckon you heard right sonny. Why? You interested in a game?"

"I don't know ... I could be, but I suspect I'm out of your class."

"Yeah, my boy, I've played with the best of 'em. What else have ya heard about me?"

"Sir, I've heard you've made most of your wealth around a poker table, and that's why I'm here: to offer you a chance to win my property."

The old man choked and twisted in his chair at the thought of a kid like Vick making such a suggestion. He laughed as he spoke. "Mind tellin' me your angle?"

"Your lumber company up against my land."

"Sonny, you must be out of your mind!" Barkin was laughing more. "I want your property, but that would be stealing. You're no match for a man like me. Why, you're still wet behind the ears, and poker, well, it's a man's game ... But you're right to say you're not in my class. People would laugh me outta' town playing against a kid." He leaned forward, staring Vick in the eye. "I play with men who know what they're doing, and not a kid who would cry if he lost."

Vick withstood the insults by staring down Barkin, letting the old man continue to ramble before finally breaking in. "Sir, I'm not trying to be rude, but what will they think when they hear you turned down my offer? They might think you don't have the guts to put your lumber company up against my land. Perhaps you're just not that sure of your game?"

Mr. Barkin sat straight up, defending his position. "Hogwash! Why don't you sign your land over to me now, and take the easy way out? I'm offering to pay ya' more than that land of yours is worth! Save yourself the embarrassment, son!"

Vick continued to stare at him, which was compelling to a sophisticated and experienced man who was not used to being crossed.

"These are my terms, take it or leave it," Vick said, without equivocation.

Mr. Barkin thought, "This boy is hard to figure out. He's either stupid or the biggest con I've ever met, and I've met a few of 'em."

Vick hated the smugness of a weasel like Thomas Barkin and thought it would be a pleasure to knock him off his pedestal. If he had learned one thing from Buck, it was how to read his opposition. Barkin was a man who loved a challenge, and would go to any length to win. However, Vick had figured him out.

He was indoctrinated with Buck's little wisdoms, as they spun through his head. "Don't look for a sucker to play against. Look for a player with skill, and then make a sucker out of 'em." He could see this was going to give him great pleasure. Yeah, the old man's wheels were turning. Vick knew Barkin was thinking of the offer as an opportunity to take Vick's land, which was worth a fortune.

Finally, Barkin showed a sign of interest. "Sonny, you mentioned your land up against my lumber company. That ain't at all fair, against a young whippersnapper like you."

"I know what you've said, but these are my terms, my land and your lumber company — may the best man win!"

"You surprise me sonny, you're awfully sure of yourself." The old man took another drink of whiskey, and smiled a devious smile for Vick's foolish bet. "Sonny, you're making it hard for me to turn ya down."

"Then, how about Saturday night? Meet ya at the saloon, say, eight o'clock?"

"Hmmm, let me have a few days to think on this. You'll hear from me soon." Barkin studied Vick, then spoke with some reservation. "We'll see son, we'll see."

Vick turned and walked out, leaving the old man in a stupor.

When the door closed behind Vick, Thomas poured himself another drink and sat there shaking his head, talking to himself. "That dumb kid thinks he can beat me at poker. Somebody oughta' tell him who he's dealing with!"

Barkin wasted no time the next day riding to town asking what people knew about Vick Porter. His first stop was the blacksmith shop, where he talked to Johnny Earl who knew everyone in town.

"All I know is dem' boys didn't have no kinda upbringing. We all thought old man Percy kilt 'em when dey' went missin'. Dats' all I know. Then I heard they wuz kidnapped."

"Thank you," replied Barkin. "Oh, by the way, you mentioned there were two boys. Do you know what happened to the other boy?"

"I done tole ya all I know. Glad I could help ya. Sho 'yo' horse don't need shoein'?"

Barkin rode toward the saloon to continue investigating Vick and his brother. No one remembered details on the boys, since Percy rarely brought them to town.

Two days later a letter arrived; Vick had Mattie read it to him. He smiled as she read that Mr. Barkin had accepted his invitation for Saturday night's poker game. Vick was instructed to bring the Deed to his property in preparation for signing it over to the winner. Deep down, Vick had known that age would never make a difference to a man as greedy as Thomas Barkin.

Mattie was concerned about Vick's challenging the sophisticated and professional businessman to a game of poker with such high stakes but Vick assured her he knew what he was doing.

When Saturday arrived, however, Vick began to second-guess his decision. The concern on Mattie's face added to his doubting. For all he knew, the old man could be a bigger con than he was, but it was too late to back out now. Time to gird his loins and con the old man out of his lumber company.

Vick walked into the saloon that evening, ready for his game, just before eight o'clock. He was handsomely dressed, like a Mississippi gambler in his Sunday best, ready to take down the man who had harassed his Pa and cut prime timber off his land.

Thomas Barkin was already there, sitting, smoking a cigar, eagerly waiting for the young stud that had dared to enter his domain, a man's game and, he was sure, to give Barkin 200 acres of prime lumber. He smiled broadly.

Vick swaggered into the saloon, standing just inside the door, dignified and looking ever bit the gentleman. "Quite impressive," Mr. Barkin thought as his opponent walked toward him. For the first time, he had a twinge of concern. This was an unusual reaction for Barkin, but the boy looked like a man with even more confidence than he'd seen when the challenge was first delivered. Young Porter's look was mysterious and a little unsettling.

Vick showed a side of himself that even he didn't fully recognize. This was the very first time to test his poker skills against a true professional, where he might even lose the inheritance he had obtained a few days earlier.

Buck's voice was present in Vick's ear as he walked toward the table where Barkin sat expectantly. "Never underestimate your opponent. If you plan to win at poker, it's not always how brilliantly you play. Sometimes it's about how inept your opponent plays, and it's up to you to take him down. The player who realizes this becomes the master of his game."

Vick remembered Buck's counsel, as he stood smiling down at the seated man, who had no idea he was about to be duped by a young man less than half his age. He greeted Mr. Barkin kindly, but after that, it was all business.

"You got the Deed to your land?" asked Barkin.

Vick laid his Deed on the table and Barkin did the same. Thomas briefly touched Vick's Deed as an aim to upset him. "That's the last time you'll touch that piece of paper," Vick thought, glad to see a sign of the old man's hunger.

Sheriff Cargill took the Deeds for safekeeping. There were at least twenty spectators watching, all seemed to be pulling for Vick, which concerned Thomas. He should have known that he was hated by the town.

Barkin studied Vick's face, as did Sheriff Orson Cargill, who had known Vick's Pa.

"He's a little too cool, and it's high time to see this cocky young bastard sweat," Barkin thought, while the sheriff imagined the sophisticated Thomas Barkin handing the Deed to his property over to the kid who had had such a difficult childhood.

The men shook hands and immediately Barkin began his tactics by trying to crack Vick's arrogant attitude, but Vick ignored his antics and banter, keeping his cool.

The old man had been schooled well with vast experience, but Vick had been tutored by the very best, how gamblers use their cool and wicked smile to control the game. This rich old man was a textbook example of that kind of gambler. Vick did not allow this professional's ruse to distract him. "A man's character is stripped at the poker table, and I'm the only one to blame if I don't read Barkin right," Vick reflected.

Vick barely looked at his opponent, as he heard whispers from the crowd say; "Vick cut off more than he can chew when he challenged Barkin. I've seen him leave here with his pockets stuffed with everyone's money." The sheriff had to work to keep the crowd quiet, as the game became intense.

The two were playing straight poker, both winning and losing. Vick intentionally let Barkin take the first few hands, while the old man played to the crowd by placating Vick, as his ego began to overtake his game.

"Tell you what son: you can have your pick of the game. You name it!" Barkin tauntingly suggested after Vick had lost a couple of rounds. The old man unconsciously tapped on the table waiting for Vick's answer.

Vick queried his opponent again by testing him. Finally he asked. "What do you want to play? Faro, Bucking the Tiger, or Twisting the

Tiger's Tail?" Vick recalled Buck's counsel in the back of his mind. "If a man doesn't know these are all the same game they're probably a bluff.

Barkin responded with, "Let's stick to Faro; it's a no brainer."

Vick smiled inwardly and thought, "I've gotcha!"

"We need a Faro board, a Dealer and a Banker," Barkin ordered like he owned the place. "Get a move on and make this happen!"

The bartender had two men move the Faro board, then glasses and a jug of whiskey for the two competitors were set near the table. "I reckon we got a man right here who will be the Dealer," he announced. One of the men stepped out of the crowd, ready to deal. The Faro board was set up, and as if on cue, another man walked through the door of the saloon, who offered to be the Banker. Barkin didn't recognize Willie Thornhill as a man who had lost his property to him several years before.

"Don't think we've met," Thomas Barkin said, shaking his hand, as things seemed to be moving a little fast for him.

"Been here all my life! I think if ya think real hard ya might remember me. My name's Willie Thornhill." The name didn't mean anything to Barkin, who also didn't notice the look in Thornhill's eyes.

"Ya got an honest man," shouted the crowd. "Willie's a good man; ya don't have a thang" to worry about."

"Willie do you know the rules?" Vick asked.

"Yes, reckon I do. Don't neither one of you worry about me, 'cause I know what I'm doin'," replied Willie.

Mr. Barkin looked a little uneasy as Willie's face started looking familiar. He decided he'd just seen him around town; he may work in one of the stores.

"Well, if Vick is okay with Willie, then he's okay with me," the old man finally stated, trying to get the crowd behind him.

The Dealer shuffled the cards and then made an announcement.

"Boys we got a side bet going on here between Mr. Thomas Barkin and Mr. Vick Porter so, their betting is between them two and shouldn't have nothing to do with the game you're playing. You all go ahead and place your bets. If your card comes up, you're a winner and if it don't the House wins. Any questions?"

As usual, they warmed up with other gamblers joining in the first few games, until they dropped out one by one. Vick and Barkin were finally left to go head-to-head. They each placed their bets and waited for the Dealer. Barkin continued to suck on his cigar, blowing smoke that circulated above his head as he watched his young adversary.

"Sonny, it looks like you ain't getting the cards," Barkin remarked, as the Dealer dealt out two cards at a time, with Barkin winning most of the bets and cheerfully stacking his winnings. Vick ignored the attitude and remained focused on the Dealer, counting to himself card after card as they were dealt. Soon he would know every card the Dealer had left in his hand.

There were very few cards left, which increased the odds of Vick winning. He was feeling the heat all right, as he waited to name the last three cards. Vick glanced at the pompous man across from him, knowing soon he would know the remaining cards the Dealer was holding.

The game was going as planned when the tables suddenly turned in Vick's favor as he won more and more bets. Now, it was Barkin feeling the heat, as the young player began raking in his winnings.

Finally it got down to the last cards. It was apparent that either of the men could walk away the winner. Now, Barkin looked at the Dealer, holding the last three cards, sweating his odds, and knowing this bet could lose as well as win.

"Well sonny, we're down to the last three cards. This could go either way as I see it, cause either one of us could be the big loser here ... I been thinking about a better offer for you. Rather than have you risk your land, I'm willing to double the price of what the land's worth and buy it from you, right here and now; what do you say?"

"Sir, I don't mean to be rude, but what kind of offer have you made your opponents in the past before you took their property?"

Pure hatred showed in Barkin's eyes when Vick brought up Barkin's reputation around the card table. Vick pretended not to notice.

"Sonny, I suggest we stay focused on this game, and not some game of the past. Do we have a deal or not?" Thomas Barkin lashed out showing signs of frustration.

"I have another suggestion," Vick said.

"And, what would that be?" Barkin was concerned with the prospects of losing.

Vick saw the sweat building up on the man's forehead as he explained his challenge. "We both put in an extra thousand, and I'll guess the last three cards the Dealer has left in his hand. It's a wild guess, but if I'm right, I'll win the Deed to your lumber company and your thousand dollars. If I miss just one card — just one card — well then, you win my land plus my thousand dollars."

"Why, you're crazier than I thought, making a foolish bet like that. Why don't we settle this the way I suggested? You'll have twice your land's value!"

Vick knew he could win anyway, but why not milk him out of another thousand? He thought.

"No, I don't think you understand. I brought you here to beat you like you've beat every man in this town. I think you've run out of luck Mr. Thomas Barkin. Here's your chance to get my land free. And you won't have to steal any more of my timber. Take the bet or leave it."

Barkin's face turned red, but he tried to hold his composure, glaring at Vick.

A thunderous noise rang out from the crowd as they chanted, Go! Go! Go! Thomas Barkin who was influenced by the crowd started counting out a thousand dollars more, placing the bills in the middle of the table with Vick's thousand. The crowd roared with approval, then there was total silence. Barkin had chewed his cigar down to a nub. The old man sweated as he sized up Vick. "The kid ain't that good; he can't be," he thought.

Sheriff Cargill appeared tableside with the two Deeds in hand and laid them on the Faro table near the Banker.

The Dealer announced, "All right gentlemen, I'm about to deal the last three cards … You heard Mr. Porter say he can guess the last three cards … a risky bet! The Dealer and all eyes turned to see Barkin's nervous reaction.

The Dealer continued, "But, if Mr. Porter fails, Mr. Barkin wins the Porter's two hundred acres, plus all the winnings … Okay, Mr. Porter, let's have it. Name the cards, and let's end this game."

Vick held the eyes of his opponent as he named the last three cards that were in question. .

"Six of Clubs, 10 of Hearts and Jack of Diamonds," Vick announced.

Willie hurriedly laid the cards down as a hush swept over the room. Necks strained to see and when they observed Vick was correct on all three, the Dealer said, "Looks like we got us a winner!" smiling as he looked at Vick.

Everyone except Mr. Barkin went ballistic. The crowd whooped and hollered, patting each other on the back, some did the same to Vick.

Mr. Barker sat overwhelmed with defeat, in shock. A voice from the crowd yelled "And Vick named 'em in the same order."

Vick expected to get the cards right but he never thought he would name them in the exact order the Dealer laid them down.

Mr. Barkin sat silent, dazed, knowing he had lost everything to a young kid. The old man was unsteady as he tried to stand. Sweat was now running down his face, dropping from his chin. "What's going on?" Barkin asked in a monotone voice. "Is this some kind of joke?" His voice was now just a whisper. He pointed to Vick saying, "I don't know how Porter did this, but he cheated!"

Barkin reached for the lumber company Deed as the Banker tried to stop him.

"You lost to this young feller, fair and square, now move your hand and take your loss like a man," the Banker said staring directly into Barkin's watery eyes.

At that moment, Sheriff Cargill came up to Barkin. "There weren't no cheating goin' on! Now, Thomas, Vick here won fair and square, and we're all witnesses." The sheriff then turned to Vick, shook his hand, "Congratulations to ya, son."

Mr. Barkin stood and shook his fist at Vick. "You set me up! You clearly set me up, you all are in cahoots with this yokel, who wants to steal my lumber company."

"Now Thomas, we don't want no trouble. You need to go on home," the sheriff instructed.

As the crowd began shouting "sore loser," Mr. Barkin was clearly on the verge of losing it. The sheriff motioned for the crowd to calm down, as he announced his verdict.

"There ain't no cheaters here, and the winner is Vick Porter, fair and square. The game's over, so be on ya way, everybody."

The sheriff handed both deeds to Vick, who did not take his eye off Barkin. He could see the old man reaching inside his jacket. Vick drew his gun and instinctively hit the floor, ready to shoot when in disbelief the old man pulled out his revolver and shot himself in the temple. The gunshot echoed throughout the saloon, as Thomas Barkin's body slumped across the game table.

No one expected to witness such a tragedy over a game of Faro. The richest man in town lay slumped over the poker table with blood running out the corner of his mouth. Blood ran from the wound on the side of his head onto the end of the table, starting to drip slowly onto the floor. The sheriff began moving the crowd out so the undertaker could be summoned. It did not take long for the word to get around town that Mr. Barkin had died by his own hand over the loss of his lumber company.

Vick immediately thought of Elizabeth, and the repercussions when he faced her. She would undoubtedly blame him for her father killing himself.

All the way home he thought about Buck, and the aftermath of what had just happened. "It was because of me," he thought. But he had not expected Mr. Barkin to kill himself!

When Vick came home, Mattie was anxiously waiting and immediately assumed he had lost everything. He looked defeated, as she tried to comfort him.

"Oh, no! What happened? Tell me, did you lose your land?"

Vick slowly shook his head. "I won, but there's no honor when a man kills himself over his loss."

"No, not Mr. Barkin! He was ruthless, but I can't believe he would kill himself over a card game." Mattie had no idea the manor was part of the bet and neither did Vick. She could tell Vick was deeply upset. "You can't blame yourself. Mr. Barkin knew the risk. How could you have known this would happen?"

Vick couldn't tell Mattie his concern was for Elizabeth and how she would undoubtedly blame him for her father's death..

For several days the town was all-abuzz about Thomas Barkin killing himself. Vick waited a reasonable time before he decided to head out to the manor and express his condolences to Elizabeth. When he arrived, the caretaker informed him that Elizabeth left town after having a funeral for her father in an unknown location. Before Vick turned to go back home, the caretaker handed him a note from Elizabeth. He explained that she had vacated the manor and boarded a stagecoach for Missouri. Vick had no idea why Elizabeth felt the need to leave him a note.

A week passed before he took the deed of the lumber company, along with Elizabeth's note, to the judge, to have it read. It wasn't until then that Vick learned the lumber company had many holdings, and the home where Elizabeth lived, the manor, was included as part of the lumber company. Everything old man Barkin owned was all lumped together under the umbrella of the lumber company. This news came as a complete shock, when Vick learned he owned the entire Barkin estate, which included the manor.

"Surely there is a mistake," he said. But the paperwork clarified that Vick was indeed the new owner. Also attached was a list of gamblers who had surrendered their property in order to settle their gambling debts to Mr. Barkin. Vick's knees buckled when the judge explained that he was indeed the new owner of the many holdings the lumber company owned.

Now, he understood why Elizabeth's father chose to kill himself, rather than face his only child and tell her he had gambled away not only her home, but everything they owned. What kind of man would disappoint his daughter by forcing her from her home after he gambled it away?

Had Vick known the manor was also a part of the lumber company Deed, he would have made the bet specifically for the lumber company. Then, Elizabeth would not have lost her home.

Vick had a flurry of questions centering on how much Elizabeth knew about her Pa's misdealing. What did she actually know of her ruthless father, who preyed on the unsuspecting and less fortunate? Vick felt sure Elizabeth was not an innocent party in her Pa's affairs.

Mattie grew suspicious of Vick's past. Something was not quite right about Vick's incredible defeat of the rich Mr. Barkin, and she was sure there was something he was not telling her. "How could a man as young as Vick outsmart and outplay someone as professional as Mr. Barkin?"

Vick picked up on Mattie's suspicion. He knew she expected answers but now was not the time to have a discussion or tell her that Elizabeth had left town. He could not bring himself to tell her that he not only owned the lumber company but the manor — the entire estate. He still couldn't believe it. What would she think if he told her he owned half the town and thousands of acres of Arkansas land. The time would come when he would tell her, but not while the pain surrounding his win was still haunting him.

After weeks of blaming himself, it finally sunk in that, good or bad, he now owned both the manor and the lumber company. Elizabeth had accepted her father's loss and was gone, so it was important to pick up the pieces and make the best of it.

Shortly thereafter, Vick decided to ride out and see his newly acquired home. It was overwhelming to have come from utter obscurity to now owning such a place. As Vick rode through the iron gates toward the mansion, his heart began to pound, sensing the richness of the Barkin estate, which was now his estate!

The lush greenery on both sides of the brick road filled the air with its fragrance, reminding him of an exotic rainforest in the Pacific Islands that Buck had spoken about. He breathed the heavy scent of abundant honeysuckle that wrapped its thick vines around the tall iron fence that helped shield the stately mansion in privacy. He admired its rich architecture and elegant walkways that surrounded it, leading to rose gardens and picnic areas near fountains and goldfish ponds.

By the time Vick reached the main entrance to the house, he was fatigued from imagining what he might see next. He had never in his life even imagined the existence of such luxury. He entered the house, and while walking through it, took time to enjoy its elegant rooms furnished with intimidating period antiques and furniture. He could not believe his fortune and wondered how a simple man, who was now wanted for seven murders, could fit into this new world that opened itself to him. If only he could enjoy his fortune without that hanging over him.

Vick tried not to think about his past as he walked into the dining room, with the majestic appearance of a European villa, the likes of which he had never seen. Off one wing of the dining room lay a large banquet hall with huge windows, where the Barkins hosted formal gatherings. There was even a poker room for Thomas' poker gatherings. Outside the windows of the hall, was a spacious brick parking area, he presumed for buggies of their guests.

He could not believe the wealth, which reflected a style of life, of which he knew nothing. Still they did share one common denominator: a love for the game of poker, but that was all. Vick stood on the balcony of the manor and scanned the array of arbors and statues that accented the gardens, and contemplated how he and Mattie might fit into this world of luxury that Elizabeth and her father had taken for granted.

It took Vick several more weeks to find the courage to approach Mattie about his new home. "I'm not explaining anything," he inwardly thought. "I'm going to surprise her and let it fall where it falls." He knew he had to be straight with Mattie, even though he could not offer her his heart or make promises to her he could not keep. These were all concerns Vick wrestled with, knowing he loved Mattie and may never be able to have a life with her.

She was sitting on her front porch when Vick rode up. As she walked toward him, without warning, he gently swooped her up swinging her behind his saddle.

"Vick, where are you taking me?" she asked.

"You'll see; hold on."

Vick spurred his horse and took off with Mattie holding on tightly. He could feel the gentle softness of her body giving him shivers as she pressed up against him. "As they rode," he thought, "This is the woman I love and if I can't be here to enjoy my wealth, Mattie will keep it for me until I clear my name." This was his only solace, since he knew within time, he would be on the run again.

The two rode in silence until they reached the lumber company where Mattie thought they were going. When they passed the building, she began stiffening with the thought that Vick might be taking her to see Elizabeth, which concerned her.

Vick stopped at the front of the manor, beside the brick platform for Mattie to dismount. He then tied his horse to the hitching post.

As they walked up the steps to the front door, Mattie was thinking how forward Vick was, intruding on Elizabeth after her father's tragic death. Vick could tell Mattie was perplexed, but said nothing. Finally, she stopped Vick and asked, "Why are we here at the manor?"

"Well, since you asked, it's where I live. I didn't know it at the time, but the lumber company owns the manor."

"Really? How can this be?" Mattie was astonished, as she tried to comprehend what Vick had said.

"I want you to try and understand. I had nothing to do with Elizabeth leaving town. I got a note that she had vacated the manor and was ready for me to move in. Mattie, I had no idea I owned the manor until the judge read the Deed and told me the manor was part of the lumber company property."

"Oh my gosh, this can't be happening! Poor Elizabeth! This is your house now?" Mattie asked, "No strings attached?"

"No mistake, it's all mine, and so are many other properties I feel I have no right to, which are all in the Deed. Mr. Barkin had it all tied together. I don't know how deep Elizabeth was into her Pa's business, but she must have known when the lumber company went, the manor went with it. Why else would she leave town?"

Vick opened the door and Mattie quietly walked in with her hand over her mouth, amazed at its beauty. She was as overcome as Vick was when he first saw the luxury Elizabeth was raised in. Mattie had been considerably less fortunate, and had never known just how well off Elizabeth and her Pa really were, until now.

"Vick, I want to be excited for you, but this was Elizabeth's home, the only one she ever knew," Mattie confided. "I feel like we are intruding. I'm sure Elizabeth did not know her father was the kind of man he was. Now, she's lost her home and her Pa. It's really sad."

"I'd like to believe that, but she was mighty thick in her father's business. I had a run in with her the day she called on me to buy my Pa's land. They wanted our property awfully bad."

Vick seated Mattie on a settee and moved a chair to where he could look directly into her eyes while they talked. She knew it was going to be a serious conversation.

"I've been thinking about something and for over a week I've wanted to do something for the families that lost their homes and land to Mr. Barkin. I have the name of every person he swindled listed in the Deed.

"What do you mean?"

"I've been told the timber on my land is worth a fortune. That's why Elizabeth's Pa was after my Pa to make a deal. If I cut the timber and sell it, that alone would be enough to pay back every person who was ripped off, and then some. The more I think about it, the more I think it's the right thing to do."

"I can't believe you would be so generous. No one else would do that," Mattie said.

"I'm not trying to be a hero. I just feel it's the right thing to do, and the sooner the better."

"Of course, I will help you, if you're sure this is what you want."

"I also need you to do something else for me," Vick added.

"Of course, I'll do as much as I can.

"I want you to take over and run the lumber company." I'm not going to beat around the bush. You know I can only read a few words and can't write 'cause I never went to school, and besides, hanging around inside an office ain't for me, anyway. I have to sign my name with an X. Mattie, I need someone I can trust, and that's you. I think you would be good."

"Vick, I don't know what to say? I've never run a business before."

"I know you can do it, that's why I'm asking. And we can get help if you need somebody working with you.

"What if I mess up and you're disappointed? I would be embarrassed to let you down."

Vick ignored her. "It's settled. You run the office, and I'll take care of the men and the outside work."

"But, I'm not educated, however I do read and write. I was told I'm good at figuring, but you have to understand, I'll be learning as I go."

"So will I, but I'm going to need you around a lot," Vick said, as he took her in his arms. "Yeah, a whole lot," he smiled.

"Oh, all right then, it's a deal. And if you like, I'll start with getting the word out that you plan to repay all the people whose land was taken by Mr. Barkin."

"Now young lady, if you will follow me this way, I want to show you a very special place." Vick took Mattie's hand.

"And what would that be?" Mattie asked, as she followed Vick down a long hall. Suddenly, they were in an elegantly furnished bedroom. Vick took Mattie in his arms, and pushed the door closed with his boot.

～

That night in the Odessa jail after reliving his connection with Mattie, Vick awoke thinking somehow he had to get back to Mattie.

He wondered if he would ever gain control of his life or if he would always be a man on the run. "What will this day bring?" he thought. "Soon I will be standing before the Circuit Judge to hear my fate."

Chapter 12

Vɪᴄᴋ ʀᴏʟʟᴇᴅ ᴏᴠᴇʀ ғᴜʟʟʏ ᴀᴡᴀᴋᴇ ᴛʜɪɴᴋɪɴɢ ᴏғ ʜᴏᴡ Mᴀᴛᴛɪᴇ ʜᴀᴅ **helped him make good to the people Thomas Barkin had taken advantage of.** There were only two hours left in his cold cell before Vick will be facing a different kind of cold. He kept reliving his past as he waited for first light.

He loved Jonesboro and wondered if the people he helped would believe he was innocent of the murders Buck accused him of.

He remembered how happy Mattie was when he told her he wanted to do something to restore the property Mr. Barkin had stolen from the people of his town.

Unable to sleep his thoughts turned once again to his past.

He remembered how the news spread like wildfire that he was repaying the men who had been ripped off by Elizabeth's father, Thomas Barkin.

The town had never heard of such generosity, and soon the effort became contagious, as the small town pulled together to help the cause. It was a noble campaign, drawing the attention of all the gamblers who had been ripped off.

That morning was very special, Vick recalled.

It was a cold brisk morning with fog hovering just above the ground when he rode out to his old home place in anticipation of the men's arrival. It was just before daybreak; the day the work was to begin. Vick first heard the sounds of mules as they came trudging through the fog. The clanging of the bits and harnesses, with occasional snickers from the mules, were all music to his ears. First came two mules, and then four, until 50 men with over 100 mules, broke through the dense fog, ready to begin work. It was like a small coalition of soldiers ready for battle, as each man stood with his mules lined up side-by-side.

Vick walked along the row of men, shaking their hands and thanking them for participating in his effort to clear the land. It was a happy occasion since the workers knew they were getting a chance to recover their land from their losses to Mr. Barkin. Vick had no idea how long his project would take, but when he saw how hard and skillful the men worked, it was no wonder the task moved faster than expected. Within three months the land was cleared, and the last timber was hauled to the sawmill. Before the men finished, and with respect for Vick, they cultivated his land planting seedlings for a new crop of trees — a gesture of thanks for his generosity.

The proceeds from the sale of the timber brought more than Vick had ever imagined. It totaled more than the "double offer" Mr. Barkin had offered for land and timber. When the time came to pay the men, they gathered at Vick's old home place to receive their earnings. The money that was set aside to pay the men was divided equally and then placed in envelopes to be given to each worker. The men opened their envelope, then looked sharply at Vick — not because they were short changed, but because their pay was much more generous than expected.

Vick's land was his inheritance, but they had no idea they would become the benefactors, which made them beholden to him. From that time on, he was honored and respected as the town's favorite son.

Mattie noticed a difference in Vick's demeanor, as he seemed more relaxed and confident. She suspected it was because of his acceptance in a town that now looked upon him as a man of importance. But, if the truth be known, he now knew what it was like to give rather than receive.

They were a couple to be admired and Mattie was making quite a name for herself, running the Porter Lumber Company. Unlike Elizabeth Barkin, she understood the workers' language, being herself a commoner. Running the company was the best thing that ever happened to her, and she soon reflected the appearance of a successful woman.

Vick loved her, and he knew that a sudden departure would be unfair to Mattie, should his past catch up with him. Their clandestine meetings and occasional sleepovers were not a problem for now, but eventually he knew people would begin gossiping, and Mattie would be the one to pay the price. More than anything Vick wanted to make Mattie his wife, but the thought of leaving her was always a concern.

During the following months, Vick embraced his notoriety of being the man who finally beat Mr. Barkin at his own game. He enjoyed his importance, but living a lie began troubling him. He knew he could not go on if he did not confide in Mattie about his past, at least some of it. She needed to know the truth, but telling her too much could jeopardize their relationship, he imagined.

One evening, Mattie began quizzing Vick about the card game he had with Mr. Barkin. He knew this type of questioning would only lead to more questions. He began explaining the less important things of his childhood, and how and why he and his brother ran away and found refuge at a cabin in Panther Holler.

"Mattie, that is where I met Buck Dupree, an Australian, who taught me how to play poker and Faro." He explained to her in detail the bond of trust he had with Buck, but conveniently left out about the treasure he had found, the mountain men, and how Buck had accused him of killing seven people. "Now was not the time to tell her," he thought. He ached for her to know the whole truth, but deep inside he was sure she might leave him.

"So, this is how you won? Counting cards?" Mattie asked.

"Guess you think I'm no better than Thomas Barkin."

"Vick, I'm glad you're confiding in me, but please don't put words in my mouth. I'm not here to judge you." She was happy Vick had finally opened up to her, but little did she know there was much more to come.

A few weeks later, after they finished dinner, Vick decided to fill Mattie in on more secrets. He was not ready to tell her about being framed for murder, but he wanted her to know about his scar, and the altercation he had with the mountain man at Panther Holler. Mattie had believed his story about counting cards and perhaps she would do likewise about the treasure. His only desire was for her to continue to trust him as he confided in her.

After disclosing some of his past, Vick brought out the treasure in a burlap sack. He had separated the items and wrapped many of the larger pieces in cloth to protect them. She had never seen such priceless pieces of jewelry and precious gems, along with many gold coins, gold bullion, and thousands of silver certificates. In the midst of the fortune lay the little red book that had been stained with Vick's blood and the bloody loose pages he had dried and put back inside the book. Needless to say she was overwhelmed.

"Why, I've never seen anything like this. You've had this all this time? It's a fortune." Her eyes kept focusing on the bloodstained book. He still felt a strong connection to the little book, she thought. It represented his struggle and injury with the man who tried to kill him," she concluded.

"Mattie, you have to promise me you will not tell anyone about this treasure."

"Why not?" Mattie asked, as she continued to query him.

"It's not safe. People would kill for any part of it."

Vick realized he made a mistake in showing her, for one answer led her to ask another question. She listened intently, but knew there was more to the story than what he was telling her. Mattie thought. "What other secrets were being kept from her?"

The next day, she had to go into town for supplies when she ran head on into a poster. The poster stated that Vick Porter was WANTED DEAD OR ALIVE for murdering seven people.

She could not believe what she was seeing. "Vick must have had a premonition," she thought.

Mattie ripped off several posters nailed in various places around town, then jumped into her buggy, lashing her whip as she drove to the manor. She was very upset, thinking Vick had deceived her. "How could he lie and keep a straight face?" She did not bother to knock. She walked in, calling out for him.

"Vick, where are you? If you're here, I need to talk to you … Now!"

Hearing the urgency in Mattie's voice, he came from his bedroom upstairs, stuffing his shirt into his pants. Mattie stood glaring at him from the bottom of the stairs as he continued to dress himself pulling his suspenders over his shirt.

She held up the posters for him to see, then threw them at him.

"How could you? I need you to explain these posters. There must be some mistake. You couldn't have possibly committed these crimes, these murders. Please tell me this is a mistake."

"Where did you find these?"

"What difference does it make? They're all over town. Did you do this? Answer me," she screamed. "Did you do this!"

"No, of course not! Buck Dupree framed me! Look, I wanted to tell you a thousand times, but each time I tried, I started thinking of how difficult this would make things for us, and I didn't want to lose you."

"You think? I need to know everything, so please start talking, and tell the truth. I want to know what else you have lied to me about."

Vick tried to take Mattie in his arms, but she backed away. "Don't touch me! How could you keep something like this from me? You need to start talking. I need to know how this could possibly happen," she said, waving the posters in the air.

He knew Mattie was hurting, but his first thought was how much time he had to explain. He walked to the window to see if the sheriff and his posse were anywhere around, then turned to Mattie and asked her to sit down. He wanted her to believe him, but now it might be too late he feared. Vick took the time and explained as much as he could, mainly swearing he was innocent.

"This is not what it looks like; I need you to understand. The sheriff will be coming, and I need time to pack." She could see the panic in his face and knew it was inevitable that Vick would be leaving her to go find Buck Dupree.

"I don't have time to console you, but I need you to believe me. I'm an innocent man!" he pleaded.

" I know you are a good man, but you should have trusted me. Now you have to go, and I may never see you again," she said as tears welled in her eyes.

"Before I leave, I need you to write something for me. I want everyone to know I am leaving you in charge and that means the lumber company and the manor. And Mattie, you have to move in and take care of things. Will you do this for me?"

"I don't know what you're asking? Everything is happening so fast."

Vick was in a panic. "Mattie, please get a pen and paper and write what I tell you. You must do this for me and for you."

He bent down to pick up the posters, as if he could read. He had expected this to happen, but not this soon. "How many posters did you see?" he asked.

"Several ... I don't know ..."

She turned and ran to the desk in search of a pen and paper. Vick took enough money from his treasure bag to last him while Mattie sat on the bed waiting patiently, absorbed in fear, watching her dreams slip away.

Tears were streaming down her face and she could barely write. She kept wiping her eyes on her beautiful puffed sleeves as she watched Vick slipping his feet into his boots.

"Don't stop writing, you have to hurry! Mattie, this is very important. I want you to hide the treasure to keep it safe and remember what I told you — it would be dangerous should anyone know about it. Do you understand?"

She shook her head yes, as she halted her writing waiting for more instructions as she watched Vick finish packing and dressing. He packed his saddlebags and grabbed his bedroll.

"I wish I had more time. I know I'm forgetting something, but I can't think right now. Listen. I want you to write that I am leaving you the manor and the lumber company with all its holdings to take care of until I return. If I don't return in two years, then you know I am probably dead, and this paper will be my Last Will and Testament. Everything goes to you, including the treasure. Hide my Will and the treasure and keep it close. Do you understand?"

She was franticly writing Vick's wishes, knowing he had no choice but to run. When she finished writing, he signed the paper with his "X" and Mattie signed acceptance as his Attorney in Fact.

"Vick, I know you have no choice but to leave, so please don't worry about the lumber company or the manor. I'll do my best to take care of everything until you return. Come back to me!"

He took time to give her one last passionate kiss as he looked pensively into her eyes.

"I'm sorry I didn't tell you sooner. I hope you will forgive me."

She longed to hear Vick say he loved her, but she knew he had more critical things to deal with, like distancing himself from the sheriff. She had many questions and wondered if the treasure was the real reason Vick was running, but she didn't really want to know.

He had his jacket and bag in his hand as he walked to the door, with Mattie trailing behind. She couldn't believe how quickly she changed from being the happiest girl in the world to the saddest. Now, her love was leaving, and there was nothing she could do but stand by as he walked out the door and possibly out of her life.

She followed him to the barn and watched as he saddled his horse. When Vick mounted up, he bent down, looked intently into Mattie's eyes, and gave her one last kiss, then rode away.

The town was stunned after reading the posters that identified Vick as being a crazed gunman who had killed seven people. He was the town hero; no one wanted to believe Vick could have done such a thing. Many walked past the posters shaking their heads in disbelief, as small crowds of people gathered, trying to make sense of the murders.

"This is a bunch of bull. Vick ain't no crazy killer," A voice from the crowd shouted.

One man stood on the porch of the post office and cried out, "Ain't no way Vick Porter murdered nobody. I don't care what these posters say."

"Ya'll know the kind of man Vick Porter is!" others yelled, "I ain't going after 'em. He's a good man and he gave me back my money that old man Barkin stole from me."

The sheriff had several men in his office, filling them in on details, as he tried to form a posse. All the men were mumbling to themselves regarding their respect for Vick and whether or not he had killed anyone, or was capable of murdering seven people.

"I think we doin' the man a favor by bringing him in. I know how ya'll feel about going after one of our own, but it's better we bring him in alive than somebody going after him for the reward and bringing him in dead," pleaded Sheriff Cargill."

"If it was anybody else besides Vick, we would go, but none of us feel right about bringing 'em in. We know he ain't no murderer, and he shore ain't crazy," a potential posse member declared.

Orson Cargill was a man of honor who took his oath seriously as the sheriff. Whether he had the men riding with him or not, he planned to bring Vick in by himself if need be.

"I know how ya'll feel, but I'm bound by the law." Orson hated being forced to be the one to go after Vick. If I can't get you men to help me bring him in ... then get outta here and go home!" He was furious, knowing he had to be the example and uphold the law. The men walked past him and out the door.

He yelled after them, "I don't need ya! I can do it myself!" He followed them out the door, quickly mounted his horse and pulled the reins so hard the horse reared up, digging her hooves into the ground. The sheriff spun the mare around as he galloped away toward Vick's manor house while the townspeople looked on with mixed emotions.

By the time Vick reached the crudely made cattle gap to enter the main trail, sure enough, Orson Cargill with his hat in his hand was sitting in wait for him.

Vick rode up to Sheriff Cargill and stopped in front of him, gently pulling his horse nose to nose with the sheriff's horse. The two men sat silently staring at one another. Vick finally spoke,

"I guess there ain't no use in me declaring my innocence, since you're here to bring me in."

"Did you do it?" the sheriff asked, looking intently into Vick's eyes.

"No, Orson, the only way I would kill a man is if it was self-defense. When I came to Panther Holler I found that family of four already dead." said Vick.

"What about the other three?"

"One was my brother who died when a limb fell on him, and the others were both self-defense," Vick stressed, "One mountain man was out to kill me and the other I killed to defend the man who framed me for these murders."

The two men's eyes were locked for what seemed a long time. "That's all I need to know. Go on ... Git the hell outta here. This ain't my fight," the sheriff said.

Vick kicked his horse and vanished in a trail of dust. Orson wondered if he would ever see Vick again.

Chapter 13

AFTER VICK LEFT ARKANSAS, HE WAS IN THE SADDLE FOR MORE THAN two months, working odd jobs in various Texas towns as he worked his way west. When he finally arrived in Fort Worth, he was down to his last dime. "Not a minute too soon," he thought to himself.

He liked the action of this new town and became fascinated with the daily cattle drives in downtown Fort Worth. Cowboys herded cattle to the stockyards where they were prepared, separated and penned, ready for the long trek north.

It was a daily routine of cows coming into town en route north to be loaded onto the Pacific Rail for transport to the slaughterhouses or for sale to ranches up north, or to be sold to ranchers expanding their herds. The trains made routine pickups throughout Missouri in towns like Sedalia, with Fort Worth being a major marshaling hub for the meat packing business.

Jobs were plentiful around the stockyards, so Vick, being a young strong cowboy, was hired immediately. The pay was good and the future looked promising, until he met a plain looking woman named Emma Norton who was there to buy. She had a dowdy appearance, with carrot red hair and freckles that covered her entire face. Her appearance and soft voice seemed strange coming from a rough Texas woman who worked and walked like a man. After Vick helped her move cattle through the shoots, she asked him to hire on and work driving her cattle since the two inexperienced Mexicans were suspicious.

Emma lived on a small ranch on the north side of Waco. Vick thought hiring on with her and being paid would enable him to keep moving in his efforts to find Buck Dupree. The Mexicans, who appeared to be shady, were not pleased that Emma had hired Vick. But he did not let their surly resentment keep him from accepting the job.

The first night of camp was near a well-known watering hole where Emma had rested her herd before. The Mexicans watched idly as Vick and Emma pitched the tents and prepared for the evening. One tent was for Emma and the other for the men, with the exception of Vick, who opted to sleep under the stars rather than squeeze into a small tent with these unsavory characters. They chose to keep to themselves anyway.

It was a warm humid evening and, after the fire went out, everyone turned in for the night. However, something had made Vick feel uneasy, causing him to have difficulty sleeping throughout the night. Just before daybreak, he woke to the sound of brush movement. The Mexicans were sneaking through camp, moving in the direction of the cattle. Vick planned to follow them and see what they were up to. He waited until they were out of sight before quietly arranging his bedroll to make it appear that he still in sleeping. Vick crept carefully to a grove of trees where he could spy on them.

He waited, watching as two strangers came riding up. He could tell these men were not Mexican, but were surely renegades in cahoots with them and up to no good. They seemed to be giving orders concerning the herd. When he saw one man point back to camp, while making a throat-cutting gesture, he hurried back to warn Emma to make a timely escape.

Emma was startled when Vick placed his hand over her mouth to keep her from screaming. She quickly dressed, while Vick saddled the horses with little time to throw their belongings together. He didn't have time to explain what was going on, and Emma, just moved fast, not asking questions.

They were making their getaway when the Mexicans returned to camp and saw them riding out before the herd. Vick fired a shot to make the Longhorns stampede, forcing the Mexicans to divert their attention to controlling the herd. But as he looked back again, he was startled to see them both gunned down by the strange riders, who had obviously turned on them.

Emma and Vick narrowly escaped death as they rode away from camp with bullets flying around their heads. The Longhorns were stampeding behind them as the outlaws gained control of the herd, turning them in the opposite direction. After they felt safe, Vick tried to calm Emma, as they traveled south to Waco, but his words were like dynamite to a dam, as Emma began to flood him with her loquacious chatter.

During their long ride to Waco, she even opened up about her husband's gambling problem and hinted there may not be enough money to pay Vick when they reached the ranch. Just what Vick wanted to hear! "I may have to challenge Emma's husband to a game of poker just to get the money they owe me," Vick thought sarcastically.

When they were in sight of the ranch, Emma rode ahead to speak with her husband in private. She wanted time to explain to him what happened to the herd before she brought Vick into the picture. Vick wanted to feel sorry for Emma, but it seemed that she would have to have known there would be a money problem when they reached the ranch.

Vick waited on the outside of the cabin, assuming Emma and her husband were trying to resolve the issue of the longhorns, when Jeanette, Emma's sister-in-law, stepped out of the cabin and looked at Vick with eyes as cold as the West Texas wind. Emma and her husband, Donny, came out to face Vick, with no thought of thanking him for saving his wife's life. He could see Emma's anticipation and embarrassment as she introduced her family to him. The unshaven Donny extended Vick a dirty hand with a limp grip.

"Howdy... Emma jest' told me ya'll let the herd get away from you."

"I wouldn't exactly say we let 'em get away. We didn't have much of a choice, since we were ambushed in camp while we slept. Didn't Emma tell you about what all happened?"

Emma's sister-in-law chimed in. "Yeah, she told us, but this is a matter for the sheriff, and we aim to get him out here tomorrow so we can get to the bottom of what happened," Jeanette said.

Vick heard the word sheriff and the blood drained from his face. "I gotta git out of here," he thought, then realized there was no way the wanted posters would have time to make it to Waco, Texas, from Arkansas. Vick tried to keep his cool, as Jeanette now looked him up and down, as if he was somehow involved with the outlaws that stole the herd.

"Emma can fill the sheriff in, but I need to move on. All I want is my pay, and I'll be on my way," Vick said.

Jeanette and Donny ignored Vick. "Tomorrow, you can give your statement to the sheriff. In the meantime, if you're hungry, we have dinner at four o'clock. We eat on time. You can make a bed in the barn, cause we don't have no extra beds in the house," Jeanette said.

"I don't think you understand," Vick intervened. But Vick was given no time to explain anything, as they all ignored him and walked into the house, leaving him standing alone outside.

Emma's husband looked as though he could be riled up pretty easily, and, since they were hell bent on him staying the night, he would have to keep his cool and wait until morning to get on his way. In the meantime, he had to think on how he was going to get the money he was owed.

Vick came to supper right on time, removing his hat at the door, and taking the vacant chair waiting for him. At the table, he was met with a hot meal and a cool reception. The Norton's could not have cared less about Vick, or what he thought, and it was apparent he would have to be clever to walk away with any of the money they owed him. After the meal, Vick put a plan into motion.

"Donny, I hear you enjoy a game of poker every now and then."

Emma darted her eyes at Vick in resentment, since he knew how she felt about her husband's gambling. Donny ignored her and nodded to Vick.

"Yeah, I play with the men in town. What you aiming at?"

"Oh, nothing in particular. I'm not that good."

Before Vick could blink an eye, a deck of cards and a jug of whiskey appeared alongside Donny.

"Don't suppose you like to play Faro?" Donny asked.

"You got a Faro board here?

"Yep, one I rigged up muh' self, since them in town is big. Mama, wha' don't ya bring out muh' board?"

"If that's your game, I'll play, but I have to tell you, I don't know it that well."

Donny loved the sound of that, and immediately felt relieved to see a way around his obligation to pay Vick.

The Faro board didn't look too bad being it was homemade and small in size compared to the saloons that Vick had frequented. He continued to bluff Donny, telling him he had left his money in the barn.

Now, hoping for an easy mark, Emma spoke up. "Don't worry, you can get it later. Let's get started," since the barn was a distance from the cabin and Donny was itching to play.

He gave Emma a harsh look, but let it slide, since Vick looked honest and Donny owed him wages anyway.

"Okay. Emma, you be the Banker, and Jeanette can be the Dealer," Donny said. Emma didn't like the idea of Donny playing but he was stubborn and she had no choice. Jeanette on the other hand was a conniving witch and was not to be trusted.

She went to the bedroom and brought out fifty crisp dollar bills she lent to Donny to bet with. Vick saw the money and thought, "This is the money Emma said they didn't have, and now I'm going to have to cheat to get what they owe me."

"Donny, what ya' say we play a modified version of Faro. I saw a game like this back in Kansas," Vick said as he started his con.

"Might be the same way we play in town. Keep talkin'."

"It's simple. Whoever wins the most bets, wins." Can't be any simpler than that. They played with coins that represented their bets. As always, Vick lost the first three games with Emma keeping tabs on Donny's winnings. Vick remembered his early training and followed Buck's pattern precisely, until it was time to make Donny starve.

As they played, Vick counted the cards until the men were neck to neck, and the last three cards were about to be dealt. Vick knew if the tables were turned, he would have to shoot his way off the ranch, since he did not have the money to pay up. So, he had to make his move.

"Well now Donny, it looks like this could be anybody's game, unless we want to make it more interesting," he said.

He remembered Barkin and how he had lured him into his web with this challenge. Donny however, was certainly not in the same class as that old man and little effort, if any, could assure Vick a win.

Donny was primed for the extra bet. Vick could see Donny wanted to know more, since he was sure that Vick stood a good chance of losing.

"What ya thanking?" Donny asked.

"Jeanette is about to deal the last three cards. It's a big gamble for both of us, but let's each put up another fifty to spice things up a bit. Then, if I can guess one of the three cards Jeanette is holding, I win. And if I can't, you win a hundred dollars instead of fifty … that is … if you have another fifty for the pot. What do you say? Are you a gambling man?"

"I ain't heard of no bet like that, but it sounds like that's a losing bet for ya."

Donny turned to Emma asking, "What do you think, mama? Do you think I ought to take a chance?"

Vick could see that Emma was annoyed. "It looks to me like you've pushed yourself in a corner. You might as well go fer' it, cause you're likely to lose, anyway. You know how I feel about your gambling!"

Vick just loved the negative energy that Emma spewed into the game.

Donny sat there thinking about a quick hundred dollars if he played along with Vick's bet. Jeanette was looking at Donny, grinning like she already had the money spent. After all, it was she who loaned Donny the money. She quickly went and got another fifty dollars and put it in the pot.

"All right! Put yore money where your mouth is," said Donny.

Jeanette looked at Vick as he said, "Queen of Spades."

"You guessing a Queen of Spades?" asked Jeanette in a voice they could barely hear.

Vick could not believe his ears when she said, "Donny is the winner."

Donny was reaching for his cash when he heard Vick calmly said, "Jeanette, don't you think it's proper to show the cards, since I'm about to lose a hundred bucks?"

Jeanette looked sheepishly over at Donny as he said, "Jeanette, show the cards."

She laid down the Queen of Spades, Nine of Diamonds and Four of Hearts, which confirmed Vick was the winner. Emma was shocked that Jeanette had lied, while Donny was mad as hell and ready to fight.

"What's this? What do you think yore doin'?"

"What do you mean, what am I doing? I think you better ask Jeanette what she was doing." Vick took his cash and was walking toward the door when Donny jumped up ready to fight. He pushed Emma and Jeanette aside then jumped Vick, pinning him face first into the wall. Finally, Emma interceded and pulled the two men apart."

"Donny, get a hold of 'yerself. This man saved my life and you ain't got no right to treat him this way. I've just about had it with ya and ya gambling. Tonight, I saw him beat ya fair and square." Donny backed off with Emma's intervention.

She motioned for Vick to leave. "Now take your money and go to the barn," Emma said. Vick did so, and left Emma and Jeanette trying to get Donny to settle down. Exhausted from the long and stressful day, he spread his blanket on the hay, and fell asleep.

The next morning, Vick was saddling his horse to leave, when Jeanette came riding up with the sheriff. She had apparently gotten off to an early morning start and fetched the sheriff before Vick had a chance to get away. She had hopes of causing trouble before he left with the money. His heart was pounding at the thought that there might be some other motivation for the sheriff's visit. Emma and Donny walked out from the cabin when they saw the sheriff and Jeanette approach Vick.

"Sheriff Thompson, this is Vick Porter," Jeanette said.

"Howdy ... Jeanette fetched me to come out here and question ya bout' some cattle rustlers. Mind me asking ya what happened? The sheriff stayed on his horse as he studied Vick's demeanor.

"Good meeting you Sheriff Thompson." The sheriff knew right away that Vick did not look like an outlaw. Before Vick could answer, Emma jumped in to explain how she met Vick, filling in the details of what happened to the herd. Jeanette could see her plan wasn't working with Emma's explanation and Vick's huckleberry smile.

"I guess we owe you for saving Emma; she's a good woman and well thought of." Vick could tell the sheriff was just doing his job.

"Ya'll was lucky to outrun them outlaws. We been tryin' to find out more about their gang since this rash of cattle rustling started in Fort Worth and around these parts."

The sheriff then turned to Vick for his side of the story. "Son, why don't you tell me what happened?"

"Sheriff, it's pretty much the same story, I was sleeping on the outside of Emma's tent when, just before daybreak, the Mexicans Emma had hired sneaked past me and headed to a grove of trees. My gut told me they were up to no good, so I decided to follow them. This is when the two strangers Emma told you about rode up and ordered the Mexicans to kill Emma and me.

"As soon as I figured out what they were up to, I warned Emma, and we hightailed it out of there. But the Mexicans were right behind us, so I fired a shot to stampede the herd. That's what saved us. When I looked back, the two strangers shot the Mexicans, and then turned their fire on us. Bullets were flying all around our head but we were pretty far away and managed to escape without being hit. If you will go back on the trail, you'll find the bodies of the two Mexicans. That will prove we're tellin' the truth."

"Ya'll are lucky to be alive. Judging by what you said. I believe those men are part of the Ellis gang. They're a bloodthirsty bunch, stealing, pilfering around and dodging the law. But we got some leads … seems their leader is a foreigner, talks with one of them accents. Ain't hardly nobody can understand a damn word he says, but the craziest thing about him is he wears a bearskin coat year round, even in the summertime!"

Vick instantly recognized the description of Buck Dupree, apparently still wearing his bearskin coat.

"The fact is, the no good has been shot a number of times, but the next day he's walking around good as new. Can't figure out how he dodges death like that … Yep, damn peculiar." The sheriff lamented.

"Do you know what they do with the cattle?" asked Vick.

"I've heard rumors, but don't rightly know. My deputy said they sell 'em to a gang of Mexicans down in Del Rio, along the Texas-Mexico border. Then I heard they operate out of Odessa. They all ain't nothin' but a bunch of renegades. When we find em' we gonna lynch all of 'em."

"Sheriff, I have an idea the man you're talking about is Buck Dupree. His accent is Australian. He wears a bearskin coat to cover his metal breastplate to stop the bullets. That's why people keep seeing him walk around after he's been shot. Some people say he's a ghost or can't die. Could be the man. That sure would explain thangs, if he's wearing a metal breastplate …" Then, as if the sheriff solved a puzzle, " So, that's why he wears that heavy coat year round," The sheriff chuckled, "Ain't that the craziest thang' I've ever heard."

Vick shook hands with Sheriff Thompson and then Donny turned and walked back to the cabin to keep from shaking hands with Vick. Emma apologized and expressed her gratitude as Vick finished saddling up to ride off.

When the sheriff asked Vick where he was headed, he said, "Reckon I'll go back up to the Stockyards in Fort Worth." Indeed he did just that, but when he got back to Fort Worth, he boarded a stagecoach, and headed for Odessa.

Chapter 14

VICK FINALLY DRIFTED OFF WHEN SUDDENLY THE LOUD CLANGING OF
his cell doors awakened him. His restless night of sleep was imped-
ed by the cold and now it was first light, and Sheriff Jensen was ready
to transfer his prisoner from the Odessa jail to the Circuit Judge in
Abilene. Vick struggled to wake up, knowing he was on his way to face
the judge who would announce his fate.

"Well, sonny, you're finally gonna git' your day in court for shooting ol' Marlin. No real love lost between him and our town, but we
ain't fer' tolerating what ya did. Even though, ol' Marlin was a rattlesnake, it ain't exactly 'poetic justice,' if you know what I mean. I spec'
you're gonna pay for shooting him in the back."

"Sheriff, I'm not interested in 'poetic justice'." How about finding out the truth? There's plenty of people who saw what happened
so why don't you start asking around. You're bound to find out what
really happened. For the last time, Marlin pulled the gun first, and I
shot to defend myself. You can screw this around all you want but I'm
innocent."

"Well, you gonna git' your chance to explain, not that it's gonna
do much good, since you'll be going before ol' Judge Murdock, who
has zero tolerance for such things. Now hurry up and git' yoreself'
ready 'cause we ain't got much time before the town starts a 'stirrin."

Vick hurriedly got dressed and stood with his hands behind him
while the deputy cuffed him. His big fur coat was thrown over his

shoulders, which hardly shielded him from the cold. Another deputy jabbed his shotgun into Vick's back, as he pushed him out the door to the open-bed wagon.

When Vick walked out of jail, the cold air took his breath. The ground was covered with thick frost, and the grass crackled under the horses' hooves as they danced around, eager to go. Before Vick could be loaded onto the wagon, two men rode up with a message for the sheriff, who had come out to see them off.

"You men — watch our prisoner, while I step inside to read this." Vick waited optimistically in the cold for the sheriff to return, thinking he might have a reprieve of some kind. Sheriff Jensen returned shortly to fill them in on the details.

"Vick, I got some good news for you. You're gonna go to Midland, just a few miles away, where you will meet the deputy marshal. There ya'll will be boarding a stagecoach to Abilene. If you want to know how we're paying for the ticket, well, we found some money in your room that I spec' you won off some poor gambler. Guess there's a little luck on your side after all."

"What's the good news?"

"Well, other words, you'd be ridin' all the way to Abilene in this open bed wagon freezin' yore ass off."

The sheriff chuckled when he helped Vick onto the back of the wagon.

"One word to you … don't get your hopes up about dodging jail time, 'cause 'yer gonna be spending time in the Huntsville prison, I can almost promise ya that!"

Vick had no idea where Huntsville prison was.

"Sheriff, when you have time to investigate, you may find you've sent an innocent man to prison," Vick repeated to the sheriff.

"Better than hanging ya! I can tell them to hang ya if you want. You know that's what they generally do when a man shoots a body in the back."

Vick shrugged his shoulders thinking, "what's the use." They had made up their minds, and there wasn't anything he could say or do that would make a difference.

"What about my gear?" Vick asked. "Did your deputy think to bring my personal things?"

"Yes, but son, ya ain't gonna need no gear where yer' going. They got special prison clothes for ya. Yep, ya gonna look downright good in them stripes." Both the deputies and the sheriff laughed, watching Vick bounce around in the back of the wagon as it pulled out.

Upon arriving in Abilene the deputy marshal escorted Vick into the Judge's chambers, knowing full well there was no chance he would escape his fate.

Judge Murdock was a wiry looking character, propped up behind a long narrow desk. And over on one side of the room was a six-man jury who were waiting to hear Vick's story. They looked Vick up and down as if he was a common criminal. Judge Murdock was only interested in facts and Vick stood accused. The escort handed Vick's gear to the judge, which included all his clothing and personal items, along with his saddle and money.

"Don't go handing this to me." Vick's face registered disbelief when he heard the judge say sell everything and use it to pay this outlaw's board.. "Young man, ya don't think we let you stay in jail for free, do ya?" Vick felt helpless as he waited to receive his verdict.

He looked at the judge, who was not a hair over five feet, with squinty eyes behind thick glasses. It was apparent the judge enjoyed his role as the judge, all based on what Vick surmised as the "little man complex." Vick realized the judge was biased, siding with the charges of shooting Marlin in the back. He finally said, "What's 'yer plea son?"

"Innocent, sir! I shot Marlin Winfrey in self-defense. We had a card game; he lost and pulled his gun on me, and I had to shoot to defend myself."

"Well now … that's your word agin' Marlin's, and I don't see Marlin here to defend hisself." The judge held up a document and began to read.

"Says here, there's no eyewitnesses. Since you shot Marlin in the back, there ain't much me or anybody else can do fer' ya, except throw yer' ass in prison."

"Judge Murdock, I can explain. When I defended myself Marlin turned, and it was the angle the bullet entered his side that makes it look like it was aimed for his back. My witnesses became money grabbers when Marlin turned over the table and money began flying around. People clamored to get the money, and then ran to keep from giving it back. I stand behind my word. It's the truth!"

"Ya stand behind your own word? Well now, that's not the first time I heard that from a common hustler, soon to be convict," said the judge.

"It's yer' word agin' a dead man who ain't here to defend hisself." Vick knew he needed an eyewitness, and without one there was nothing that could be done.

"Son, we're bound by the law, in this here courtroom, so jury have you reached a verdict fer' this man?"

The jury deliberated about 2 minutes and then turned to the judge.

"We find this here man guilty," shouted one of the jurors.

"Vick Porter, without no eye witnesses, I have to give ya twenty years hard labor. Yer' gonna be escorted to the prison in the morning. Good day, and have a nice life!"

The judge slammed the gavel on the table, and then walked out of court, leaving Vick standing dumbfounded in shackles.

The deputy marshal locked Vick in the Abilene jail for the night, and the next morning, Vick was loaded onto a stagecoach bound for the prison in Huntsville.

Chapter 15

Elizabeth Barkin, heartbroken after her father's death, had **unanswered questions of why her father committed suicide.** She tried not to focus on Vick Porter, and the role he played in her father's death, but having lost everything, her family's fortune and the manor she was raised in was overwhelming to her. She hoped one day to have answers to those haunting questions.

Leaving Arkansas and traveling to St. Louis, Missouri, to live with her Aunt Connie was life changing for Elizabeth. Leaving the manor, she took one last look, thinking she would never see it again. She took only a trunk of clothing and what money she had. The reality was that she was leaving all the comfort she had known and also Jonesboro, the town she had grown to love.

Traveling, she thought back to when she was a little girl and recalled Vick when he was a boy. "Yes, I'm sure I remember him and his little brother loading feed in the back of Mr. Percy's wagon. How ironic that this poor boy has ended up with my family fortune, leaving me destitute."

She had adored her life there, but without her father, she felt lost and vulnerable to the emptiness that now seemed to plague her. Her only option was to join her aunt. Besides, facing Vick Porter, the man whom she thought responsible for taking away her father and all the things she owned and loved would be heartbreaking. Seeing him would be like throwing salt on an open wound.

Elizabeth questioned why her Pa would risk their property in a card game, knowing how much Barkin Manor meant to her. She knew he loved to gamble, but it did not make sense that he would risk their entire fortune in a silly card game, unless there was a reason she did not understand. Her father was an astute businessman, and was never known to be so careless. It was unimaginable how he could turn the gun on himself, forsaking her, his only child. She vacillated between hating Vick Porter and being furious with her father for being so reckless.

It was on a late summer afternoon, a beautifully clear day when her train came rolling into the station where her Aunt Connie was waiting to greet her. Even though Elizabeth could not actually remember her Aunt, something about her was strikingly familiar, familial resemblance to her father. They recognized one another immediately, and she instantly felt at ease and safe.

She soon learned although her father and Aunt were brother and sister that they were totally opposite from one another. Elizabeth's daddy was arrogant and self-centered, while Aunt Connie was soft-spoken, considerate and mild mannered. She radiated the warmth that Elizabeth had sadly never experienced with her father. Indeed, Elizabeth and Aunt Connie resembled one another so much that they could have easily passed for mother and daughter.

Elizabeth was fashionably dressed, all beautifully tailored to fit her small frame, contrasting with the country-styled dress her Aunt wore. Later, she noticed that all her Aunt Connie's clothing had small collars, with skirts hanging down just above her dress boots.

She was quite the lady, but even at their first meeting, it was apparent she had led a difficult life, the exact opposite of Elizabeth. Concerned with their difference in lifestyle, Elizabeth feared she would not fit in and had made a terrible mistake coming to St. Louis.

Connie, on the other hand, admired Elizabeth as a rare redheaded beauty. She greeted her niece as if she had seen her just last week, when, in fact, she had not seen Elizabeth since her birth. They spoke briefly and then set off on the journey to a small home in a rural neighborhood, several miles outside of town. Here, houses were scattered about in a five-mile radius.

As Aunt Connie sped along in her buggy, wild rabbits scurried, hiding behind bushes upon hearing the approaching horses. Elizabeth looked at the somewhat barren countryside with few trees. The road they traveled was difficult and many times, her Aunt had to leave the road to dodge the deep ruts.

The home was a very small, modest two-bedroom farmhouse set on approximately five acres of land. It was typical frontier architecture, with a living room and bedroom on one side, a breezeway in the middle to separate the kitchen. One other bedroom was located on the opposite side of the house.

There was even an outhouse, which was foreign to Elizabeth, for she had never used one. This was a depressing discovery for her, but she tried not to show it to her sweet Aunt. The manor had two water closets and other facilities offering comforts and conveniences she had never been without.

Elizabeth's first thoughts were how little Connie had, how much she and her father had owned, making her wonder why he hadn't looked after his sister and helped her financially. The stark difference in lifestyles was the first clue that something was amiss in her father and Aunt's relationship. Elizabeth's heart went out to Aunt Connie, who seemed to be happy and making the best of what she had.

Connie, on the other hand, was saddened at seeing her niece grieve. She wanted to reach out to her, but she realized Elizabeth needed privacy. Pressing her niece about her Pa's suicide could be very upsetting to her.

During the weeks that followed, Connie learned more and more about her brother's estate. She grew increasingly curious as to why her niece would leave the beautiful manor to live with her in such meager surroundings when she had hardly enough to care for herself. Despite such a drastic difference in their lifestyles, Aunt Connie wanted her niece to know that she was there for her as much as she could be. She was now in her sixties, and the hardships and struggles of a pioneer woman living alone, had left her in poor health.

Elizabeth who was trying desperately to fit in had never known a hard day's manual work in her life; and learning to do the chores on a small farm was quite a challenge for a young woman who had been brought up in luxury. After several days, she shed her haute couture fashions and settled for clothing that was more suited for farm life.

In spite of Elizabeth's severely diminished economic status and depressed state, she adapted rather quickly to their daily farming routine and growing their own food. Most difficult for Elizabeth was the lack of social activity to balance the humdrum of their daily lives. Afternoons were filled with quilting in the parlor, until Aunt Connie learned that Elizabeth was not a quilter. After spending a half-day ripping out her niece's stitches, her aunt encouraged her to develop another talent, such as painting roses. Before long, they both laughed as they agreed that neither quilting nor painting was Elizabeth's forte.

The one question Connie did not inquire into was the manner in which her brother Thomas had acquired his wealth. As the months passed, Connie and Elizabeth became very close, but not close enough for Connie to confide in Elizabeth about the estrangement she had with her brother. She would change the subject when her niece began asking sensitive questions about Connie's childhood as related to Elizabeth's father.

She would never be able to tell her sweet niece that her father, Thomas, was responsible for the death of Elizabeth's grandfather, Mitchell Barkin. Thomas was always a selfish man and, when Mitchell who was an invalid was left alone the day before he died, it was all attributed to Thomas for ignoring him and failing to bring in wood to keep his crippled father warm. The elder man developed pneumonia after the night of extreme cold and lived only two days. Remembering that horrible time, Connie relived the altercation between her and

Thomas after he neglected their father by gambling in a saloon, winning, and not wanting to leave.

Prior to Elizabeth's birth, Connie and Thomas had finally had enough of each other. From then on they avoided each other like the plague. At that time, Connie was living in St. Louis and Thomas was involved with unscrupulous dealings that she would not be a part of. Shortly thereafter, Thomas's wife died giving birth to Elizabeth. She had heard Thomas was away when Elizabeth was born. She often thought her brother neglected his wife much like he did their father.

Connie's only regret was not having a part in Elizabeth's life. As it turned out, her niece never knew what a scoundrel her daddy really was.

At the end of each day, when their chores were finished, the two women would retire to the front porch and spend hours talking about various subjects. They especially loved to discuss literature and history, since both women were educated. Elizabeth soon realized how privileged her life had been and how she had taken her good fortune for granted.

It had simply never occurred to her to question her daddy about how he acquired his wealth. Additionally, she had done some work at the lumber company but did not see any of his crooked dealings. She never believed the claims were true that her father was cheating people out of their land for their timber. She was certain he accumulated their wealth through the sweat of his brow, legitimate sources and his business acumen.

After a year had passed, Elizabeth began getting homesick for Arkansas. She even conjured up daydreams about Vick, how handsome he was and how different he seemed from the time she first laid eyes on him as a boy. She remembered how rude he was the night he stood her and her father up, which made her question her own sanity for dreaming about a man responsible for her father's death.

Gradually, through Connie's influence, her attitude began to change even the values she held dear. "I had no right to treat Vick as

I did," she decided. "I might have even changed the outcome of what happened to my father had I not been unapproachable to this young man. Why didn't I give Vick a chance to explain about that evening when he failed to show for their appointment?" she reflected. "From now on, I'm no better than anyone else." She became ashamed that she had been so privileged that she had set herself apart from others less fortunate.

Elizabeth tried to adapt to the months of hard work, but ultimately decided it was impossible for her to succumb to the idea of being poor the rest of her life. She knew that in time, she would have to move on since she was not cut out to be destitute and poor; plus she had the drive and ambition to build her own future and do something good with it.

Connie was shocked when Elizabeth finally divulged how and why she lost her inheritance. "My brother had not changed since childhood," Connie remembered. To satisfy her suspicion, she wrote the County Clerk in Arkansas and asked for clarity on the circumstances surrounding the death of her brother. She also asked for any information regarding Vick Porter, who had somehow been connected to his death.

She was thinking of Elizabeth and the options she may have if it could be proven that her niece had been unfairly taken advantage of. She became even more disturbed upon hearing Elizabeth grieve over what her daddy had done, and what had driven him to kill himself. "How could he have taken the coward's way out and left his daughter penniless?"

Connie refused to add to her niece's grief by commenting on how she really felt about her brother and his selfishness. She did not want to say anything disparaging about her brother, because it could affect Elizabeth the rest of her life and destroy all of her fond memories of her father.

She eventually asked Elizabeth what she knew about Vick Porter. She explained, "Vick is very handsome, and I believe he was raised in a poor environment, with little or no education. I think I saw him once when he was a boy. I remember his eyes." She further explained how upset she was when Vick was invited to the manor, only to have him flagrantly stand them up with no explanation.

"A man who would do something like that had very little up-bringing," Connie, agreed. When she received her reply from the city clerk's office, everything negative she expected to hear about Vick Porter was just the opposite.

The clerk's letter proved Connie wrong about Vick Porter's character. She was surprised to learn he was considered a model citizen and town hero for his unselfish act of restoring property to the folks in their town, who had been taken advantage of by her brother, Elizabeth's father.

Connie needed to know the facts before she addressed any of her personal issues concerning Elizabeth's daddy. She wanted to tell her niece what she had learned, but reconsidered, since it might appear that she was meddling in Elizabeth's affairs. Out of respect for her niece, she did not intend to invade her privacy. Aunt Connie decided, it would serve no good purpose to show the letter to her. "I will tuck it away and allow her to continue to live her fantasy, fueled by the good memories she had of her father."

Elizabeth lived with her Aunt almost two years when she began thinking more seriously about moving on. However, before she had a chance to discuss her plans, Aunt Connie had a massive stroke that left her paralyzed and in a vegetative state. Connie required a caretaker, and, since her niece was her only family member, the responsibility for Connie clearly rested with Elizabeth.

Shortly after Connie's stroke, Elizabeth went through all of her Aunt's private papers and came across the letter from the county clerk's office telling her what a model citizen Vick was and how her father, Thomas Barkley had swindled ranchers and farmers out of their property.

She was angry learning the truth in a letter, when her Aunt could have told her what kind of person her father really was. "What a fraud he was and what a mockery my life has been, knowing the truth of the man I cherished as my father," she thought.

She was embarrassed, knowing what the townspeople must have thought of her. Her life had turned out to be a lie all because of the father she was raised to adore. "How dare he!" Elizabeth challenged. After weeks of reflection, she wrote to Vick, apologizing for the way she had misjudged him during the time her father was trying to manipulate him into selling his property.

Within a month, Elizabeth received a response from Mattie, explaining what she knew of Vick's past. It was a very long and informative letter, containing all the details of Vick's past that were now public knowledge. She was concerned to hear he had a bounty on his head for murder and that he had been on the run for about five months. At the end of the letter, Mattie reached out to Elizabeth and asked her to return home to help run the lumber company, which both knew she was capable of doing.

She was stunned, hearing about Vick and thought Mattie's offer was very gracious, since this would give her the opportunity to make things right with the town she had lived in since she was a little girl. Her only problem was Connie, who was clinging to life. She could not turn her back on her at a time she needed her the most. She had grown to love her Aunt like a mother. Elizabeth had been her lifesaver; she could never leave her to die alone.

Elizabeth mailed a sweet letter to Mattie, explaining the situation to her, thanking her for the generous offer. Mattie wrote back and sent money for Elizabeth to get a caretaker to help bring Connie to Arkansas, but before the money arrived, Connie died. Elizabeth used the money for her Aunt's funeral instead of a ticket back to Arkansas. After the burial, she took time to liquidate the property she inherited, and soon had more than enough money for the train and stagecoach fare back home.

This time she was wearing her homespun clothes and worn shoes. The young beauty, who had once thought she was on top of the world, was just an ordinary woman without the means to take care of herself. This was the new image she would portray to a town that previously thought Elizabeth had everything. Finally boarding the stagecoach, she felt like a queen, having treated herself to a meal in a boarding house for the first time in nearly two years.

When she arrived back in her hometown after a long stagecoach ride, Mattie was there to greet her, looking ravishing. It seemed the tables had turned. It was now Elizabeth who was in commoner's clothing, while Mattie was a woman of wealth and substance.

As Elizabeth stepped off the stagecoach, Mattie greeted her like a member of her family. The young ladies hugged and then Elizabeth turned to Mattie as though she was seeing her for the first time.

"My dear sweet Mattie, how can I ever repay you for reaching out to me?" It was evident that Elizabeth had changed for the better, and all Mattie sensed was a sweet gentle nature that she had never realized Elizabeth had possessed. Mattie immediately felt at ease.

"Well, I'm glad you're back. You should have never left in the first place." Mattie stated.

"I can't believe you would do this for me," Elizabeth said, taking Mattie's hand in hers.

"Then you don't know me, do you? Let me get your bags." Mattie turned and was about to go.

"No Mattie, please." But it was no use arguing with Mattie. When she got back to the buggy, she was carrying Elizabeth's one tote. "I tried to find your suitcases but there was just this one tote. Did they lose your belongings?"

"No, this is it. I travel light these days." Elizabeth brushed it off. Ordinarily, she would have been embarrassed, but she had already faced her demons and was quite comfortable being of meager means, if it was meant to be. Mattie was embarrassed that she had brought attention to the one bag. She then tried to help Elizabeth into the buggy, but refusing, she climbed in with ease. Mattie walked back to the other side to drive the buggy back to the manor.

"Elizabeth, I don't want you worrying about anything."

"Mattie, I failed to tell you, but I won't be staying in the manor. Perhaps tonight only, but tomorrow I plan to find a place of my own in town. I have a little money saved from my Aunt's estate, so I'll be all right."

"I beg your pardon, but that is out of the question. I have your room ready, so that's that. You have a home and it's with me." Elizabeth noticed something different about Mattie. She was not only full of confidence, but she was glowing.

The girls talked on their way back to the manor. "This is strange coming back to Arkansas. I really missed my home after I left," Elizabeth said, and then she caught herself speaking of the manor like she still lived there.

"I'm sorry Mattie, I didn't mean to refer to the manor as my home."

"Well, it is your home, and it always will be. You know, Vick never wanted you to move out, and had you stayed, something would have been worked out."

"Mattie, you are very kind, but I don't know if I'm ready to go back to live in a house that holds so many memories. I thought my daddy was a good man, and now I've found out my entire life was a lie. It's hard to accept."

"Dear, you're not to blame for what your father did. This is a new beginning for the both of us. Why don't we concentrate on the present, and let the past stay in the past! You're back and that's all that matters."

Mattie reached over and patted Elizabeth's hand, as if to say everything will be all right.

"You know, I have another reason for inviting you to come live with me. I hesitated to tell you this so soon, but I don't want to keep anything from you.

"I don't understand."

"I'm pregnant! Six months, and I can't hide it much longer."

"Mattie, are you sure?"

"Oh yes ... I'm sure! Do you think you can deal with this?"

"Is the father ..." Elizabeth hesitated.

"I know what you're thinking, and yes, Vick is the father. I know he loves me and desired to marry me, but with his past, he never asked, and he doesn't know about the baby. You are the first person I've told."

Elizabeth could not help but have a pang of jealousy since she had secretly dreamed of Vick. She quickly refocused for Mattie's sake.

Mattie began to cry as she told the story leading up to Vick leaving. Elizabeth reached over to comfort her but all the emotion she had bottled up was more than she could stand. Finally, Elizabeth took over the reins and slid in the driver's seat to let Mattie cry it out for the first time since Vick left. "Don't fret over this, we'll figure things out." Elizabeth tried to comfort her by giving Mattie a quick hug. "You don't worry about a thing. I'm here now ..."

By the time they got to the manor, Elizabeth had reassured Mattie that they would see her pregnancy through, and she would stay on as long as Mattie needed her. Arriving at the manor, she stopped the buggy and just sat looking at the home she was raised in. She had so many emotions. Her wonderful home was no longer hers. The manor looked the same, and when Elizabeth walked through the door of her childhood home, she felt nothing. She was glad for her thoughts were now of her father and how he acquired his fortune in order to lavish them with wealth she no longer felt connected to. As far as Elizabeth was concerned, Vick Porter and Mattie were the owners of the manor, and she was a guest. Her previous life felt distant, as if it had been a dream.

Chapter 16

WHEN THE SHERIFF WALKED UP TO VICK'S CELL SHORTLY AFTER **sunrise, he found his prisoner motionless on the cot, staring at the ceiling.** Within minutes Vick was on his way to hell.

By the time Vick arrived at the prison in Huntsville, Texas, he had to accept that his past had finally caught up with him. He was now considered a hardened criminal, deemed guilty of killing eight people, the latest of which was Marlin Winfrey. The iron-caged wagon rumbled to a stop in the filthiest part of Huntsville, Texas where Vick would spend a life's sentence after his brief trial.

Vick was guided into the prison where he stood in line with a dozen other prisoners, for a shakedown after which he was led to a room where locals were bargaining for field hands as part of a work-release program.

The warden had just received news that the prison had purchased the Clemens Farms in the far west side of Walker County and that Vick and his band of brothers, most of whom were black, would be under guard, hoeing and pulling weeds in the cotton fields near the prison.

Vick cooperated with the program, but he was not cut out for prison life. "There's no way I'm going to make it in prison," he thought with dismay.

Word spread that Vick was in for killing eight people, making him a target of other prisoners who protect themselves with the "kill him before he has a chance to kill me." He was in a precarious situation that just got worse.

Vick's nights were spent thinking about Mattie and wondering how she was doing, taking care of his responsibilities back in Arkansas. He had no idea Mattie was carrying his child and that she had reached out to Elizabeth to return to the manor and help run the lumber company.

He felt helpless, since he was illiterate and could not write Mattie to tell her where he was. The months were passing quickly as he toiled in the fields. Having told her he would return in two years if he was alive, if the word did not get out that he was in prison before then, Mattie would think he was dead.

On a cold overcast morning in the early spring, Vick was finally going to get the chance he'd been waiting for. He must have had a premonition, because the day started with an eerie yet exciting feeling that something was about to happen.

The other prisoners chatted as they rode to the far north cotton patch to do their day's work. They kept smiling and different ones would glance at Vick. Yep, something was up, Vick imagined. Just as the wagon stopped and the men started to gather their gardening tools, one of the prisoners stuck Vick in the side with a homemade knife. He crumbled to the ground in excruciating pain, with blood gushing from his wound.

Fortunately, the wound was not that deep; but it was bad enough to make his assailant and the guards think he was going to die right there on the ground in front of them. With no idea how things would play out, Vick just laid as still as he could.

For weeks, all he had thought about was escaping and getting as far away from Huntsville as possible. He knew he would be killed long before his 20 years were up.

One of the guards punched around on Vick. "Is that convict dead?"

"No, but it won't be long; you need to get him to the infirmary fast," said the bossman.

Hearing that, Vick pretended to be unconscious, just grunting in pain as a couple of guards threw him back onto the wagon. Vick continued to lay lifeless, taking shallow breaths, with no idea how serious his wound actually was.

Lying there alone, he thought about rolling off the wagon and slipping away, but would not get far with the shackles. He waited silently. Before long, the guard climbed aboard, turned the wagon around, and started in the direction of the infirmary. He took off rather fast, as if trying to impress the other guards.

As they got closer to the hospital, Vick saw it was backed up to a wooded area that would provide cover for his escape. Vick was desperate to make his move and knew he had to strike —there might never be another chance.

Vick opened an eye just enough to see the guards shotgun on the seat beside him. The guard was paying attention to the road, not worried about his unconscious charge. When the wagon rounded a corner and they got out of sight of the work area, the guard reined the horses to a slower pace. The rapid change of speed caused the shotgun to slide off the seat.

From the back of the wagon, Vick saw it sliding toward him. He held his breath, hoping the guard would not think to grab it as they were jostled around by bumps in the road. As the gun fell and slid toward him, Vick lunged to grab it, and instantly had the guard at gunpoint.

"Stop the wagon and get down. Slow like, you hear? I don't want to hurt you, but I don't have a thing to lose. You got any other weapons besides the one on your hip?"

"No. Don't shoot — I ain't done nothin' to you!"

"Do as I say, and you'll be just fine. Now, undo your belt and set it up here on the wagon where I can reach it … Now … grab that key ring and come around to the back of the wagon, easy like, and don't make any fast moves!"

"Yes, sir. Guess you want me to remove those shackles, don't you?"

"You got that right, and hurry. I don't have time to waste."

Vick got the pistol from the holster and held it on the guard while he unlocked the shackles to free Vick.

He slipped down off the wagon and stood with the guard. "Okay, now, how about moving the wagon over in those trees. Move it and don't think I won't use this!" He ordered as he grabbed a rag from the wagon.

"I hear ya, jest give me time to get this 'dang thang' turned around."

As the guard turned the wagon, Vick watched him with the gun handy while he wrapped the cloth around his waist to stop the bleeding. Soon, the wagon was out of sight and they had again exited the wagon.

"Now unhitch that horse," Vick commanded. His wound hurt, but adrenalin masked the pain. He was scared but had no alternatives — he would be a fugitive or could be killed escaping.

As soon as the horse was unharnessed, Vick assessed the situation. It would be hours before anyone would be looking for the guard, the wagon, or the work party.

"Take off your clothes," he commanded.

"What?"

"You heard me. I said take off your clothes!"

"Okay, okay … just point that thang' the other way."

As soon as the man was undressed, Vick ordered him to sit under the wagon.

"Okay, now sit back against the wheel and stick your hands through those spokes toward me."

Vick quickly, but carefully, tied the guard's hands. He knew ropes well from his childhood, so he made sure the guard would not be going anywhere until he was missed. Vick quickly stripped out of his prison uniform and changed into the guard's clothes that were a couple sizes too big.

"Raise your rear," he commanded as he slid his discarded uniform under the guard. He then tied a gag around the guard's mouth and asked, "Can you breathe okay?" The guard nodded "yes."

With that he strapped the gun belt on, picked up the shotgun, and escaped on one of the wagon horses with a cheery farewell.

The guard was shocked at how well Vick treated him. "This ain't the actions of a man that's killed eight people," the guard later explained to the warden. "He even made it comfortable for me, while I was sitting there waitin' to be found."

Huntsville was known as the most secure prison in Texas. When the warden heard that one of his prisoners had escaped, he was embarrassed and eager to get Vick back as quickly as possible, hopefully, before the story spread too far. It was a sensitive situation, since the escaped prisoner was wounded and had been found guilty of multiple killings. He immediately called for the Texas Rangers to hunt down Vick.

Despite all odds and the cut in his side, Vick outmaneuvered hounds and Texas Rangers through bayous, swamps and snakes until he crossed the Sabine River into Louisiana. After Vick crawled out of the last swamp he had leeches on his back and chest. When he felt the blood suckers, he shuddered at the thought. Vick never knew such things existed.

The next day he hitched a wagon going to New Orleans.

His wound proved not to be deep, as the crude knife had glanced off a rib, sparing his organs. Vick treated his injury as best he could, during the trip to New Orleans; a likely place to find Buck Dupree.

Two weeks later, Vick was in New Orleans, in the process of winning a hefty pot, when both his brief spell of freedom and nightlife abruptly ended. Sitting in a popular poker parlor, he looked up at the barrel of a .45 that suddenly appeared in front of his nose.

"It's no use son, there's eight of us, one for each murder you committed, a voice behind him said. "We were tipped off by a man claiming to be a Texas Ranger who followed you here, but no longer had jurisdiction."

Thus, Vick was taken to the Orleans Parish Prison. A hasty investigation determined that he would serve a life sentence for murder, in one of the harshest criminal systems ever known.

Despite Texas' efforts to have Vick extradited back to Huntsville, the courts of Louisiana trumped up their own charges and required Vick to serve hard time in the New Orleans Prison.

Chapter 17

VICK STEPPED DOWN INTO THE MUD, ARMS AND LEGS WEIGHTED DOWN
with shackles, as he began to serve his sentence. He was strip
searched, given harsh warnings, and degraded, and got one well-
placed blow to the ribs with a short club. Vick didn't respond when
the warden proudly told him he would be spending the rest of his life
working at hard labor with a chain gang on the railroad.

"There are many things to love about life," Warden Carson in-
toned, "but you will never experience any of them again." The words
sunk in as Vick picked himself up out of the mud, holding his searing
ribs.

"However long or short your life may be, I can assure you, beyond
question of one thing: It will be filled abundantly … with misery."

The Orleans Parish Prison was made up mostly of Vermillion
Parish slaves who had been convicted of heinous crimes, many of who
had been framed just as had Vick. There were very few white men
serving time there, but regardless of race, they all had the same hollow look in their eyes.

Like everyone who had spent any time in Louisiana, Vick had
heard stories of the tortuous treatment of inmates and how few survived more than just a couple of years once they were behind these
walls.

The old Orleans Parish Prison had burned to the ground years
ago, taking nearly a third of the inmates with it.

The new prison was built near a run down part of town with small vacant houses that evidently had received storm damage. Several of these rundown buildings were used for gambling, so there were men coming and going around the new prison.

After the old prison burned, surviving convicts were transferred to the new building with surroundings more humane than the original, but the guards were still brutal. There was a stench about the prison that only a new inmate could detect, hence the claim that you could always tell a new arrival by the sickly scowl on his face.

"Oh, you'll warm to that smell. In time, it'll be a comfort even … like home."

Vick was standing naked in front of the warden, holding his side and trying to catch his breath. He decided right then that he could not live the rest of his life in that hellhole. Or was it just that he wouldn't live for very long?

The warden began to read Vick's file, taking his time, pouring over every detail. Finally, still engrossed in the pages, he spoke.

"You been busy …"

Vick knew when not to speak. And the two guards with those short clubs behind him were waiting for the slightest transgression.

"… doing your share …"

"Not a word, not a movement," Vick reminded himself.

"… of killing."

The warden finally looked up at Vick. "It says so, right here." Vick knew that the cardinal rule was to not "speak when spoken to" but rather "answer when asked." The warden was baiting him, and the grunts were eager for Vick to slip up.

"You shot a man in the back over a card game … killed two mountain men … killed a family of four …" he looked up at Vick, wide-eyed, "and then killed your own brother!" The warden shook his head as he looked up at Vick, who just stared at the ground.

"What's wrong with you son? Are you enraged at the world 'cause your Pa didn't like you?"

"I was framed, I never killed my brother." Vick spoke in a whisper.

Both grunts lunged forward and clubbed Vick across the back. He went down hard.

The warden stood very erect with stoic ease and great dignity.

"That would be, 'I was framed ... Sir', now wouldn't it?"

Vick struggled to speak through the pain, but there was no air left in his lungs. "Sir, if I could explain ..." he finally got out.

"This is the wrong place to proclaim your innocence, boy. You're here to pay for your crimes and with the list you got ... well, I suspect we gonna be burying you. I'll tell you like I tell every other prisoner, make yourself at home, but just know that not too many residents survive our hospitality, if ya know what I mean."

The warden called back over his shoulder, "Skinny!"

Out of the shadows stepped a strange and unsettling creature. He was shockingly thin, with dull, grayish skin clinging tautly to his bones. His eyes were eerily deep set, forming shadowy holes of nothingness.

"This here's Skinny. Now, I know what you're thinking. He looks ugly and stupid. But I assure you, the human parts that The Good Lord has taken away, He has replaced, tenfold ... with viciousness. Skinny here, is gonna be in charge of you. So you just might want to take being good seriously."

The warden walked over to Vick and motioned for the grunts to pick him up off the ground. Vick stood naked, motionless, and un-moved, as the warden looked deep into his eyes.

"I can tell a prisoner with an attitude ... that I don't like. That usually means we will be seeing each other again very, very soon. Now get him outta' here."

"Which cell block, Boss," asked Skinny in a thin and raspy voice.

The warden grinned, "Put him in with ol' Greasy. They'll make a good pair. Maybe they'll kill each other and we won't have to feed 'em."

Vick dragged his leg irons along the stone cell block floor, won-dering what life would be like with a cellmate named Greasy. When they finally reached Vick's cell, he noticed there was a bunk bed and one small chair, two blankets and a chest, not to mention a pot, and the biggest colored man he had ever seen. The stench from human waste was overpowering.

"Greasy, I got company for you." The guard unlocked Vick's chains, opened the door to the cell, and pushed Vick's naked body inside. Vick flinched as Skinny struck him with his whip … just because.

"This fella killed three more people than you did, Greasy. Looks like you got some catchin' up to do. Then to Vick he said, "Have a happy life, corpse."

The guard threw a black and white striped uniform and a blanket to Vick. Greasy caught the blanket and shoved it into a makeshift chest that contained all his own personal property.

Vick slipped into his striped uniform, and acted unconcerned. He looked at the expressionless giant who was waiting for Vick to make the first move. After a moment, Vick decided to take the bull by the horns, so to speak.

"The name's Vick Porter," he said offering his hand.

Few things on the planet could have mattered less to Big Greasy. The massive man did not respond. Vick looked into his small, bloodshot eyes, but he saw virtually nothing there. The most notable aspect of Greasy's personality was that he smelled to high heaven. His bulbous, ratty hair, looked as though it had never been washed. Greasy had remained seated the entire time, but Vick guessed him to stand nearly a head taller than his own six foot frame, and so very much wider. His shoulder-to-shoulder width could hide two normal sized men, and his arms were about the size of Vick's legs.

There was nothing left for Vick to do but climb onto the top bunk and wait for night to pass. He had hoped no one would find out the heinous crimes he had been convicted of. That kind of reputation can bring out challengers who want to make a name for themselves, or, in Greasy's case, make them feel like underachievers.

There wasn't much sleep for Vick that night. Not because of fear, but rather, because his mind was turning over and over, and a plan was already beginning to form.

The next morning, before daybreak, the prisoners walked into a room that barely resembled a dining room. All were in shackles and moved slowly through the line, waiting for the cook to slop out a spoonful of food. They all appeared underfed and angry, as they were pushing and shoving. Tired hungry men tend to do that. Many looked at Vick like they were ready to kill him over his food, or maybe just to enhance their own reputations.

"You got a problem with people living?" came a voice over Vick's shoulder.

He realized he was a marked man, they knew his death count, and the results of that were about to begin. Vick never turned around, just kept moving. Greasy kept an eye on Vick, not about to miss a thing concerning his new roommate. After all, Greasy had only five murders to his credit, so whatever happened was almost surely going to involve him in some way. Greasy was definitely going to see to that.

After Vick was served his food, there was one chair left, and it was beside Greasy. Vick knew his only chance at survival was not going to come without some pain.

When Vick sat down, without hesitation, Greasy took Vick's food and poured it onto his plate. The room fell deadly silent, as every eye waited to see what would happen.

To everyone's amazement, Vick did nothing. He sat at the table in complete contentment twiddling his thumbs. That wasn't what had been expected. Gradually, all the men turned back to their plates, and began to eat, but not without disappointment.

It wasn't that Vick didn't want to make a scene, and it wasn't that he didn't have much of an appetite for that barely edible food. Nor was it because of the slightest fear of Greasy.

It was because of his plan. And it was working exactly the way he had envisioned it the night before, in his cold, dank bunk.

On Vick's first day of work, the prisoners were loaded onto a big wagon driven by a team of mules, and taken to the railroad. There were only three white men on the work gang. It was a cool morning, but by midday, Vick was wishing for the slightest cloud to temper the beating sun.

The men were swinging picks and heaving railroad ties as the humidity and stifling heat sucked away their energy. No one got water when they thirsted. It was up to Skinny to break for water ... when he saw the men had suffered enough he would shout out, "Water break in five minutes," just so the men would have to wait a while longer. If anyone asked for water, he would deliberately make them wait until everyone quenched their thirst, and he got what was left, if any.

Skinny was especially slow with the water that day. He was busy standing watch over his new convict, making sure he knew the meaning of backbreaking work. It was apparent Vick had the muscle for manual labor, and knew how to pull his weight.

"Looks like you done time before, new boy. A man works like that in this heat, oh he's been caught killin' at least once before. You kill some people we don't know about? Yeah, I bet you did!"

And so Vick's infamous reputation continued to expand.

When Skinny's back was turned, one of the prisoners whispered to Vick to pace himself. "Hey, new boy," he whispered, "slow yourself down." The man explained that everyone would have to keep up with the workload of the fastest man on the job. Vick complied.

If no one did their duty and no one asked for water, then the hours, days and weeks on the chain gang simply melted one into the other, and time passed with a numbness Vick could never have imagined. After a month, he began having conversations with some of the men who had been in prison for a long time.

"Anyone ever try to escape?"

"Ain't nobody ever made it, but they tried. And those that tried got caught and tortured," they explained. "Word has it that there is a 'disciplinary chamber' somewhere underground, a few lived to tell about. Some said it was beneath the warden's quarters and that he personally supervised all the correctional sessions."

Vick was told that when those surviving prisoners were finally released from "discipline," some weeks later, they were never the same. Even though they both lived for a couple of months after the attempt, something inside them was dead long before their bodies gave out.

Vick's main concern was to bring as little attention to himself as possible. Surprisingly, Greasy warmed up to him after several months of working side by side on the railroad. Even more than any of the others, he seemed to respect the eight notches they all thought Vick had on his belt, as a seasoned killer.

One of the men asked Vick what he used to do before he was caught. The only thing he could say was that he was a gambler, thinking that may spur some interest with the warden or the guards.

One prisoner got nerve enough to ask Vick about the men he killed and why. He answered by telling them he did not talk about his past. He knew that he was now respected as a murderer, but if anyone ever found out that he'd never wantonly killed anyone, things could change drastically, and his days might be numbered.

A couple months had passed by the time Vick learned there was a program whereby convicts could be leased out to plantation owners. The owners would come into the prison and bargain for prisoners to come to their plantations and cut sugar cane or pick cotton. As soon as Vick heard about this, he asked Skinny about working in the lease program. Skinny laughed.

"You must be crazy … you're a killer. Ain't no killers ever worked on a plantation." Skinny spit and shook his head.

Realizing it was a lost cause trying to make headway with Skinny, Vick never tried to deal with the "little tyrant" again. He'd have to try someone with a little more clout.

Every three months the warden would have all the prisoner's cells searched for contraband. On occasion, the warden would come along, too, mostly to order the beating of at least one prisoner, just to keep the fear level high. Vick decided he would use this chance to ask the warden to let him work in the lease program.

"Never! Your record is too bad to work on a plantation. Forget it!"

"Warden, I hear you're a pretty good poker player," Vick said as he passed by during a search.

"Some people say I am … I like to play now and then. Why, you that good?" asked the warden.

"Some say I am."

The warden sized up Vick for a moment, then started to walk away. "Well, maybe someday we'll see just how good you really are."

"Anytime, Warden."

The warden stopped in his tracks, then looked over his shoulder and gave Skinny a nod. The guard swung the club end of his whip into the back of Vick's leg, and he crumbled to the floor.

"Oh, you have plenty of time," the warden was heard saying, as he chuckled and walked away.

A few nights later, Skinny approached Vick's cell to fetch him. Greasy snapped awake at the noise of the ring of keys opening their cell door and got nervous, showing signs of distress, making Vick uneasy.

"Outlaw, you're coming with me," Skinny said to Vick in his raspy voice, pointing ahead.

Vick quickly slipped into his uniform then followed him to the warden's office. Skinny knocked, they heard a pleasant reply inviting them to enter. The warden sat patiently with a bottle of whiskey and a deck of cards.

"Sit down, Mr. Killer. I hope I did not interrupt your sleep?"

Vick sat at the table on the opposite side, waiting for what would come next.

"I been thinking about your challenge. Now is your chance to show me what you got. You ready for a little game?" Warden Carson asked.

Vick looked at the whiskey and deck of cards then shook his head "yes." He remembered the many nights he and Buck used to drink themselves silly playing poker.

"It's been a long time since I've played; I'm a little rusty," said Vick in his mellow voice.

"Come on, now, humor me … Skinny, pour Vick a drink, a man's gotta have a little whiskey in 'em while he plays." The warden sucked on his cigar and sat back in his chair as the smoke circled above him.

Skinny looked at the warden as though he had been insulted, being asked to pour a convict a drink. The warden noticed Vick's composure, and even though his prisoner hadn't seen a bath in a week, there was something regal about him.

They played for hours, while the warden studied Vick's handling of the cards. It was interesting how professional Vick seemed, sitting there in the prison garb, winning most of the time. Vick was quiet, never sharing any secrets or any information of any kind. Those secrets might be needed when it came time for the real challenge.

Vick knew this game wasn't just about the warden wanting to play cards. This was about something else. He just didn't yet know what. He knew he was being tested with every hand he played as his superiors watched him with great intensity. And, strangely, that made Vick feel right at home. As it turned out the warden's young inmate was a surprise to him.

After the card game, Vick was escorted back to his cell. Skinny instructed him that he was not to tell anyone he had been playing cards with the warden.

"It might not go so well with the other prisoners, if you know what I mean."

That went without saying. Just as he was stepping into his cell, Skinny hit him on his back so hard that Vick was knocked to the floor.

"Let that be a lesson to ya," Skinny said, as he quickly locked the cell door, then snorted and chortled as he skittered away.

Greasy jumped up to see how bad Vick was hurt.

"Dey mean som' bitches," said Greasy as he helped him to the top of his bunk.

Vick didn't say a word. His cellmate was impressed at how Vick could keep his cool.

"Why dey got it in fo you?"

"Forget about it," Vick said. They got nothing. It's all about nothing."

Greasy sat back on his cot and marveled at Vick's fortitude. From that time on, Greasy had Vick's back, and the other prisoners knew to let Vick be.

Once a week the warden would have Vick brought to his office, and when he returned to the cell, Skinny would hit him in the mouth or the shoulders, on the back, or the ribs. Vick would never show any emotion. It was a game he was getting very good at, and one he now knew he could win.

On one occasion, Greasy stood right by the cell door glaring at Skinny as he was about to put his key in the lock.

"Stand back Greasy!" hissed the hated guard. Greasy didn't budge as Skinny started to get anxious and agitated. "I said step away from the door, ya animal!"

Vick motioned for Greasy to step back, and finally he did. Skinny unlocked the door and Vick calmly stepped into the cell and waited for his blow. But this time there were three in quick succession. And Vick couldn't help but let out a grunt as he hit the floor, almost unconscious. Skinny slammed the cell door and locked it in a panic.

"You do what I say!" Skinny barked at Greasy before he hurried away.

Greasy rushed to see how badly his friend was hurt. "He's a dead man," Greasy said under his breath.

"I fight my own fights," replied Vick, smiling up at Greasy. "Don't let it bother you ... and I'll hurt less." Greasy lifted Vick up with little effort and placed him on the top bunk.

Later that night, they talked and Greasy opened up about the early days before prison. He confided that he was an honorable man before he was accused of murdering five men while defending a young colored man he knew was innocent.

Greasy alone killed all the men in self-defense, but his pleas of innocence fell on deaf ears after the rumors circulated that the standoff ended up in a blood bath. Greasy was found guilty and sentenced to 99 years in the Orleans Parish Prison. Vick listened as he continued to talk telling about being tortured by Skinny and left for dead several years before Vick had been incarcerated. Seeing Vick taken out of his cell brought back bloody memories and deeply alarmed Greasy.

Vick wanted to confide what he was really doing, but he knew he couldn't take a chance on Greasy and the other prisoners misunderstanding his special treatment. If that ever happened, they might all turn on him. And then he could be killed or thrown in the "hell hole" he had been warned about.

One evening, Skinny came for Vick and escorted him to a room outside the warden's office. There was a tub of water and civilian clothes lying on the back of a chair, even a mirror where he could see himself. Vick wondered what was up.

"Wash yourself and change into these clothes, cause the warden has a job fer' ya."

After Vick was dressed, Skinny gave Vick a bankroll of cash and told him he would be playing poker with some local men who were good gamblers. And so to apply a little pressure, he was told to win or get punished. Vick was taken outside the prison walls and driven by wagon to a small frame house that was set up like a gambling parlor. When they entered, he was introduced as an off-duty guard who wanted in the game.

The warden felt a bit uneasy when he saw the men sitting at the Faro table, all set up and ready to play. Obviously, he had not known the other men had planned to play Faro. But Vick returned the warden's gaze with confidence and said, "Gentlemen, it's a pleasure."

Vick's voice surprised the warden and for the first time, he knew he was in the presence of a professional. The guards looked at the warden who returned their glance by shaking his head with approval, while Skinny slithered away with resentment.

Vick had no intention of losing and taking all the men's money would certainly endear him to the warden.

There was a Banker who had been brought in by the men to oversee the game, and a Dealer to distribute the cards. One of the men playing was later discovered to be the town sheriff.

"Yes, this was going to be fun," Vick thought to himself. He hadn't forgotten what Buck had said: "It's more about playing the men than playing the game. In fact, playing the men is playing the game."

When the men seated themselves, Vick proceeded as if he was in charge.

"I see you men want to play Faro, but there's a couple of new games that might be more interesting. "And what's that?" Asked one of the gamblers. "Bucking the Tiger" or "Twisting the Tiger's Tail," said Vick.

"How about we stick to playing Faro, 'cause we got the Banker and Dealer here ready to go," one gambler said.

"Yeah, Faro is better for me," another man insisted.

Vick chuckled underneath his breath that the men did not know the new games were nicknames for Faro. Just as Buck had taught, if they don't know the games are the same, chances or they're not that good of a player. Vick smiled as the men stumbled through the game. He let a few bets get away just to keep the excitement going, while the warden looked at him warily. When the time was right, he bet hard and fast, as the other gamblers lost. It was just like old times, and it never felt so good!

The sheriff had been watching Vick suspiciously from the beginning, but as the game continued and Vick had won the majority of his bets, no one could see evidence that Vick was cheating. Luck was with Vick as he wrapped up a nice win for the warden, who liked how Vick handled himself with the sheriff right across the table.

The usual set up at the end of Faro would have to wait until another day when more money was involved. Vick was clever enough not to reveal all he knew his first game, and reserved the big win for a high stakes game in the future and make a big win like he did when he outsmarted Thomas Barkin back in Arkansas. He smiled thinking, "the warden hasn't seen anything yet. Just wait till I show him my magic." Vick sensed the warden's hunger for more money, and he was the one who could give it to him for a price.

It wasn't a long evening, but out in the real world, it would have been a lot shorter. Here, Vick had to play both sides of the "game." On one hand, he wanted to win as much money as possible for he could see the greed in the warden's eyes. Vick knew he was being looked at as a means to make more money than any prison system employee could ever dream of.

On the other hand, Vick knew that the action in this little backyard game was just the beginning. If he took too much too soon, he'd never get a chance at any bigger fish. The men were all gracious, and congratulated Vick for his win, while Warden Carson although thrilled, began wondering who Vick really was. "Something about Vick ain't right." He remembered Vick saying he was innocent and wondered if Vick really was framed.

"I got bigger plans for this man and he ain't going nowhere," the warden thought. And so it was, the warden became very protective of his prize convict.

Step by step Vick's plan was working; he was on his way to gaining more control of his life behind bars. It was either make life bearable in prison or die a miserable death waiting to get out, his only options.

Once everyone was gone, Skinny quickly rushed in, as if his presence was a necessity. He felt it imperative that he search Vick thoroughly, in case he was attempting to keep part of the winnings for himself. Vick invited the search, and of course was found honest, which seemed to please the warden.

Back at the cell, Skinny unlocked the door and allowed Vick to walk through as he had always done. This time, however, just as Skinny raised his whip to give Vick the traditional blow, Vick turned and looked him dead in the eye. It was a look of confidence and power. It was a look that marked that a transition had taken place, and things would never go back to the way they were. Vick said it all with the piercing gaze of his steely eyes.

Deeply unsettled, Skinny lowered his whip, locked the cell door and scurried away in silence. None of this transitional moment was lost on Greasy. It was here that he began to reassess his opinion of Vick's position in this prison.

Chapter 18

Elizabeth loved being back in Arkansas, although she was embarrassed, knowing of her father's deception. It took several months for her to relax and be herself, even though no one held her responsible for her father's miss-dealings. When Elizabeth ran errands in town, she rarely took time to tarry. She was often seen scurrying about in a modest print dress, too embarrassed to associate with people from her past. Her appearance was far from the prim and proper dress that she used to wear.

Months passed, as she watched Mattie suffer through her pregnancy. She knew things were not right when Mattie, who was normally anything but lazy, preferred to remain in bed rather than do some of the simplest tasks.

She was at least three weeks short of full term when Elizabeth returned from the lumber company and found Mattie standing in a puddle of water and in active labor. Not knowing what to do next, Elizabeth helped her get back into bed, then called for Frank, the gardener. She asked if he would take the buggy and fetch the midwife who lived nearby.

Normally very level headed, Elizabeth was now near panic from hearing Mattie's continuous pleas for help. "Mattie, I don't think we have time for the doctor. I sent Frank for the midwife; she'll have to do."

"Elizabeth, hurry: the baby is coming! ... I don't care who delivers the baby! Just hurry!" Mattie cried out in pain.

Dr. Robert Lewis, more of a medicine man than a medical doctor, was well respected and in spite of his lack of credentials, Mattie planned to have him deliver her baby. Much of his medical practice was based on what he learned hands on and by trial and error, rather than years of formal medical training. But he knew the business of delivering babies, and that's all that seemed to matter in their small rural community.

Elizabeth paced the floor while Mattie continued to groan, pushing to deliver the baby naturally, but the baby would not budge. By the time the midwife arrived, she knew the baby was not coming without a doctor's help.

She again turned to Frank, and he drove off at top speed.

While they waited, Mattie lost consciousness several times. Both women sat by her side, wiping her face with a cool cloth as they watched her drift in and out of consciousness mumbling about things that made no sense. Fearing she might die, Mattie came around long enough to speak with Elizabeth. "I need to talk with you privately." Elizabeth looked at the midwife, who immediately left the room.

"I'll be right outside the door if you need me," she said.

"Mattie, you should save your strength. When the baby starts coming, you will need all the strength you have," Elizabeth suggested.

"No, we need to discuss the baby," she said in a weak voice.

"Mattie, you're going to be fine. Please don't try to talk."

"Elizabeth, in case I die, will you promise to raise my son as your own?" Elizabeth had not thought that far ahead assuming Mattie would survive childbirth and raise her own child.

"Mattie, you know you don't have to worry about that! Of course I would, but you're going to be around to raise him yourself."

This was the first time Elizabeth allowed herself to think of Mattie possibly dying.

"Thank you, Elizabeth, I knew I could count on you … but there is something else …"

"I don't understand?" Elizabeth said.

"It's about a treasure I've been keeping for Vick. The most beautiful treasure I have ever seen." Her voice got stronger as she continued. "He told me it would be dangerous if anyone knew; that's why I have never told you."

Elizabeth listened as she kept wiping the perspiration from Mattie's forehead. "She felt sure Mattie was imagining Vick had a treasure hidden somewhere."

"Elizabeth, if something happens to me, give the treasure to the baby when he is old enough. It's hidden in the secret closet. You remember, don't you? … that closet under the stairwell. Promise me you will never tell anyone, for it would be dangerous if Buck Dupree found out you had the treasure." "Who in the world is Buck Dupree?" she thought.

"Mattie, don't worry … I promise." She would have promised anything to settle Mattie down.

Growing up, neither Elizabeth nor her father ever used the secret closet. "She must be hallucinating, for Mattie was talking like she already knew the sex of her baby. She wanted Mattie to stay focused and remain calm, thinking it might help her.

When Dr. Lewis arrived he could see his patient was in trouble and tried to be of comfort to Elizabeth as he checked Mattie's pulse and began his examination.

He turned to Elizabeth and urged, "We need hot water and towels, plenty of 'em.".

He immediately knew he would have to take the baby and called the midwife back in to help.

"Mattie's heart ain't gonna make it if I don't take the baby," Dr. Lewis said. "Mary get plenty hot water ready and come over here."

"Already got it," said the midwife. "Right here!"

"What do you mean, take the baby?" asked Elizabeth.

"I got to take the baby Cesarean."

"You mean operate and take the baby?"

"Ain't you ever heard of a Cesarean before?" asked the doctor working with Mary to prepare Mattie for surgery.

"I guess so, but this is the first time I've known of a Cesarean around here. Have you done this before?"

"Once, on a horse!"

"What happened to the horse?" asked Elizabeth, then realized it was her voice that had asked such an odd question.

"Never mind the horse," said Dr. Lewis. "Old man Riley's got one of the finest colts this side of Missouri and she's spry as they come."

Elizabeth took a deep breath and prayed that Mattie would live to raise her baby. The umbilical cord had been wrapped once around the baby's neck. When he was delivered, Dr. Lewis slapped him on the butt, and Mary tied off the umbilical cord. After hearing the baby's cry and getting a glimpse of him, Elizabeth had no doubt that she could love Mattie and Vick's child. In the meantime, the doctor and Mary worked feverishly to stop Mattie's hemorrhaging and close the incision. There was a lot of blood, but they finally finished.

After bathing the baby, Elizabeth laid him tenderly next to Mattie.

"Might even make her wake up," she thought, as she continued to wipe her friend's forehead and whisper reassurances.

"Dr. Lewis, can you tell me anything about her condition?"

He looked at Elizabeth with very sad eyes.

"I can't tell you for sure whether or not she'll ever open her eyes, but Mattie's got a lot of spunk, so let's hope for the best. I've known this girl all her life; she's one strong woman, just like you. You take good care of her and keep her laying down and she might surprise us. She has been through a lot, lost a lot of blood."

"Dr. Lewis, thank you so much. It' a shame Mattie's husband couldn't be here by her side."

"You mean to tell me Mattie and Vick got married?" Both Dr. Lewis and Mary questioned simultaneously.

"Yes, Mattie married Vick before he left town. We thought everyone knew about it," Elizabeth lied.

"Too bad the man got himself in such a mess of trouble. Does he even know Mattie was having his baby?" asked the doctor.

"No, Vick left before Mattie knew she was pregnant."

"Glad you are here to help out. She's gonna need lots of looking after, 'cause the prognosis don't look too good. Give her a little toddy if she continues to run a fever, and let me know if she gets worse. Lizzie, I hate to leave you, but there ain't nothing I can do until she wakes up. I'll best be going, since I got a couple house calls to make. Mary will stay with you, and I'll be back to check on Mattie first thang' in the morning."

Elizabeth walked the doctor to his buggy, while Mary stayed upstairs with Mattie and the baby.

Frank was waiting anxiously to give his approval. "I heard the baby cry. How's she doing?" he asked as he climbed onto the wagon.

"Don't really know yet," the doctor answered. "She is going to need a lot of rest. All we can do now is just hope for the best. A little prayer won't hurt anything, either. The baby is healthy and a pretty good size. You need to get some goat milk into him until Mattie wakes up and can feed him."

Elizabeth waved as Frank and the doctor rode away.

The young mother remained unconscious, while Elizabeth took care of the baby. Mattie laid in a state of sleep until one afternoon on the third day, she surprised everyone by waking and asking for her baby. Elizabeth was ecstatic to see Mattie open her eyes.

"You have a beautiful baby boy, waiting to be named. You've been asleep long enough." Mattie tried to smile, as Elizabeth brought him to her. She opened the blanket to examine her new baby, and looked up at Elizabeth with tears in her eyes.

She spoke in a whisper. "Don't you see how he favors Vick?"

"He does have a great likeness to his Pa. Have you thought of a name?" asked Elizabeth.

"I want to name him Victor Cain Porter and call him Cain," she whispered."

"I'm sure Vick would be proud." "I think so," Mattie said. " I wish there was some way we could let him know. Have you heard anything from him or where he could be?" she asked.

"Not a word, but I'm sure he's alright.. Don't you think we should have heard something from him by now? I hate to ask, but didn't you say Vick couldn't read or write? If that's the case, this may be the reason you haven't heard from him."

"That must be the reason," Mattie agreed.

"The main thing right now is, the doctor wants you in bed with a lot of rest, and not to worry.."

"As long as Cain is healthy, that's all that matters," she whispered.

"You gonna have to mind the nurse, and that's me!" Elizabeth teased her. "Thank you Elizabeth. How can I ever repay you?"

"You already have. I'm so glad you opened those beautiful eyes."

Elizabeth had never shown the affection she had for Mattie, even though she had liked her from the start. After the ordeal they had been through together, and the faith placed in Elizabeth to raise Cain should something happen to her, she felt incredibly close and spontaneously bent down and kissed Mattie on the forehead.

The women became like sisters, regardless of any social barriers that had once divided them. As the months passed, Elizabeth and Mattie were both mothers to Cain. Within a few months, the baby was scooting himself across the floor and showing signs of becoming a very active child. He was the best entertainment the women could ask for, as they spoiled him with their combined love.

Elizabeth thought, "I couldn't love a child more if he were my own."

Mattie was still weak and sickly, while Elizabeth ran the lumber company and the manor at the same time, plus carefully supervising Mattie's task. She treated her like a princess, waiting on her hand and foot during the months of her recovery. Soon, Mattie was well enough to care for Cain herself, and Elizabeth was free to spend more time running the business.

The Porter Lumber Company continued doing well under the leadership of Elizabeth, but she had a particularly difficult problem dealing directly with the loggers. Her Pa had always shielded her from the men because of their dirty habits and unsavory language. Spitting on the floor was quite common among the loggers, and Elizabeth disliked being around their snuff dipping and tobacco chewing when she had to clean up after them. They had a daily flow of loggers coming and going through out the day and it became a real chore for her.

Elizabeth and Mattie decided they needed an overseer for the loggers, a man who understood and could deal with them.

Mattie continued to improve but Elizabeth remained concerned noticing how difficult it was for Mattie when she bent down to pick Cain up. One morning, Elizabeth drove her into town for an appointment with Dr. Lewis. It was her first trip since her surgery, and she decided to use the opportunity to talk to the doctor about the kind of person they needed to help run the company. He had become like a father to the girls.

"Well, I can certainly understand why you need a man around all those logger fellers," Doctor Lewis concurred. "Ain't no place fer two women telling them men what ya expect outta 'em. Don't rightly know if ya'll can use my nephew, but he's coming in from Little Rock, and I'd like to see him find something he would be good at. He graduated from college, but he's not quite ready to settle down and raise a family. He's about ya'lls' age and might fit right in. This is just a suggestion, and ya don't have to pay no mind if ya have someone else yer' thinkin' of."

Knowing what a problem Spencer was, while growing up, the doctor had some reservations, however, he wanted his nephew to have a chance with people that knew he was from a good family. "This will help Spencer to mature," Dr. Lewis thought.

Elizabeth and Mattie agreed to hire him, and within two weeks they had a new employee: Spencer Lewis. He was tall and nice looking enough with his full head of hair and brown eyes, but wasn't anything to write home about.

Unbeknownst to the women, though, Spencer still had unresolved issues and was far from the man his uncle had assumed he had become. Mattie and Elizabeth wanted a strong man to lean on when high-pressure decisions needed to be made, and they hoped Spencer was the man for the job.

They all knew he had no experience in the lumber business, but he was well educated and felt he could do a good job. His first priority with the business was to make a good impression, because he wanted Elizabeth to like him. He was smitten with her beauty from the beginning.

Spencer thought he and Elizabeth could have a lot in common, but she kept their relationship strictly professional, not at all looking for a romantic connection with Spencer. When they first met, she thought he was nice looking, but she found herself making comparisons to a man she had no right to covet. Unwilling to accept her feelings, Vick Porter had more of her heart than she wanted to believe.

She hadn't dared to allow herself to care for a man that had been so elusive with her, but Mattie's chatter about Vick had stirred a romantic desire in her that she had tried to suppress. Even if, heaven forbid, Mattie were out of the picture, Vick had too many skeletons in his closet to deal with, and it would be fruitless to waste her time. Even knowing this, Elizabeth still found it difficult to stop thinking of Vick. There was no chance anything good could come of a relationship with a man who was partly responsible for her father's death. Elizabeth was ashamed of herself for having these thoughts. Mattie's talk about Vick only made things worse.

One day, while Elizabeth was off running errands, Mattie dropped by the lumber company. She stopped just outside Elizabeth's office door and heard noises. Leaning forward she observed Spencer opening drawers and going through Elizabeth's desk, never realizing that

Mattie was nearby. He stopped rummaging, sat down in Elizabeth's chair, and propped his feet up on her desk. "This will be my office when the bitch is gone," then he laughed.

To be sure she was hearing correctly, Mattie slipped quietly into the office. She listened as he rambled on about the day he would own the lumber company.

When Spencer heard someone behind him, he jumped to his feet concerned to see Mattie standing there observing him make a fool of himself.

"Oh, Mattie, I didn't know anyone was around. Don't mind me as I am a little dramatic at times … Uh, I used to act in college. Sometimes my imagination runs wild."

"So it seems! What are you doing in Elizabeth's office?"

Spencer ignored Mattie and got up to bring her a chair. "Elizabeth should be right back. Make yourself comfortable. I have work to do."

"As comfortable as you were making yourself in Elizabeth's chair?"

Spencer gave a nervous chuckle, and left Mattie to wait for Elizabeth. When she arrived back at the office Mattie got up and shut the door for privacy. Spencer observed this and assumed she was spilling the beans on him. He immediately thought his position would be more secure if Mattie was out of the picture.

"What a surprise to see you in the office," Elizabeth said, giving Mattie a hug.

"Well, you're not the only one who was surprised, because when I came in, Spencer was sitting in your chair talking to himself about taking over the lumber company. He called you a terrible name, one that I wouldn't want to repeat, but you should know. He called you a bitch."

"You must be kidding … I don't believe it! Are you sure you didn't misunderstand him?"

"No, I know what I heard. Dr. Lewis said he was sometimes a little dramatic, but this was over the top."

"Well then, there's the answer. I think he is harmless and I doubt he would do anything to hurt the logging business, since his uncle recommended him to us."

"You're probably right, but keep an eye on him … I hope you don't mind me dropping by; I was getting a little stir crazy at home."

"That's a good sign. I'm glad you're up and about."

Spencer was eavesdropping but couldn't quite hear what Mattie was telling Elizabeth. At one point he slammed his fist into the palm of his hand, mocking what he'd really like to do to Mattie.

The ladies visited for a while but when Mattie opened the door unexpectedly, she caught Spencer turning to go to his desk. She knew he had been listening to their conversation, but doubted he had heard anything, since she and Elizabeth were not talking above a whisper.

All the way home she kept thinking about Spencer, and if he was a man they could trust. There was a lot at stake, and she had no idea what someone like him could do to hurt the company, or Elizabeth.

The next morning, Mattie was not feeling well, She began experiencing shortness of breath and asked Elizabeth to send Frank to fetch Dr. Lewis. When the doctor examined her, he knew he had to talk with Elizabeth about Mattie's failing heart.

"Mattie, I want you to have complete bed rest. No getting up, not even light chores. You stay put. You hear me?"

"I can't! when I have a toddler to take care of."

"You let someone else take care of Cain. That is, if you want to get better," the doctor chastised.

After Dr. Lewis left, Mattie had another serious discussion with Elizabeth.

"I want to thank you for all you have done for me. You have been more than just my friend. I couldn't have made it without you."

She was glad it was near dark, so Mattie could not see the tears in her eyes. She had a foreboding feeling that Mattie was dying. It was so unfair for Cain to be without his mother. Mattie was feeling melancholy as she opened up to Elizabeth about Vick, telling her of his childhood with an abusive father. She detailed his whole life, right up until he had been forced to run, leaving Mattie with the lumber company and the manor.

"Elizabeth, I have been waiting till the right time to talk to you about my personal affairs."

She looked at Mattie, knowing how hard it was going to be to have the same conversation they had before.

"You have been like a sister to me: Coming here and relieving me from all my responsibilities. Helping me with the lumber company, nursing me back to health, and now helping me take care of my son. You are like a second mother to Cain. I'm thankful I've had the time with him but Elizabeth, I have to ask you if you'll be Cain's mother after I die." Elizabeth was taken completely off guard.

"Mattie, I hate for you to worry about this. You remember, we talked about me caring for Cain. And I will; you can count on me."

"I know, but my time is running out and I need to do this, so the transition will be easy for you and Cain. I want everyone to know this was my decision for you to raise Cain. So I'm asking if you will adopt my son before I die. I want to make sure that after I'm gone, he will have a mother." She paused to rest a few seconds.

"I have drawn up the papers and want you to sign them as soon as possible, if you agree. The paperwork is all prepared concerning the lumber company and the manor, which will be yours, if Vick does not return home. I know you will do right by Cain, because he will be your son in every sense of the word."

"When did you do this?" Elizabeth briefly looked over the legal papers.

" I don't know what to say ... are you sure? I have not thought along these lines, and I'm afraid you have taken me completely by surprise. Of course, if anything ever happened to you, without question I would take care of Cain, but you're always going to be his mother. I want you to know that."

"Well then, I won't take 'no' for an answer; you're as much his mother as I am and all you have to do is sign."

Elizabeth sat quietly, as tears welled up in her eyes but Mattie was not through.

"I have one more thing I have not shown you, if you will please help me to the closet under the stairwell." Elizabeth was puzzled as she got up to help Mattie… Inside the closet Elizabeth saw a sack filled with something. She then remembered Mattie talk of a "treasure" under the stairs.

"Ooh, my!" Elizabeth said. "I've never seen anything like this. Mattie, this has to be worth a fortune."

"You do remember, don't you? I promised Vick I would keep it hidden until he returned. No one was ever to know about this."

"Mattie, you told me about a treasure during your childbirth, but I thought you were delirious and didn't know what you were saying."

"Elizabeth," Mattie expressed. :"We must not tell anyone about the treasure. Do you understand? Vick said that people may hurt us to get to the treasure. Do you remember me telling you about the man who taught Vick how to play poker? He must never know or find out about the treasure. Everything stays between us and in this room."

"Mattie, I'm puzzled. How can a mountain man come across a treasure like this?"

"I thought the same thing when I saw it."

Elizabeth kept staring at the treasure, shaking her head yes. She could not believe what she was seeing.

"Mattie, Vick probably does not realize what he has here." She saw Mattie struggling to breathe, and suggested she go back to bed.

Later, when Elizabeth entered Mattie's room to close the curtains, Mattie had fallen asleep. Elizabeth had no idea someone was outside the window watching them.

That night, lying in bed, she thought of all the changes that would take place when Mattie died. How unfair it would be for her friend to be taken so young, leaving her infant son to be raised by another woman. Mattie would never be able to see Cain grow up and become a man.

Thoughts of being a mother and the possibility of having to face Vick, further racked her mind. The poor man would face a triple shock when he found out he had lost Mattie, had a son, and that Elizabeth, was now Cain's mother. How strange it would be to find that the daughter, whose inheritance he won in a card game had been given his most prized possession, his son.

She was just musing, "If Vick is the father and I became the mother, would we be ..."
Elizabeth would not allow herself to think of what Vick would think.

Chapter 19

"Greasy, are you awake?"

A blood-curdling scream woke Vick in the early morning hours.

"Yeah, I hear 'em ... dey' got a man in de' hole."

The guards were whooping and hollering, celebrating the pain of a convict being tortured.

"It sounds like they're killing him and the guards are making it worse."

"Don't let 'em hear you say dat," Greasy admonished. "Remember, I told you what they do if dey' get it in fer ya."

Vick lay there hearing scream after scream, wondering how long they would keep it up until they killed the man.

"Just so ya know, dey' might as well kill em' when dey' get through with 'em. Dey' put me in de' hole once 'cause I punched a guard. Don't ever want to go der' agin'."

"What did they do?"

"Dey' chained me to a wall, left me fer' days n' most of the nights. I had one piece of bread a day and a little water, that's all, and the third day, dey'give me a meal dat' taste like old food but I was' glad to git' it."

Suddenly, the screams stopped mid-scream.

"It sounds like it's over for him," Vick said.

"Dey' may as well kill him if dey cut his balls off, so don't' git' on the bad side of de' warden."

"No, they wouldn't do a thing like that."

"I told ya … just so ya know."

Vick fell back on his cot, thinking how inhumane it was for the guards to mistreat the prisoners that way. It was never that bad at home with his Pa. This was the first time, since he entered prison, that Vick felt vulnerable.

"Greasy, I ain't made to be locked up like this, and when I get a chance, I'm runnin'."

"Der' ain't no way out, men tried and men died. So git' used to it. Git' some sleep. Tomorrow gonna' be another bad day. I been meaning to ask you, where de' take you when Skinny comes after you?"

"It's not safe for me to talk, maybe soon."

"Yo' business … 'night."

The next morning there was a lot of clanging on the bars and whooping and hollering by the inmates. This was all new to Vick. He later learned that this was a standard protest whenever the prisoners learned that one their inmates had been sent to "the hole." When Vick and Greasy made their way to the food kitchen, most of the prisoners were sitting at the table, starring at their food instead of eating it.

"Nobody eats after a man's been in the hole. Dar's been some tales goin' around what they put in the food after a man's been tortured. Git what I'm sayin'?"

Vick cringed, then whispered under his breath, "How much worse is it going to get?"

Greasy and Vick made their way through the line, but passed on the eats. About that time, two new convicts stepped in line to fill their plates. The cooks smiled and then laughed as they watched the men eat.

After breakfast they were marched to the wagons, with the exception of Vick, who became nervous not knowing where he was going.

"Am I about to be punished for something?" he thought. Skinny began punching Vick in the back with his gun, and directing him to another wagon.

"Git your ass in the wagon and don't ask no questions."

Vick climbed into the wagon with a puzzled look on his face.

"The warden wants you to work on the plantation 'cause we got a shortage of men." Vick imagined it was an excuse to take him to the plantation. The two new prisoners, plus all short-term prisoners were on the lease program, along with Vick, as the wagon began moving out to the plantation. It was a long ride, and the men had plenty time to talk. One man mentioned he was from a tiny town in Texas, and had gotten into some trouble over a woman he didn't know was married.

"I know about Texas, lived in Fort Worth for a time," Vick said.

"I lived all my life in Waco. You ain't heard of Waco, have ya?"

"There must be a lot of cattle rustling in that area, 'cause I had a herd of Longhorns stole from me just south of Fort Worth."

"Yep, sounds like you met up with the Ellis gang — a passel of thieves, rustling cows and terrorizing ranchers. They been riding and rustling for a couple of years, robbing banks and causing all kinds of chaos. In fact, one of the gang is married to a church lady. He's been shot at least ten times, but they say the man won't die."

"What do you mean?" asked Vick.

"They say the sonavobitch has been shot through the heart a couple of times, and the next day he's walking around like nothing happened."

"Do you know his name?"

"No, don't reckon I do."

Vick felt sure he may be on to something, but little can be done when a man's in prison.

"What's this man to you?" asked one prisoner.

"Just curious, I used to know a man that wore a metal breast plate for protection. Sounds like the same man."

"Maybe, but what I hear, he's a mean bastard with his knife. All of his victims have their throats cut." Vick knew from their information that it was Buck who was riding with the Ellis gang.

By the time the men got to the plantation, the sun was almost unbearable, but Vick was smiling inside. The warden had finally taken him off the chain gang to keep him in tip-top shape for his next game.

Each of the prisoners tied a dirty piece of material around their heads to shield themselves from the sun, as they marched into the fields to pick cotton. Vick thought, "These petty outlaws with short sentences don't know what heat is."

When Skinny got to Vick, he pulled him aside and told him he had another job for him.

"Warden told me he didn't want you chumming up to the prisoners, 'cause you might talk. You work over around the plantation house pulling weeds and doing some planting. I saw you talking to them men over there ... Keep to yourself. Hear?"

Vick worked awhile and the plantation owner came up to him and introduced himself.

"Look's like you're doing a mighty fine job. We can use good men working for us. Play your cards right and I might teach you something about growing cotton. By the way, my name is Hop Babcock."

Vick started to shake hands but instead pulled back since they weren't supposed to have body contact with the outside. Funny, that Mr, Babcock said, "play your cards right," for that is exactly what he did to con his way to working on the plantation."

"I can handle this until I make my escape," Vick planned. He had remembered what Greasy had told him about talking to people. "Don't trust nobody, cause if dey' git' a chance dey' talk and ya end up in de' hole."

Back at the prison, Vick would wait in his cell until supper. Then afterwards, every few nights, Skinny would come to the cell and fetch him to go to the warden's office to play cards.

Greasy would look at Skinny like he could kill him, but would never say a word. Little did he know that Vick was becoming a regular "sugar tit," bringing in money the warden wasn't used too, which had vastly improved the warden's lifestyle. Vick was beginning to win some "serious" money, and by doing that more and more poker games were organized. Night after night Vick would lie in his bunk until Skinny came and got him for another game. A few nights later, Vick was prepared to go to the warden's office when the cell door opened and, as usual, it was Skinny, ready to give Vick his first wallop.

Before Vick could flinch, Greasy was on top of Skinny, beating him with his fist. Vick had never seen such a fight, with blood flying everywhere, and it was all Skinny's.

The guards heard the commotion and came running with their guns shooting Greasy between the eyes. He fell like a huge boulder, hitting the cell floor hard and flat. Vick was in shock seeing Skinny unconscious, now face down, blood all over his upper body.

They tried to remove Vick from the cell, but not before he knelt down and closed Greasy's eyes. Vick stood by while they laid Skinny on a quilt and hurried him off to the infirmary, leaving Greasy who had died instantly until later. When the guards escorted Vick to a private cell near the warden's office, he cried, knowing Greasy had lost his life trying to protect him. He felt pain from the guilt of not being honest with his friend, who thought he was being punished, when in fact, he was playing poker with the warden.

Vick later found out that Skinny was the one that abused Greasy by cutting his testicles off and the beating Skinny got was payback.

"The sonavobitch got what he deserved for treating another human being like that." Skinny died of severe brain damage, and the story got out that they threw his body to the gators.

The warden put a halt on the games until he could find a replacement, someone he could trust. Skinny had worked with the warden for years, while the other guards were not particularly close to the warden.

Vick's main concern was how losing Skinny was going to affect his job working on the plantation. It took awhile for the warden to find a replacement and during that time, there were no outside poker games. Vick spent evenings in his cell playing solitaire, or, if he was lucky, the warden would call him to his office for a game of poker.

Months passed, and Vick was becoming more comfortable working at the plantation. Hop Babcock was known to be the owner of one of the largest farming plantations in New Orleans. He trusted Vick and noticed the difference in Vick's quality of work than the other convicts who had worked on the lease program through the years. After a year, Hop had taught Vick everything about shipping and raising cotton. Life was as good as it was going to get for a convict, and Vick worked hard to win favors among the guards and also Hop Babcock who never knew Vick was in prison for killing 8 people.

Chapter 20

ELIZABETH SUSPECTED IT WAS BECAUSE OF CAIN THAT MATTIE REFUSED to give up. She saw her friend week after week cling desperately to life, when death would have been much sweeter, not to mention easier. Each day Elizabeth felt Mattie's pain so acutely, that it was like she was dying herself. She loved her like a sister and would have done anything to have her well and whole.

The reality of what was happening had gradually sunk in, and Elizabeth questioned whether she would be ready to take on the entire responsibility of running both the lumber company and the manor, now that she had a growing son to take care of. Even worse, she was afraid of being forced to turn the company over to a man she did not trust: Spencer.

Having helped deliver Cain and raise him from birth, Elizabeth felt confident in shifting roles from caretaker to mother. Of course, he would miss his mother, but no more or less than he would miss Elizabeth.

The one thing that Mattie repeatedly asked was to instill in Cain the knowledge that his Pa was a decent man. She wanted him to know and be reassured that none of the accusations against Vick were true. He would undoubtedly hear this over and over. She made Elizabeth repeatedly promise to do this.

They were sure that Vick was not even capable of murdering one person, let alone seven, proving that he had told the truth, and had been framed by Buck Dupree. Mattie knew that people would talk no matter what, but she wanted to make absolutely certain that Elizabeth remembered to teach Cain the truth about his father.

Cain was growing like a weed, when one unexpected morning Mattie slipped into a coma and never woke up. Dr. Lewis and Elizabeth were with her when she took her last breath. It was difficult to see her dear, sweet Mattie slip away.

The strangest thing happened. Mattie opened her eyes one last time to lock on Elizabeth, as if to say "I will miss you." She then died peacefully with a faint smile on her lips.

"If there was a Heaven, her face made it clear that she had gone there." Elizabeth imagined.

The doctor, checked her pulse, bent down, and listened for any sign of breath. He even looked for moisture on a mirror, still hoping for the best, but Mattie was gone. Elizabeth could hardly believe her friend was dead, when so many times she had come back from death's door. She turned to the doctor, buried herself in his open arms, and cried.

Dr. Lewis, normally avoided getting attached to his patients, but all three of them had been through so much together and they were more like daughters than anything else. He'd grown to care deeply about both, and Elizabeth's obvious devastation, multiplied his feeling of loss. Mattie was at peace now, but Doc was worried about Elizabeth.

Everyone that knew Mattie loved and respected her, and when they heard she had died, the town could not do enough for Elizabeth and Cain.

When the graveside services were held for Mattie, it was a bitter cold day after one of the worst ice storms Elizabeth could remember. Only a few people showed up for the service, but her dear friend, Dr. Lewis, and Spencer were there, along with Sheriff Cargill and his young daughter, Lucy, who had just lost her mother. Elizabeth thought how fortunate she and Cain were to have the ones she depended on most come to comfort her.

Spencer was happy that Mattie had finally died and that he was rid of her so he could make his move on Elizabeth. Many times, Spencer had imagined stealing inside the manor and snuffing the life out of Mattie before she died.

Elizabeth did not remember being as shaken when she lost her father or Aunt Connie, but it physically took something out of her when Mattie died. At the service, Elizabeth looked over and saw Spencer holding Cain tightly against him as they shivered in the cold. "He's a decent fellow … I should give him a chance," she thought.

By the time they arrived back at the manor, it had warmed a bit and friends had tables of food set up so everyone could rest in comfort. They were all there for Cain and Elizabeth, who had finally earned the respect of the town she had imagined, were against her for what her father had done. It was obvious they cared for her and Cain.

By mid-afternoon, the wind died down and the sun came out, just in time for the crowd to disperse in relative comfort. When they left, Spencer asked if he could stay and visit with Elizabeth. He was surprised when she agreed; Elizabeth hoped she hadn't made a mistake. As they sat in the parlor by the fire, he comforted her, and for once she thought she might have misjudged the man who Mattie was so sure had ulterior motives.

"Elizabeth, I'll always be here for you," Spencer said. She looked at him sweetly, but she knew she could never feel any affection for him, no matter how many years he might pursue her. The only man she had feelings for was Vick but she felt guilt because of Mattie.

Taking care of Cain was a blessing for Elizabeth. After just a few months, it was amazing how quickly and completely she was able to fall into the dual role of being a mother, while running the lumber company. She had to rely on Spencer more than she intended, because taking care of Cain took up the majority of her time. For a while, everything seemed to work smoothly.

Elizabeth marveled seeing her son grow into a young man. Time had passed so rapidly but Elizabeth's life remained the same as she focused all her attention on raising and educating Cain. She was very proud of her son finishing school two years early in order to enter law school. She imagined his choice of vocation was to help clear his Pa's name when the time came. Neither Elizabeth or Cain knew that Vick was alive and incarcerated in the New Orleans Prison for near twenty years. The years rolled by and Cain had become an accredited lawyer. He was about to begin his law practice in Jonesboro, or at least that's what Elizabeth thought.

During the time Cain was in school, Elizabeth had continued to hold Spencer at arm's length. She began seeing changes in him that concerned her, but imagined his eccentricity was because of his age. Spencer had many failed relationships during this time and each time they failed Elizabeth could feel his pressure. He would always hope she would change toward him and he might move right in.

Through out those early years she had become quite the businesswoman, running the lumber company with precision, knowing her industry inside and out and becoming recognized as a leader in her community.

Even so, she had turned most of the duties of running the business over to Spencer, resigning herself to civic duties. She worked only a half-day in the office now, mainly to keep an eye on Spencer to make sure he followed her instructions.

It seemed like only yesterday that Cain was a young boy, but now he was over six feet tall, a grown man who had earned his law degree. He was extremely handsome, and possessed the best of Mattie and Vick's features. When he walked in a room every young woman would turn their attention toward him. Elizabeth was ecstatic when Cain had made the decision to come home and begin his career. Her only wish was that her son would meet and marry a local girl so she could enjoy a family she had never had.

But, after his schooling, all Cain could think about was finding Buck Dupree and making him pay for lying about his Pa. He was determined to find out what had happened to Vick and had no qualms about his need to find the man who destroyed his father's life.

Indeed, Elizabeth had followed Mattie's dying request and taught Cain well, about his Pa, maybe a little too well, sometime embellishing Vick's accomplishments. Little did she know that she had created a young man who was determined to bring the very dangerous Buck Dupree to justice?

Spencer, on the other hand, had become more and more of a pest to Elizabeth, who had to fight him off each time she went to work. After years of disappointing relationships, Spencer's old desires always brought him back to Elizabeth.

He kept pushing to take her out in spite of her insistence that she would not mix business with her personal life. Spencer was becoming too close for comfort, but Elizabeth hated to fire him. She still felt an allegiance and an obligation to Dr. Lewis, who was a dear friend and now very elderly. Spencer kept intruding on her space, still trying to break through her barriers, hoping she would finally give up. This frustrated her, but she needed him to stay on and run the company.

Cain had been home a week when, after finishing supper, he asked to see the treasure that had been hidden away for years.

They looked through the treasure when Cain noticed the red book with stains on it.

"Mom, doesn't it make you feel strange to see Pa's blood on this book?"

"It always has. I don't know why he kept the book when he couldn't read. Perhaps it's because it was part of the treasure and contained his blood.

It was a warm night, and after they put the treasure away, Cain went to bed, leaving Elizabeth alone in the study. When she walked toward the window to close the curtains, she was startled when she thought she saw a figure. It occurred in just a couple of seconds, which she questioned was real or was nothing more than her imagination. The next day, when she went to the office, she told Spencer of what happened.

"It's that big house you're living in. You need someone taking care of you ... It's probably nothing. I wouldn't worry."

"Someone was watching me. I could feel it"

"I've told you that you should get married and have a man to take care of you."

"I have Cain; that's all I need." Elizabeth replied.

"He's not always gonna be around. One day, your boy's going to have his own life to live, and where will you be then?"

"Spencer, I've lived in the manor all my life, and after all these years, I have a 'peeping Tom.' It doesn't make sense."

"It may be a sign," Spencer said.

Elizabeth stared at him incredulously as he continued.

"You know, it may be time for you to think about marriage."

Spencer began to inch closer to Elizabeth, and before she could stop him, he had her in his arms kissing her. She struggled and pushed him away.

"Spencer! You have no right to force yourself on me like that!"

"Elizabeth, I can't help my feelings for you. Why won't you give us a chance? You know I care for you!"

"Just stop it, now! You were hired to do a job ... and I'm not part of it!

You work for me and the only reason you're still here is because of your uncle. So please, don't let this happen again."

"I see, so this is the way it is ... I thought you had feelings for me."

"You thought wrong!"

She turned and ran out of the office, leaving Spencer with his mouth open. He peered at her from the window as she climbed into her buggy and rode away.

After she was out of sight and hearing distance, he shouted, "You'll pay for this, you spoiled bitch!"

Chapter 21

A MAN CAN DIE A SLOW DEATH IN PRISON. AFTER ALL THESE YEARS, Vick had lost hope of anyone finding him, dead or alive. The last vestiges of hope had come and gone long ago and now, he had become nothing more than the warden's puppet in order to stay alive.

As for Mattie and his few friends, all he had were memories that were now becoming blurry. He would think of the nights he slept with Mattie in his arms and dream that she was next to him, but these were fleeting ruminations that were beginning to pass as quickly as they came. He would think of his boyhood and his brother Sam, but even those memories were fading. Thus, the days were long and the nights were lonely, as he felt his life slipping away from him, with the uncertainty of ever being released from prison. Now, he imagined what she would look like, near forty, even more beautiful. Finally, he often wondered if she had waited for him. "Surely, she would have married someone else by now," Vick thought.

If only he had been able to write, he might have gotten a letter past the warden and into the hands of someone who could help him. He had even considered getting a fellow prisoner to write it, but none seemed any more literate than he was.

Vick often thought, "I'm still here, trapped behind these walls, waiting for my big break should it ever come." He knew he was lucky to be alive after all the guards that had come and gone. The only thing that kept him alive was playing poker and thinking of Mattie.

Vick remembered when Frank Buckalew came to work for the warden after Skinny and Greasy died. It had been nearly twenty years ago but after Greasy killed Skinny, the poker games stopped a while, along with the cash that Vick managed to win for the warden. "We gotta git these poker games going again; time's a wasting," the warden would say. Vick would spend his lone time thinking up new strategies he would use the next time he played. Poker had become his life during the nineteen years he had been in prison. It was really the only thing that kept him sane in the loneliness of a dark cell, where a man, pondering over his existence, would think of many things to pass the time. Vick remembered even the lyrical murmur of the gamblers as they counted out the crisp dollar bills, preparing their money for the pot. Other times he would hear the sounds of gold pieces or pesos falling onto the table. He had given up after being imprisoned what seem to be a thousand lifetimes.

Vick loved the cotton business and had been taken under the wing of Hop Babcock, to learn the business. Many times, he wanted to confide in Hop but that was strictly against the rules for prisoners to get close to plantation owners. Vick had become the exception as far as learning the business until the warden learned that Vick had crossed the line and had become more of a friend than a prisoner to Hop.

"You're not only a good man but a good friend," Hop would say to Vick but he would never let on that he was incarcerated for something he did not do. He remembered Greasy's warning to trust NO one.

Frank Buckalew was relentless after he saw what he thought was Vick cozying up to Hop. Finally after all the years of imprisonment, he was back on the chain gang.

"You pull your weight, or they bring your body in with the surviving prisoners at the end of the day," the warden would say to make a point with the prisoners.

Frank mistreated prisoner after prisoner, but somehow managed to ignore Vick, who remained as innocuous as possible to everyone.

He was soon convinced that Frank was following the warden's orders, but did not know why, when suddenly he was pushed in with the other convicts to work on the railroad rather than the plantation were life was easier.

As the weeks passed, the days were longer than ever. The hot sun bore down on their backs, as they wielded their picks at a pace set by Frank. There was no slacking, just steady, hard labor. The uninitiated began to shed their shirts so they could work without being restrained, which only made matters worse. No one was permitted to drink water or relieve himself until Frank said it was time. This torture was made even worse because the men had no idea when or if he would finally call "timeout."

One occasion Frank took special notice of Vick. "Pride ain't good when you're a prisoner. The bastard needs a warning," Buckalew decided.

He noticed Vick was pacing himself in throwing his ax. "Hey you, pick up your pace. You ain't working fast enough."

Vick gave him a nod of agreement, and began slinging his pick ax at a higher rate of speed, which no prisoner could keep up with. The perspiration was pouring off his face as he toiled. The other prisoners watched as they worked, knowing he would not last long at that rate. Vick was severely dehydrated from lack of water, but could not slow down. The others thought Vick was trying to kill himself, but the fact was, he was just angry, and with each blow of the pick, he imagined he was hitting Buck Dupree. Finally, even Frank grew concerned since the Warden had plans for Vick. He stopped at Frank's command.

"Everybody hold up and break for water," the guard announced.

The men ran to the wagon like a bunch of thirsty corpses, skinny as hell from hard work and lack of food. Vick intentionally waited until the last man drank, since Frank was watching.

After Vick drank and walked away, the guard stopped him and said, "Ain't you forgetting something? You ain't said thank you."

Vick hesitated briefly and then said, "Thank you." Frank laughed, showing his shiny gold tooth. He felt powerful but Vick had a plan and it was working.

That evening he was near collapse when he fell onto the hard cot that seemed as comfortable as a feather bed. He still had his pride and self-respect, however, he was smart enough to know if he wanted to live he must continue to conform.

Before Vick had much time to rest, Buckalew came to his cell and escorted him to the room outside the warden's office to freshen up and dress for a game of poker.

"Tonight?" Vick could hardly put one foot before the other.

"That's what I said. The warden wants you pronto, so hurry!"

Vick was beyond exhaustion, but knew he had to please the warden. As soon as he walked into the office it was evident that Vick was overworked. "Frank, you put Vick back on the plantation, ya hear?" Vick thought, "gotcha."

Buckalew nodded to the warden, then gave Vick a dirty look.

Even though Vick was tired, playing poker was his only enjoyment.

He lived for the games, and the minute he stepped out of prison he smelled the various aromas of the New Orleans air. The smell of chicory gave Vick a sense of normality. It was there, drinking whiskey and winning money for the warden, where he felt most alive. The minute Vick stepped inside the parlor he felt like a man again, alive and confidant.

"Vick it's going to be an important evening for ya. Big plantation owner from Texas gonna be here, by the name of Johnson Petty. They say he's one of the wealthiest men around. I hope you're on your game, because if you're not, you will be back working on the railroad!"

Buckalew grinned when the warden threatened Vick.

"No pressure, huh, Warden?" chided Vick. When Buckalew started walking toward Vick after he heard his remark the warden lifted his hand for his guard to stop.

"Just do what it takes to win. That's all I'm asking ya." Vick nodded and sat down at the table.

At 8 o'clock sharp, the gamblers began coming in, and it didn't take more than a glance to know who the successful plantation owner was. Vick looked at the handsomely dressed Mr. Petty and gave a nod.

Vick had always been advised to never use his correct name, so when Johnson Petty introduced himself and looked at Vick for a response, Vick used his regular alias Buck Dupree in case someone might know Buck and recognize the same similar techniques in Vick and Buck's game. Perhaps Buck himself, would hear of a man in prison using his name, Vick hoped. It was a weak plan but it's all he had.

"Shall we get the game on the road?" asked the warden.

It was apparent to Johnson that the warden was speaking for Vick, the man he thought to be Buck, and wondered what their connection was. Each time Johnson would ask a question, the warden would answer, which was distracting to a man like him. "Sir, why don't you allow the man to speak for himself?" Johnson finally asked.

"We came to play and not answer forty questions, so let's git on with it," said the warden. Johnson kept looking at Vick like he knew something was a little off. The idea that this Buck character might be from the prison, entered Johnson's mind, but then he thought better of it.

As the pressure mounted, Vick knew he was not only playing with a professional, but also playing for his life. This excited him, as he wondered just how good a poker player this Mr. Johnson Petty really was.

They continued to play straight poker with Vick winning some and losing some. The warden began looking at Vick like he better pull a magic rabbit out of his hat, because things were not looking so good. The warden had only been privy to what Vick wanted him to know and this was part of Vick's game.

"I got some fine whiskey here. How about another round?" asked the warden, after seeing Vick had lost yet another hand. "Maybe this is Vick's payback since I had him working on the railroad," the warden thought.

"Perhaps the men are tired of poker and would like to try another game," Vick said as he continued to act out his charade.

"Ain't doin' much good this way. Sure, bring it on," said one of the men.

Johnson had already won most of the money, and Vick could tell he was concerned with risking his winnings, but the evening was still young and a true gambler wasn't about to turn away from a table when the night was still young,

"I see you all have a Faro table; anyone for a game of Faro?" Johnson asked. The warden was showing distress, but said, "Sure, I'll have a couple of men be the Banker and the Dealer.

Several gamblers dropped out of the game when they saw the warden push the large Faro table in the middle of the room. As usual Vick began by testing his opponent: "If you men would rather play something else we could play Twisting the Tiger's Tail, or Bucking the Tiger."

Johnson looked at Vick for a moment as if he were going to be the man who would finally recognize that the three games were one in the same. He then said, "No, we'll stick with Faro."

"Well, Faro it is," said Vick smiling that "gotcha" smile.

The gamblers began placing their bets on the board, while Vick intentionally bet wildly, all the while narrowing his odds by card counting. The warden was getting nervous, seeing Vick make such dumb bets. This was good for Vick, in case anyone thought he was in cahoots with the warden. It was apparent the warden was nervous and Johnson sensed it.

Everyone else paced their bets, winning and losing, but Johnson Petty was sitting pretty with the majority of the money. He noticed the careless bets Vick was making, and decided that the man was a fool, precisely what Vick wanted. Vick's ploy all along was to set Johnson up for the kill, making a bet on Johnson's winnings.

When the Dealer was left holding the last three cards, Vick interjected, "Well men, how about making this a little more interesting?" This was the most words Johnson had heard from Vick all evening.

The warden looked at Vick as if to say, "Oh, holy hell, what are you gonna' do now?"

Johnson, who had a stoic look on his face asked, "What do you have in mind?"

The warden once again darted his eyes in the direction of Vick, hoping he would take a hint, not to bet any further.

"It's a wild bet, winner take all. My winnings combined with your winnings, plus another thousand from each of us for the pot." Vick counted out his money and pushed it in the middle of the table along with his winnings.

"Any of you other losers are welcome to do the same."

"You're making it hard for me to refuse," Johnson said. "You're mighty sure of yourself, but I for one think you're stupid, making a bet like that.

The other players began to stir. "Ain't nobody here got that kind of money, so it's all yours."

The warden was thinking, "I'm gonna' kill me a prisoner as soon as this game is over." He was sure that Vick was trying to get even with him and Buckalew, "and he's about to throw his winnings and another thousand to the pot."

Finally, it was down to Johnson and Vick. The rich Texas gambler took a long puff on his cigar, blowing smoke into the air reminiscent of Thomas Barkin who had fallen for the same trick.

"I haven't figured you out yet, but I'm going along with the bet. Now, what?" Johnson taunted.

"Every dog needs a last chance, and since there's three cards left, I'm betting I can guess all three cards the Dealer has left. Johnson laughed as he said,

"Ha! Have at it."

The smooth businessman turned to the crowd and took another puff, while waiting for Vick to make a fool of himself. The crowd hushed and everything became still.

"All right men, we got us a bet. Buck here, says he is going to guess all three of the remaining cards. Okay Buck, let's have it?"

Vick looked Johnson in the eye and for a moment he didn't mind cheating the man who looked at him all evening with his smug arrogance.

"Jack of Clubs," Five of Hearts and the King of Spades.

The only sound now was the heavy breathing of the men. Some sat with their mouths agape, while others twiddled their cigars, as they waited. And the warden was about to have a heart attack. He had never seen Vick make this kind of bet and Vick had waited for almost twenty years to blow the warden's mind.

"Why gosh dern," said the Dealer, as he dealt the Five of Hearts, King of Spades and Jack of Clubs. "We got us a winner. Buck Dupree just won the pot.

Johnson put his cigar down and then stood looking at the man he thought was Buck Dupree. For a moment the warden saw fire in the eyes of the Texas gentleman who was trying to control himself.

"Okay, what's going on here?" Johnson said as he looked at the warden.

"You think I'm not wise to what just happened? Your man, Buck Dupree is a thief!" Johnson pointed to Vick.

"Look, Mr. Petty, this was a guess, and since you had the most to lose, you think I'm cheating," Vick said, in an attempt to defend himself.

The man kicked the chair and walked toward the door. He stopped, and looked back at the warden. "Are you in on this?"

The warden was as shocked as the crowd and ignored Johnson. The gamblers who were witnessing the game began calling the Texas gent. a sore loser.

He continued to yell at the warden, while walking out. "You're not answering because you know I have you pegged. Johnson's eyes fell on Frank Buckalew, when he was leaving. Vick imagined Frank was enough to scare Johnson off.

The guard looked at the warden for an okay to take care of him, but not knowing Johnson's connections, the warden backed Buckalew down.

At last, Vick had made his mark and the warden was spellbound. He did not know if it was the luck of the draw, or if Vick actually had cheated Johnson. This was by far their biggest win, and this amount money was worth the risk. As the warden sat counting his win, he tossed Buckalew a few dollars. For Vick, his reward was returning to work for Hop Babcock's plantation.

Before Vick was taken to his cell, the warden said, "Vick, I don't know who you are, and really don't care, but you sure made us a hellava lot of money tonight. He laughed and patted Vick on the back. Suddenly, Vick was not so tired, as his adrenalin was flowing.

"Vick, have a seat, this calls for a drink!"

The two sat and basked in their win, while finishing off the bottle of whiskey. Hatred and loathing filled Buckalew's thoughts when he wasn't invited to join them.

Chapter 22

ALTHOUGH TIME HAD PASSED AND VICK HAD BECOME INVALUABLE TO the warden, he still felt every moment of each day, while he was imprisoned. The poker parlor had gained in popularity, and gamblers were coming from all parts of the country to New Orleans by way of the riverboats.

Frank's connections would lure men of every description to the poker parlor for a game with Vick. The warden, who once applied pressure on him, now realized the parlor needed credibility in order to keep people coming back. So occasionally the warden would arrange for Vick to lose. He tried to be careful of the parlor's reputation for the place had developed quite a name for itself, namely because of Vick.

After years of winning and losing, Vick overheard the warden and Buckalew talk about throwing gamblers to the gators after they had been stripped of their winnings. There was a bayou that weaved around back of the prison and Vick had imagined there were more than just gamblers who were tossed to the gators. He assumed the bodies of the prisoners who died from heat exhaustion or simply gave up from overwork, were tossed to some hungry gators as well.

Anyone planning to escape thought twice wading through the bayous and swamps of Louisiana. Not only would they have dogs and guards to deal with but the hungry gators as well.

After hearing the rumors of gators, it circulated about gamblers who went missing, and Vick figured Buckalew and the warden had fulfilled their plan. Thus, there came a new kind of pressure on Vick, knowing the men that won would most probably be murdered as they left the parlor. Vick wrestled with the thought of the men being eaten alive by the hungry reptiles.

His only refuge was thinking about Mattie and the years he had been away from her … He wondered how she was getting along, and whether she had gotten remarried. He never imagined Mattie being dead. The harsh reality of his incarceration was he might never be freed unless someone visited the parlor that knew of him. Certainly, the warden, who was getting rich, was not about to let him go especially since he had become accustomed to the handsome income Vick provided him.

∽

At home, Elizabeth, had finally faced the reality that Vick was never coming back. For almost twenty years she held tight to a dream that she now knew would never materialize. During the early days, her devotion to Cain eclipsed the need to find someone to love, but that was no longer the case. Her son was a man now, and it would be up to her to find a suitor for herself.

During the time Cain was away at school, Elizabeth had tentatively begun to explore other possible options that interested her. Cotton had become big business in the south, which sharpened her ambition to generate a business other than lumber. She had read many success stories about profitable cotton plantations and wanted to learn more. She had also traveled to Memphis to do shopping, which kept the dream of owning a cotton plantation alive. There were many cotton fields from Jonesboro to Memphis and on into Mississippi.

Elizabeth had proven that she was a businesswoman in her own right, so venturing into Cotton seemed wise at this time in her life. As she further investigated the cotton business, she became fascinated with a man by the name of Johnson Petty, who owned plantations in Memphis, Tennessee, San Augustine, Texas and fields throughout Mississippi. After reading of his success and the fact that Johnson was an eligible bachelor, she began planning a way to meet such a man. She did her research and found his wife had died in their Memphis home.

Through the years she had thousands of wasted acres in the lower part of her state, stretching from Ft. Smith, Arkansas, to Tennessee. She thought growing cotton might offer the best solution for putting those wasted acres to use. Still, she knew nothing about cotton except what she read in newspaper articles and other agriculture publications.

The Alluvial Plain of Arkansas, one of the most agriculturally productive regions in the world, is referred to as all flat land in the lower part of the state, which covered many of those wasted acres. Although it was rich farmland, Elizabeth had never cultivated, or even taken the time to find what would best grow there. After extensive inquiry, she decided on cotton, since it was a cash crop, and the flat land in Arkansas and Tennessee seemed to be considered best suited for its cultivation. This inquiry interested her but the price of cotton had flat-lined throughout the industry and it would take some time to reap the benefits. Nonetheless, being very wealthy and smart to boot, Elizabeth had the means and the time to bankroll the business until the market reestablished itself.

~

Cain had been home for a while, when Elizabeth wanted to do something to introduce her son back into the community, after all he was an eligible bachelor and Jonesboro had grown into quite the town. By now, she was known for her parties and one favorite was the Gardenia Ball which was coming up. She thought this party would be excellent in her effort to fuss over Cain. In planning, she took it a step further by inviting Johnson Petty as the keynote speaker concerning cotton. This would provide the ideal opportunity for her to get to know this exciting man, plus educate her audience on the topic of cotton and the industry. She imagined her guest would never know the real reason for having Mr. Petty as their guest speaker.

When she introduced her idea to the committee, most of them complimented her on her selection.

Although Cain never knew his father, they shared many of the same characteristic and disliked being singled out. He could have cared less about a big "to-do" over his graduation from a prestigious school. But, when told of his mother's intentions, he became sucked in just like everyone else in town.

He didn't know all of what she was up to. In fact, no one seemed to suspect her ulterior motive was to meet Johnson Petty and find a suitor. Elizabeth was a determined woman, but she had a sensitive side and people who knew her loved her for the desire to help people who needed work. She convinced herself that being successful in the cotton business would afford her a way to help folks who were still trying to find plantations to reside and work on.

Elizabeth learned that Johnson Petty was owner of the Magnolia Plantation outside of Memphis, and also the owner of another farm called Pecan Plantation in San Augustine, Texas.

In the final days before the Ball, Cain had the idea that since his mother was financially fit she should purchase an automobile. She thought about it, then realized it would be a perfect way to impress Johnson Petty. She had never thought of having a Model T, but the fact that such a man would be at her event made it a good investment for her secretive desire. It would show him how progressive she was, both in business and her personal life.

Indeed, after a few lessons behind the wheel of her new Model T, Elizabeth was driving everywhere. The new car made her the talk of the town, as she ran from shop to shop making last minute arrangements.

Her new confidence had a negative effect on Spencer. His bitterness from all the years of his repeatedly rejected advances now turned to a bitter hatred. Busy planning the Ball, she left a picture of Johnson Petty along with a related newspaper clipping in her office. Spencer saw it during his regular rummage through her personal papers, and became obsessed with jealousy.

He wanted to punish her to get even. The more he thought about it, the worse it got. He imagined taking her to bed and watching her squirm as he forced himself on her. He had to have her, and, when she finally gave in to his advances, he would choke the life out of her.

At the same time, Elizabeth was having her own thoughts about a relationship. Johnson was her new fantasy. "Finally, I have another man I can dream about. For years my thoughts have been wrapped up in a dead man, and now it's time to put to rest the ghost that has continued to haunt me."

She was happy to think she might finally be free of Vick, but her tall handsome son, Cain, was his spitting image, looking almost exactly as she remembered Vick when they were young.

She was impressed with Cain's drive and focus when it came to something he was passionate about and she imagined Vick to be the same. Cain was unstoppable when he thought he was right and there was no consideration for compromise. As his adoptive mother, she had always done everything to make him strong for fear that, without a father's influence he might turn into a "Mama's boy." She wanted him to be a man's man and was glad to see he had grown up with the spirit and intelligence that had made him capable of being on his own.

Elizabeth was a typical mother, encouraging her son to be a gentleman. When he came out of the dressing room, looking tall and handsome in a brand new tuxedo, she was taken back to the time his father threw her off his property. She remembered that day, even though he was angry, Vick charmed her in a way that no man ever had.

"Oh my, Cain. The women are going to have to take a number to dance with you. You are indeed your father's son!"

"Did you ever take a number to dance with Pa?" Cain asked.

"No, I didn't. You know the story. Mattie was the one your father loved. She loved him and he loved her. But, I did notice what a looker he was, and you ... why, you look just like him. I wish both your father and mother could be here to see you now."

Cain smiled, and said, "My mother is here," as he pointed to her. He kissed a tear from her cheek before walking back into the dressing room to change.

No matter how Elizabeth tried to deny her feelings for Vick, they were still there, which would give Johnson Petty little chance for her affection.

That night, with all the memories of Vick, she thought it was time for them to revisit the treasure that had been hidden away. She imagined this would be a good way to honor the promise she had made to Mattie and remind Cain what a good man his Pa really was. When he was younger, Cain did not seem interested, but now, as a man, Elizabeth thought he might want to sell some of the priceless pieces of jewelry and use the money to set up his law office and maybe even make a donation somewhere.

Late that night, as the two sat examining the treasure, Cain once again picked up the little red book.

"Mother, don't you think it's ridiculous keeping this blood stained book with these valuables."

"You remember what I told you about how the mountain man tried to kill your father? Those bloody pages helped save him."

"Ma, I don't know if I ever told you this, but this treasure reminds me of how much I hate Buck Dupree."

"Cain, you must not fill your heart with hate. Buck was the man your Pa hated and for good reason. I don't want you eaten up with negative feelings. Your father is probably dead by now, and I know he would not want you ravaged by a hatred you can do nothing about. I didn't bring the treasure out for you to get all stirred up about Buck Dupree."

"Well, I've been meaning to tell you before I established my law business that I'm going after Buck myself."

"You're planning on what?"

"You heard me." Elizabeth had never seen Cain so upset about trying to find his father's enemy.

"Cain, please don't do that! Your father and Buck are probably both dead by now."

"We don't know if Pa's dead. Why, he could be out there needing us and here we are living in this big house. What have you done to try and help?"

"I've raised you to be the man you are today, and I've done a mighty good job! You've made something of yourself. You should have seen how your grandfather lived!"

"The grandpa that swindled the town out of their land so he could get rich?" Elizabeth had never heard such defiance and felt like slapping Cain, whom she had never raised a hand to. "Don't you ever talk to me that way, do you hear?"

"Ma, you can't hide the truth. I know all about what happened with your Pa."

"If you want to talk about grandfathers let's talk about your grandfather Porter. Do you know he used to tie your Pa and his brother to a 20-foot rope, leaving them alone so he could go to town and drink all day? He was an alcoholic and treated his kids like animals. Don't ever talk to me about things you know nothing about. At least my father loved me and provided for me, even if he did do things I'm not proud of."

Cain started to walk away from his mother, but he stopped short of leaving to have the last word. "You can kiss my attending the Ball and my tuxedo goodbye, because tomorrow I'm leaving to look for my father. This is not something I just dreamed up yesterday; I have been thinking about doing this for a long time."

"Then go! What can I say ... you are your father's son. I won't stand in your way. Just one thing, let me know how you're doing now and then!" Elizabeth began to cry, knowing she could not change her son's mind.

Cain walked out of the room, leaving her to return the treasure to its special hiding place.

Cain had just gone upstairs when Elizabeth went to the window to close the curtains. As she gazed out, she saw a shadow that quickly vanished, but there was no doubt this time. He had seen Elizabeth and Cain arguing, and even spotted the secret closet where they kept the treasure. She ran to Cain's room and told him she had seen someone spying on them.

"What did they look like?" asked Cain.

"I don't know, it was dark but I clearly saw the shadow!"

"Mom, you were upset. Maybe you imagined someone spying on us."

"Why try to convince a man?" She thought.

That night Elizabeth tossed and turned, as a dark figure stood in her bedroom watching her sleep.

"What a beauty!" The man was about to bend down and kiss her but she turned suddenly and ruined the moment. All the years of rejection had taken its toll on Spencer who was standing over her ringing his hands. He wanted her but he also knew Cain might hear, and then there would be an altercation. Seeing Spencer act out some of his fantasies would leave no doubt in a mind that he was delusional.

Elizabeth had drifted off into a deep sleep as she dreamt of the first time she met Vick. He was smiling at her and beckoning her to come to him. Just as she reached out to touch him, she woke up. She thought she felt someone close by.

"Vick? Vick, where are you?" Elizabeth cried out. She had no idea moments earlier that Spencer was standing over her obsessed with her beauty and his desire. When she opened her eyes and looked up, Cain was there. "Mother, wake up, you're calling out for Vick. You screamed Vick, Vick!

"Cain you misheard I was calling for you. Someone was in my bedroom. I felt them standing over me, watching while I slept, but I couldn't wake up."

He sat down on the bed and held his mother while she shook with fear.

"I know you don't believe me, but I know someone has been watching me. I'm sure of it."

"Mother, listen to me. You have been here alone since I have been away, and I imagine you have been frightened, but I really don't believe anyone has been spying on you. Why don't you try and go back to sleep. We'll talk about this in the morning."

"What's the use? She thought. Now, she would not be able to sleep the rest of the night. As she lay thinking of who might be spying on her, she thought about Vick. "What if Cain's right and Vick was still alive?" she thought.

The next morning Cain was in the kitchen, noisily packing food to take with him on the trail. Elizabeth startled him as she walked in.

"I know you're wondering what I'm doing, but I really am going to go find Pa. If I can't find him, then I'm going after Buck Dupree."

"Where are you heading first?"

"Did Mattie ever tell you anything about where Pa was heading when he left?

"All I remember her saying was something about him going to Texas. Maybe even to Louisiana where there's lots of gambling."

"Then that's where I'm going."

"Son, do you know how far it is to Texas. You're going to be in the saddle a long time unless you take a stagecoach."

"But, I'll need a horse for tracking."

Elizabeth sighed and shook her head. "What do you know about tracking? Buy a horse when you get there."

"It's time I learned about tracking, so don't make fun."

"Seriously, I am not making fun. You have money, so take a stage-coach." "Okay, I'll take a stagecoach! Satisfied? You think you'll be all right?"

"Cain, I know you've wanted to do this for a long time, but ..."

"Don't worry about me, I'm not going to try and stop you. Why don't you take a piece of the treasure that your father might recognize if you find him? Better yet ... take the little red book! That way, you won't be leaving yourself open to be robbed, and he'll probably remember the book."

"Good idea! I'll take the book."

Cain went to retrieve it from the treasure, but everything including the book was gone.

"Mother, did you move the treasure?"

"No, we put it away last night, and it should be in the closet where it always is."

"Well, the whole thing is gone!

Evidently, what happened to you last night was real, and someone came in and stole it all! They would have to, because how else could it disappear when we know we put it back?

They were both in disbelief, racking their brains. A cold wave seemed to go through their bodies. Neither of them could imagine who could possibly break into the house and steal the treasure.

"It had to be the person I saw at the window. He was probably watching us the entire time and saw where we hid it."

"How in the hell are we going to find out who did this?"

Elizabeth and Cain were in shock, and realized there was no way either could prove they ever had a treasure.

"Mother, think hard. Do you have any idea who could have done this?"

"I have one good guess, but I can't go accusing someone without proof," Elizabeth said.

"Then find proof, because I can't leave until the treasure is found." She grabbed her wrap and purse, then flew out the door.

"You stay here, I have an idea who might have done this."

Cain followed her to the door and saw her get into her Model T. She drove hard and was exasperated by the time she got to Dr. Lewis' office. She barely stopped the motor before jumping out of the car.

"Well, well, what a pleasant surprise. You look upset, what's going on?"

"Have you got a minute?" she asked.

"For you? ... as long as you like. What's wrong, honey?"

"I don't know how to say this, but it's about Spencer. I know he's been spying on me. I can't prove it, but I know he's the one doing the spying. I have seen someone hiding outside my window a number of times and I know it's him."

"Spencer? He's been working for you for many years. Why do you think he's spying on you?"

"Something just happened, and I think Spencer is involved."

"Tell me, what you are accusing him of?" asked the doctor.

"I believe he stole something very personal of Cain's that belonged to his Pa."

"What would Spencer want with something that belonged to Vick?" "It's a treasure that's worth a fortune ..." she hesitated. "We've kept it hidden for years because of its value and we're not sure what to do with it, because it was Vick's. Last night, when Cain and I finished with the treasure, I saw the shadowy figure again – someone spying on me. He must have seen the treasure and were it was hidden." "And you think its Spencer? Tell you what Elizabeth, you go on back to your house and let me get to the bottom of this. If Spencer has Cain's property, I will personally see it returned. I hope there's some mistake."

"I hate this for your sake, but I do not think I'm mistaken."

Elizabeth walked from the door with the doctor as he left. He climbed into the wagon and gave the horses one swift pop. Dr. Lewis was not wasting time, as the buggy disappeared out of sight, heading in the direction of Spencer's small house.

When he arrived, he hurriedly walked in the direction of Spencer's door but he first went to the front side window that was sheltered by a hedge, and hid for a moment, so he could see into the bedroom window. Sure enough, there on Spencer's bed was a piece of jewelry, sticking out from a blanket that appeared to be shielding something.

"That has to be what she's talking about!" he thought, and promptly walked back around to the porch, beating his cane on the front door.

"Answer the door Spencer! I know you're in there."

He went back and parted the bushes again. This time he saw the unsuspecting Spencer examining the gold pieces, obviously assuming that his uncle would decide that he was not there and would simply go away.

"Well, well, Spencer, it looks like Elizabeth is right about you," his uncle thought. He walked to the door again and rapped louder with his cane. "Come on, you open this door Spencer, and make it quick!"

Startled at hearing his uncle shout at him, Spencer carefully hid the knapsacks away, leaving one piece of jewelry exposed. He walked sheepishly to the door and opened it to find his defiant uncle pushing him aside to come into the tiny living room.

"You haven't changed much, have you Spencer?" His uncle pushed past him. "I thought Elizabeth was wrong when she said you had been spying on her. How could you steal from her, son?"

His uncle was so angry he failed to see the evil in Spencer's eyes.

"I don't know what you're talking about. I haven't stolen anything from Elizabeth!" Spencer shouted.

"You're lying! Dr. Lewis pushed Spencer aside and headed toward the bedroom where he had seen his nephew looking at the treasure.

"Hold on! You can't just force yourself in here like this!" Spencer shouted. As he was trying to stop his uncle from pushing past him, the doctor lost his footing and fell on the floor.

He was stunned as he looked up at Spencer, "You were always a bad seed. Here I thought you had changed, but now I can see you haven't!"

The doctor was trying to get back on his feet when Spencer walked over to a small chest and pulled out a pistol.

"So you think I'm a bad seed, do you?"

"You are just like my brother, conniving and wicked as they come," Dr. Lewis said.

"Then you might like joining him in hell."

His nephew turned and pointed the gun at his uncle, this is when Dr. Lewis noticed how bloodshot Spencer's eyes were.

"Spencer, don't be a fool; my God, for once in your life do the right thing!" he pleaded. "Spencer, I think you might be sick. Let me help you?"

"I am doing the right thing," Spencer said, as he aimed and fired the gun, hitting his uncle in the face at point blank range, spraying blood and bits of bone and flesh everywhere. Standing over him, he stared in disbelief at what he'd just done, seeing the blood run out the side of his uncle's mouth. Finally catching up with the reality of the situation, he bent down just as his uncle drew his last breath.

Spencer finally realized that other people had to be on to him as well, and was thinking about how to hide the doctor's body, when there was another knock on the door. He walked to the window and looked out at Elizabeth's Model T sitting beside his uncle's buckboard.

"Well, well ... not a moment too soon. Two birds with one stone!" Spencer thought.

She knocked louder, and then shouted, "Spencer, I know you're in there, so open the door. Dr. Lewis? Come on, one of you two, open up!"

She hesitated as she heard the sound of something being dragged across the floor. Still getting no response, she moved to the same front side window that Dr. Lewis had peered through not long before, and saw the piece of jewelry hanging out from the spread on Spencer's bed.

Returning to the front door, she again shouted, "I know it was you who stole our property and I want it back! Open the door."

Spencer barely opened the door, peering out through the small space and saw Elizabeth standing alone waiting to come in.

"What have you done? I see it all over your face!" said Elizabeth.

Before she could say anything more, Spencer opened the door, grabbed her, and pulled her into the living room. As he spun her off her feet, he struck her, knocking her unconscious. Panicking, and running in circles trying to find a rope to tie Elizabeth, Spencer was so undone with what happened, he spat obscenities as he picked up her limp body and started to tie her in a straight-back chair.

"You little bitch ... always the prim proper lady who never gave me a chance. Think you're too good for me, eh? Well you've had your chance. Now, it's my turn." Still unconscious, she heard none of it. Momentarily, Elizabeth began to regain consciousness and started struggling, as Spencer continued his efforts to tie her up, her hands already tied behind her in the chair. She lashed out with her foot, inflicting a painful blow to Spencer's right shin. He swore and called her a "bitch."

"Where is Dr. Lewis? What have you done to him?" she cried.

"You'll find out soon enough."

After Spencer gagged Elizabeth, and tied her feet, she could neither get away nor kick him. She stared at him in utter disbelief, as he dragged his uncle out of the closet. Elizabeth's eyes focused in horror on the poor doctor. Unable to utter a word, her eyes filled with tears as she saw her friend who had been such a good friend; like a second father for twenty years, now lying dead on the floor.

Spencer hurriedly gathered his belongings and tied the knapsack back, scooting them out near the front door. Then he brought what looked like some kind of fire agent Elizabeth had never seen before.

She struggled violently to free herself, seeing that he intended to burn the house down with her and the doctor in it. She looked at him with terror in her eyes, as he poured what now looked like some kind of tar, all over Dr. Lewis' body and then around her chair.

"Now you know what I really think of you! Too bad you'll never know what it's like to be with a real man."

Spencer lit a match and threw it on Doctor Lewis, causing his clothing to go up in flames.

Finally, Elizabeth was able to wiggle the gag from around her mouth, she shouted, "Spencer, don't do this! Your uncle loved you just like a son!"

Spencer rushed to the door, picked up the knapsack of treasure, and took one last glance, as the flames consumed the doctor. The stench was awful, as the raging fire now jumped from the doctor to the curtains. Elizabeth struggled to free herself before the kerosene vapor could attract the flame and burn her clothes. Spencer was still standing there, watching her struggle with the ropes. The chair fell over as she writhed her whole body, freeing her feet.

"You were always a hot mama, Elizabeth. You're getting what you deserve." Spencer slammed the door behind him, and ran from the burning house. Throwing the knapsack up and over his horse, he mounted up. "That should be everything," he said aloud.

Looking back toward town, he was surprised to see Orson Cargill, the town sheriff and his deputy, Charlie B, riding at high speed toward him. "Damn it! They must have seen the smoke," he thought, as he spurred the terrified stallion into motion, the horse now weighted down with the heavy knapsack of treasure.

The sheriff waved frantically at his deputy and yelled to get his attention. "You go after Spencer while I try to get to Elizabeth!" Sheriff Cargill jumped off his horse that hadn't yet come to a full stop, and ran to the door of the burning house. As he turned the knob, it flew open violently, he was knocked backwards, and a sheet of flame singed his hair and eyebrows. The stench, smoke, and intense heat were overpowering, as he ducked down to escape the inferno that had engulfed the interior, and was now racing to consume the air from the open door.

He could see nothing, and was about to give up and get away, but thought he heard a voice through the roar of the flames. Then something moved in the opening. He was sure now.

Fortunately, Elizabeth had pushed herself all the way across the floor in the overturned chair, to the closed door, but struggle as she might, she was unable to get to the handle. "I think I can get it open if I can stretch that far. If I can just get ..." she was thinking, as it miraculously flew open violently, knocking someone back away from it! She yelled the word "help" as loud as she could, and scooted herself halfway through the opening.

The fresh air felt like a cool spring on a hot day. Somewhat rejuvenated from the oxygen, she shouted again, as she pushed herself still further out onto the front porch.

"Help me please! Spencer?!!"

Sheriff Cargill, on his hands and knees, crawled back across the porch toward where someone was now clearly moving.

"A chair?" he thought, then shouted, "Lizzy, are you there?" Now struggling forward, he reached out and grabbed it ... "Yes, it is a chair!" he thought, as he held on and dragged it quickly back to the steps. With chair in tow, he dragged Elizabeth along by her hands, as both of them narrowly escaped the hungry flames roaring out across the porch. The doorway was now invisible in the flames. Struggling back to his feet and recognizing Elizabeth, the sheriff picked her up and staggered out into the yard toward where her car and the horses were waiting. She was limp in his arms, but showed no signs of having been burned anywhere on her body. Even her legs and feet looked okay.

Elizabeth looked up at the sheriff, as he untied her hands, freeing her from the chair at last. "Oh Orson! Thank God it's you! I was afraid ..." She didn't need to finish the sentence. Both of them realized that, within moments, Elizabeth's clothing could have ignited.

As it was, however, she was below the flames that shot out as Orson opened the door. Elizabeth, save for some sore and strained muscles from her struggle, along with abrasions from the ropes and dragging herself, was completely unscathed; physically, at least.

"Is Dr. Lewis in there? I see his buggy," the sheriff asked.

"Dead ... before the fire even started," came her raspy reply. "Shot!"

"Spencer?"

"Yes, I think so," she answered. "He was dead by the time I got there."

Meanwhile, the deputy had ridden at breakneck speed, trying desperately to catch Spencer, until their horses were nose and nose. Spencer kicked out at the deputy's horse, trying to keep from being jumped, but the heavy bag of treasure slowed his horse, he had no chance of getting away. The experienced deputy had no trouble jumping Spencer, sending him flying off of his horse in a rolling fall. Spencer hit the ground with so much force it knocked the breath out of him, but he recovered quickly and was already reaching for his gun by the time the deputy could rein in his horse and turn back. Spotting the gun, the lawman, smooth as silk, drew his gun and drilled Spencer near his heart. As he watched, the dying Spencer dropped his gun, fell forward, and rolled face up, with a crazed look in his eyes.

"At least I ... took ... that bitch ... with me," he said with four deep breaths.

"Sure hope you're wrong on that one, you sorry bastard," the deputy answered, but the only response was a blank stare. He was gone.

The deputy retrieved both horses, the saddlebags, and then struggled with the body finally draping it across his horse, then led them back to the burning house. By the time he got there, Elizabeth was just standing there with Sheriff Cargill, both watching Spencer's house burn to the ground. She started to cry as Orson went over to help his deputy place the two saddlebags of treasure in the Model T. Spencer had transferred most of the treasure to his two large saddlebags.

"Are you all right Elizabeth," the deputy asked her, with obvious concern.

"I'll be okay," she sobbed. "What about Spencer?"

The deputy nodded his head toward the horse, and she knew that he was dead. When the sheriff walked back over to her, Elizabeth broke down in his arms and began crying in earnest.

"Thank you for helping. You saved my life! I feel terrible about Dr. Lewis," she blurted out between sobs. "He was like a father to me and Mattie when she was living."

"At least we were able to catch that Spencer fellow before he could hurt anyone else. Almost got you though!" "Me too, as it turned out!"

"Best you git in that Model T and head home, 'cause I know Cain's gonna be wonderin' what happened to his mama," the deputy said. "Nothing more anyone can do out here."

"Orson, you've always been here for me. When Mattie died, you and Lucy came to the funeral, and now you've saved my life."

Elizabeth knew Sheriff Cargill was a good friend, but she had no idea that he had allowed Vick to escape over twenty years earlier. It had always been Orson's personal secret that no one else knew, and as far as he was concerned, it would remain so until Vick came home.

Chapter 23

Cain was shaken when he found out that his mother had narrowly escaped death, and even more upset to learn it was her long time employee, Spencer, who was spying on her and had stolen the treasure. He felt he would be indebted to Sheriff Cargill for the rest of his life. For, once again, Orson had displayed extraordinary courage by crawling into a blazing fire to rescue Elizabeth. Had it not been for his swift actions with total disregard for his own safety, she would have perished.

The sheriff was more than just a brave upholder of the law. Being an honest man, he now had another secret to keep. One for Elizabeth, who did not want the public to know about Spencer's stealing the treasure that resulted in his death, and the other was for Vick Porter, the man who the sheriff allowed to escape twenty years earlier rather than face a hanging.

The treasure was considered a private matter between Elizabeth and Cain, and it was no one else's business. Beside, allowing people to know about a treasure would possibly place Elizabeth and her son in harm's way. The less people knew, the safer Cain and Elizabeth would be.

No one could have imagined Spencer to be the kind who would murder anyone, much less the uncle who had done so much for him.

The town was all a buzz about how Elizabeth got caught in the crossfire of the incident between Spencer and Dr. Lewis. They figured she had walked in on Spencer in the heat of the moment after killing his uncle, and he had to cover it up by trying to kill Elizabeth too — of course, there was no mention of the theft.

That quickly became the most common story, and the sheriff allowed it to circulate, a perfect cover up.

Cain was especially grateful to the sheriff for saving his mother's life, but blamed himself for dismissing her when he didn't fully believe that someone was spying on her. He knew she needed him now more than ever, and he couldn't leave quite as soon as he planned.

By the evening of the ball, everyone seemed to have settled down. The guests arrived at the manor in formal attire for the night's celebration. Elizabeth looked absolutely stunning, as she walked slowly down the stairway, carrying her long train with one hand, and taking Cain's arm with the other. Everyone applauded her as she entered the ballroom, not just for hosting the event, but also out of respect for a woman who only a week before, had narrowly escaped death.

As each guest arrived, Elizabeth held her breath in anticipation that the next one might be Johnson Petty. After the announcements were made, the music began again, as they all walked into the beautifully spacious ballroom; with seats and tables placed uniformly around the room.

The wait staff carried glasses of champagne from the refreshment tables, serving the guests as they stood talking among themselves. Others carried delicious hors d'oeuvres, as the evening went on. But still, no Johnson Petty. Elizabeth's tension was relieved when suddenly, the music stopped so two late guests could be announced: a tall handsome man and his lovely daughter. Johnson was more refined than she expected.

"Mr. Johnson Petty and his daughter Eileen, from Memphis, Tennessee," the host announced. People clapped in recognition that the keynote speaker had finally arrived, while Elizabeth observed Cain's reaction to the beautiful Eileen. Cain looked especially handsome in his tuxedo, and there was no doubt that he noticed the young beauty standing in front of them, waiting to be introduced.

"This Ball was supposed to show off Cain, who seems rather taken with the young woman who has yet to pass my approval." This show of interest surprised Elizabeth, since she had never seen Cain so obviously impressed with a girl before. At first, Elizabeth was disturbed that Johnson had not mentioned that he was bringing his grown daughter to the event. But when she saw Cain's reaction to Eileen, she knew there would be no problem seeking Johnson's undivided attention. In fact, when she saw how her son's face lit up, she actually became very pleased with the situation. This could be exciting in more ways than one, she thought!

Elizabeth was more radiant than Cain had ever seen; and for a moment, he thought, it must be because of the tall impressive stranger, that had arrived late. He is certainly handsome, but he was not the man Cain envisioned for his mother. Elizabeth noticed within ten minutes of meeting Johnson that he could never be compared to Vick, however he could run a close second.

Early in the evening, Johnson asked Elizabeth for a dance, during which time he asked her to excuse any feeling of intrusion for bringing his daughter at the last minute. He added that Eileen was going through a tough time after losing a close friend. She understood, and assured him that there was no problem.

Elizabeth and Johnson made a beautiful couple, and conversation came easily, as they seemed to enjoy each other's company. After they danced, he asked her to join him on the terrace, so they could exchange information about the cotton business.

"I don't know when I've enjoyed myself so much," he said. What a beautiful place! Have you always lived here?

"All my life. It's been a wonderful home to raise Cain."

"I'm sure ... you're evidently a great contributor to your town, if not the entire state."

"Thank you, Mr. Petty.

"To you, I'm Johnson."

"Very well, and please call me Elizabeth."

"Elizabeth ... very fitting. I think we have a few Elizabeth's in our family tree," Johnson shared.

She was very impressed with his background, and was just beginning to open up when Cain walked in and disrupted the moment. He addressed his mother and then Mr. Petty, although they had not been introduced.

"Mother, I've been looking for you. And Sir, I've already seated your daughter for dinner."

"Just one minute, Cain before we go. You haven't been formally introduced to Mr. Petty." Cain walked over to the distinguished gentleman and shook his hand.

"Nice to meet you, Mr. Petty. I'm glad you could come. I understand you have lived in Texas ... I was on my way to Texas but decided to put it off another week," said Cain.

"Oh, then you'll be visiting in my state! What will be the occasion?"

Cain intentionally avoided the question, and Johnson wondered why.

"I didn't realize you lived in Texas; I thought you were from Memphis."

"I do live in Memphis, but I have another plantation in San Augustine, Texas. I'm actually from Texas and since the death of my wife we're there most of the time."

"The only plantation in Texas I've heard of is the Pecan Plantation. Would that happen to be yours?"

"Yep, that's the one. Most people think, since it's named Pecan Plantation that it's a pecan farm, but I can assure you its cotton. We just happen to have over 600 pecan trees, that we harvest each year. You and your mother should make a trip out to our annual Pecan Festival."

"Thank you for the invitation ... Mother, I think we should be seated. Shall we?" Cain led the way for their new guest and his mother as Johnson held out his arm to escort her.

The wealthy cotton farmer was obviously proud to have Elizabeth on his arm, as they strolled into the banquet hall to join Eileen.

Many people were being seated, but when the handsome couple entered the room, all heads turned toward them. There was no denying that Johnson thought Elizabeth was not only a beautiful and charming woman, but also quite powerful.

The night could not have gone better for the handsome Texan. He was engaging, charming and a great speaker. After dinner, everyone was congratulating him for coming and sharing his knowledge. He explained how cotton was now the most lucrative commodity in the country, and that even the smaller farms had their place in the industry.

He was very cordial to everyone, but managed to return his attention to Elizabeth in between guests. The man clearly had savoir-faire and was absolutely enchanting to all present. When the crowd began to dissipate, Elizabeth and Johnson walked back onto the terrace, where they happened on Eileen and Cain.

The gnawing question of why Cain was going to Texas was still in the back of Johnson's mind.

"Cain, you mentioned you were traveling to Texas next week. Are you going on business or leisure?"

"Nice of you to ask, Mr. Johnson, thank you. Actually, I have a twofold reason for going. One, to find my father, whom I hope is still alive, and the other is to hunt down the man who can clear my father's name."

Elizabeth looked sharply at Cain for being so outspoken with a man he hardly knew. She saw the sudden interest directed toward Cain and this bothered her.

"Did you say, clear your father's name? Was he in some kind of trouble?"

"I hadn't intended to bring this up tonight, but that is the reason I'll be leaving for Texas. I hope to find my father, or the man that framed him."

"Who in Texas framed your father? Perhaps I've heard of him."

"I doubt you've heard of a man named Buck Dupree? Or my father Vick Porter."

Elizabeth tried to give Cain a look of disapproval to deter him from bringing up his father, but he either ignored her or missed her signal. She was not sure which it was.

"You did say Buck Dupree?" Johnson asked, somewhat stunned at hearing that name.

"Yes sir, Buck Dupree. You seemed surprised when I said his name."

"I am surprised, because I did play poker against a man in New Orleans with that same name. Yes, I am sure it was Buck Dupree. There is a small poker parlor outside the Orleans Parish Prison, where they regularly play poker. That's where I met Buck Dupree. But I've never heard of Vick Porter."

"Did you notice if Buck had an accent?"

"The man barely spoke a word until he introduced himself. Some other man, who I think was the warden, seemed afraid to let him talk."

"And you're sure the name was Buck Dupree?"

"Quite sure, young man … because I questioned his integrity."

"Integrity? That's not surprising, knowing the background of this man."

"We played Faro, and I think he set me up. In fact, I know he did — He was very polished and I should have known he was a card counter when he said he could guess all three cards the Dealer was holding at the end of the game."

"It's him, Mom, I know it has to be him! There are too many similarities."

There's something very shady about that operation, and I should have listened to the rumors circulating about that place. I suspect your man, Dupree, is a prisoner who obliges the warden by setting up and cheating the gamblers. He got me for quite a sum. Ordinarily, I could have reported what happened to the authorities, but I can't have my name and my profession involved with such a racket. You understand, I'm sure."

Cain showed his excitement from hearing the new information about Buck Dupree.

"In fact, I am going back to New Orleans at the end of the week on business. If you would like to join me, you might want to do some query of your own."

Cain seemed excited about the possibility of joining Mr. Petty to New Orleans.

"Just one minute, Cain. I hope you're not thinking about traveling to Louisiana to see Buck Dupree." Elizabeth stated.

Cain turned to Johnson. "Mr. Petty, do you think you could get me a card game, so I can see if we have the same Buck Dupree?" Then, turning to Elizabeth, "Mother, I hope you won't give me trouble about this. I have a feeling we're onto something. One way or the other, I intend to see if he's the man I'm looking for."

"Cain, you can't be serious." said Elizabeth, almost pleading, then turned to Mr. Petty. "Johnson, we haven't heard from Cain's father for almost twenty years and I think he is quite possibly dead."

Johnson could see he had opened a can of worms and that he should not have mentioned Buck Dupree.

Cain interjected, "That's one reason I want to meet Buck Dupree … to see what he knows about my father, Vick Porter."

"Cain, you must make it okay with your mother … if she approves, you can accompany me to New Orleans, but if Elizabeth is not on board with this, then I have to withdraw my invitation," Johnson stated.

The way Cain looked at Elizabeth made it clear that there was no stopping him. They exchanged a knowing glance, Cain smiled, her face showed concern.

"Mother knows I have to do this … But Mr. Petty, do you think the warden will suspect something if you go back?"

"You might be right. We'll have plenty of time to discuss it. I didn't mention, but I must take my daughter home first. I'm speaking of the home in Texas, of course."

"Mr. Petty, do you mind if I call you 'Johnson'?"

"Please feel free."

"Well Johnson, I do need your help: I'm afraid I don't know a thing about poker.

Johnson was visibly amused with his innocence; Eileen beamed and looked radiant. Elizabeth recognized right away that Eileen was looking forward to Cain traveling to Texas with them.

"I don't know if we told you, but Cain is a lawyer," Elizabeth said.

"Well my boy, this is getting very interesting, indeed." Johnson smiled and patted Cain on the back. "Good for you, son. One of my best friends is a lawyer in San Augustine. We go way back and now he's the governor of the State of Texas."

"Cain, did you hear that? If you would stay home long enough to practice law, instead of traipsing around the country … "

"Don't say anymore, please, Mother," he smiled. "I still think Pa is out there alive somewhere. And I might be on the trail to find him. I have to do this or I could never live with myself."

The next morning, Elizabeth walked in on Cain looking through the treasure.

"What are you doing?" Elizabeth asked.

"I'm thinking about taking several pieces with me. What do you think?"

"Do whatever you want, but I'd be very careful if I were you."

Cain replaced the pieces in the knapsack and in so doing, the bloodstained book fell out. "Here Mom, I don't think we need this book." Elizabeth took the little red book and placed it on a table.

"I never knew why Pa kept it, in the first place. If it had been up to me, I would have gotten rid of it a long time ago," he said.

Although Elizabeth did not want her son to go with Johnson, she knew she could never win an argument with him. It was the lawyer in him she supposed. Cain would be safe, however, traveling with an upstanding man like Johnson Petty.

The next morning at daybreak, Cain had his bags packed ready to go. Her heart ached, seeing them leave, and wished she had been invited to go along with them.

As they were about to leave, Elizabeth presented Johnson and Eileen with a basket of food, left over from the banquet.

"Why, thank you Elizabeth," he said, brightening. "You're very gracious to think of this."

She felt a wave of excitement as he held her hand and kissed it. She looked deep into his eyes and felt he would have taken her in his arms had they been alone.

A teary-eyed Elizabeth waved "goodbye" and watched Johnson's brand new Model T pull out. Her concern for Cain was heavy on her mind and she knew the manor would be lonely without him.

Even though Buck Dupree was likely imprisoned in New Orleans, Elizabeth was deeply concerned for Cain's safety and did not want him to meet the notorious outlaw face to face.

Chapter 24

Elizabeth had been duly impressed with Johnson Petty, but she had mixed emotions. Her feelings about him had waned a bit. The wealthy cotton farmer was definitely sophisticated and handsome, but she had noticed something of a flaw about him.

He was taking her son on a potentially dangerous trip, which was unexpected, and her feelings had changed somewhat when he suggested Cain go with him, without first talking to her about the New Orleans trip.

Was it a "male thing?" no need to get permission from a mother because Cain was an adult, or did she expect too much from a man she hardly knew. She disliked the idea that Cain might be encouraged to play poker with a convicted felon placing him in danger. She wasn't sure she would want Cain to be influenced by a man like Johnson, no matter who he was or how wealthy.

"One minute I'm hot and one minute I'm cold, perhaps I'm too smothering," Elizabeth thought.

She wanted to give Johnson a break, for he was charming, wealthy and had great connections but she was a protective mother and wanted to shield Cain from making mistakes. After a long, loving hug and tearful kiss "goodbye," she had walked back into the house and busied herself with tidying up.

For unknown reasons, she turned her attention toward the little red book that had been among the treasure. It had never interested her before that moment. She didn't know if she was restless or bored, but she picked up the book and curiously began thumbing through the pages. She could see it was written in terrible scratch, using words she hardly understood. She quickly assumed the book belonged to one of the murdered children.

As she read and deciphered some of the words, it became clear that it was a young girl's personal diary. A couple of pages were torn ones that Vick said he had used to absorb the blood when the mountain man slashed his face. But the other pages, with careful study, were legible enough to read.

She remembered the story Mattie had shared with her about Vick fighting for his life during the altercation with the mountain man who had killed the family of four. Vick was the one who discovered their bodies when he arrived at Panther Holler. As she read more, it became clear that the diary had belonged to Janie, the oldest child, who, along with her brother, was viciously murdered.

As Elizabeth continued reading, tears welled up in her eyes as she imagined what Janie and her family must have gone through. Each and every word carried an impact, especially since the last part of the diary must have been written a few minutes before the murders.

The notes the young girl had scribbled were barely legible, but "it's important that I understand what Janie had to say," Elizabeth thought.

What follows is Janie's diary, as read by Elizabeth:

December 25, 1893 — *My name is Janie Ballard and I got my diary for Christmas today. My family don't have much and most of the time it's just me, my brother Mark and my mama who live by ourselves. My Pa is always gone and there ain't no one to take care of us so we do the best we can. Goodnight diary.*

January 2, 1893 — *Me and Mark can't go to school no more cause mama says it takes money to send a kid to school. That ain't fair, if you ask me 'cause everybody ought to be able to go to school.*

We ain't got no friends either but we can hear them kids yelling when they running in the woods. One day, I maybe gonna' have a friend, but now it's just me and Mark that play together. I know how to write and spell but I don't know nothing when it comes to counting numbers. Goodnight diary.

May 5, 1893 — *Every day we do the same thing. I ain't written in my diary for a long time cause there ain't nothing to write about. It's almost time for my birthday again. Mama says Pa is coming home to move us up in them Arkansas hills. She says things is going to be different but I heard that before, and nothing ever changes. I reckon I'll be ready to move though when Pa comes home cause I ain't old enough to strike out on my own. I'll try to remember to write in my diary again soon. Maybe when we git moved to Arkansas. Goodnight diary.*

June 3, 1893 — *I'm writing again today, 'cause mama says Pa might be home tomorrow. She's packing stuff in sacks so we can move when Pa comes. Goodnight, diary.*

June 16, 1893 — *I ain't written in my diary for a few weeks. I hate moving even though we ain't got much to move. We made it to Arkansas. Ain't nothing here. We ain't got no schools and we ain't got no people around us. The house has a sign saying Panther Holler, so I guess that's the name of this place we live in, Panther Holler. Mark says it's alright but it's 'cause he don't know no better. As for me, as soon as I'm sixteen I'm getting out of here. No sense living in a place that don't have no people. Goodnight diary.*

June 20, 1893 — *Today something is happening. Pa is acting up and mama acts like she is scared of Pa. They been ripping through the house looking for something and I don't know what. I asked them what they trying to find but they say it ain't none of my business.*

I did hear them say something about a man coming and he ain't going to like it if they don't find the loot. Pa says it's a big loot, whatever that is. Pa thanks somebody came in the house and got it, but I never seen nothing Pa's talkin' 'bout." Goodnight diary.

June 21, 1893 — *Pa is really mean to mama. He took her by the arm and made her fall on the kitchen floor. He thanks me and Mark hid the loot and he's a tearin' up everything. Me and Mark found a hiding place and that's where we play most of the time to keep from being hit. It's our secret place. Goodnight diary.*

June 24, 1893 — *Mama says Pa ain't going to be home much 'cause he don't want to see that man who is coming to see us. Pa acts like he's afraid. I hope that man ain't going to be mean to us. I told Mark we going to hide if we see him being mean. Goodnight diary.*

June 25, 1893 — *Pa's been away and is supposed to be coming home soon. I hope he comes 'cause Mr. Dupree came and mama's been having to cook fer him. He talks funny. Mama says he is from another whole country around the other side of the world! He says he's my Pa's partner and he's there to wait for Pa. He don't seem happy. Me and Mark stay out of the way 'cause he don't act like he likes us. I told Mark I don't trust him. I sure hope Pa gets home tonight. Goodnight diary.*

June 26, 1893 — *Bad things have been happening all day. Me and Mark have been in our secret hideout and I'm having a hard time trying to get Mark to stop crying. I don't think we are safe here. Mr. Dupree has been asking mama something about loot that's lost. We don't have no loot, but he thinks we are lying. I tried to keep him from hitting mama but he grabbed at me when I broke away and ran out the door. Mark is scared and I am too. I told Mark we got to be real quiet so Mr. Dupree won't see us. Goodnight diary.*

June 30, 1893 — *Pa rode up today and Buck Dupree grabbed him and is beating him bad. I cried when I saw Mr. Dupree cut my mama and there's blood everywhere. He is standing over Pa now with a knife. Mr. Dupree is acting like a madman and he's cutting my Pa. Mr. Dupree has blood all over his coat and he's coming after me and Mark. He's done killed mama and Pa. He's calling our name. We don't know what to do. I hope he ain't going to hurt us. Me and Mark are going to run if we can ...*

Elizabeth was crying, feeling the fright and horror the two children must have endured seeing their parents murdered and trying to run before they were murdered. She put the book down and began pacing the floor. "Cain has to know this diary clears Vick! He doesn't need to see Buck Dupree.

She ran to her room and began throwing clothes together, "I'll take a stagecoach to the train depot in Little Rock then on to San Augustine, Texas, hopefully in time to intercept Cain and Johnson before they leave for New Orleans," Elizabeth said, to herself.

At long last, Cain felt he was doing something to clear his Pa. He had already fulfilled one plan in order to help his Pa and that was to become a lawyer and use the law to his advantage. During their journey to San Augustine, Johnson and Cain spoke nonstop about Buck Dupree.

Eileen had been behind the wheel of the Model T, driving as the men talked. She resented her father taking all of Cain's time, teaching him how to play poker, when it should have been clear that she needed time to get better acquainted with Cain. "After all, they have plenty of time to visit when they drive to New Orleans," she thought.

Finally, Eileen had enough of men talking and stopped the car. "Pa, you are going to have to drive the rest of the way, I'm sleepy."

"I would think all our talking would keep you awake," Johnson responded.

"Well, it's having the opposite affect and I'm about to fall asleep."

Johnson knew perfectly well what was going on with Eileen, and agreed to take the wheel. The young couple wasted no time getting into an endless conversation, laughing, giggling, and flirting back and forth, enjoying themselves immensely. Watching the two of them interact so nicely, Johnson knew they would make a nice fit, but he had reservations about Cain's father and needed to find out more about this young man's background. Johnson, too, was protective, and wanted the very best for his daughter and any future grandchildren that might come along. "Cain's handsome all right, but my family cannot afford a scandal."

When Johnson finally turned off the main road and drove the tree-lined road to the Petty plantation, Cain was taken aback at its enormity. He, and those he knew, had always thought the manor he grew up in was a large estate. But it was nothing as huge as the Pecan Plantation and the vast cotton fields surrounding it.

After the two men unloaded the suitcases from the Model T, Eileen led the way into the house. The outside of the home was beautiful and stately, but when Cain stepped inside the front door, he was even more awed by the opulent interior. To his right was a huge dining room fit for a king, and wonderful oversized antiques filled every room. Cain thought, "I wonder who the Petty's entertain to have the need for such a huge and elaborate home. And they say they have one just like it in Memphis. Mama might be right about the cotton business."

Eileen continued showing the way, as Cain observed the paintings and silver that were displayed in the huge ornate cabinets that aligned the hallways.

"I'm overwhelmed. Your home is beautiful. Are you all here enough to enjoy it?"

"We go back and forth to Memphis. When you see the home in Memphis, it's pretty much the same, except we have more trees than you see here. Come along, I will show you to your room."

As Eileen led Cain upstairs, Johnson realized that he might have to break his daughter's heart, if and when he had to put an untimely end to her new friendship with Cain. They walked into a chamber that was much more than your usual bedroom. It had a warm ambiance which, when, combined with the beautiful young woman standing in front of the fireplace, nearly took his breath away.

"We have plenty of wood, if you would like a fire. We keep one going this time of the year."

Cain thought the room was amazing, with couches and chairs along the wall surrounding a beautiful feather bed. "If I had Eileen to myself, we would never leave this room," he thought. Cain felt himself blush slightly at the thought. She did not seem to notice.

"Eileen, you're spoiling me; I may not want to go home!"

She laughed, and patted Cain on the shoulder, thinking to herself "that might not be much of a problem at all." When her hand touched his shoulder, he knew Eileen was special. A shudder went up and down his spine. "This is definitely chemistry," he thought.

"Cain, why don't you take a little time to relax and make yourself at home? There are things I have to do before we have the staff start dinner. I don't know how hungry you are, but dinner is always served at seven. You can have a snack now, if you want."

Eileen looked very comfortable in her role as the perfect hostess, and Cain imagined that someday he might have a wife just like this lovely girl.

"Thanks Eileen, but I'll be fine until dinner. If you don't mind, I think I will take a quick nap. Would you mind knocking on the door, in case I over sleep?"

"I would be happy to, Cain," she said. Eileen loved this handsome man asking her to wake him, and as she closed his door, she felt a warm connection to him.

Cain took a moment to look over his room, then walked to the window and looked out over the vast cotton fields. He was in awe of the plantation and its operation, as he saw workers picking cotton and placing bushel baskets on top of flatbed trailers that were driven by mules to a cotton gin.

His eyes focused on Johnson as he walked to a worker he assumed to be the foreman. He could see his fiery temper demonstrated toward the man who cowered down to him. "I would sure hate to get on his bad side," Cain thought. "I'll have to make sure I don't rub him the wrong way."

He looked down along the long narrow road they had driven in on and realized what Eileen was talking about when she had described the "huge pecan trees, whose long limbs hovered over the road."

The entire place is like a beautiful painting, he thought.

Looking to the other side, Cain could see through the open loft doors into the barn where the hay was stored. For a moment, he allowed himself to think how comfortable he could get in this kind of setting.

It seemed to Cain that he had just nodded off, when he heard a soft knock on the door.

"Cain, it's time to wake up. Supper is almost ready."

"Thank you, Eileen, I'll freshen up and be right down."

After hearing Cain's deep mellow voice, Eileen stood with her ear to the door as a rush of excitement came over her. She took a moment to be sure he was moving around before she smiled and walked away.

The Pettys were very extravagant, and, when Cain walked into the dining room, it was set up like they were having a party. Everything was perfectly placed with the very best china and silver, not at all like he was used to. Cain and his mother had settled into a modest lifestyle without the frills, not nearly as impressive as the Petty's, and Cain wondered if Eileen would be happy stepping down a peg or two, should they become more than just acquaintances.

During dinner, the butler brought Johnson a letter that was apparently important, for he eagerly opened it and took time to read it. He would read and then pause, looking at Cain as if the letter had something to do with him. Surely, it was his imagination, he thought.

After dinner, Johnson asked Cain to join him in the library for a cigar and after-dinner drink. Once again, Eileen thought her father was being unreasonable by taking Cain away from her.

He asked Cain to follow him as he led the way into the library where he went to a large humidor filled with the finest cigars Cain had ever seen.

"Do you smoke, Cain?"

"Yes sir, on occasion." He liked Johnson treating him as one of his peers but the fact was Cain hardly knew how to light a cigar.

"I think you will enjoy this cigar; it's one of my favorites." Johnson handed Cain a cigar that he awkwardly took and smelled, as if he knew what he was doing. Johnson observed him carefully, thinking Cain to be naive and sheltered. He liked the fact that Elizabeth had done such a splendid job raising her son, but he wasn't sure Cain or Elizabeth would fit into his circle of friends, especially after reading the investigative report that he had just received about Cain's family.

"Cain, we've talked about our trip to Louisiana, but I don't know much about you or your mother."

"Not too much to report, having lived in a small Arkansas town. I've had a relatively quiet life," Cain said. "Ma is not my real mother. She adopted me. My real mother died when I was a child, but Elizabeth is all I know, and I couldn't ask for a better mother. She's done everything for me ... she has always been there."

"Can you tell me about your Pa and what kind of man he was?"

"Only what I've heard, as I never met him. I think he was a good man, though, with an unfortunate childhood. I don't usually speak of my Pa, but since you asked, I'll tell you what I know. Cain left nothing out, and told the entire sordid story of Elizabeth's father and how poor Vick was, having been raised by an alcoholic father.

Cain had no idea he was exposing his family in such a negative way that Johnson was completely turned off with the thought of possible relationships developing between him and Eileen.

"Sounds like there were some questionable dealings in your family on all sides, but you seem to have turned out well, especially with the worthy profession as a lawyer." Johnson was beginning to wonder what was coming next, now knowing that all may not be as he originally thought in the Porter family. "How about your real mother? What was she like? Was her family anything like your fathers?

"I really don't know much about my mother, but she must have been a good person, because Ma and my real mother were like sisters. They were both very good at running our family business."

"I imagine it was hard on Elizabeth when your mother passed leaving her to run that big lumber business your family is known for."

"I never think of that, we just do what we have to do to make it. Don't get the wrong idea about my Pa either.

"This concerns me about your father having to act in an unscrupulous way to survive. A man always has a choice, and you seem to sidestep that issue where your Pa is concerned. Am I reading you right, when I say this?"

He was a good man who was forced to revert to the survival mode after he was accused of murder.

Cain was beginning to feel like he was under interrogation and did not like the tone of Johnson's voice, as he spoke accusingly about his father.

"No Johnson. I don't mean to be indignant, Sir, but you are mistaken about this. Perhaps you do not understand. My Pa had been framed and had no real choice. He had to either run or be hanged for crimes he did not commit. I believe in a situation like that, any man would have done the same. Even you … Or me!"

"Didn't you tell me, or perhaps it was Elizabeth, that your Pa won that lumber company from your grandpa in a card game, who after losing, committed suicide out of shame?"

Cain ignored the question and started to turn and walk away. His only concern was finding Buck Dupree and he needed Johnson in order to do so.

"Look son, I think we need to get to bed early. We have a long drive ahead of us tomorrow. So, I will see you in the morning?"

As Johnson shook hands with him, Cain had the last word.

"You know Johnson, all families have their little secrets. I have noticed that when people brag about their family tree, they are very careful to prune it first!" With that, he walked out of the library and up the stairs to his bedroom, leaving Johnson standing there, unable to stop himself from admiring Cain's self-confidence and straight-forwardness. He thought to himself, " Regardless of where he came from, I think that kid's going to amount to something one day, but not with my daughter." And, after extinguishing the light, Johnson headed upstairs to bed.

The following morning, the men packed the Model T, but before they left, Eileen appeared to bid them farewell.

She extended her hand and asked, "Will I see you again?" and smiled from ear to ear.

Cain smiled but did not answer since he was still harboring disappointment from the night before when her father acted so obnoxious.

As she saw them drive away, Cain put his arm out the window and waved sending chills over her with the feeling he cared.

Johnson Petty could tell Eileen liked Cain, but after last night's discussion, he doubted he would give his daughter the approval to marry him.

By the time Elizabeth arrived in San Augustine, Cain and Johnson had already left. She was terribly disappointed. The thought that Cain was on his way to New Orleans to face Buck Dupree, a ruthless murderer who had even killed innocent children, made her heart sink. Unbeknownst to all involved, the little red book could have cleared Vick long ago. Right there in his own house was the diary of a little girl, containing the secret that would not only clear Vick, but point the finger at Buck Dupree.

Now, here Elizabeth was, holding Janie's diary, filled with the notes of a teenage girl describing that fatal day when Buck Dupree murdered her and her family. How ironic that the proof they needed was under their very noses all this time, and they had no idea.

Since Elizabeth could not talk to Cain, she told Eileen all about how she had uncovered the truth about who murdered the family and now proved Vick to be innocent.

"Why, Elizabeth, that's wonderful! This is incredible news. "Now that we have evidence that Buck Dupree killed those people, my father can contact the governor and exonerate Vick."

"Are you sure?"

"Yes, because it was my father's money that put him in office."

"Do we have to wait for Cain and your father to return, or can we contact the governor now?"

"Elizabeth, I'm sorry but my daddy would kill me if we did that. I hope you understand. The two women hugged and retired for the night.

Chapter 25

THE TRIP TO NEW ORLEANS WAS LONG AND GRUELING, PARTLY BECAUSE it took Cain and Johnson half the trip to finally warm up to each other. The indignation Johnson showed the night before, when he spoke critically of Elizabeth, left Cain frustrated and disappointed.

"Why would he be so critical of my mother," he wondered. "He convinced himself that his budding friendship with Eileen had to be the reason for Johnson's rudeness.

He knew her father was wrapped up in himself, so he began asking him questions about his past.

"Johnson, last night you questioned me about my background. Perhaps you would like to tell me how you got your start in cotton farming? You've obviously been very successful with it."

Johnson was not happy about the questioning, but decided to warm up since they were only a few miles from New Orleans.

"Well, since you asked and seem interested, the cotton business has been in my family's blood for years, and when the business grew, I reinvested in land throughout the south. That's all I do. What else?"

"What about Eileen's mother who died?"

"We met when I was twenty-four and married soon after. Look Cain, I think we need to make a plan before I walk into the poker parlor again. I want to make sure you know how dangerous it is that I'm sticking my neck out for you. Let's just hope they don't suspect I'm there for another reason."

"Are you having second thoughts?"

"No, but I've avoided telling you about the gators. I've heard some bad rumors about gamblers being robbed and thrown to gators. I didn't want to say anything in front of your mother."

"Gators?"

"Don't be alarmed. I don't know if the rumors are true but if they are, I have to know you're standing guard just in case."

"I see … but this is shedding a different light. Johnson it's up to you, but you can count on me no matter what."

"That's good, now the first thing I need to do when we arrive is make contact with the bartender. Hope he's there, cause if he isn't we might have a delay."

When Cain and Johnson arrived in New Orleans, it was a warm humid night with a light mist of rain. The Model T made its way downtown were the folks were dancing and playing music. Occasionally, Cain would look in the direction of the saloons, but he didn't want Johnson to think he was a wide-eyed kid who had never seen a half naked women. He was intrigued by the Barkers who were beckoning people to come in for their shows. Cain had never seen show girls parading the streets.

When they finally reached the hotel, Johnson began namedropping about friends he had in high places, mainly Winthrop Rockefeller, who built the hotel where they were staying, the Le Downtown du Vieux Carré. He could see that Cain enjoyed the finer things but Johnson had already decided that he or his friends would never accept Cain's family with questionable character.

Meanwhile, Cain was enjoying the hotel, with its plush chairs and elegant furniture. He was clearly thinking how easily he could enjoy the luxury, if he were as wealthy as Johnson.

He briefly allowed himself to think of Eileen and what future they might have should Johnson allow them to get to know each other. "Next time, I'll let her know how I feel," Cain thought.

After the men went to their separate rooms, it was difficult for Cain to sleep, knowing that within hours, he might be seeing the face of Buck Dupree for the first time — a man who had remained elusive to him and his Pa for over twenty years.

The warden had already received word that Johnson Petty was returning for his second go-round. He wondered if it was to win back his money or if it was for some other reason. One thing for sure, the warden didn't want trouble. He remembered Johnson's threats when he was there before.

"I don't like the man returning and if he pulls anything, we know what to do with him!" The warden reminded Buckalew.

Vick had continued to provide the warden with a very lucrative lifestyle and one the warden was not willing to give up at any cost. It was most unusual for a guest to return to the parlor after being cheated the way Johnson was.

"If the man didn't learn his lesson the first time, we'll clean his clock again," the warden thought. A man like Johnson Petty is lookin' for revenge since he got his ass beat."

Despite the rumors surrounding the parlor, it was still a draw to gamblers and that's what the warden was banking on. Many who passed through the doors of the parlor had bought a one-way passage to the gator swamp, yet the poor suckers kept on coming.

Vick was told it was going to be a big night, and the warden was making it extra special for a certain guest.

Buckalew was anticipating the evening, since the warden had refreshed him on who Johnson Petty was. "Did you tell Vick to get ready to play tonight?" asked the warden.

"Yeah, he's ready. I told him he needed to be on his game."

"Ain't you afraid of this Johnson Petty winning? He's a damn good poker player," said Buckalew.

"Vick knows what to do."

"What if Vick can't beat him?"

"Then we feed the gators… but just be careful."

Back at the hotel, Johnson spent the entire day trying to win Cain's trust, in case his actions from the night before were still gnawing at him. He didn't want any distractions or mix-ups where his safety was concerned, and it was also important that no one suspect that their real reason for being in town was to have a meeting with Buck Dupree.

"Cain, no one can know we have a connection. Do you understand? Remember, you are to be my eyes on the outside, in case someone jumps me when I come out. You sure you can handle that?"

"Don't worry; I got you covered."

"You know where to park the car and then find your way close enough to the building. If I run out, be prepared to jump whoever is after me. Don't mean to keep repeating myself, but you have to be on your toes, because this is dangerous. You have the gun?"

"Yeah, right here." Cain patted the gun he had in his jacket.

"Have you ever shot a gun before?" Cain didn't want to answer, since he had never learned to use a gun.

"Don't worry, I can pull the trigger if I have too."

"Well, for my sake and yours, let's hope so, and if you shoot don't shoot me." Cain smiled but Johnson didn't.

∼

Vick was waiting in his private cell, ready for the evening, when Buckalew came with a last minute message.

"Shave that beard off. The warden wants you to have a clean face tonight, and don't forget to use a different name; we don't want anyone remembering that Buck Dupree name the last time you played."

"Yeah, yeah, but why shave my beard?"

"Remember the rich cotton farmer from Texas that lost his money ? We don't want him recognizing you."

When Vick entered the room the warden looked at his shaved face and scar and decided there was no way Johnson could recognize Vick. "This is good." he said. "Johnson Petty will think you're a different gambler."

Vick was eager. This was a game he had been waiting for — a return guest who might be there for reasons other than playing cards. Vick was still young looking although he had been incarcerated for nearly twenty years. He knew the warden would be surprised to see how severe his scar was, since it had always been covered with his beard.

Right on schedule, Johnson and Cain drove the car to the parlor. Before Johnson was dropped off, they stopped short of the place, so Cain would know where to park and stay out of sight. He parked and then got close enough to get a good look whenever Buck entered the parlor. He found himself a perfect place to see anyone coming or going, without being noticed. Waiting patiently, he saw Johnson enter the door. Afterward, three other men wandered in, none of who came close to the description he thought Buck might look like. Shortly thereafter, another man approached the parlor that Cain thought was likely to be Buck Dupree. He entered through the same door with two other men, one he assumed was the guard and an older, chubby man who carried himself like a lawman —an odd trio. Cain's heart began to race as he saw the man's face.

"Something's wrong this man can't be Buck Dupree." Again, Cain would have no clue this man was actually his father. However, though the man was Vick, Cain did not see the scar since he could see only one side of the man's face. Later, he thought the man may not have been Buck at all, but someone else." Perhaps he missed Buck Dupree all together, or it may have been the wrong night." Vick, who Cain thought might be Buck was not at all like Cain had pictured, since he was fit and healthy looking. "This man can't be Buck Dupree.

Johnson was seated and warming up when Vick walked in. The tall, handsome man did not look like a prisoner at all, and for a few seconds Johnson thought he was looking into the eyes of someone else, someone familiar as he tried to place the man.

"Well gentlemen, what do we want to play tonight?" asked the warden.

"I think we need to at least introduce ourselves before we begin playing," said Johnson Petty.

"Let's get the pleasantries over with. We're here for a game," said the warden.

Names were exchanged around the table until it was Vick's turn.

He hesitated and then said, "My name's Vick Porter."

The warden could have been knocked over with a straw. His face turned white as a sheet when he heard Vick use his real name, which was a sure give away for anyone who wanted to prove the warden was using prisoners for his own personal gain. The warden gave Vick a hard look that seem to say, "just you wait." He was not alone in his surprise as it was shared with Johnson Petty, who did a double take when he heard Vick say his name. *"My God this is Cain's father,"* Johnson thought.

Johnson put on his best poker face to hide his dismay and realization that this man was not Buck Dupree. And now that he had the information, he was stunned as to what to do, other than finagling a reason to get the hell out of the parlor.

He remembered an old trick that usually worked for him when he canceled a game. Johnson reached into his coat pocket and felt around as if he was searching for his cash.

"Gentlemen, this is embarrassing, but it appears that I left my money back at the hotel. I trust you will allow me to come back at another time?"

The warden looked at Buckalew, unbeknownst to Johnson and shook his head "no." which meant not to throw Johnson to the gators. As much as he hated he would have to save the win for a better day when Johnson returned. *"Ain't no sense killing a man, when I got a chance to make a killing,"* the warden used to say. Johnson was smooth as he walked calmly out the door, heading straight for the Model T, wanting to get as far away from the parlor as possible. By the time Johnson opened the car door he was visibly shaken and Cain noticed.

"Let's get out of here!" said Johnson.

As he started the car, Cain asked, "How did it go? Did you see Buck Dupree?" He was directing questions at Johnson faster than he could devise a plan.

Johnson had to think, but he knew he could not tell Cain that Buck Dupree was, in fact, his father.

"I saw Buck Dupree go in. Did he say anything? I thought you would be playing for hours." Cain said excitedly.

"Son, I must have made a mistake — there was no Buck Dupree. Now, drive on!"

Cain drove away talking as he went. "What do you mean, you were so sure? Was the same man there as before?"

"Yes, but I misunderstood his name. Somehow, I thought he said Buck Dupree, but it was someone else. I'm sorry we've come all this way, and I've misled you. I had a feeling the warden was up to something, so I invented a reason to get out. I told them I left my money at the hotel by mistake. Thank God, they bought it."

"I guess it was nothing but a wild goose chase," Cain said, not hiding his extreme disappointment.

"Can't win 'em all son, we simply do the best we can," replied Johnson, trying to sound cheerful. In the dark, Cain couldn't see the worried look on Johnson's face.

"What next? We going back to the hotel?" Cain asked. "Right now, I can use a drink, just drive!" Cain could hardly believe the evening was ending without information that could help him.

He continued to talk about what happened after Johnson went into the parlor. "Buck Dupree must have already been in the parlor before we got there. There were some men I saw, but they didn't fit Dupree's description you gave me. I only saw two men, but nothing like I imagined. Johnson thought. "*Glad he didn't see the man's scar?*"

"I saw one who didn't look like a prisoner, but the man with him sure could pass for a guard. Creepy looking man."

"I'm glad you listened to me and kept out of sight," Johnson admonished. "Damn, I sure thought we were onto something,"

"Cain, I have to be honest with you. You're a good man, but don't waste your time and your life running after a dream to clear your father's name. No one remembers Vick Porter, and if they do, they remember what they want to remember about him. You said yourself that Jonesboro holds your Pa up like a hero, because of what he did for the landowners who had their property stolen by your grandfather. The other people don't matter because they didn't know your father. One piece of advice — start living your own life."

"Perhaps you're right, but I have never thought my Pa was dead. Don't ask me why, but something inside tells me he's out there and needs my help. That's why I became a lawyer, so I could help him"

"Son, nobody can help your Pa."

Cain had no idea that the man he trusted could be so devious and withhold information that could free his father from prison.

Johnson finally felt he had justice against the man who called himself Buck Dupree, for ripping him off only a few weeks before. "Let him rot in jail and pay," Johnson smiled inwardly. The man is no good to society after being locked away with criminals for all these years.

When they arrived back in San Augustine, they were quite surprised to find Elizabeth waiting for them. Cain couldn't quite grasp why his mother would be at the plantation, unless there was something wrong. Elizabeth walked hurriedly toward her son, hugging him as soon as he got out of the car.

"What's going on? Why are you here in San Augustine?" Cain asked.

"I had to come. I have some very good news for you. I tried to get here before you and Johnson left for New Orleans." She looked toward Johnson Petty, nodded a greeting, and then turned her attention to her son.

Johnson was listening, wondering why in the hell this woman was here without an invitation.

"Thank God you're back safe and sound. I was so worried about you going near that horrible prison."

"You came all the way to San Augustine because you were worried about that?" Cain asked.

Johnson was wondering the same thing.

"Cain, the book your Pa had with the treasure. You know ... the little red book with your Pa's blood on it? It happens to be a personal diary that belonged to a little girl by the name of Janie, who identifies that killed her family. She tells everything, all of the accounts that led up to the time she and her family were murdered. She named Buck Dupree as the one who killed her family. This proves your Pa is innocent. It's all in the little diary, every last detail! Now, we can clear your Pa with Johnson's help, if he's alive. If not, we can clear his name."

Cain was elated knowing that his Pa would finally be exonerated from murdering the family. Elizabeth glanced at Johnson who did not look happy.

"Your father and his little brother must have arrived at the cabin shortly after Buck killed them," Elizabeth said. She turned to Johnson, as if to receive support.

"Johnson, Eileen told me that you could get the governor to clear Cain's Pa. Is this true?'

Cain turned to Johnson, "Is that true? Can you have the governor clear my Pa?" Johnson was so angered for being put on the spot that he looked at Eileen with piercing displeasure.

"Cain, I ... I don't know. All we have is a book that tells a story and I'm not sure that's enough to have your Pa's name cleared of murder. Not just one murder, but seven. Let me think of the best way to approach this. Give me some time and, after you and your mother are back home, I'll contact you again."

He observed Johnson backtracking and didn't quite know what to think. It was certainly a side portrayed by Johnson that was confusing to Cain who was a lawyer.

"Mother, I think Johnson is tired from a very long and discouraging trip. Why don't we talk again in the morning?"

"I think Cain is right," said Johnson.

Johnson was sickened that Elizabeth was as involved as Cain about clearing Vick Porter's name. At that moment he felt like he'd had enough of the Porter family. "I want both of them out of here," he thought, and now was not soon enough.

Elizabeth walked with Cain into the house, while Johnson pretended to go to his room and rest. She was perplexed with the indifferent and cold man Johnson had become, certainly not the reception she expected from a man who was bent on helping her son.

Poor Eileen noticed her Pa's rudeness and was concerned as she followed Cain and Elizabeth into the library. "Cain, if you and Elizabeth will excuse me, I think your mother would like some alone time. Anyway, I have chores to do. Will you excuse me?"

"Sure. We'll have time to catch up."

Eileen smiled and shut the door behind her.

Cain was excited about the news his mother brought him. "What about this diary?" Cain asked.

Elizabeth butted in. "First, tell me everything, I have been dying to know what happened."

"Nothing happened, it turned out to be a wild goose chase. I will say one thing about Johnson, he made sure I was safe." Cain tried to praise Johnson for something, still wondering what was on Johnson's mind.

"Well, at least he took care of you," Elizabeth said. "What about Buck? Did you see him?"

"I saw men but I couldn't tell if any of them were Buck. Johnson said he got the man's name mixed up. It was a total waste of time."

"Cain, don't you think that's strange? Remember when he said, he was sure the name of the man was Buck Dupree? There is something going on we don't understand. Perhaps he's trying to throw you off!"

"Throw me off, about what? Why don't you stay out of this. We went there with all the good intentions and when Johnson saw the man it wasn't Buck. Now, leave well enough alone.

Well, did you see a man go in the prison?"

"Yes, but the man I saw didn't look like a prisoner."

"What do you mean, didn't look like a prisoner?"

"I just saw his profile. I kept trying to see his face but he never looked in my direction. "Did you notice Johnson's reaction when he heard I had read the diary that could clear your Pa? He didn't act like he was interested at all. Something else is going on with him. I feel it!"

"Look, I'm tired and Johnson's tired. Our trip was long and disappointing, so don't go stirring something up."

"You think what you want, but something is going on with him. I can't believe you didn't sense he was hiding something. Perhaps Eileen can shed some light about her Pa. I know she's waiting to see you."

All the time Cain was talking to his mother, Johnson was looking for Eileen until he found her on the veranda. "Who you waiting for? Thinking about Cain?" Johnson said sarcastically.

"No, I've been waiting for you. I could tell you were not happy about the new evidence Elizabeth found to clear Cain's Pa. Why would you act like that?"

"I see … now, Elizabeth has you all hyped up with this so called 'new evidence,' that I dare say would not prove anything. Eileen, why did you tell Elizabeth I could get the governor to clear Vick Porter's name before you spoke with me? You should never speak for me. Now, I have problems, because you opened your mouth about something you know nothing about."

Eileen was almost in tears. "I thought you would want to do whatever you could to help Cain. Am I mistaken?"

"Am I mistaken at how involved you are in Cain's and his mother's affairs?"

"Why would you say such a thing? I thought you liked Elizabeth and Cain?" Eileen showed her displeasure at her Pa's attitude toward their guests and the new evidence.

"Haven't you figured this out? This family has way too much baggage. Young lady, I have spent a lifetime raising you to choose someone with character and a good name. Vick Porter and Elizabeth are the kind of people I don't want to associate with. You act like you have feelings for this boy, but this family is no good. People won't care that Vick Porter is innocent. All they will care about is shaming you and your children if you marry into a family like this. I don't want that for you, no matter how much you feel you care about Cain. I've made up my mind, and I'm not going to ask the governor to exonerate Vick Porter, regardless of what new evidence they have."

Eileen stood and faced her Pa. "I can't believe what I'm hearing. If Cain knew you felt this way, he would never want anything to do with this family."

"You must listen to me. Cain doesn't realize what kind of man he would be letting out of prison."

"What are you saying? Do you know where Cain's Pa is? You said he was in prison. You know something, don't you? What is it?"

"I didn't mean for that to slip out, but since it did, you need to know. I saw the man who is passing himself off as Buck Dupree, only this time he said his name was Vick Porter. He's in the New Orleans Prison and I'm going to leave him there. When he introduced himself as Vick Porter, a couple men who I think is connected with the prison were dumbfounded."

Eileen could not believe what her father was saying. All she could do was shake her head "no."

"Daughter, this has to make an impression on you. Cain's Pa has been living with hardened criminals for almost twenty years. He can't be a good man, living all those years with the likes of what's behind those prison walls. I don't want any association with a man like Vick Porter, and if he gets out, no telling how this could hurt his son. And I forbid you to tell Cain any of this. If you want to remain friends with him, he must never know, and that goes for Elizabeth, too."

"How can you keep something like this from Cain, who would give anything to find his father?"

"To protect him … and to protect you … and whatever comes of this relationship. You have to promise me you will never tell Cain what I have told you. Do you understand?"

Eileen broke away from her Pa and ran into the house, right into Cain's arms as he was coming down the stairs.

"Eileen, is there something wrong?"

"Oh, I don't know, you know women … we can cry over the tiniest thing," she replied.

Cain touched Eileen's face and wiped away a tear. "I know one thing. It makes beautiful eyes awfully red when they cry. Why don't you tell me what's got you so upset?"

"Cain, you're very sweet, but I think you need to be in bed. You and father are tired, and I don't want you up worrying about me."

"Not before I do this." Cain took Eileen in his arms and kissed her sweetly. After she felt his lips on hers, she knew she had to keep her father's secret, for fear of losing him. She pulled Cain into a small sitting area, a room, which she knew would afford them the privacy she needed for what was about to happen. She was very vulnerable now that she was carrying her father's secret.

Cain, hardly knew what hit him. He was as disappointed as Eileen and when she began to initiate her advances he followed her lead.

"Eileen, are you sure? I don't want to take advantage of you when you're upset. I know something is wrong."

"No Cain, it's just that I am so happy to be here with you."

Cain kissed her again and again before he knew they were making love. Eileen was sweet and special like no other. He unpinned her hair and watched it fall around her shoulders. Soon the reality of what happened hit him, but it was too late. Cain, saw this lovely beauty half-dressed lying on the floor and there was no turning back. "OH, Eileen, I'm so sorry, I didn't mean for this to happen." He thought she would be embarrassed but she wasn't.

"Cain, please it was as much me as you. I knew you would be leaving. I don't know how you feel about me but I couldn't let you leave without showing you how I felt."

He knew they made a mistake, but what was done was done and the young lovers talked until dawn sharing their dreams and ambitions. It was the wee hours of the morning when they parted but by this time they had committed themselves to one another and were talking about marriage.

The next morning, Elizabeth and Johnson were waiting. Breakfast was served late, affording time for Elizabeth to visit with Johnson while Cain and Eileen were still sleeping.

His attitude was the same as the night before, cold and distant. She was dying to know what changed between the time he and Cain left Arkansas, until they returned to Texas from New Orleans. She became more disturbed seeing this side of a man who might have interested her.

She tried to break the ice. "I hope you don't mind me showing up without an invitation. I suppose we will be seeing each other from time to time, since our children appear to enjoy each other's company."

"Oh, is this what you perceive with our children. I only see courtesy where my daughter is concerned."

"I'm sure our children will work things out, but what about you and me? You seem very distant, since the last time I saw you. I'm very puzzled."

"I'm sure you are imagining something wrong when there is not. Perhaps what you see is how busy I am."

"Then do accept my apology. Johnson, it was not my intent to barge in on you, but in the light of this new information, Cain and I will be leaving in the morning."

"I see, then tomorrow it is."

Elizabeth thought, "this man will not give." She was sure he was hiding something.

"Oh Elizabeth, before you go … I am sure Eileen told you the governor is an old time friend of mine, but the matter of your new evidence will take time, however, between you and me, I'm not sure there is anything that can be done to clear Cain's father."

"I understand perfectly. Please excuse me."

She stood, then walked away, wishing she had never met him. She stopped briefly and looked back at him, wondering what was really going on with him.

The next morning, Elizabeth and Cain were packed and waiting on Johnson who was out riding his horse over the cotton fields. This only rubbed salt in Elizabeth's wound, since it was another way to insult her. Everything he did was a personal affront to her.

He came in just before time to head to the station for Elizabeth and Cain to catch the stagecoach home.

Eileen was sweet, bidding her farewell, but Johnson was less than cordial. She tried to ignore his cold indifference.

The first leg of the trip home, Elizabeth and Cain barely spoke to each other. He was reliving the night before, when he and Eileen made love, while Elizabeth brooded over all her expectations that had gone awry.

Finally she spoke. "Cain, I need to talk seriously about Eileen. I hope you are not getting involved with her. I see how you two look at each other, and if you think I'm going to sit back and see you make the mistake of your life, well, you're wrong. Johnson will not stand for you dating or developing a relationship with her. Also, if you did I would be miserable having this man anywhere close to me. There are plenty young women around that live a lot closer than Eileen."

Cain had no idea his mother was so resentful with her suspicions about Johnson, and now she had turned on Eileen, who he had very strong feelings for.

Elizabeth went on and on about how disappointed she was with Johnson. Finally, Cain had enough. "Mother, you're all worked up! Johnson was very nice to me on our trip, and it wasn't until we returned home, that I noticed a difference in him. Have you thought you may have feelings for him, and they are not returned?"

"Hogwash! Don't say another word. It wasn't me that caused him to act indifferent. It had something to do with Janie's diary.

"What you're saying doesn't make sense. Why would he care about a dead girl's diary?"

"I don't know, but I plan to find out."

"One thing that you and Johnson do agree on, is me wasting my life trying to exonerate my father. He may be right! And how many times have I heard you say the same."

"Johnson told you that?"

"Yes. What difference does it make to clear Pa's name if he's dead."

"Remember one thing Cain, I've read the diary, your Pa is innocent and if you've changed your mind about clearing him, then I will do it myself."

Elizabeth reached into her bag and pulled out the little red diary, giving it to Cain.

"After you read this, I want you to tell me if you feel the same. Whatever the outcome, I will respect how you feel, either way."

Cain took the diary from his mother and began thumbing through the blood- stained pages until his eyes rested on Buck Dupree's name. After seeing his name, he could not resist reading the awful details of the family's tragedy. He sat speechless as he imagined what it was like for a young girl witnessing the murder of her family and then being murdered by a butcher.

Elizabeth watched her son's face turn white, as blood drained from it. That's all it took for her to know that Cain would not stop until he cleared his father.

The more Elizabeth thought of Johnson, the more she was sure he was hiding something.

As the stage rolled back into town, Elizabeth could not have been happier. But foremost on her mind was Johnson's attitude toward the information she had that would clear Cain's father.

"If Johnson won't help me clear Vick's name, then I'll do it myself. Elizabeth knew she would have to be the one to start the ball rolling, and the first person she wanted to see was Orson, her old friend.

The sheriff was often considered a joker because of his big yarns, but if there was anyone Elizabeth could trust, it was him. He was a dedicated lawman and had her respect.

The next few days were filled with hours of catch-up around the lumber company, since she no longer had Spencer. Cain was involved with his own plans setting up his law office and it appeared she would be the one to clear Vick's name. She knew her son was touched by the little girl's diary, but it wasn't until she saw Cain with a gun around his waist that she knew he had plans of his own. This was all the more reason for her to visit with the sheriff. She knew Cain knew nothing about guns.

She drove to town and parked in front of Orson's office then walked in.

"Well, well, if it ain't Lizzie. I shore hope the water ain't a rising. Do you know how long it's been since you stepped inside this office?"

They hugged each other and the sheriff pulled up a chair for her to sit. "What brings you to town? You been feeling all right?"

"Orson, I want to thank you again for saving me from the fire. That was the most courageous thing anyone has ever done for me."

"Well thank ya, but that man Spencer was the devil himself. Glad I made it in time."

As the two friends talked, Elizabeth poured her heart out to him about what happened with Johnson, and how frightened she was for Cain, who was now wearing a gun.

"Seems strange, the way the man acted toward ya, Elizabeth."

"Orson, I couldn't get over how the man changed…and just like that!"

"I think yer' right about one thang. He's a hidin' somepin' from you and Cain."

"I don't understand what could he be hiding?"

"Can't tell ya that, but I been around a long time and dealt with some cagey fellers. He sounds jist' like a man that knows somepin' he ain't wantin' to share. Yep, he's a hidin' somepin'."

"It doesn't make sense to me." Elizabeth said.

"Wish I could help ya, Lizzie, but if I wuz a guessin' man, I'd say it's about Cain's Pa. Yep, I think he knows thangs' about Vick he don't want you and Cain knowing about. That's what I thank."

Elizabeth was appreciative to the sheriff for his counsel, and hugged him for taking the time with her.

The sheriff walked her out to her Model T. "Anytime Lizzie, anytime."

Before she drove away, the sheriff turned and held up his hand for her to stop. She waited until he walked over to talk with her.

"Lizzie, I thank it's bout' time I told ya something I ain't told nobody before. I always knew Vick was innocent, and that's why I let him go, all those years ago. Don't suppose ya knew that, but I didn't have the heart to bring him in when I knew the man didn't have a killin' bone in his body."

"You did that for Vick?"

"Now you know! I ain't never told nobody about that 'cause when I took the job as sheriff, I swore to uphold the law and at that time the law said to bring Vick in ... but I couldn't do it!" The sheriff was shaking his head. "Nope, I just couldn't bring myself to arrest 'em."

Elizabeth took the sheriff's hand and squeezed it.

"Thank you, Orson. Your secret is safe with me."

Elizabeth had no idea how much she endeared herself to the sheriff by confiding in him about Vick.

When she got back to the manor, Cain was rereading the diary. He reflected on all that had tragically transpired over a secret treasure, written by a little girl who was tragically murdered.

"If only my Pa could have read this, how simple things would have turned out for him. He would have had a normal life," he woefully muttered to himself.

Cain's hatred for Buck Dupree intensified each day he remained home. "Buck Dupree was out there somewhere, and if he ever knew that mother and I had the treasure, he would come looking for us. I have to find a way to protect us," he thought.

Elizabeth found Cain with the gun strapped on his hip packing to leave. "He has made up his mind," she thought. She wondered why he took to wearing that old gun that she doubt he could aim…much less shoot.

The next morning Cain took his gear outside before saddling his horse. Much to his surprise, Sheriff Cargill was waiting for him. Orson had his hat in his hand like he had the day he let Vick ride out of town.

"Howdy Cain! Ya goin' someplace?"

"Well, if it's not Sheriff Cargill. What are you doing out here?"

"Ya can call me Orson, ya ain't no boy no more."

Cain smiled to see the sheriff had paid them a visit before he was about to leave.

" I been rollin' somepin' over in my mind about yer' friend Johnson Petty, and I came to talk to ya.! But it looks like ya goin' someplace. Ya ain't plannin' on goin' by yerself, are ya?"

"Planning on it," said Cain.

"Ya ain't a plannin' on taking the law into ya own hands are ya? I see ya got a gun on yer' hip."

Cain looked at the Orson and smiled. The sheriff knew Elizabeth was concerned about her son.

"Orson, I can see you got something in mind," Cain said. "Ya rightly do son….Ya can't break the law if the law's with ya."

Cain smiled, thinking he could use the company. "So, you planning on tagging along to make sure I stay inside the law?"

"Yes indeedy son! I came out here to talk to ya about Johnson Petty, the man ya mama spoke to me about, but since ya leaving, I spec' we kin talk 'bout him on the way. I don't guess ya mind goin' by my place to git me a few changes? Where we goin' anyway?"

"Can you afford to be away from town that long?"

"I reckon I can, but I can't afford nothin' else, cause I'm a little short"

Cain smiled. *"The man is worried about money for the trip when he saved my mother's life a few weeks ago?"*

"Don't worry, I got money." He assured the sheriff.

"Well, then we covered, ain't we?"

Elizabeth was feeling better, knowing that Orson would look out for Cain.

"I'll git old Charlie B to take over 'fer me. Everybody's kinda tame these days. Anyway, where we off to?"

"First we're going to see the governor of Arkansas. And when we're done there, we're going to New Orleans. By the way, have you ever stayed at the Le Downtowner du Vieux Carre'?"

"What ya talking bout? Ya gonna have t' talk English if ya want me tailin' along with ya."

Elizabeth laughed, knowing Cain was going to have his hands full with Orson. "Now, take care of yourselves." Elizabeth admonished.

Cain hugged his mother, jumped on his horse and turned toward the gate with a wave.

"Cain, you take care of your horse and don't ride him too hard," Elizabeth called after them. Cain leaned over and patted his horse.

"Ma' will you please stop worrying?" He asked.

The sheriff tipped his hat at Lizzie and nudged his horse into a trot. Elizabeth watched as Cain gave Lucky the rein to run. When they got a distance away, Elizabeth heard Cain and the sheriff yell.

"Yehawwwwwww,"

"Now we're talkin'," Orson shouted. Elizabeth watched until they were out of sight.

Chapter 26

Vick wasn't surprised when Buckalew showed up at his cell to take him to the warden's office. He knew he was going to pay a price for introducing himself as Vick Porter to Johnson Petty, but he didn't know how much of a price or when.

Buckalew taunted him for three days before he finally came to his cell and dragged him off his cot. Vick landed sprawled on the floor after Buckalew shoved him in the warden's office.

"Here he is! You want me to take care of him?" asked the guard.

"Not so fast Buckalew. Me and Vick, need to have a little understanding." The warden was livid, and had it been any other prisoner, the man would be dead. He took a moment to peer at Vick over his eyeglasses, as if he was enjoying seeing his prisoner sweat.

"You knew punishment was coming but you didn't know when. Well, it's now! You'll think twice before you use your real name again."

Vick started to speak but thought better, when he saw Buckalew coming toward him.

The warden got up from his desk and stood over Vick, who was trying to stand. He nodded at Buckalew to use a special strap designed to inflict severe pain. He had been threatened before with the strap, but this was the first time Vick had to experience what many other prisoners had often been exposed to and feared daily.

Vick was powerless with the two men standing over him. The warden was smoking his cigar and watched Vick agonize in pain as Buckalew thrust the strap in such a way that caused Vick's body to tremble.

"Don't kill em', just beat em' till he wishes he was dead."

Vick grimaced, anticipating how sharp the pain from the strap would be. Buckalew lifted Vick's shirt to ensure more punishment. The second lash drew blood, as the long leather tentacles wrapped around Vick's torso leaving large welts. Whatever the instrument of his current fate, Vick's mind escaped to another place where he found refuge with Mattie as she stroked his brow.

Ugh!" Vick whimpered as Buckalew swung the strap again. The intensity of the pain was far worse than he had imagined. The warden held up his hand to stop momentarily.

"You disappointed me the other night when you used your real name. We had an understanding, and you went against me. You possibly cost me even more when that feller' goes back home and talks to ... we don't know who. This could be trouble for me 'cause the man seemed thunderstruck, and I say it's something about you. Do you care to tell me why you decided to use your real name?"

"I was told to use another name, and I couldn't think what to use and it just slipped out," Vick spoke slowly in a whisper, barely able to form a sentence. "No harm intended."

The warden nodded to Buckalew. "This should be a reminder that, when I tell you something, you do it." At that point, Buckalew dug his foot into Vick's side with such force that he momentarily lost consciousness.

When he came to, he found the warden bent over him, holding his head up by his hair. The warden's face was so close that Vick could feel his hot breath as he growled obscenities at him. Vick could hardly see because his bloodshot eyes were beginning to swell closed. "You look at me when I talk to you."

Vick nodded and gasped, "Yes sir."

"Now, we're gonna close the parlor down for a while in case that Johnson Petty feller tries to start trouble. Just remember, you've cost me and whenever you cost me, I collect that amount from your hide."

The warden started playing with Vick's mind. "Just remember, you never want to corner anything as mean as Buckalew, because he can be a nasty sonavobitch' and he's itchin' to … well, I'm not gonna say, because that'll be our little surprise when the time comes."

"I'll give you one hint: When you learn to walk again, you might be sore for a long, long time. Now, if Greasy was here, he could tell you all about it." The warden and Buckalew looked at each other and laughed.

Vick knew for the first time he was in the presence of pure evil.

"How about a little reinforcement of what I'm talking about?" He looked at Buckalew and smiled again.

Buckalew straddled Vick and used all the strength he had to administer several brutal lashes. This time, Vick crouched in a fetal position, moaning and trying to catch his breath. He had never experienced such punishment. He wanted to speak but he couldn't.

"Let this be a lesson to you! You ruined it for me the other night, now, this'll ruin it for you! Get him back to his cell! I'm through with him!"

"How am I gonna git him back to his cell when he can't walk?"

"I don't care … drag him if you have to! Just get 'em outta here."

Buckalew picked up Vick's left leg and began dragging him back toward his cell. Luckily for both, it was not far away.

"You ain't nothin' but gator bait. That Johnson feller left early and you cost us. Better get some sleep, 'cause tomorrow you're gonna be slinging a pick," Buckalew said as he slammed the cell door shut, leaving Vick lying in agony on the floor. All Vick could do was lie there, and wonder whether or not Johnson Petty had recognized him as Buck Dupree.

"Finally, my plan might be working," he thought. A faint smile penetrated his pain.

Chapter 27

Cain was glad Sheriff Cargill accompanied him to Little Rock. He had never had a father image, and having the sheriff with him brought something he sorely needed: Hope!

"Reckon the governor will see us?" Asked Orson.

"I ain't leaving till he does," said Cain.

"We got all the proof we need right here in this little girl's diary to get yer' Pa exonerated."

"I wish he was alive to hear when his name is cleared," Cain lamented.

"Well, now, don't ya go gittin' negative on me. Yer' Pa could be out there some place waitin' fer you to find him. Cain, ya have to keep thinkin' Vick's alive until ya find proof he ain't."

"That's the reason I need to go to the New Orleans prison and see for myself if Buck Dupree is there."

"I spec' if that's what ya want to do, you'll do it!"

When the men hit the main trail, the horses began making good time.

The sheriff was quite a character. Cain could see why his mother liked him, plus he helped him with a little target shooting along the way.

"Nothing wrong with a little gun knowledge, just in case a man has to defend hisself," the sheriff instructed. However, the sheriff could see that Cain would be much better handling the law than a gun.

In spite of their age difference, the two became fast friends. Most of their time was spent laughing and talking, as Orson cracked Cain up with one tale after the other. His constant entertaining made the trip go faster. By the time they got to the governor's office at the Arkansas State Capitol, the sheriff had become edgy and a bit nervous.

"Now Cain, I ain't good at this sort a thang", so don't spec' me to talk when we see the governor." This was the first time Cain had seen the sheriff so uptight.

"Orson, I wish you would relax. The governor is a man just like me and you, so no need to get all nervous and worked up about talking."

" I learnt' one thang" in my life that has worked for me; and that's talk low, talk slow, and don't talk much. Jest sayin'."

"I want you to rest easy. I'm not going to pressure you to talk. You're here with me and I'm the one that will talk with the governor. Why you so worried?

"Well, I ain't never met no governor before."

Cain wanted to laugh, but he could tell his friend was serious.

By the time they got to the governor's office, the sheriff had turned from being quiet to a regular chatterbox, talking non-stop. Now, anything but silent, the sheriff's loud squeaky voice reverberated throughout the building, attracting the attention of the governor's aide and God knows who else.

"What the hell?" the aide said, hearing a strange voice carry, as they were coming down the hall toward the governor's office. As they approached his desk, the sheriff tipped his hat and gave the aide a big grin. He seemed almost intoxicated.

"Gentlemen, can I be of assistance to you?"

"Sir, we're here to meet with the governor," Orson said proudly. Cain noticed reluctance from the aide and realized the sheriff might be a hindrance.

"Have you an appointment?"

The governor walked out of his office just before Cain could answer.

"Is there a problem out here? I thought I heard a commotion of some sort."

The sheriff looked around, as if he was looking for someone who was causing a problem. "This is Governor Wade," the aide said.

These men want to see you sir, but they don't have an appointment."

He looked Cain and the sheriff up and down, and thought they both looked harmless.

"That's okay, Jason; I have a little time. How can I help you gentlemen?"

"Nice to meet you Governor Wade," said Cain. The sheriff only grinned and nodded.

"Sir, my name is Cain Porter, and I'm here to talk to you on behalf of my Pa, who is a known fugitive."

The sheriff stood holding his hat, and sporting a faint smile, showing a slight separation in his front teeth. His sweaty forehead, clearly accented from his tight hatband, had left his hair quite crumpled. In contrast, Cain was standing tall, handsome, and prominent.

The governor quickly formed the opinion that the sheriff was Cain's Pa, and was indeed the fugitive in question.

"Gentlemen, come in my office and have a seat."

Governor Wade pointed out two chairs in front of his desk for the men.

"Thank you for seeing us, Governor," Cain said with reverence.

"You caught me at just the right time, since my docket is clear until later. What did your Pa do?" The governor continued looking at the sheriff, but neither Cain nor the sheriff had any idea that he thought Orson was the fugitive.

"I'll get right to the point. I am an attorney in the State of Arkansas, and my Pa was a young man when he was wrongfully accused of murder. The murders happened over twenty years ago, at which time my Pa found a family of four murdered. I recently found definitive proof that will clear him of any responsibility for these crimes.

"And what proof is that?" The governor asked.

"I have a diary that identifies Buck Dupree, the one who falsely accused my Pa, as the killer. You'll see for yourself, when you read young Janie's first-hand account of what happened."

Orson was so nervous he did not realize that he was whistling under his breath, until Cain touched his leg to get him to stop. He immediately caught himself, and sat up a little straighter in his chair. All this time, the governor was still examining the sheriff's demeanor, wondering if he was really innocent of murder.

"And, why isn't your Pa in jail?" the governor asked, as he looked in Orson's direction.

The sheriff looked at Cain in near panic.

"Governor, I'm sorry for not having properly introduced ourselves. It seems you've mistaken our town sheriff as the fugitive. This is our town sheriff and we are from Jonesboro, Arkansas. I invited him along to substantiate my evidence and the character of my Pa." Orson gave another smile and nodded slightly, but continued to squirm in his chair.

"Oh, I see. Who is your Pa then, and where is he?"

"Sir, my Pa is Vick Porter, and I think he's dead. He left home long before I was born, so I never had a chance to know him."

"I see … so if your Pa were alive, he would not know he has a son?"

"That's right, sir."

"Now let me get this straight. This gentleman is your town sheriff and your name is Cain, and you say you have proof of your Pa's innocence?"

"Sir, I do, right here with me. And by the way, this is Sheriff Orson Cargill."

"Good meeting you, Sheriff Cargill."

"Nice to meet ya," said Orson.

"Now, tell me how you know your Pa is innocent?"

"Governor, I recently discovered a diary written by a little girl by the name of Janie who was killed, along with her mother, Pa and little brother. She names Buck Dupree as the killer, and he is the person who accused my Pa of those four deaths and three more murders."

"Did you say seven murders?" Governor Wade asked incredulously. Sir, if you will give me a chance, I will explain."

"Please do!"

"We've had the diary of Janie for years, along with a number of other items that were part of a treasure-trove left with my mother for safe keeping when my Pa left home to find Buck Dupree and prove his innocence."

"So, you say this Buck Dupree is the man who actually murdered the family, then accused your Pa?"

"Yes sir, that's exactly what I'm saying, and even though I think my Pa is dead, I want to have him exonerated and his name cleared."

"Let's put first things first. Where is this diary you are speaking of?"

Cain pulled the diary from his saddlebag.

"Sir, I'm sorry about the blood stains on this book. They are over twenty years old."

"Not a problem! You also mentioned something about a treasure?"

"Yes, my Pa left the treasure with my mother, and I have no idea of its origin or what it's worth. It's been with our family over twenty years and we suspect Buck Dupree killed his partner and the family mentioned in this diary because of the treasure.

"And your Pa had the treasure along with this book? Did you bring it with you?" asked the governor.

"No sir, it would have been too dangerous because of its value and it's plenty heavy. The treasure is a mixture of items that amount to great wealth."

"What do you mean by, 'mixture of items?'"

"Well, if I had to say, it looks like a series of robberies from wealthy estates. We have two large sacks of an accumulation of gold bullion, coins, silver certificates and unset gems, along with many pieces of jewelry. My Pa was so young, he didn't know what he had. He was young when it came into his possession."

"How did your Pa end up with such a valuable stash then? Where'd he get it?"

"From a mountain man who my Pa thought had stolen the treasure from the dead family."

"You mean the family that this Buck Dupree killed?"

"Yes, exactly! He thought the mountain man was the one who killed the family and took it from them. In fact, at that time, my Pa was just a boy and was nearly killed by this beast of a man."

"Need I ask what happened to the mountain man?"

"My Pa was fourteen years old when he killed him in self-defense. Later on, he was also forced to kill the man's friend, as he was about to kill Buck Dupree, who was Pa's friend at the time."

"Wow, this can be confusing, but I think I can see why you would want to have your Pa exonerated. That's quite a list of bodies for a man who's innocent. I would say it was also self-defense, if he was trying to protect this Buck Dupree."

"Yes, he was trying to save his friend. The blood on the diary came from my Pa's face when the mountain man tried to kill him. He had a scar that covered one side of his face. Janie's diary could have cleared him years ago had we known it was a diary. All these years we thought it was just a book. My mother only recently read it. That's why we're here, hoping to clear this up and exonerate my father."

"What about the other man your Pa was accused of killing?"

"He was his brother who was killed in a storm. He was younger than my Pa and was hit by a falling limb at Panther Holler. My mom says that my uncle ran into the storm after they found the family's bodies in the storm shelter."

"I think I get the picture."

"Governor, I personally think Buck Dupree and Janie's Pa were in cahoots with each other and got in a fight over this treasure. Buck probably thought his partner lied to him about the mountain man stealing the treasure, when he was actually telling the truth. That's what made him mad enough to kill the family."

"Mr. Porter, I hope no one knows about this treasure, because if this Dupree guy learns you are Vick Porter's son, he may figure you have his stolen items and could come looking for you. Get what I'm saying? If he's killed this number of people, one or two more will not make a difference to him. You all wait here while I get my aide to see if we have any information about any high profile robberies about twenty years ago in that area of Arkansas. In the meantime, I'll take a look at this little girl's diary."

The governor left the room, and Cain and Sheriff Cargill were left alone to wait. Cain couldn't believe how easy the governor was to talk to, and felt comfortable waiting, knowing he may be able to accomplish clearing his Pa.

"Sheriff, I've been meaning to talk to you about Johnson Petty. I think you're right about him withholding information. From the time Johnson came out of that gambling parlor he acted different. He treated me differently, and Mom noticed it right away when we returned from New Orleans. Something had to be eating at him."

"Cain, there ain't no tellin' what he knows about yer' Pa or about Buck Dupree. I got a feelin' the man's a liar, and I'm usually right about such thang's. I can't explain why."

"We'll find out soon enough, when we go back to New Orleans. Not to change the subject, but I'm tired of talking about Johnson Petty. How about your daughter? You haven't mentioned anything about Lucy. I haven't seen her in years. How is she doing?"

"I got me quite a little gal. You know I lost Lucy's mama when she was jes' a tiny little thang. Lucy and me was at your mama Mattie's funeral all those years ago. Don't spec' you remember how cold it was that day. Lucy was real little, and you were a young thang' 'yersef. Yeah, Lucy has more spunk than anyone I know! She's been away in what they say is a 'finishing school'." She always laughs when I ask her what she plans to finish when she comes home."

Orson had a jovial laugh as he talked about Lucy.

Cain remembered Lucy as a plain girl, rather tomboyish who did not know how to take care of herself. He suspected it was because she didn't have the influence of a mother. He could never imagine her as a proper lady.

"You ain't seen my Lucy since she's all grow'd up?"

"I was a couple years older than Lucy, but I remember her," Cain said.

"Yep, if ya ever know Lucy, it ain't likely you'll forgit' her." She was a regular tomboy all the while she was growing up. Talk about somebody that can tote a gun! Them people doin' the finishing has quite a job if they spec' they're gonna make a proper lady out of Lucy." Orson and Cain had a good laugh.

There was plenty of reminiscing but most of Cain's time was spent thinking about Eileen and whether they would have a future if he found out Johnson was lying. "Wouldn't really be her fault though," he decided.

After a while patience was getting the best of them, and Cain began to pace the floor, looking at the certificates on the wall and touching small mementos sitting here and there. He would hate if it turned out that he and Orson had ridden all the way to Little Rock for nothing, if Janie's written testament didn't clear his Pa of the charges, nothing would.

The sheriff had his hat off, twiddling his thumbs, waiting for the governor.

Governor Wade was clearly the most prominent person the sheriff had ever met, and Cain imagined there would be some tall tales circulating back home when he returned.

Nearly two hours had passed, when they finally heard footsteps coming down the marble floor toward the anxious men. The sheriff jumped to his feet.

"Do you reckon that's him?" They were both standing as the governor walked back into the room with a solemn look on his face.

"Cain, the diary of this young girl was very compelling. It was a painful account of a terrible crime, and I don't know that I have ever been so touched as now, after reading the words of this young girl. It was like a voice beyond the grave spoke to me. Two children should never be put through what Janie and her brother went through. I have two young children of my own, which made this account even more horrifying."

"Governor, it sounds like you had the same reaction I had, and to hear Janie name Buck Dupree as the murderer, made it mandatory for me to do what I could to vindicate my Pa and this family."

"I know children don't lie about something like this, and I do believe Buck Dupree is the killer. I also believe in you as an attorney, and also you Sheriff Cargill, for being here to support Mr. Porter, here."

The sheriff spoke up, which surprised Cain. "It ain't jest Cain I'm supportin'. I know Vick Porter personally, and he is a hero in our town."

The governor allowed Sheriff Cargill to continue; he could sense Orson was not a man motivated by money even though he could have used the money for his trip.

"Yep, nobody in Jonesboro ever thought Vick Porter coulda been a murderer in the first place, an' we'd all sure appreciate ya takin' the time to clear Cain's Pa of all them murders that Buck Dupree did."

"Thank you Sheriff Cargill. I believe you." Cain and the governor shared a smile.

"It's going to take me a little time to do this, but I'll have the paperwork ready in the morning. In the meantime; you all can stay at the Carriage Boarding House for the night, as my guests."

"That's mighty nice of you Governor Wade," said the sheriff, shaking his hand.

"In the morning before you men head home stop by my aide's desk and sign the paperwork to exonerate your Pa, Mr. Porter. Hopefully, by then I will also have news about the treasure you spoke of. I wish your Pa were alive to know what a fine son he has, and also a good friend like Sheriff Cargill here. We need more good men like you.

"Thank you Governor, but I need to ask one more favor."

"What favor is that?"

"I think Buck Dupree is in prison in New Orleans, and I need to see him. Could you arrange a meeting where I can talk to him face to face?"

"You sure you want to do that? "

"I have to, because he is the only one who can answer some questions I have about my Pa."

"I don't know if you're aware that this falls under the jurisdiction of the governor of Louisiana. We'll have to send a telegram and see if we can arrange for you and the sheriff to have that meeting. When I find out, I'll let you know. Sheriff Cargill, please leave your information with my aide tomorrow when you come by and we will send you word as to whether a meeting can be set up with Dupree."

The sheriff was wide-eyed as he heard that he was included in Cain's plan to visit Buck Dupree in prison.

"You've been a great help, sir. I don't know how to thank you," said Cain.

"If the Louisiana governor can arrange this for you, it will be interesting to know how Buck Dupree reacts when he meets the son of the man he framed."

"Thank you, Governor," added the sheriff.

With that, both Cain and the sheriff shook the governor's hand fervently as they started to leave the office.

"Mr. Porter, aren't you forgetting something?"

Cain turned, as the governor handed Janie's diary to him.

"You should always treasure this diary, as it is what exonerated your Pa."

"Thank you sir, I will do that. I wish my Pa was here to thank you personally."

As Cain and the sheriff left the governor's office, they discussed the possibility of going home instead of heading straight to Louisiana, since it would likely be a while before the governor would have an answer from New Orleans.

The next day, after a hearty breakfast, Cain and the sheriff stopped by the aide's desk to pick up the Declaration of Innocence that officially pardoned his Pa and cleared his name. What a great day it was to know that after all these years, they had finally accomplished Cain's goal.

Thanks to the expert investigation of the aide, who was now a lot friendlier, the governor made a point to be in his office when Cain and Orson arrived. Governor Wade had answers to many of the questions Cain had about the origin of the treasure.

The research yielded some good news and he eagerly shared his findings. "It seems that both Buck Dupree and his partner were members of the Johnny Doyal gang, one of the most notorious groups renegades in the South but were never captured."

"During and after the War Between the States, many Yankee soldiers pilfered gold and silver serving items, plus heirloom jewelry from the southern mansions. The federal marshal's actually recovered a good amount of the items from those soldiers to return to their owners. The Doyal gang learned through one of the deputies that it was being moved from a military building in Savannah, Georgia, to a more secure bank vault downtown. The gang ambushed the marshal's men outside the bank and killed the marshal, every one of his guards and several innocent bystanders, including women and children, right in the middle of town! The leader of the Doyal gang was also killed. It was a terrible gunfight with bodies lying everywhere.

Most of the gang members died, too, but Dupree and his partner survived and made off with a fortune. One source reported that just outside of town, the two split up. After that, the trail went cold. All told, the value of that items the two took should be at least a half million dollars, according to estimates in our report.

Cain was stunned. "I had no idea!"

There were rumors of Buck Dupree being in Texas, Louisiana and Arkansas, but the federal officers never were able to track him down.

"Mr. Porter, I think what happened was Janie Ballard's Pa was Buck's partner. He had the treasure when he and Buck split up. Apparently they were to meet some place and divide it."

"You think that place was Panther Holler?"

"Yes, I'm sure. What better place could there be? Remote, isolated with no witnesses around. Besides, Janie wrote that her Pa was expecting Buck. Her Pa no doubt, was robbed by the mountain man and that's why Janie never knew of a treasure. So very sad." Officials didn't know the name of Buck's partner until you brought in Janie's diary. Now we know his last name was Ballard.

I'm sure there's a lot to this story we don't know. For instance, how did the mountain man get his hands on Janie's diary? Cain said he had even wondered the same thing, but decided the mountain man must have come back to the cabin and found it by Janie's body.

"But at least we know where the treasure came from," the governor said. "One day, after you have your meeting with Buck Dupree, you can come back and fill me in. Until then, keep the treasure safe. You have kept it safe all these years, so a few more months won't hurt. When I find out more, I will let you know."

"Thank you again, Governor Wade. I really appreciate all you have done to help us."

"You men take care. You'll be hearing from me soon." He patted both the men on their backs and walked them out the door.

Cain was happier than he had ever been and couldn't wait to get home and tell Elizabeth the news. "Cain, you know Elizabeth ain't gonna like you paying a visit to Buck Dupree in that New Orleans prison."

"I know, but it's about time Buck met Vick Porter's son.

Chapter 28

CAIN AND ORSON HAD BEEN IN THE SADDLE MOST OF THE DAY WHEN **Cain's horse trotted on ahead.** Out of nowhere, a large hawk swooped down in front of Cain, frightening him and spooking his horse. He ducked just in time to keep from being hit, as his horse reared up, sensing danger. He couldn't understand why the hawk kept circling

"Did you see that?"

The sheriff watched as the large bird swooped toward them again.

"Are you all right? That thang' almost knocked you off yer' horse. That's the biggest damn hawk I ever seen, an' I ain't never seen one do nothing like that!"

"Me, either!"

Orson followed the hawk with his eyes. "Look! He lit in that pine tree. See 'em?" he said, as he pointed toward the bird in the midst of several large pines.

"He must have been flying along, not paying attention."

As they traveled, they had time to talk about everything, including Cain's infatuation with Eileen.

Every now and then they would see what looked like the same hawk circling in the sky and would comment that the bird seemed to be following them.

Cain finally asked Orson about his daughter. "How long has Lucy been gone?"

"Almost two years now. I'll be glad when she gits home, so I can eat some good cooking. That daughter of mine knows all 'bout cooking. She's learnin' all that proper lady stuff, jest don't want her rubbin' it off on me, cause I am what I am."

Cain laughed at the sheriff's reaction.

"Sheriff, Lucy couldn't change you if she tried."

"Ya got that right!"

After several nights sleeping under the stars, they finally arrived back in Jonesboro.

"Cain, how bout' riding out by my place, so I can unload my thangs."

As they approached the cabin, they were surprised to see smoke coming out of the chimney.

"Looks like somebody's nestin' in my cabin! Wonder what's goin' on?"

About that time Lucy came running out to meet her Pa. Cain was sure he had not ever seen this beautiful girl before. He had time to look her over good before he realized Lucy had changed from the dowdy young girl he remembered into a beautiful woman. He was only a few years older than her, and had not remembered her being such a striking beauty. She was utterly breathtaking to him.

"Why, I'll be danged if it ain't my girl. She ain't suppose to be home until the summer," the sheriff said.

"Lucy girl, whatcha' doin' home?"

"I surprised you, didn't I, Pa?"

Cain felt guilty looking at another woman when his heart was with Eileen, but Lucy was so striking that he couldn't keep his eyes off her.

When she walked toward Cain and extended her hand, it was like a bolt of electricity went through his body, something he didn't remember happening when he first met Eileen.

"Cain Porter, it's been such a long time, how nice to see you." Lucy trembled as she felt the warmth of Cain's hand in hers. She noticed how the boy with the huckleberry smile had developed into such handsome, mature man.

Of course, the sheriff did not recognize how finishing school had brought out the best in Lucy, changing her from a shy, plain tomboy, to a confident young lady. She had no idea the impact she made on Cain, as he tried to conceal his thoughts. The only problem was that she was a little too late for him, since he had committed himself to Eileen.

This pert beauty with her long blonde hair and blue eyes was like sheer sexual magnetism to him and he felt guilty for even giving her such a thought. There was also the issue of his friend, Orson, whom he respected, although he was still reluctantly drawn to his daughter, and for the first time in his adult life, Cain felt like he was out of control.

Lucy's beauty had scrambled his logic and clouded his judgment so quickly that he knew he could become vulnerable to her charms if he was not careful. Finally, after what seemed to be an eternity, he was able to speak.

" Lucy uh, how have you been? I heard you were away at school."

"I've just graduated," she said.

They stood there looking at each other, both trying to figure out what to say next.

He started to say how she had matured, but was just able to say, "You are so, uh ... grown ..." Neither one of them was making very good conversation, since both were drawn to each other.

All the time Cain was thinking, "I don't remember having this feeling with Eileen."

"Lucy, I'm sorry if I spoiled your surprise."

"It serves me right for not letting Pa know I was coming home. By the way, how is Elizabeth doing?"

"She's the same, always busy running the lumber company and helping out when she can. I've been telling her she needs to slow down and find some help."

"Perhaps you two can slow down long enough to come to supper one night. I promise you a good meal," Lucy said.

Cain thought, "I'm not playing this game, when I'm committed to another woman."

Lucy kept talking, but Cain was so mesmerized by her, watching her lips move, admiring her eyes, that he could hardly keep up with what she was saying. "This is not going so well for me," he thought.

"Well, will you talk to Elizabeth about dinner?"

"Uh … yes, sure! I'll talk to her and get back with you, if that's okay?"

The sheriff could see what was happening with Lucy, and feared she might be opening herself up for hurt. He liked Cain, but he was fully aware that there was another woman in the picture.

"Cain, that's all right if you and Lizzie are busy, but I have to say Lucy's a mighty good cook." He hated to see his daughter disappointed.

"I'm sure she is. I'll talk to mother and get back to you in the next day or so."

"I hope you all can make it," she said.

Lucy extended her hand once again. Another bolt of electricity went through him. "Dang it," he thought. "This is not suppose to happen when I'm in love with Eileen."

As Cain rode out past the sheriff's makeshift cattle guard, he turned to see if Lucy was still looking. There she was, peering at him with big blue eyes that were as piercing as the noonday sun. He quickly looked away, thinking to himself, "Oh boy, am I in trouble. This girl is dynamite."

When he arrived at the manor, Elizabeth was almost finished pruning her rose bushes. When she looked up and saw her son, she dropped the shears and ran toward him.

"Cain, I've been on pins and needles waiting to hear if you saw the governor?"

"Better than that, if Pa were alive today, he would be a free man."

"I can't believe that Governor Wade exonerated your Pa. That's wonderful! I want to hear every detail. Where is Orson?"

"Oh, he wanted to come but Lucy surprised him," he answered. Cain dismounted and they walked arm-and-arm into the house.

"Lucy just returned from finishing school. She's nothing like you remember."

"She was always a cute girl," Elizabeth said.

"Ma, I've been thinking about what you did for Pa."

"What do you mean?"

"Well, if it wasn't for you, none of this would have happened. If you hadn't read Janie's diary, we might not have been able to exonerate Pa."

"Son, all I care about is it's over and you finally cleared your father!"

"Well, it's not quite over yet. The governor is arranging for me to meet Buck Dupree."

Cain could see the disappointment and fear in his mother's eyes.

"Don't give me that look Ma. You know this is something I have to do."

By this time they were in the library, seated so Cain could share the details with his mother.

He gave the Declaration of Innocence to Elizabeth, who handled the papers as if they were sacred. She read it quietly, and then gave Cain a big hug.

"Reading this, it doesn't seem real. Your Pa would be so proud. Elizabeth hesitated and Cain knew what was coming next.

"Son, you've done your part."

Cain did not allow her to finish. "Please don't start this again. You know I have to do this."

"I don't get it! What more can you want, the man's already in jail?"

"I want to see his face when I tell him my Pa beat him. He's a butcher that killed an innocent family, and I want him to know Janie had the last word when she wrote his name in her diary. That's what I want!"

"Well, it looks like you've made up your mind. Would you do me a favor when you go, and please take the Model T and me with you?"

"Are you sure you want to go?"

"Absolutely! I've lived a lot longer with the name Buck Dupree than you have, and it's about time I did something to support you."

"Well, you're going to have to let up if you go. I don't want you hampering whatever I need to do when I get there."

"You can do whatever you want, but I need a vacation."

"By the way, Lucy Cargill invited us to supper. I told her I would check with you first and let her know. And I also invited the sheriff to go to New Orleans with us. So what do you think?"

"About the sheriff or Lucy?"

"About going to Lucy's for dinner."

"I think we should, don't you? I haven't seen Lucy in years. So, Lucy has really changed? I bet she's cute as a bug."

"Cute? Beautiful is more like it!" Cain caught himself. "

"Look? Hmmmm, what look is that?"

"I shouldn't have mentioned Lucy."

"In fact, I have my own plans for Lucy. She might work out fine taking Spencer's place in the lumber company, which would free me up to do more with my cotton business, and perhaps do a little traveling. She's pretty tough. I'll see how she works out while we're gone, and if she does, I'll offer her a permanent position."

"Where is the Bible?" Cain asked.

"That's a quick change of subject! If you would try reading it more, you might know. What are you going to do with the Bible?"

"Put Pa's exoneration papers in it … or, if you keep on about Lucy, I might need it for more reasons than one!"

"So how about our trip? You do want the sheriff to join us, don't you?

"Of course! Now back to what we were talking about before you changed the subject."

In preparation for dinner for Elizabeth and Cain, Lucy was giving her Pa last minute details on her expectations.

"Now Pa, you know how important it is for this evening to be perfect."

"Now Lucy girl, don't be trying to make me into somepin' I ain't. Jest calm down."

Lucy peered out the window just in time to see Elizabeth and Cain drive up.

"Pa, they're here! Now, please, behave yourself?"

The sheriff rolled his eye as Lucy took one last look in the mirror in the living room.

When she opened the door and invited Elizabeth and Cain inside, they were pleasantly surprised with the stark contrast to the outside. Lucy had an artistic touch. Elizabeth admired her creativity in turning something as old and mundane as the cottage, into a comfortable home.

The moment Cain saw Lucy; he was smitten with her again. She looked radiant.

Trying not to be obvious, Elizabeth noticed a spark of interest between her son and Lucy. She had not remembered how confident and self-assured Lucy was and the meal was outstanding. Elizabeth looked for anything that could give her hope that Cain would fall for someone other than Eileen. She dreaded the thought of Johnson Petty being in her life. "What more could Cain want in a wife than a young beautiful girl like Lucy who lived in the same town." she thought.

Elizabeth was sure her idea of Lucy taking Spencer's place would work. She had planned to make Lucy a job offer after supper. Elizabeth was very eloquent as she spoke,

"Lucy, I'm planning on going to New Orleans with Cain and your Pa, if he'll agree to go with us, and I would like to know if you would work for me at the lumber company, while I'm gone."

Lucy looked at her Pa, and waited for his nod of approval.

"I'd appreciate if you can fill in for me. You know, I've reached an age where I want to travel and do some other things," Elizabeth said. She had caught Cain completely off guard. "How else could his mother complicate matters?" he thought.

"Thank you, Elizabeth. I hadn't thought about working at the lumber company, but yes, I would love to."

"My girl can handle it fer' ya Lizzie," said the sheriff.

Elizabeth went to Lucy and gave her a big hug.

"Nice to have you aboard, Lucy. We open before daylight for the loggers. I hope you're an early riser?"

It was apparent Elizabeth had made Lucy very happy. Looking at the excitement in her face, Cain kept comparing her to Eileen.

When they arrived back at the manor, Cain thought his mother looked like a cat that had swallowed the canary. He wondered if she hired Lucy for herself, or if she hired her for his benefit. "I'll find out soon enough," he thought.

"What are you smiling about?" he asked as they walked upstairs.

"Oh, nothing. I suppose I was thinking of our fun evening with Lucy and the Orson."

"Just don't get any ideas about matchmaking, you hear?"

"I want you to do me a favor, Cain?"

"Here it comes. I knew you had something going on in that mind of yours."

"Well, I do, but it's not what you think. Don't you think you should pick Lucy up, since it's her first day of work?"

"I knew it! You're meddling! Get used to it mother! Eileen is going to be your new daughter-in-law, and Johnson will be giving her away to me. If you don't want me to rush into marriage, you're going to have to back off and quit pushing Lucy on me! Understand?"

"All I asked is if you would pick Lucy up for her first day for work? My gosh, why would this get you so rattled? Don't you want to make a good impression?"

"I made my first impression when I was seven years old. Remember, I've known this girl since we were kids."

In spite of the night before, Cain picked Lucy up for work the next morning. As she walked out, and saw him standing with the car door open, he took her breath away.

"My, my, this is a surprise. You didn't say anything about picking me up this morning."

"I wanted you to know that we Porter folk know how to treat a new employee on her first day of work. Are you ready for this?"

"Why, thank you. This is really a nice gesture." Lucy couldn't believe Cain was so thoughtful that he would come and pick her up.

"When mother mentioned I should pick you up, I wondered why I didn't think of this myself."

"*So, it was Elizabeth's suggestion that brought Cain there to pick her up,*" Lucy anguished.

Somewhat disappointed, she found it difficult to carry on a conversation. No matter how much refinement and schooling she had, her insecurities overwhelmed her. The sharp contrast between her modest way of life and the opulence, money and style of the Barkin's brought back the insecurities of her early childhood.

When Lucy walked into the Porter Lumber Company, Elizabeth was impressed. She was totally professional, yet animated, and spirited, coming across like a breath of fresh air — much like Elizabeth, herself had been when she came home from finishing school. Lucy appeared to be just like her, enthusiastic and confident.

One thing she found especially impressive was Lucy's ability to handle the loggers, most of whom had a rough exterior like the sheriff. She was firm and yet friendly with them, which gave her an edge. Elizabeth couldn't have been happier, seeing she had such a capable employee filling Spencer's shoes.

It had been only two weeks, when at long last the notice came by special delivery that the governor had arranged for the meeting with Buck Dupree. Cain was ready to go, and Elizabeth found she was equally excited. However, Orson was reluctant, knowing he did not have money and proper clothing for the trip.

"I shore preciate' ya'll wanting me to go, but I may have to take a rain check this time."

"I don't want any back talk! The governor is expecting both of us, so you're going. Cain reminded the sheriff. "Not only that, I need you to keep me out of trouble."

"I'd like to go but it'll cost me a year's pay for one night."

"You don't worry about the expense, we have it covered, and besides, how many sheriffs get to meet the governor of Louisiana?" Cain asked.

"Well, I supposin' you're right about that. Oh, okay, guess I'm gonna be stayin in that thangma jigger hotel after all, whatever the dang name of that place is."

"You think you can get yourself ready by the end of the week?"

"I reckon I'll be ready, since I don't have much to pack."

"Well, I got a surprise for you. Lucy bought you a complete wardrobe to take along to meet the governor."

"Better not be none o' them monkey suits or them purdy boy shoes, 'cause she knows I won't wear 'em." Cain smiled and hoped he was not making a mistake encouraging the sheriff to tag along.

"We'll pick you up the end of the week, so no back talk when I say to get your things packed."

Of course, Lucy did a great job choosing clothes for her Pa. When Elizabeth and Cain pulled up to the Cargill cabin, he was waiting on the front porch in his new suit, shoes, and shiny new pocket watch, with the beautiful chain draped from one side of the suit to the other. "Right in style," Cain and Elizabeth thought.

"Hope ya'll satisfied with all these fancy clothes I'm a wearin.' I feel outta' place, and probably look like some circus clown."

Elizabeth thought Orson looked quite nice all dressed up.

When they arrived in New Orleans the sheriff was sitting on the edge of his seat as Cain drove up and down the main street of the French Quarter with scantily dressed women of every description.

"I ain't never seen nuttin' like this. Downright shameful, I say."

"Orson, this is called the French Quarter. The women are what makes it famous."

"I'm with the sheriff, I think it is awful, seeing women dressed so provocatively."

"Here ya go agin', talking dat' fancy talk, Lizzie."

"It means the same, sheriff," Cain said.

As they arrived at the hotel, Cain dropped Elizabeth and the sheriff off while he went to find a parking place.

The Captain of the hotel was there to take their luggage. When he took Orson's bag, he was at first concerned that the man was stealing his suitcase. Elizabeth intercepted his thoughts with that 'certain look' to let him know that what the Captain was doing was customary. He followed along in silence as they were escorted to their different rooms.

The next morning, the sheriff was up and dressed waiting for Elizabeth and Cain in the lobby. He had his hair parted in the middle, combed and oiled down like he was waiting to be photographed.

"It's 'bout time ya showed up. I was afraid one of them women of the night might latch on to me."

Elizabeth laughed, and thought, "So much for the new clothes, because he was still the same Orson Cargill."

The sheriff followed along as Cain led the way to the dining room. When they arrived, the tables were donned with white tablecloths set for a breakfast feast. The sheriff felt guilty enjoying Elizabeth's and Cain's hospitality, while Lucy was home working.

After breakfast, they drove to the governor's mansion and were escorted to Governor Hall's office.

"We shore got this down pat, don't we?" the sheriff said. Cain tried to keep from laughing, knowing Orson was referring to their recent visit with Governor Wade in Arkansas.

When they entered the governor's office, he made everyone feel welcome as Cain introduced the sheriff and his mother. What neither of them knew was the governor had a plan of his own to expose Warden Carson's poker parlor operation.

When the governor heard that Cain and the sheriff were coming, he decided to wait and enlist their help in his efforts to take the warden and his men down.

"Mr. Porter your timing is perfect for me to enforce my plan. That is, if we can agree that you and the sheriff will assist me. I need your help to gather information for me.

"Won't it be dangerous?" Elizabeth asked.

"There's always a chance something could go wrong. I've heard that men have been reported missing because of the warden and his men, but that's all the more reason we have to stop them. Having someone like Mr. Porter and the sheriff who are here from out of state will be much more convincing and safer. Ma'am, we need someone trustworthy like your son and this fine gentleman to help end the corruption. When I heard your son was coming to visit one of the inmates, I felt it was time to join together to put an end to the rumors I have heard about the warden."

"Governor, when I asked to see a convict named Buck Dupree, we did not come here to help you expose the warden. This makes a big difference. I don't feel right asking the sheriff to endanger himself, becoming involved with some kind of secret operation."

"I see, but let me ask you this: Do you think your Pa would back down, if he had a chance to bring Buck Dupree down? You can help us close this poker parlor, and also save lives. What the warden is doing is illegal, immoral and downright wrong, by anyone's standards, and what we need is proof in order to move forward. You can provide that by helping us."

Cain was surprised when the sheriff spoke up.

"Ya can count me in, but only if ya promise to give Cain a chance to meet eyeball to eyeball with this Buck Dupree feller."

Cain jumped in, as he saw his mother was about to speak.

"Mother, I don't want you saying anything about this. I know what I'm doing. I'm going in with the sheriff."

Elizabeth shrugged, trying to bite her tongue to keep from interfering.

"Cain, when you and the sheriff are safe on the inside, you can rest assured I will have my men ready to move in and arrest the warden. Excuse my French in front of a lady, but I want that scumbags head on a platter."

Cain's mind was racing, thinking about what Johnson Petty had told him about gamblers being thrown to the gators.

"I need to know if we go in that place, that you will protect us. I've heard the rumors about gamblers who go missing. I think you've heard the gator stories."

"Who told you about gamblers being thrown to the gators?" asked the governor.

"I'd rather not say if you don't mind. He's a wealthy plantation owner who had rather not become involved."

"Cain, you never told me about gators! Are you saying Johnson knew about gators when he lured you to New Orleans?" Elizabeth asked. "Oh my, I'm not about to let my son and our sheriff do your dirty work, Governor. If something happened to either of these men, I would never be able to live with myself."

"I'm sorry Miss Barkin, but these are my conditions.

The governor turned to Cain and appealed to him to calm his mother down.

"Mother, please!"

"Don't ya worry, Lizzie, I'll take care of Cain," Orson said.

Elizabeth knew it was a waste of time trying to make sense to Cain when his mind was made up.

Before they left the governor's office, Cain and the sheriff were given clothing so they could play the part of successful riverboat gamblers. Cain was still concerned that he may not be able to pass himself off as a professional because of his age.

The governor made it clear to Cain and the sheriff that Agent Adams would escort them secretly to the poker parlor. He also gave them each a bankroll of their own to flash when they entered the card game.

Elizabeth could sense Cain's nervousness, and became more and more stressed about her son and the sheriff becoming involved in the governor's plan.

"Cain, please don't do this. I think you are asking for trouble going into a place like this. I'm concerned; you remember what Johnson said, "It's dangerous."

"Please mother, you promised me you would not interfere. I knew you should have stayed home."

The sheriff turned to Elizabeth. "Lizzie, remember … I'll be there to take care of 'em."

Elizabeth knew the sheriff was very capable, but she did not know if under these circumstances he could help Cain. She hugged them goodbye and prayed they would return.

By the next day, the warden had already heard the news that two "riverboat gamblers" were staying at the hotel in town, ready to play. He wanted everything to go without a hitch, but fell uneasy after hearing they were professional riverboat gamblers. He wondered if he had overestimated Vick, taking on men who had possibly played with Wyatt Earp and Doc Holliday.

After the warden talked to Buckalew, they decided it best to poison the professionals before they left the parlor. This would be administered a little at a time to the whiskey and after 4-5 drinks of arsenic, by the end of the evening they'll be dead. As the warden went over last-minute details of what he expected, the guards saw he was more uptight than usual about Vick's performance, in case the professionals had some tricks of their own. The warden continued to fill Buckalew in.

"I want Vick on his game tonight, you hear? Everything's riding on 'em."

"Don't worry, he knows this is a big night." Bucklalew replied.

"I'm counting on everybody doing their part. Make sure you got that whiskey mixed and remember, I don't want 'em dead until the end of the game. It better be a big night. I'm counting on getting out of this place someday."

"Ya, gonna take us with ya, ain't ya, Warden?" One of the guards asked. "Sure, sure, when I leave you all leave with me. We just need a few more big breaks like tonight, then we'll take care of Vick. I don't want to leave anyone that'll talk."

The warden sent Vick a package of nice clothes and shoes, wanting him to look like a wealthy professional. After nearly twenty years, the poker parlor had gained notoriety during its years of operation, and Vick had seen hundreds of gamblers of all kinds for him to fleece. He was highly suspect of the warden's puppets and how they exaggerated when they wanted to peak Vick's excitement. One rule Vick always played by was to prepare for the worst, and if the best happened, great.

He was impressed when he saw the clothes were nicer than normal, knowing something was up, which made him a little nervous, going up against some of the best, apparently. "This has to be an important night for the warden to go to this much expense," he told himself. Vick was now feeling extra pressure to win, which could work against him. Vick's playing had worked well over and over all these years, but, in the back of his mind, he felt he could slip up and lose badly, which would result in Warden Carson not needing him anymore. He, too, could be fed to the gators. *Could this be that night?*

Cain also wondered if this could be the night ... the night he came face to face with Buck Dupree. He knew the success or failure of their plan, was riding mainly on him; his disguise as a shrewd gambler with cold nerves and unshakable composure. Meanwhile, beneath his cool exterior, Cain had become very nervous. He was going over in his mind everything Johnson Petty had taught him about poker. There was little time to focus on the sheriff, while trying to orchestrate his secret mission. How ironic it would be to pull the same trick on Buck that Buck had pulled on Johnson Petty. Cain smiled under his breath as he thought of Buck's possible reaction.

Chapter 29

IRONICALLY AT THE SAME TIME THE GOVERNOR'S AGENT WAS SUPPOSED to meet and accompany Cain and Orson to the poker parlor, Buckalew, showed up before the agent and intercepted Cain and Orson before the governor's agent had a chance to meet up with them.

"*They're like little lambs being led to slaughter*," the ruthless guard chuckled to himself. "*After I take care of 'em there won't be much left. Yeah, they'll make a fine meal for them hungry gators.*"

Cain and the sheriff were totally unaware of the grim fate facing them.

Elizabeth saw Cain and Orson leave with Buckalew who she thought looked of questionable character. "This couldn't be one of the governor's men," she thought.

What neither Cain nor Buckalew knew, was that Sheriff Cargill had strapped two pistols under his disguise, just in case.

Although Orson knew the risk involved when he and Cain left with Buckalew, there was really nothing either could do but play along and hope Orson's pistols would not be discovered. As they rode through downtown New Orleans, Buckalew tried to carry on a conversation, but his passengers chose not to partake.

Meanwhile, Orson was subtly motioning to Cain, as if to say they were okay, but Cain didn't know what the old gent was up to. "*How incredulous it was to have been here with Johnson Petty only a few weeks earlier, and now, because of my persistence, I'm back with Sheriff Cargill about to see Buck Dupree and possibly be dead because of our hasty departure.* Cain imagined.

The road to the prison was not very far out of town, but the further they drove, the more the landscape seem to change in their favor. Cain caught the idea, too, and gave the sheriff a nod when he recognized they were getting closer to the parlor.

The small house, was typical in architecture for the region, located just outside the prison. Across from the location was a series of old buildings that were vacant and barely standing, a good place for a stake out that was not going to happen, since their plan ran amuck.

By the time they saw the place, and no sign of the governor's back up. Cain thought, *"we're dead men walking."*

Here they were, posing as professional riverboat gamblers, when neither one of them hardly knew how to shuffle cards. Cain thought, *"Too bad. It looked like we could have nailed the warden for sure. Now, this could get ugly in a hurry."*

For the last twenty years, poker had been a gold mine for the corrupt warden and his select guards, all of who were maintaining a double life. A prison warden by day, poker parlor operator by night with his front man, Buckalew, organizing the games. He was able to pull off his scheme because gambling at the parlor was a private affair, making the games especially popular and elusive to authorities that might have shut it down. The mediocre existence as a warden paled when compared to the power, intrigue, and easy money of the parlor; it had quickly come to mean everything to him. His primary job had become secondary as greed set in.

Vick's talent for counting cards had been the only thing that made it possible for Warden Carson to taste a life of luxury, and live beyond the means of a warden's salary. After the first smell of success, he was willing to do most anything to protect what had become his golden egg. Even murder had become necessary. He kept his guards just hungry enough that they would do most anything to stay on his good side, including killing and robbing. All he had to do was toss the men a couple dollars and they would roll over to make that extra money.

It had taken almost twenty years for the Louisiana governor to finally hear of the corruption surrounding this crooked warden and his poker parlor business. The disappearing men in that area was the motivator that brought it all to light. He wanted to shut it down and arrest Carson in the worst way, but not without sufficient evidence to convict him put him and his men away for the rest of their lives. This is when the participation of Cain and the sheriff was about to make it possible for him to make the obvious arrest.

Orson Cargill's only real concern was to honor the promise he made to Elizabeth, that he would take care of her son. Nothing else mattered, and he was ready to use the pistols if need be. "If we can keep thang's' under control until the governor's men show, this might work," he told himself.

Buckalew continued with the small talk as he led his riverboat gamblers to the front door of the parlor. The governor's plan had backfired, but the two men were still intent on their quest to meet Buck Dupree face to face, at any cost. Cain's earlier thought that he and the sheriff might have to fight their way to safety, came roaring back as they stood at the door ready to go in.

As they entered the poker room, the sheriff's countenance had changed from the witty, laughable character, to the serious riverboat gambler that was the mainstay of their cover. He walked with a strut, and there was no question that the sheriff had become the master of his disguise.

Buckalew informed Cain and the sheriff that it was customary to do a search before the games began. While the sheriff waited patiently, Cain held his arms out and was searched. When it came time for the sheriff's turn, he held his arms up and dropped a gold coin that rolled across the floor, resting against the wall. He planned for the distraction and started walking toward the coin, but Buckalew got there first. When he picked the coin up, he offered it back to the sheriff, who refused it saying, 'Keep it … this is the least I can do for you coming after us."

"Thank you!" Buckalew said with a rare smile, sticking the coin quickly in his pocket, forgetting about the search. "This is a more generous offer than the warden had ever given me." so the guard thought.

All was working well for Orson so far, as Buckalew led them to the poker table to await Buck Dupree. The guard figured Orson was rich and generous and passed him as unarmed. When the men were seated, the sheriff continued to case the room, looking for another way out.

Cain just sat there thinking about why Johnson had lied about Buck Dupree. He obviously knew Buck was here and yet he lied. "Why would he do that?" he wondered.

Buckalew only thought of the other gold coins the riverboat gambler might have on him. "Just before I throw their bodies to the gators, "I'll strip search 'em. He had seen enough men die at his hand to become fixated on death and had actually come to enjoy seeing his victims draw their last breath. The gators had become friends who appreciated a meal that was offered with such pleasure. He smiled under his breath, as he imagined them begging for a bullet after feeling the affects of the arsenic.

Cain was now sure Orson had something up his sleeve, because he was normally a cheapskate and would never be so generous when it came to money. "With no governor's men for protection, and only an unarmed old man with me, we don't have much of a chance," Cain thought.

When Warden Carson entered, he seemed overly friendly as he talked to Cain and the sheriff, thinking they were fresh from the boats. He questioned the men about weapons. Buckalew quickly answered for them, to let the warden know he had done his job. "Don't worry. They're clean. I searched 'em."

The sheriff silently took a deep breath, confident with his hidden pistols.

"So you men are in town for a night of poker?"

"We got a shortage of gamblers tonight but the man we have coming can give you a run for your money. Hope you men will enjoy the evening." The warden did not want to be encumbered with a room full of gamblers when he intended to poison and rob the gamblers.

"We hear this is the place," the sheriff answered.

"Well, we're glad to have you. Let me get you boys a drink."

He turned and nodded for Buckalew to get the jug. The sheriff gave Cain a grin as if to say, "Son, don't worry. I got it under control."

Cain nodded to the sheriff and began clumsily shuffling the cards. Orson very carefully unbuttoned his jacket to get ready for what might lie ahead.

Buckalew was in the next room, smiling as he mixed the whiskey with the arsenic. He picked up the jug to take a whiff, and grinned. *"Can't smell nothin' but whiskey."* The men continued to make small talk while waiting for Buck Dupree. Meanwhile, Vick was being escorted from his cell to the parlor. There was something special about this evening — mystery filled the air. "Who were these important guests?" Vick wondered.

Buckalew met Vick outside the door and gave him the last bit of instructions before they entered the parlor. "You're not going to like this, but no whiskey for you tonight, understand? Don't forget and mess up like ya did before when you used your real name. You're Buck Dupree, ya' hear? We got some of them fancy riverboat gambler's waiting for you, so keep your mind on the game."

Vick nodded "yes," but hated the thought of a poker night without a drink. Having a drink of whiskey now and then in this hole was all that kept him sane. Besides, he played better with a little buzz going on. He sure didn't have to be reminded about the beating he took, and he knew what the warden was capable of if he wanted to make his point. He remembered the shame Greasy felt after being castrated, cringing at the thought. He imagined the warden and Buckelew had a plan he didn't know about and it probably had something to do with the whiskey. "They're probably going to poison the poor suckers."

Vick looked the part all right, as he transformed himself from a rugged unkempt piece of scrap wood that lived with his ruthless fellow convicts, into a gentleman. He moved his hand that in no way resembled a convict's calloused hand over the fiber of his new clothing, and his cadence was that of a self-assured gentleman as he headed to the parlor. He picked up his cigar and walked with Buckalew into the parlor.

No one would guess this handsome, refined man entering the den of iniquity, was none other than Cain's Pa, and not the murderer Buck Dupree.

Just as the sheriff began making a poor attempt at shuffling, a tall handsome gambler walked in the door. Vick's only thought was to win. Cain and Orson looked at the man they thought to be Buck Dupree, then back at one another. Things didn't match up to either of them.

This man was well dressed, sported a beard, and did not look like one of the warden's prisoners, which puzzled them to no end.

Surely, there was a mistake. For a moment they thought all was in vain and now they were risking their lives for nothing, because this could not be Buck Dupree. "Perhaps Johnson was right," Cain thought, momentarily relieved to know he might have misjudged the father of the woman he planned to marry.

The sheriff studied the gambler they were going up against, deciding that someone of this man's stature could not possibly come from a prison environment. If the warden was using prisoners to forward his criminal activity, they surely couldn't look like this man; they would have to look totally different, something like Buckalew, the warden's trusted guard.

"Maybe we are being set up and this guard is really Buck Dupree," the sheriff thought.

Cain was confused, too, until the guard introduced the gambler as Buck Dupree.

"Buck here can give you a game. "Ain't no gamblers showed up Buck. I got a jug for ya here."

Vick gave a sharp look at the men sitting across from him, hoping they would not drink the whiskey. This is when he saw the striking resemblance of his dead brother, Sam, in Cain's face. Cain mistook Buck's look as intimidation. "He's an arrogant sonavobitch," Cain thought, as the sheriff continued to study the gambler's movements.

Finally, Vick, who was supposed to be Buck, looked up, and began to speak. The man's voice broke at first, but it sounded somewhat familiar as his voice became strong and clear. As much as he wanted to hear an accent he didn't.

"I've heard that voice before," Cain thought, not realizing the stranger's voice sounded like his own.

Vick didn't know what to think about this young man who favored his brother Sam. "*The kid's likeness is so much like Sammy's, and if he drinks the whiskey he will be a dead man, just like the brother who had meant so much to him.*" A warm feeling came over him, as he thought of the uncanny likeness to what Sam might have looked like as an adult.

For a moment he allowed himself to travel back to his childhood, when he and Sam were living at home with the Pa who had mistreated them. There again was that unmistakable bond that transcended time as he thought of a brother that had died many years ago. A man learns how to reminisce in a millimeter of a second in prison, a technique he developed as he longed to escape its walls. "That's the one thing no warden could take away from a man who was able to project himself beyond the walls of the prison," Vick reminded himself.

Vick quickly explored his memories and even thought of Hawk, his young Indian friend who he saved from the panther. He remembered how he believed Hawk when he said, "*I'll always be your protector,*" *after he had courageously saved his life. "If only that was true; I could use Hawk now.*"

He snapped out of it when he heard the warden say, "Okay boys, and let's get on with it."

Vick was curious and asked, "Gentlemen, you may want to introduce yourselves."

The warden wanted to kill Vick for acting so personable.

"I'm John Henry and this is Ben Thornell," Cain said, using their phony names. He continued trying to shuffle the cards, which was not going well for him. Vick noticed.

"Buck, what's your pleasure, Twisting the Tiger's Tail, Faro or Bucking the Tiger?" Cain asked, before the Faro board was set up. That was Vick's biggest clue that these men were not who they purported themselves to be.

He was speechless, almost dropping his cigar. "No one has ever used that trick, except Buck Dupree and me. Vick continued to study the men without the warden's knowledge. "This kid hardly knows how to shuffle the cards. Something is going on, those eyes, there's something about those eyes that I know," Vick ascertained.

The sheriff was trying to figure out the same thing. He noticed a familiarity about Vick he could not put his finger on.

Vick remained frozen trying to determine what in the heck was going on. "He wondered if he was losing his mind altogether, mixing dreams with reality … both of these men look so familiar. Where could he have met them? The young one, so much like Sam."

The warden came over to pour the first round of whiskey, as a cue for Vick to get the game moving. Cain picked up the jigger of whiskey, while Vick was in a quandary as to what to do. He thought, "I can't allow a young man who looks like my brother drink that stuff, no matter who he is."

Everything seemed to be happening in slow motion, while Cain waiting for the Faro board to be set up. He was about to touch his lips to the poisoned glass of whiskey, when the sheriff jumped up and pushed the game table over, shocking Vick back to the moment.

"This man here ain't Buck Dupree … this man is Vick Porter!"

Pulling the pistols out of his coat Orson quickly tossed one to Vick, who easily caught it an went into action. He turned just in time to clip one of the guards.

The warden and Buckalew were scuffing around trying to figure out what was happening, while three more guards entered the room and began to draw their guns. Cain was standing there looking on, close to panic. Vick, with the instinct of a gunfighter who now had a gun, jumped Cain and held him to the floor. Before Cain knew it, Vick had him in a roll.

The guards reached for their guns, but Vick and Sheriff Cargill were as coordinated as if they had worked together for years. The warden and the guards never had a chance, for Vick and Orson were faster than greased lightning. They were crawling under tables, seeking refuge from the bullets that the sheriff and Vick were firing. A gun battle ensued. Some people were hit, and others were trying desperately not to be hit.

Cain was oblivious to what was happening and wondered, *"Why is Buck Dupree helping the sheriff?"* It had not registered that Buck Dupree was none other than his father, Vick Porter.

After Vick rolled Cain across the floor he hastily crawled behind the overturned table while the sheriff and Vick exchanged gunfire with the guards, blasting away at the lanterns filled with oil. The warden was crouched behind another table returning gunfire.

Amidst the bullets the guards continued to scatter. Some laid still, either dead or playing possum. But it didn't fool the sheriff, who continued to shoot just above their heads, penning them down.

The sheriff blasted the last reservoir of oil near a guard who went for his shotgun. When the oil spilled all over him, he immediately erupted in flames, screaming in pain as he ran out the door.

Vick hit the floor, rolling toward the other guards as they were trying to flee, wounding or killing them before they left the parlor. Cain worried that the sheriff might be killed and still wondered why he was working with Buck Dupree. Cain was embarrassed that he did not know how to safely use a gun and at that moment, seeing these two men go up against a room full of men, he resolved to learn to use a gun. The last scene Cain remembered was the sheriff bouncing off a table, then rolling and tumbling like a twenty-year-old, nailing Buckalew with a bullet in the chest. The guard grunted and said, "Damn, you hit me ..." then fell with a thud.

Vick shouted, "Orson, leave Buckalew to me," but it was too late. Just as the gunfire stopped, four of the governor's men came running in with guns drawn. Vick thought the men were more guards from the prison and was turning to fire when the sheriff jumped him, throwing him to the floor. "No more, Vick, don't shoot. It's over."

The sheriff was laying on top of Vick looking him square in the eyes. Vick was staring up at Orson, amazed. Vick said, "Orson, I can't believe you're here. What took you so long?"

The sheriff laughed, "Yeah, it's me all right ... I knew that voice of yours, the minute I heard it. Damn, you're a hard one to find. Took me twenty years, but reckon you're going to be a free man after today."

Cain and Vick exchanged looks, but neither of them quite understood what was going on. As they looked around several guards were found dead, but two were squirming in pain. The warden knew his world had come to an end. He was still hiding, crouched behind a table, waiting for his chance to slip out of a window. Seeing Carson's reflection in the window, a state deputy with gun drawn said, "Warden Carson! It's over, stand and put your hands in the air! Now!"

The warden placed his hands behind his head as so many of his prisoners had done over these decades, and slowly stood. He held his head in total disbelief. The thought of hanging was a mighty grim fate.

The governor's deputies held their guns on the warden, who tried desperately to make one last ploy, saying "Easy boys, you've made a mistake. I'm the warden, and this man here is my prisoner," pointing at Vick.

Cain was taking it all in, as he saw movement out of the corner of his eye. He turned and saw the wounded Buckalew reach his gun and turn it toward Cain. Everyone had assumed Buckalew was dead. Once again, Vick pulled Cain out of the way, and shot Buckalew right between the eyes. Cain, shocked from being handled, jerked himself away, completely confused, and dazed by what just happened. Vick walked over to the vicious, fallen guard, who was bleeding profusely. Buckalew tried to say something, but he died choking on his own blood.

One of the governor's officials walked over to Vick and patted him on the back.

"Are you all right?" Instead of Vick speaking, it was the sheriff who spoke up.

"I reckon, we are. We could have used your help a little sooner, but me and Vick took care of everything," he said, laughing.

The officer in charge walked around looking at all the men who were dead and wounded.

"Yeah, I'd say so. The warden's about the only one left alive.

Vick and Cain were still in the dark, trying to figure just who each person really was, and exactly what had just happened, while the warden was being handcuffed.

"Get this scum out of here," the official said to his men, motioning at Warden Carson.

He had a snarl on his face as he was led past Vick. "Looks like you're going home, why don't you have a drink on me and celebrate?"

With that, Vick walked over to the jug of tainted whiskey to pour a jigger full. He couldn't smell the content and decided there was another way to find out if his suspicions were correct. He walked up to the warden and threw it in his face. "You sorry sonavobitch, you were planning to poison them."

With the whiskey all over the warden's face and clothing, he looked comical as he turned his head side to side, frantically trying to wipe the poisoned whiskey from his eyes and face onto his shirt, while handcuffed behind his back.

"This is my way of finding out if the whiskey is poison," Vick said.

The sheriff laughed and said, "You ain't changed a bit!"

"Boys, bring that jug. We're gonna need it as evidence," the agent said.

Cain was staring here and there, still trying to figure out what had happened, "*how did the sheriff know this man who was supposed to be Dupree, and why were they working together.*"

They watched as the warden was led out of the door and into a prison wagon harnessed up to a mule.

Finally, the governor's agent approached Sheriff Cargill. "It looks like you all had an army of men behind you."

"No, just me and Vick here. Sir, thank you for coming. I don't reckon we know your name ..." Orson said.

"I'm Agent Adams and I'm happy to meet you all in person. I'm sorry we missed you at the hotel. A lady told me that you all left with a man who looked a little shady. I figured it must have been with one of the warden's men. That's why we're here. I reckon we owe you and Mr. Porter a debt of gratitude for your bravery. I don't know how you were able to pull this off. Vick, you are free to go."

He turned to Cain, who was still wondering why on earth the sheriff was working with Buck Dupree. "Cain Porter, I suppose you want to know what's going on? And you too, Vick!"

"Yeah, I reckon I do," they both said simultaneously.

"Well son, we didn't rightly know how to handle this. We thought about telling you that we suspected your father was using the name of Buck Dupree, but we couldn't take a chance. If you had known you were meeting your father today, you might have acted different and gotten yourself killed, so we let you and the sheriff think you were playing against Buck Dupree, who you were here to see, anyway."

Vick and Cain stood in awe unable to comprehend what was happening. The governor's agent knew Cain was trying to absorb the details as he tried to explain. "Vick, I want you to meet your son Cain. And Cain, this is your father, Vick Porter, who is not Buck Dupree."

Cain turned as white as a sheet, as the two just stood staring at each other. Neither did anything at first. Cain thought he was hearing things, stood wide-eyed and looked at Orson questioningly, then back at the agent.

"Did you say this man is my father? Vick Porter?"

"That's right, and Vick, this is your son, Cain."

"Just a minute, there must be a mistake. I don't have a son." Vick responded.

The sheriff saw the confusion on Vick's face and came to his aid. "Vick, you were always on the stubborn side, but yes, this is your son, Cain. After you left, Mattie had a baby.

Vick's mind was spinning a mile a minute, as he looked at his son and thought of the enormity of what had just happened. What should have been a happy occasion was dampened by the fact that neither of the men could absorb that much information all at once.

Vick was thinking, *"If this really is my son, I should feel something, but I don't feel anything. How can this be?"*

Agent Adams tried to explain to Cain about why they had to trick him. Cain listened, but all he could think about was why Johnson Petty lied to him about not knowing his Pa was in prison.

His mother had been right all along about Johnson. He must have found out my Pa was in jail and for some twisted reason decided not to tell me. I wonder how he is going to feel when we go to Texas first. I want to see his face when I call him a lying sonavobitch. The sorry bastard could have gotten me and the sheriff killed. These thoughts swirled around in Cain's head.

Remembering Vick's actions in the gunfight, Cain thought, *"Vick must have had the instinct of a father by shielding him from being shot. He kept trying to listen to the agent, but all he could think of was Vick saving his life."*

He heard the agent continuing, "Cain, I want to tell you that after Arkansas Governor Wade contacted us, we had to do a little investigating ourselves. We found out the man using Buck Dupree's name was your Pa, Vick Porter, and he was being held in prison, and was being used in the warden's poker scheme.

"We're sorry to keep this from you and you, Sheriff Cargill, but we couldn't have you blowing our cover. Once again, we apologize. I suspect if you hadn't contacted us when you did your Pa might have spent many more years in prison because of Warden Carson. He wasn't about to give up the wealth he was making off of your father."

Vick was definitely in overload, trying desperately to focus, but all he could think about was Mattie. "*She must have had a baby soon after I left town,*" he thought. Everything was happening so fast he hardly knew how to react. This was his son and he was at a loss for words. He imagined it was as big a mystery to Cain as it was to him, so instead of grabbing and hugging one another, they both continued to stare at each other.

The agent turned to Cain and gave him a pat on the back. "Cain, lucky for you, the sheriff was with you. He was a brave man bringing his guns in a place like this."

Chapter 30

CAIN, WAS STILL SHAKEN AND CONFUSED, STANDING QUIETLY OBSERVING the relationship between Orson and Vick. Why didn't Orson tell him that he and his Pa were such close friends? He was mesmerized as he studied Vick, so tall and regal looking. After being locked up for twenty years in one of the most corrupt prisons in Louisiana history, one might expect to see a broken man. But instead, Cain saw a handsome, well-spoken, and evidently well fed gentleman-type, who seemed to be anything but a prisoner.

Trying not to seem aloof, Cain walked closer to the men, while they stood patting each other on the back and shaking hands.

"Good to see you, Orson!

The sheriff smiled broadly and patted Vick on the back as he glanced at Cain. "The minute I got a good look at you, , I knew you were Vick. Ya hardly changed at all, 'ceptin' for yer thick beard."

Vick put his arm around the sheriff and walked toward his son. Cain gave Vick that huckleberry smile that Vick had always been known for, then shook hands.

"Well, I don't rightly know what to say. Reckon I'm as surprised as you, learning you're my son. I thought I was looking at my brother, Sammy, who's been dead almost thirty years. That smile gave it away, but I couldn't quite figure out what!

Cain had heard of Sam, but he still did not know what to say. Finally, he spoke. "I remember hearing about my uncle and how he died. I hope you don't mind if I call you Vick, since we just met."

"No, not at all. I wouldn't expect you to call me anything else."

"You caught me off guard though, when you wrestled me to the floor. I owe you. One of those bullets would have hit me, if it hadn't been for you," Cain said.

"Well, I couldn't let them shoot you before we had a chance to meet." His son didn't appear to catch the joke.

His main fear was breaking the news to his mother about Vick being alive and well. There would be no time to prepare her, and he was concerned that hearing the news would upset her. The fact was that he knew very little about Vick and his mother's relationship, since she tried to shield him from all the details as to why they hadn't got along when they first met. She had always thought that the least Cain knew the better, and concentrated on teaching him that his Pa was a good man, incapable of murder.

"Mind if I ask how you knew I was in prison?"

"Vick, we don't want to disappoint ya, but it was Buck Dupree we were here to see. We had no idea Buck Dupree was goin' to end up being you."

"I guess that lie finally paid off.

"What lie is that?" Orson asked.

"Calling myself Buck Dupree. Just don't start calling me Buck now." Vick's smile turned stoic, when he noticed Cain was still preoccupied.

It was apparent the two strangers had difficulty communicating. Orson could read Cain like a book, and he knew it was his mama he was thinking of and how he was gonna break the news to her about Vick being alive. That is going to be interesting, knowing their history," he imagined.

"Vick, your son here is a lawyer, and he's the one that got them charges agin' ya dropped. Ya owe it to him that you're a free man."

Vick turned Orson, smiling broadly, "Guess that means you won't be arresting me when we get back home."

The sheriff chuckled hearing Vick crack a joke, although Cain remained unfazed.

"I was jest lookin' at how much y'all favor one another. There ain't no denying that y'all are blood related 'cause you look jest alike."

Vick blushed as he tried to hide his embarrassment.

He looked at his son who was definitely preoccupied and thought developing a relationship with Cain was going to take some work.

Imprisonment had definitely taken a toll on Vick, even if it wasn't visible. Perhaps one day he would share what he had been through, but for now, all he wanted was to forget the last twenty years and enjoy being free.

"You two showing up when you did, proved to me one thing: Regardless of how you begin your day, by nightfall everything could change. I want to thank you for finding me."

"Vick it wasn't just me, there was someone else that had a big part in your being free," Vick broke in, assuming that the "someone" was Mattie, Cain's mother.

"What about Mattie? Is she home or did she come with you?" Vick asked. Cain had no idea how to reply and turned to the sheriff for help. Orson walked over to Vick and placed his hand on his shoulder.

"Why don't we get outta here and talk back at the hotel. You know, twenty years is a long time, and thang's' happen. Do you want to have some time to get your thang's together?"

"Thanks Orson, but I'm set. I don't want any reminders."

Vick knew he was about to receive some bad news; possibly that Mattie was married. The sheriff put his hand on his shoulder and led him out.

"Vick, do you mind giving me a minute to talk to the sheriff?" Cain asked.

"No, not at all. Go ahead, and take all the time you need."

Vick was sure that Cain was trying to figure out how to tell him Mattie was married. The sheriff and Cain walked away so they could be private.

"Son, I know what' ya gonna say. It's about Lizzie ain't it"?

"Orson, I need some time. There's a saloon next to the hotel. Why don't you take Vick in for a drink and give me time to break the news to Ma? I also need some time to place a few things in Vick's room that he might need."

"Ya mean clothes and thang's like that?"

"Yeah, we look about the same size. You know, mama's going to panic when she hears he's alive."

"I'll give ya' all the time ya' need."

The last thing Vick wanted was to have Cain concerned about him. He was free now and that was all that mattered. "Anything else can slide. After all, letting things slide has been what's kept me sane all these years."

It had been only a few minutes when the governor's agent drove up in a shiny new Model T to escort them back to the hotel.

"How about this?" the sheriff asked, pointing at the car.

Vick ran his hand over the automobile fender but did not say a word. Ordinarily he would have been excited with the mechanics and luxury of the car, but he chose to control his excitement and not act like a kid in a candy store. "I'll take one day at a time," he thought to himself.

Cain sat up front with the governor's agent, while Vick and the sheriff sat in the back. No one spoke a word on the drive back to the hotel. Downtown New Orleans was beautiful at night with bright lights that held Vick spellbound. Almost immediately, he felt right at home; feeling like a million dollars with the clothes and bankroll the warden had given him. "Things could not have worked out better," he thought.

Vick saw Cain walk toward the hotel entrance as the sheriff steered Vick to the saloon next door.

"Vick, I reckon we need to talk," Orson said.

Vick was sure it was about Mattie being married, never imagining that his joy was about to be wiped out by sadness brought on by something far worse.

"Why don't we grab a table in the far corner where we can talk? And don't 'git your hopes up 'bout places like this back home, 'cause there ain't none. Our town has grown some but not a whole lot.

"Vick smiled," as he thought of Mattie.

Orson found a nice little corner and sat down, motioning the bartender to bring over a bottle and glasses. Vick's eyes darted from the array of whiskey and glasses under the lantern light, and saw they were in a large saloon. Simple things were exciting to him, such as the wooden stairway that led to the rooms he imagined were for the ladies of the evening.

"Why don't we get on with this Orson. I know Mattie is probably married by now. No woman's going to wait this long for a man."

"Vick I don't rightly know how t' say this, but it ain't what ya think. A lot happened after ya left. When Cain was four years old, his mama died." The sheriff saw the blood drain from Vick's face, as he struggled to compose himself.

"Mattie's dead?"

"Yes." "Yeah, Mattie is dead." The sheriff sat quietly allowing him time to absorb the news.

Finally, Vick spoke. "All these years I thought she was alive. I wouldn't have made it without thinking of getting out and back to her. I kept hanging on, thinking one day I might get out of prison and we'd be able to pick up where we left off. I can't believe she's dead."

"I hated to be the one to tell ya, but now ya know."

Vick hung his head and thought, "The two people I've loved the most are dead. First Sam and now Mattie."

"I know ya' wonderin' how she died. It was her heart, and, after she had Cain, it was' too much fer her. She hung on as best she could fer him, and she always hung onto the hope that you might return home some day."

The sheriff grabbed the whiskey bottle and a glass, to pour Vick a drink.

Next door in the hotel, Elizabeth awaited news from Cain and the sheriff. When she saw her son walk into the hotel without Orson, she knew something was wrong. She was seated at a rosewood desk in a room off from the lobby, writing when Cain approached her. Elizabeth was almost panicked.

"Cain, please tell me that Orson is okay, and nothing has happened to him?"

"Don't get all worked up, the sheriff is fine. He's next door in the saloon, so I can talk to you alone." He belabored how to tell his mother that Vick was alive. "*She's not going to take this well,*" he thought.

"You're scaring me, what happened?"

Cain sat down opposite Elizabeth, almost afraid to speak. "I don't know how to tell you this but, when we went into the card game, the man we thought was Buck Dupree turned out to be my father."

"What?! You mean Vick?"

"Yes, Vick. Apparently, he was calling himself Buck Dupree to draw attention to anyone that might help him from the outside."

"He's been in prison all this time?" Elizabeth asked.

"Yes, he's been right here in the New Orleans prison for almost twenty years."

Elizabeth's reaction was not at all what he expected, which was somewhat confusing to him.

"Cain, are you sure it's Vick? Are you positive it's him?" Elizabeth didn't even fully realize she was thrilled at the good news.

"Without a doubt, he looks and sounds just like me. The sheriff recognized him right away and called him by name. There was something else that happened ... Vick actually saved my life during a gunfight." Cain continued to examine his mother and the way she responded to the news.

"Oh my, I knew this was dangerous. Did you get hurt?" she asked as she looked him over and saw no bandages.

"I'm okay, but the warden was arrested and Orson and Vick took care of the guards."

"I can't believe that Vick is alive! Oh, and I'm so glad you're here and safe. Are you sure, honest to Pete sure that the man is Vick?"

"Yes, I'm sure, and I might add you're taking this quite well." Elizabeth tried to control her exuberance, knowing Cain had no idea of what her true feelings for Vick were.

"I'm just glad you're okay. You know what this means, don't you? Johnson Petty knew all along that your Pa was in that awful prison. And he lied to you."

"Now don't go jumping to conclusions we'll find out soon enough."

"Mom, knowing the history between you and my Vick, I must say you are surprising me.

"I have no idea what you're talking about."

"You seem excited as if your long lost cousin has returned. We're talking about Vick Porter and you're smiling."

"No son, what you see is how happy I am that you know Johnson Petty is a liar. Where is your Pa now? Does he know about me and where I'm living?"

"Calm down, I don't want you getting all crazy on me. I think the sheriff is filling him in. They're in the saloon next door, and I'm sure he knows everything by now."

"I can't believe all this time he has been alive in that horrible prison. Cain, I'm sorry but I can't see Vick now, not tonight."

"You're not leaving? ..."

"I need some time. I'll see you in the morning." she said as she turned from Cain and went to her room.

Orson had no idea how Vick would be affected by Mattie's death. He poured him a drink.

"You think I need a whiskey?"

"Yeah, cause there's more to come."

Vick looked stunned. "More?"

"I think you better hear me out," said the sheriff. "Remember all them years ago when I let ya ride on instead of arresting ya?"

"How could I forget? It's likely I would have been hung if it wasn't for you."

"When I let you go, that was the first time I ever broke the law, 'cause I knew ya was innocent. When ya left, ya didn't know Mattie was pregnant. Poor girl didn't know what to do raising a child and running a lumber company, so she reached out to Elizabeth for help."

"Elizabeth?… old man Barkin's daughter?"

"That's right, Lizzie came right away, Mattie asked her to move back into the manor to help her run the house and the lumber company. I don't know what Mattie would have done without her. Now, I'm about to tell ya something ya might not understand."

"Orson, spare me if it's about Elizabeth Barkin."

"No, it ain't what ya thank. Now, you listen to me."

"It can't be any worse than finding out Mattie died, so let's have it and don't hold anything back."

"If ya say so. Anyway, Mattie asked Lizzie to adopt Cain before she died."

"Are you kidding me? You mean Elizabeth Barkin is now Cain's mother?

"I know, ya ain't liking that Cain's been adopted, but she's been a good mother to him, educating and even helping ya git exonerated."

"Elizabeth Barkin helped me? Imagine that! So that's who Cain was talking about when he said there was someone else who had a part in my freedom. I'm really surprised, especially since I remember the history we had with one another. What you're telling me now doesn't even sound like the Elizabeth I knew."

"I spec' ya might find in life we all change, sometimes for the better and sometimes for the worse, but in Elizabeth's case, she's changed for the better, and … you two got off on the wrong foot way back there."

"I reckon she's going to think I'm not fit to be Cain's Pa."

"Let's jes wait and see how thang's' work out."

The sheriff could see Vick's confusion. "Anyway, after Elizabeth left the manor, she went to live with her aunt in St. Louis, and they was poor as mice. When Mattie needed help, she found out where Elizabeth was and contacted her to come back and help her run your company.

"When they didn't hear from ya, they figured ya wer' dead. After Mattie had Cain, she started having trouble and that's when she found out she was gonna die. They was like sisters them two. Elizabeth nursed and took care of Mattie until she drew her last breath. Mattie had Elizabeth adopt Cain before she passed away."

"Who would have guessed, and I thought it couldn't get worse."

"Now, don't go acting up."

"What do you mean? We're talking about Elizabeth Barkin!"

"Vick, she's been a good mother to Cain … She loved him, educated, and took care of him like her own. So … don't ever make her feel she ain't Cain's mother 'cause she is, and always has been ever since he was born, helping Mattie with him those first four years."

"Orson, I knew you had some news, but I didn't expect a twisted tale like this. You've sprung too much information on me. I don't know if I can handle all the problems you just handed me. Maybe we should do like we did twenty years ago and let me ride on. I don't want to come between Elizabeth and Cain. And I'll never be more than a stranger to him." "Now you listen here! Ya ain't riding on nowhere. Ther' ain't really no reason to run now. I know this is all a big shock to yer' system, but it was my place to tell ya, so now all you have to do is deal with it."

"Are you sure this is all, nothing else?"

"Well, maybe one other thang'. She's made you into a very wealthy man with yer' Porter lumber company and that cotton business she's leaning to, but I reckon she can tell you all about that when she sees ya."

"I'm not ready to see Elizabeth tonight, maybe never. I know you and Cain may want me to march in and greet her with open arms, but it ain't going to happen. So please, you go and talk to Cain about this. It's going to take me time."

"This here is somepin' ya gonna have to hit head on, cause ya done wasted too much time in that prison."

Cain walked in to the saloon where the sheriff and Vick were talking.

Vick took another drink of whiskey and looked up to see Cain standing over him.

"I suppose you know the story by now?" Cain asked.

Vick took a big gulp from his glass and the whiskey went straight to his head. He went into overload and nothing was going to stop him from saying what he wanted to say.

"Cain, you and Elizabeth don't need to worry about me barging in and taking over your lives. I just want to thank you both for having me cleared, but I am not here to cause either of you any problems. I can make it on my own." Vick was like a whipped pup, stunned at all the news. Orson patted him on the shoulder as they sat there, and they had more rounds. The sheriff was doing most of the talking, while Vick drank and Cain listened."

"Vick, I have to' tell ya one other thang". Elizabeth knows all the good thangs ya did and she's ashamed of what her Pa done. She don't hold you responsible for him killing hisself. I jest hope ya can give Lizzie the break she deserves."

"Orson, I think we've had enough talk for one night. All I want to think about is how lucky I am to be a free man and sleep in a real bed."

Vick got up and dropped enough money on the table to cover the tab and a nice tip, patted Cain on the back and started for the door.

"I don't know about ya'll, but I'm beat," Vick said.

"Well, wait for us. Cain's got yer room key."

Vick stopped long enough for Orson and Cain to catch up.

"Vick, before you go to your room, I hope you don't mind, but I shared some clothes and my shaving kit with you. I think you'll find everything you need in your room," Cain said.

For some reason Cain's words didn't set right. It may have been the whiskey talking or a mixture of emotion that caused him to have an outburst. "Cain, I don't know if you know, but underneath my beard I have a big ugly scar. If you don't mind, I'll keep my beard."

"Vick, hang on a minute! Cain, weren't telling' ya that ya need a shave. The boy was just trying to let ya know he was helping."

Vick took the key from Cain and kept walking until he got to his door and stopped.

"I want to set something straight; I've been told what to do for over twenty years. I've been directed and kicked around like a dog, so let's try to stay out of each other's business. See you in the morning."

The sheriff and Cain were left stunned as Vick closed the door to his room.

"Cain, don't take nothing yer' Pa said to heart. He'll be all right. Once he has time to thank an sobers up, he'll be just like his old self.

"Thanks for warning me, but the man's got an attitude."

"I jest unloaded a lot on your Pa; give em' time. I had to tell him bout' yer' real Ma 'dyin."

As Vick entered his nice fresh hotel room, it was like turning on a new switch. His attitude immediately changed from depression of hearing the news of Mattie's death, to the reality of freedom. "Life is bitter sweet. Free!" he thought.

Vick walked through his room touching and feeling the fine furniture, marveling at the difference from where he had lived only a few hours before. It was breathtakingly quiet, no more clangs from the iron bars that had closed behind him for the twenty years he slept in a dark dank cell.

He sat on his bed and gave it a few exuberant bounces, knowing from now on he would be sleeping in comfort without the sounds of prisoners interrupting the solitude of his thoughts, with screams and obscenities throughout the night. Only the night before he had been sleeping on a hardwood bed with just a blanket, but as of tonight, his entire life had changed. "Things don't have to work out," Vick thought to himself. "I'm a free man and that's all that matters." He looked in his closet and found clothing that Cain had shared with him and felt ashamed that he had been so ungrateful.

Lying there in his soft bed after a hot shower, Vick remembered how cold and unapproachable Elizabeth had been. "I haven't thought of her in years, and now it seems she is the center of my thoughts."

The next morning when Vick opened his eyes, it took a moment for him to realize where he was. He had to pinch himself to be sure he wasn't dreaming. His only thought was his freedom, something he thought would never happen. His only hurdle was accepting Mattie's death, but there was no need to continue to mourn her passing, when she had been dead nearly as long as he had been in prison. The most important thing was to enjoy now and his new life of freedom.

Cain wondered if the meeting between Vick and his Ma would cordial. He had seen Elizabeth in action before, and knew she was very capable of being territorial where he was concerned, and for his Pa's sake, he hoped she would be civil.

When Cain knocked on his mother's door, he could see that she had been crying. Her eyes were red and puffy, although powdered to conceal any evidence she had been upset. Other than that, Cain thought she looked to be in her thirties. She looked absolutely gorgeous.

"Did you sleep well?" he asked, trying to defuse his concern that she had been crying. Elizabeth immediately put her glasses on so not to be obvious. "I'm all right Cain. Please don't read much into this. I'm just fine. Are you ready to go?"

"Mother, I hope you will keep an open mind. They're going to meet us for breakfast."

"By 'they,' I suppose you mean Orson and Vick. And please, don't worry about me. I know how to handle myself."

"Are you up for it? I don't think Vick is going to give you a hard time."

"I'd rather hear that from him. Now, are you ready for breakfast?"

"Lead the way," Cain said. He knew his mother was wound up as tight as a fiddle.

Elizabeth patted her son on the cheek, picked up her umbrella and a small tote, and walked bravely down the stairs straight toward the breakfast room. When she got to the door she paused, took a deep breath, and walked slowly toward the table where the men were seated. But before she got there, she could feel her knees become weak. All she saw was the back of Vick's head and suddenly reality set in. She had no idea what she would say or how she would act.

Vick and the sheriff rose from their chairs when Orson saw Cain and Elizabeth walking toward them.

When she reached the table, she looked at Vick and gave him a faint smile, while holding out her hand. Instead of squeezing it as a welcoming gesture, he placed her hand to his lips as if to wave a flag of surrender. This shocked Elizabeth, who had not expected such charm, and surprised Vick, who had not planned to kiss her hand.

As Vick graciously pulled her chair out for her, she said, "Thank you Vick," in a shy melodic voice.

Her first impression was that he was even more handsome than she remembered. She recalled Vick as a very attractive young man of nineteen, but this more mature man made her tremble within.

She felt her heart race as she sat looking into the eyes of the man she thought was dead. *"And here he is alive,"* Elizabeth thought.

Vick had no idea what kind of effect he had on Elizabeth, especially since he had not allowed any other woman but Mattie to occupy his thoughts until now. As he studied Elizabeth, he was reassured that she had indeed changed, just as the sheriff had said. Being in prison for twenty years degraded Vick, so that he never felt he was anything but ordinary and certainly not someone that would appeal to Elizabeth. He had not given much thought to women, for Mattie had been his world, and another woman had simply never captured his thoughts. However, seeing Elizabeth again was very sobering. He was now sure that she was not the same as he remembered in the early days.

"It's good to see you again Elizabeth," Vick said with a low mellow voice that excited her. She was as much a mystery to Vick as he was to her. What he wanted more than anything was to be straightforward and transparent. However, the waiter interceded and poured coffee for everyone before Vick could muster up the courage to speak. Thus, they ended up making small talk for a while, until Vick sensed the time was right.

"Elizabeth, I hope you don't mind me getting right to the point. I'm glad we have witnesses to hear what I have to say ..."

She held her breath thinking, *"He is so serious."*

"In case you and Cain are wondering, I want you both to know I'm not going to create problems for you. I can take care of myself and make my own way. Right now, the most important thing to me is my freedom and what I intend to do with the rest of my life."

The sheriff could read the look on Cain's face. He was thinking his Pa might be leaving. "Now you're forgetting something, Vick. You have a son that needs to get to know his Pa. He's gone through a lot to get you exonerated and, ya thanking 'bout moving on right away? This ain't fair to Cain."

"Orson, if that's what Vick wants to do, I don't want to be the one to stop him," Cain said, trying not to appear disappointed.

"Please, I'm not finished, don't put words in my mouth" Vick broke in. "I've had time to think this morning, and Elizabeth, I know you feel a little awkward that I'm the father of Cain! That's certainly understandable, but you've done such a good job raising him, that there is no way I want to interfere with you. I have my freedom, thanks to Cain and Orson."

Cain was grateful for what Vick said, but he needed to set the record straight about his mother's participation in winning his freedom.

"Vick, I think you need to know it was my Mother who found the proof that cleared you. She read the little red book that was in with the treasure."

"I don't remember a book. What book is that?"

"Don't you remember the bloodstained book you tore pages out of to stop the bleeding on your face?"

Vick had to think back. "Now, I remember, he said.

"I don't know why it took us so long to read it, but when Mother and I forgot to put the book back with the treasure she read it and found out Buck was the one who murdered that poor family. It was the little girl's diary. Her name was Janie, and she wrote about everything that happened right up until the minute before she and her little brother were murdered."

Vick sat speechless for a while, trying to absorb all the details.

"I don't quite know what to say. All these years and the truth was right there under our nose. Elizabeth, thank you."

She responded, "I only wish we would have read it sooner."

"I can't imagine what the children went through before Buck killed them," Vick mentioned.

Orson went on explaining about Elizabeth being responsible for Vick winning his freedom.

"After Lizzie read the diary that's when me 'n Cain went to see Governor Wade in Little Rock who dropped all them charges agin' ya."

Vick looked at Elizabeth and thought again, "this is not the woman I remember." Her eyes were different. They were the eyes of kindness and suffering, yet strong and intelligent. "I'm sure this can't be the woman I remembered."

"Vick, I do want you to know how much I loved Mattie. She was a wonderful person and the best mother to Cain. Before she died, she asked me to adopt him and it has been the best decision of my life. He is my son and there is nothing I wouldn't do for him."

"I don't know about ya'll, but I'm tired gettin' a little homesick. Now that we have everthang' all squared away and Vick here is out of the 'clinker,' do ya know when we might be goin' home?" Orson asked.

"Well, not before we have breakfast." Vick answered. "Orson, it's been a very long time since I've had your kind of breakfast."

"Well, let's git' on with it, so we can git' home."

"You're all going to have to consider making one more stop with me," said Cain, as breakfast was being served.

"Oh, no you don't, Cain! You can't ask me to take another step in that man's house!"

"One more stop. Me and Mother need to pay a visit to Johnson Petty." Vick was stunned hearing Johnson Petty's name.

"Excuse me Cain, but did you say Johnson Petty?"

"I figured you would recognize the name," Orson said.

"Better yet, how well do you know the man?" Vick asked.

"I knew him well enough to trust him. It's a long story, but the bottom line was Johnson knew who you really were and didn't tell me. I was in Louisiana with him the last time you saw him. There's a lot more to the story but him and me came to New Orleans to have a game with Buck Dupree, who later turned out to be you. I need answers of why he lied."

"So that's why Johnson came back? Actually, I didn't play poker with him the last time he was here.

"But that's not all; I'm committed to marry Johnson's daughter Eileen. Now you can see why it's imperative that I get answers. Vick, since you remember Johnson, are you sure he knew who you really were?"

"He knew all right for I took the beating of my life for using my real name. I recognized Johnson right away. The first time I played against him, I said, my name was Buck Dupree. Then later, when he came back, I used my real name. This is when I got in hot water with the warden, who nearly beat me to death. My plan was to alert and confuse Johnson by using my real name, hoping he might think something shady was going on and help me. But when help never came, I decided he simply did not want to get involved."

"If he had been truthful, you would have already been out and me and the sheriff would not have risked our lives. Guess he didn't know that we would find out. To me this is the ultimate betrayal," Cain said. "And I need to know why."

"The man had quite a temper. He has no idea that I saved him from being killed."

"I heard they robbed the gamblers then threw their bodies to the gators," Cain reported.

"Well, I didn't want to mention that in front of your mother. All I can say is the warden's men were animals, and when they smelled money they would do anything to keep it. If Johnson would have beat me, he would have been thrown to the gators as soon as he left the parlor."

Elizabeth cringed when she realized how close to death her son and the sheriff had come.

"Thank God this is over, and to think that Orson and Cain could have been victims. I know this sounds harsh, but I could care less what happened to Johnson."

"Now Ma, why can't you tell the truth and admit you have a thing for Johnson Petty." Cain looked at his mother and instantly knew he had said the wrong thing.

Vick saw Elizabeth's face turn from a soft ivory to beet red. "Why would she have been so embarrassed," Vick wondered.

"Cain! How could you embarrass me with such nonsense?"

"Mother, you do act like a woman in love."

"You couldn't be more wrong. I despise him for lying to us. He knew your father was in prison and he kept it from you. I still don't know how you could want to be in a family with this kind of deception."

"You seem to forget I have feelings for Eileen."

Vick saw that Elizabeth was in a tight spot and needed some help. "Cain, I think you should never speak for your mother. Can't you see you embarrassed her?"

Elizabeth could not believe Vick was so thoughtful to correct their son. "He was definitely his own man," she thought.

When breakfast was over Vick asked to speak to Elizabeth privately. "Orson, would you and Cain excuse us? I think I would like to talk with Elizabeth alone."

Neither the sheriff nor Cain could believe how engaging Vick was with Elizabeth.

"Do you mind having coffee in the parlor so we can talk?" he asked.

Elizabeth led the way, with her umbrella and tote, to a cozy area in the tearoom. She and Vick sat in a private section of the room that reeked of romance with all its lace and frills.

It was an exciting room accented with ivory lamps and antique beaded shades, with dimly lit kerosene lights. As Vick pulled the chair out for her, his body faintly brushed against her arm, which sent chills through her body.

Vick wanted nothing more than to clear the air with Elizabeth, and let her know that he did not want to disrupt her life. He knew she must have reservations because of him winning their wealthy estate in a card game resulting in her father committing suicide. It was best to solve the problem before they left New Orleans if at all possible, he thought. He had no idea of the feelings she had for him.

"Elizabeth, I hope you did not mind but I … uh, we … need this time together for many reasons. One, so I can explain to you what happened with your father and me."

"Vick really, you don't have to go into my Pa's past. I know the whole story and I don't blame you at all. My Aunt Connie, with whom I lived after I left the manor, I found out all about my Pa. Aunt Connie shared some dark secrets with me about what she knew about him. He was not the man I thought he was. I've tried to forget how many people he wronged..

"What my aunt didn't find out about you, I found out later from Mattie after I came to live with her. She told me what you did for our town, giving the men back what my father had stolen from them. This took a remarkable amount of courage and unselfishness on your part, and it really impressed me about the kind of man you are. I've always felt that way. Mattie explained everything and you don't owe me any explanation."

"Thank you Elizabeth. I appreciate your understanding."

"And as far as my father, I discovered I truly never knew him."

"If you don't mind, there is one thing that has puzzled me all these years about you, and that's when you failed to show up for dinner all those years ago. Remember the time you were invited to dinner and never came?"

"Yes, I do actually. I have very few memories that far back, but this is one I do remember. I don't mind telling you now, but back then you would never have understood. I was getting ready to leave to meet with you and your Pa, when Mattie showed up at my door crying about a relative who died. I don't remember who it was now, but she was upset and I didn't know how to tell her about you and your father having supper waiting for me. Mattie kept crying and I tried to console her. I don't know if you knew, but Mattie was the one who took care of my Pa when he was dying until I returned home. So Elizabeth, that's what happened. I just couldn't ask her to leave. I know it's twenty years too late, but I do apologize."

Elizabeth smiled, "I accept your apology, but why didn't you tell me so I would have understood?"

"Truth? Because I thought you and your daddy were basically un-approachable. I doubt that either of you would have believed me. I knew the kind of man your daddy was, and realized that he was not the forgiving type."

"You're probably right, but I think I would have understood if you had made more of an effort. And for your information, I was never like my father."

"If I could go back and do things over, there would be a great many things I would have done differently. I know you have to be concerned about the manor, but don't be … it's all yours and Cain's. I've been living in an 8-by-8 cell all these years, and I can find my way without imposing on you or anyone."

"You will do no such thing! That house is big enough for all three of us."

Vick was somewhat surprised.

"Elizabeth please, I know how people talk and I don't think I can put you through that. Don't worry about me, I'll find a room in town and give you and Cain the space you need. Enough said. I've made up my mind!"

"You know the house is yours, anytime you want it," Elizabeth offered.

"This is something you didn't know, but the manor was always yours. Now, it's yours and Cain's.

Elizabeth did a good job of concealing her feelings from the clueless Vick, as they continued to talk well into the afternoon, which they both enjoyed immensely. She talked about the Porter Lumber Company and the status of her cotton business.

Chapter 31

EARLY THE NEXT MORNING CAIN AND VICK LOADED THEIR AUTOMOBILE and left New Orleans, headed toward the Piney Woods of East Texas. Elizabeth was in the front seat with Cain driving and Orson and Vick sat in the back, enjoying the sights as they drove through the streets of downtown New Orleans.

"One day at a time," Vick thought, as the little car loaded to the brim — mostly with Elizabeth's bags — pulled out of New Orleans. Vick's main concern was how he was going to fit into a world that had moved on without him. *"The woman I love is dead, and our son has been raised by another woman. My future is yet to unfold,"* he thought.

Leaving Louisiana and crossing into Texas, the Model T made its way northwest, and headed down the narrow road to San Augustine. They would pay an unexpected visit to Johnson Petty, and get to the bottom of why he lied, deceiving Cain about Vick being in prison. They would then head northeast to Arkansas.

All manner of wildlife scampered across the road: squirrels, armadillos and even a deer or two, as the little car hummed over hill after hill. Vick had not seen animals in such abundance since before he was imprisoned. It brought back memories of the good old days when he would leave Panther Holler and camp out overnight, hunting for his meat in the wild. He had always loved hunting, and killed enough to cook and cure in the smokehouse. These were some of his fondest memories he had growing up after running away from home.

Of course, those were the days prior to Buck Dupree turning his world upside down. Seeing all the wild game gave him an itch to get back to what he'd missed all those years.

Confronting Johnson Petty was not as important to Vick as it was to Cain, who was determined on finding out why Johnson had lied about him knowing Vick was in prison. One thing that Vick learned being in prison was, "not to sweat the small stuff. Twenty years is a long time to be denied the simple pleasures of life. *"Let them worry about Johnson Petty, if that's what is important to them. But for me, I'm a free man, and I intend to make up for lost time."*

He imagined how different things could have been if Mattie had lived. *"Certainly life would have been much simpler now that I have a son. I probably would have married her, reclaimed what was mine and gone on to being a Pa to Cain."* But life takes a direction of it's own. Now that Elizabeth has adopted my son, I really don't have much claim on anything. I may never get those lost years back or have a relationship with Cain," Vick imagined, *"and if not, I need to be prepared to deal with that."*

Being a father was going to be an adjustment, but the strong resemblance between Cain and his brother, Sam, seemed to be the force driving Vick to keep an open mind. Cain definitely looked like a Porter, but he did not have any of their mannerisms. "He must have taken after Mattie's side of the family," Vick thought.

As for Cain, his primary concern was his relationship with Eileen. Yet, Cain knew it was important for him to make room for a relationship with his Pa. It would be important for him to balance his time for the sake of the family.

"You asleep back there?" Cain asked. "Vick …what do you think about Texas?"

"I'm enjoying the scenery. You know, I was in Texas over twenty years ago when I left Arkansas… Orson I think you remember that day."

"That must have been when I let you go instead of bringing you in and let em' hang ya. Did you ever run into old Buck in your travels?" Orson asked.

"Yeah, as a matter of fact, I did. It was down past Fort Worth when I was herding a bunch of Longhorn steers. I was hired on working for a woman who lived in a little town called Waco. Yes, her name was Emma I believe. That's when I got a glimpse of Buck. As a matter of fact, we almost got ourselves killed, escaping by the skin of our teeth. It turned out that the other two hired hands working with us were in cahoots with Buck and a man I assumed was his partner. Fortunately, we slipped away from our camp before they were able to kill us.

Elizabeth wondered who Emma was and what she might have been to Vick.

"Did you get a good look at Buck?" Asked the sheriff.

"No, but wearing a bearskin coat year round will give you away every time, and that night it was mighty hot."

"Why you supposing Buck wore that coat when it was hot as blue blazes?"

"Oh, you probably didn't know, but Buck had a metal breastplate he wore for protection. His coat concealed it. That's the only thing that kept him alive."

"If that ain't the damnedest ... like the armor them Spanish fellers wore." Cain looked at his mother and smiled at the sheriff's innocent humor.

"Vick, I hope you don't mind me dragging you along to confront Johnson about lying to me."

"Cain, a man's got to do what he has to do. He did you wrong and you aim to get to the bottom of why he lied. Makes sense! But what you don't want to do is go in half-cocked and let him get the upper hand on you. My advice would be to know in advance how you intend to approach him," Vick instructed.

"Cain, I don't know why you need to see Jonathan at all," Elizabeth challenged.

"Maybe not now, but when I finish with him you'll be glad that I came."

"Cain, you'll do fine; don't worry... Believe me; I've had my share of conflicts. The only difference between the two of us is that girl you're fond of. I suspect if things are serious, you're going to do your best to make it right by her Pa."

"Exactly, if he gives me a chance. But I'm dang sure not going to cave like I did before."

"The last time Cain talked to Johnson, he didn't have his mother to back him up. If he tries anything, he'll have to deal with me," Elizabeth said.

"Yeah, Johnson ridiculed me plenty, especially about Mother's Pa killing himself. This time I'm going to have the upper hand."

Each mile they traveled made Cain angrier. "How could I have been so stupid believing Johnson? Mother was right about him all along," he thought.

Vick looked over the vast cotton fields as they entered the road that led to Johnson's palatial home. The fields brought back memories of the early days of prison, when he worked as a lease hand for Hop Babcock. "Hop was a decent man," Vick thought.

If it hadn't been for the cotton fields, he would have received the same harsh, inhumane treatment administered to the other prisoners by guards like Buckalew. Seeing the beautiful manicured fields, Vick recalled how he maneuvered his way to work on the plantations. There was something about the richness of cotton that interested him, and he learned all about the business during his first five years of prison, thanks to Hop.

When the Model T drove up, Eileen was sitting on the veranda, knitting. Her idle hours were spent thinking mostly about Cain, and when he drove up unexpectedly and got out of the car, she ran straight into his arms and kissed him right in front of everyone.

Elizabeth saw a look of disgust on Johnson's face as he walked around the corner to see who was there, just in time to see Eileen display her affection. "The man is still as arrogant as he was the first time I met him," Vick observed.

Elizabeth held her breath when she saw Johnson approaching her. She hated him for what he had done to Cain, and did not want Johnson to touch her, but instead of taking her hand, he openly ignored her, obviously meant to be an insult.

Vick enjoyed seeing Johnson squirm as he tried to figure out who Vick was. "There is something strangely familiar about this man ... I know I've seen him before, but where?"

When Cain mentioned New Orleans, it hit Johnson like a ton of bricks, that the man in question was Vick Porter, Cain's father. "*How in the heck did he get out of prison,*" Johnson wondered.

It took only a few seconds before the pieces began to fit. "There's no point in flinching," he thought; "*they probably know the truth about my lying to Cain.*" Thus, Johnson remained as unreadable as he was when he played poker. "Never let 'em know the hand you're playing," was Johnson's motto. He didn't care about Elizabeth and Cain, but he did care what Eileen thought, especially since she knew he had been deceptive.

The sheriff was as wise as an owl and quite adept at reading people. "*Johnson ain't got me fooled one bit. I need to be ready if thang's go bad,*" he thought, resting his hand on his gun..

"I presume you're all here to talk," said Johnson as he led the entourage into the library. Eileen followed, upset that she could feel conflict in everyone's attitudes, and afraid that her Pa's temper could ruin things between her and Cain.

"Well gentlemen, I'm sure you all did not come this far just for a leisurely drive, so let's get right to the point."

Cain finally spoke. "I would have preferred this to be a social visit, but in view of what's happened, I need to hear why you lied to me about Vick being in prison?"

Eileen looked stunned. Johnson tried to act restrained, since he was outnumbered, but he was clearly angered by Cain's aggression.

" We just came from New Orleans where we had a meeting with the governor of Louisiana to arrange to meet with Buck Dupree in prison, who turned out to be my father, Vick Porter. I'm sure you remember this man, as he introduced himself to you only a few short weeks ago, as Vick Porter. You know, my father who I have been searching for."

"Yes, sure I remember." Turning to Vick, he said. "You're the outlaw that ripped me off with your card counting. Yeah, it's no mistaking you're him. Passed yourself off as being Buck Dupree at the time. So you think you finally know who you are? Which is it, Buck Dupree or Vick Porter?"

"Johnson, what I did, I did to save you … but what you did, was plain wrong, lying to Cain when you knew who I was!"

"You think people like me are going to accept you? I saw the real Vick Porter sitting in that den of iniquity enjoying every minute of what you pulled on me. Vick or whatever your name is, you might have fooled your supporters, but you don't fool me. Your son and my daughter would be much better off if you had died and rotted in prison. When you live with scum it rubs off on you."

Vick felt the need to defend himself in front of Cain and Elizabeth.

"Johnson, what you saw was a man in prison for a crime he never committed, trying desperately to stay alive until someone could free him. Everything you saw was self-preservation, an attempt to stay alive. What you fail to understand is that I had to beat your ass to keep you from being thrown to the gators. Those men you sought out to play poker with would have killed you in an instant if you had won. Your daughter here would never have seen or heard from you again. You wouldn't be standing here talking like you know who I really am."

Johnson was surprised at how well versed Vick was, since he hardly spoke when he played poker with him. Of course, Vick had been taught the ways of a gentleman by Buck, who molded him so well.

Otherwise he might have died within the first six months in prison, had the warden not recognized what he had in Vick.

"What I saw in you was a no-good cheat," Johnson proclaimed.

"Johnson, I'm not going to argue with you further but one last thing: I had no choice over what I did in prison, but what you did outside of prison was clearly the calculated tactic of a selfish man out for his own gain. You knew after you accompanied Cain to New Orleans that I was the man you met in the poker parlor, yet you withheld this from him, and because of that, could have gotten him killed and the sheriff, too." Now, if you will … ask yourself what kind of man you are and father to a daughter who I imagine would want a father she can respect.

Cain was very impressed with his Pa's reasoning. He thought, "Vick would have made a great lawyer. Perhaps I'm more like him than I thought."

"Johnson, why would you do something like this?" asked Elizabeth.

He looked back at Cain and Elizabeth with pity, as if a con artist with a mysterious past had taken advantage of them.

"My intention was to protect Eileen, and whether you believe it or not, to also protect Cain from his father who happens to be you." Johnson turned toward Vick. "You're no good and your son has a chance to make something of himself. I thought I would be doing Cain a favor. Why would I want Cain or my daughter connected with you, after you've been living with convicts for twenty years? You can't say it hasn't rubbed off on you. What good will you ever be to society? Because of you, your son will always have to embrace the stigma of a convict as a father.

Elizabeth had finally had enough of Johnson. "My son has already made something of himself, and over a lifetime he will be a better man than you will ever be," she replied.

"Vick, how about telling your son about Odessa. You remember the man you shot in the back? I think that's what landed you in jail to begin with. Let's see … wouldn't that be eight people murdered instead of the seven you were accused of killing? And how about when you broke out of the Huntsville prison? Do you think I haven't had you checked out? You have a lot more baggage than these people know about," Johnson argued.

Cain looked at Vick, but he was not about to let Johnson see him squirm. "Vick? Do you care to explain this to your supporters?"

"No, I don't. Perhaps later is a better time."

Cain was very confused at Johnson's accusations of his father.

Vick was thrown off guard. He glanced at Elizabeth, who was standing with her mouth open. "Cain, I'm not going into this right now; it is not the place. We will talk later, when we get home."

"So, it's true?" Cain said. "You shot a man in the back?"

"Cain, this is not the time or the place. I said, I'll explain later," Vick was more firm. The sheriff could see the mess Vick was in and spoke up in Vick's defense.

"I think it's about time I said a few thang's that none of you know about. You see, Vick told me all about that little incident when we were having our talk the other night. And before you start stirring something up about Cain's Pa, well, you should all know that those charges against Vick didn't hold up."

Vick could not believe how the sheriff was digging himself a hole, lying to Cain and Elizabeth, and possibly making matters worse.

"Just watch out what ya say 'bout Vick, when ya don't know all the facts."

Johnson hated that his facts could be wrong, thus strengthening the relationship between Cain and Eileen.

The sheriff was so convincing that Johnson wondered how his sources could have screwed things up so badly. He was disappointed and felt foolish."

"And who are you to know so much about this man?" Johnson asked.

"I'm the sheriff from Jonesboro, Arkansas, and I helped get Vick freed by the governor of out state. Anything else ya want to know?"

Johnson could see that the sheriff was fidgeting with his gun and decided not to push things.

Eileen felt terrible, seeing her dreams slip away. She was ashamed of how her father treated the man she loved, and her heart went out to Cain, seeing him in such turmoil.

"Daddy, I told you this was not a good idea, keeping Cain's father a secret. I should never have listened to you. Can't you see how you've hurt this family?"

Cain was shocked at hearing Eileen's confession.

"Eileen, you knew about this and kept this from me? You knew, and allowed your father to manipulate me? How could you?"

"I wanted to tell you before when you were here, but Daddy said it was for the best. I'm really sorry. I was confused and didn't know what to do."

"Do you know your lie almost cost me and the sheriff our lives? We were almost killed."

Cain's response took Eileen by surprise. "I'm so sorry. I had no idea you were in danger; I know now that I should have told you. Please forgive me," she pleaded, looking into his eyes.

Cain wanted to wash his hands of the whole mess and get out. Elizabeth was determined she was going to have the last word when she saw Johnson smile.

She walked over to Cain and put her arm around him. "Son, we wanted to tell you about Odessa and what happened, but thought it best to wait until we got home. Johnson has upset you about your Pa, but I am the one who asked Vick to wait until we were home before we explained about the mistake in Odessa."

Vick thought, "They're both digging a hole. The fact is Cain may never trust me again when he finds out the truth."

"Is there anything else I need to know?" Cain asked.

Vick was filled with gratitude that Elizabeth and the sheriff would stick their necks out for him, but now, he might have a bigger problem when he has to explain what really happened in Odessa.

"Just for the record, there is no way I am going to allow my daughter to marry into a family like this."

"Daddy, how could you?" Eileen cried out, but she could see in Cain's eyes that the damage had already been done. "Please don't say anymore."

Eileen was remorseful and clearly hurting, but there was no way Cain could forgive her, not now anyway. All he felt was disappointment, even when she ran over to him and began to plead for his forgiveness.

"Eileen, you should have told me. That's unforgivable. I can't deal with it. I think your father is right. It could never work out for us. I have to say goodbye," Cain concluded. He turned and walked out of the house with everyone but Johnson following him.

"Cain, Cain, please wait! We need to talk about this!"

He looked at Eileen for a second, then turned and walked toward the car. Everyone climbed in quickly and Cain drove away, leaving Johnson standing there trying to console Eileen.

Cain took one final look, and knew in his heart that it was over.

The next day, Lucy was waiting when they drove up to the sheriff's modest cabin. "Don't you all want to come in for supper? I've got enough for everybody."

She could see they had an extra guest with them, but making room for one more was never a problem for her.

Cain was still reeling from the episode with Johnson, but Lucy's bubbly personality was just what he needed to help forget the pain.

"Lucy, I want you to meet Vick Porter." Elizabeth said. "You've heard of Cain's father, haven't you?"

Cain was relieved that his mother took charge and introduced his Pa. He was still having a difficult time calling Vick by name.

"Oh my, welcome home, Mr. Porter." Vick got a nod from Elizabeth that everything was okay with him.

"Good to meet you Lucy. I've known your Pa for a long time."

Elizabeth thought it would be good if they stayed. "Are you sure you want us all here for supper? Perhaps you're not prepared for all of us," Elizabeth suggested.

"For goodness sakes, don't be silly. I've got plenty cooking. Not another word!"

Lucy tried to help her Pa out of the back seat of the car, since he had been sitting for such a long period of time.

"Now jest take yer' hands off me. I ain't no invalid."

"Pa, don't go acting ornery; I know how stiff your legs get."

The sheriff was trying to move fast, but it was apparent Lucy was right. "Dad blame it girl, there ain't a stiff bone in my body."

Vick was amused at Orson struggling to get his legs moving, as he hobbled inside the cabin.

"Come on in everybody. Lucy knows how to put them scraps together. I've taught her well", said the sheriff.

Lucy was a perfect hostess, serving her simple but nourishing meal to everyone, while Cain sat back and watched Vick scarf down the delicious food she had prepared. Certainly this man would not kill for the sake of killing. Everyone deserves a second chance," Cain thought.

After supper they visited for a while, then Cain drove his mother and father to the manor. Elizabeth knew it was going to be strange for Vick, after being away for so many years.

When they drove up to the beautiful estate, he was amazed to see the manor had remained the same. He immediately thought of Mattie and what she had meant to him, but he had to accept the fact that she was dead and his life had to go on. Prison had taught him to appreciate the present because tomorrow might never come.

Vick had been unsure of his mortality while living among evil men in prison. But what it had taught him, was to appreciate every minute, for in a moment life could be over. Although he had to say goodbye to Mattie, he knew it was her memory that had kept him alive during some of the darkest days of his life.

He could now see that Cain was her gift she had left for him. Whatever the future held, Vick knew he had a son, and the most important thing to him was to make up for lost time. His future was right here with Cain and possibly … he would not allow himself to finish the thought.

How strange it was for Elizabeth to see Vick walk up the steps to the manor that had been her home since a child. Momentarily it had slipped her mind that after her father's death Vick lived in the manor, while she was living with her Aunt Connie in St. Louis.

Vick would have loved being alone in the manor long enough to sort out his thoughts, but Elizabeth had regained her home and it was up to him to find another place to live.

She hardly seemed like the same person to him. He tried to remember if she was ever that provocative and appealing? Perhaps she was all along, and I failed to see her because of Mattie." Vick had wonderful memories of Mattie, but now, it might be time to make new ones.

Vick and Elizabeth were standing near the stairs before they each went to their separate rooms, when he spontaneously asked, "Elizabeth, are you always going to save me?"

The way he said it was very touching, clearly coming from the heart. "Of course!" she said, smiling. Her heart skipped a beat as she answered.

Before they said goodnight, they stood at the door like they were waiting for a kiss, but each thought the other would think it was too forward.

After Vick entered his bedroom and closed the door, he stood for a moment breathless, thinking how beautiful Elizabeth was and how he wanted to hold her, but he imagined it was because he was a free man and hardly remembered what it was like to be with a woman. "Am I imagining this or is there really something between us?" he wondered.

He moved around the room, trying to remember things that he had forgotten over the years, but everything looked the same. He picked up a picture of the young Elizabeth and thought, "How little she has changed. She has the same face and the same smile. I'm the one who's changed," Vick thought. He sat on the bed thinking how she answered his question about saving him. For the first time, it was Elizabeth who filled his thoughts, rather than Mattie.

Chapter 32

THE NEXT DAY, CAIN WAS MAKING HIS EARLY MORNING COFFEE, **engrossed in thought, when Elizabeth walked in on him.** Caught in mid-draw, he holstered the old gun strapped around his waist.

"Cain, I thought we talked about you and that gun."

"We did, and I listened. But don't worry, Orson's been showing me a thing or two." His feeble attempt at handling his pistol like a real gunslinger, in front of his mother, left him somewhat embarrassed.

"So how you doing with your gun?" Elizabeth asked somewhat sarcastically.

"Now, don't be so catty. I may never be fast, but at least I'll learn to shoot."

Cain took his coffee and headed outdoors to the barn to avoid having words with Elizabeth. "I'll be back in awhile. I have some errands to run."

She had no idea what was going on with him, but the idea that he had a gun strapped to him worried her.

Now that Cain knew the history behind the treasure and its value, he became keenly aware that his family might be in danger. He had seen, first hand, Spencer try to kill his mother over the treasure. If anyone caught wind that Vick was released from prison and had a hefty stash, they might come calling. And if they did, he wanted to be ready. If the truth be known, Cain probably had an itch to be like his Pa. He had seen how the sheriff and Vick handled the warden and his men, while he watched helplessly. "Next time, I want to be ready," he thought.

After he corralled his horse, he rode nearly two miles to a secluded area where he could target shoot without being seen. He wanted to keep his shooting a private matter, especially after recently learning only the basic techniques. He found a quiet area near a trail, surrounded by a grove of trees. Cain surveyed the area for outsiders and then began fumbling around trying to remember what the sheriff had taught him. "This is going to take a lot of work," he thought.

Time flew by and he lost himself in his newfound love of shooting. He never wanted to be known as a dangerous man, but handling a gun gave him a sense of power. Deeply entranced by the seclusion and sound of gunfire, he was unaware of an unknown presence spying on him from the bushes.

The man had come up on Cain while he was practicing. Noticing his futile attempt to do a quick draw, he chuckled to himself. As he sat there watching the show, he removed his coat.

"The kid's really bad," the stranger thought to himself, careful not to distract this greenhorn for fear of being shot.

The extremely unkempt gunman spit snuff and chewed on the butt end of a cigar. "The kid needs to know how a real man uses his gun."

The middle-aged cowboy hadn't intended to interrupt, but when his horse snorted, Cain turned sharply toward the source of the noise. The man walked his horse out of the bushes in the direction of where Cain was standing.

Cain laughed nervously seeing he must have had an audience.

The man's face was stern looking, and hard to read, as he walked his horse a few feet more.

Slowly taking his cigar out of his mouth and spitting, the stranger began to talk.

"I don't rightly intrude on a man with his gun, but you are handling your gun all-wrong. His horse danced around, eager to go, but the cowboy held tight to the rein.

"How old is that damn thing you got there? Mind if I take a look?"

Cain thought the man looked interesting, and noticed he had an accent. "Perhaps he's from Ireland," Cain thought, as he walked over to him handing him his gun, grip first, as he sat on his very tall horse.

"First lesson to you, don't ever give your weapon to a man you don't know."

"You look friendly enough," Cain said.

"And don't assume anything," the stranger said, as he lectured, while examining the weapon.

Second lesson: You should know your surroundings, because I've been standing in that grove of mesquite, watching you for the last ten minutes." He finished with a chuckle, biting down on his cigar.

Cain wasn't happy that he had been spied on, but no harm done," he thought.

After examining the gun, the man handed it back.

"Are you planning to kill somebody or tis' this a hobby? Wait don't answer that! 'Cause if not, you're planning your own funeral."

"*The man's getting rather cynical,*" Cain thought, as he began to get irritated.

"Right now, I want to get good enough in case I have to kill someone," Cain responded, trying to keep his temper intact.

The man had a hearty laugh, but Cain did not like the amusement, especially since he was the butt end of his joke.

"Judging from what I just saw, you wouldn't stand a chance in a gunfight."

"It sounds to me like you know a lot about guns," Cain said sarcastically.

"Yeah, I reckon I do. I learned a long time ago, a pair of six shooters would beat a pair of aces anytime, and I got me two of 'em." He showed one gun in his holster and one in his belt. These are my two best friends.

"*Whoa, this man is serious,*" thought Cain.

"I've never had the need for a gun until lately; that's why I'm practicing."

"But what you have wouldn't kill a thing, not even a rabbit. I doubt you could kill a rabbit if it hopped right in front of you, the way you kept missing your target."

Cain continued to study the man, thinking the stranger was obnoxious, out of line, and talked too much. He had always respected the proverb of "never missing the chance to keep your mouth shut," and clearly, he missed the Sunday morning service when they taught that lesson," Cain thought.

The man holstered his gun so Cain could see. "That's quite a gun you have."

"Yep, but it ain't for a hobby, if you know what I mean." The man's smile turned a bit wicked.

"Well, if you have any more advice, I'm appreciative. If not, I best be moving along."

Once again, the man's attitude changed to the light side, as though he was talking to an old friend. Cain sensed that this man was trouble. Call it the power of discernment or whatever, but he could feel the man was unpredictable, one who could be dangerous if he got his dander up.

"Thank you for your advice, but I need to be on my way."

"Just a minute before you go."

Cain felt a shudder come over him as the man's tone of voice changed again.

"Come on over here, and let me teach you a thing or two about using a gun. You need to know this, and then you can be on your way."

"Cain thought, "I may be a dead man before this is over," but he walked toward the man, trying to act confident. At the same time, the man was dismounting his horse.

"First off, get you another belt and holster. One that fits around your waist comfortable, like mine." He pointed to his gun and holster, then gave his gun to Cain to feel.

"Go ahead, feel it, rub your hand along the butt and the barrel of the gun. Now, a gun like this is what you want."

"You're right. It's mighty nice." Cain was sure the man heard him swallow, as his heart was in his throat.

"Now, if you want to take a gander, I'm going to show you something. You see that limb up in that tree?" The man pointed to a tiny branch at the very top of the tree.

He then placed his gun back in the holster, and within a twinkle of an eye, he did the quick-draw, clipping the limb off then resting his gun back in his holster. "Now, that's what you want. You keep practicing until you can do that."

"Wow, you're really fast." Then it hit him that this man may be a professional killer, and it would be best to get out and fast.

"When you can draw and fire like that, you've mastered the art," he said.

Cain walked to his horse while the man was still talking.

"Be sure and remember, you got to feel your gun. Be loose and do what's natural to you. Keep working at it until it's natural.

The man walked over to his horse and hopped on like a twenty year old. As he was about to ride away, the man stopped and said, "Remember one thing, we're not born, we're made. So keep on practicing. Good luck to you!"

The man rode a few feet, and then stopped again. Cain thought, "oh no, here we go again, but he had no choice but to stop and listen.

"I beg to differ about something I said earlier, the stranger told him. I do know one man that was born a fast gun, and he was the quickest draw I ever seen. I ain't seen him in over twenty years, but when I do, I aim to kill him!" The stranger yanked his horse around then spurred him and took off.

Something about those last words sent shivers over Cain. Though he noticed a heavy bearskin coat strung across the horse's haunch, he watched the man ride away; having no idea he had just met Buck Dupree.

Chapter 33

ELIZABETH, ANXIOUS TO SEE LUCY, WAS UP AND OUT OF THE HOUSE **before Cain and Vick awoke.** She drove to the lumber company bright and early to see how Lucy handled her job, while Elizabeth was gone to New Orleans.

"What an improvement," she thought, when she parked her car in front of the old building that was now spruced up with new flowers along the walkway leading up to the entrance. She could hardly believe it was the same place.

As soon as Elizabeth walked in the door, Lucy began apologizing for telling Hattie Mae, the town gossip, concerning Vick's homecoming. "I shouldn't have told her about Mr. Porter being freed."

"Why would you worry? They are going to know sooner or later."

"You don't understand. Pa came by and said the town was planning a welcome-home party for Mr. Vick because I opened my big mouth. I'm so sorry."

"Don't spend your time getting all worked up about that. It'll be fine. I'm sure Vick won't mind a little party."

"Lucy, you've made a vast improvement around the building. I noticed all the work you did out front and now, I'm wondering how I ever got along without you. You did a wonderful job while I was away."

"Unlike Spencer, Lucy was very focused and tried to please her," Elizabeth thought. About that time, the loggers filed in for their schedules, while Elizabeth watched on with pride, seeing Lucy handle the men as though she had worked there for years.

Mid-morning, Vick and Cain came by the lumber company to see Elizabeth and admired the tremendous work she had done, while he was away in prison.

"This place doesn't look the same. Somebody's been busy." Cain said.

"I wanted Vick to see what all has been done since he's been away. But it looks like it's in better shape now than it was when we left for New Orleans."

Vick appeared to be impressed with the office and the work that had been done.

Elizabeth pointed at Lucy, who had a big smile on her face. Cain noticed how much better the office looked.

"Is there anything you can't do? You cooked a wonderful meal last night and reworked the office. This is great! Good job, don't you think Mother?" *Cain was being a little flirtatious*, Elizabeth thought. "Yes, Lucy did a marvelous job." Elizabeth added.

Lucy seemed somewhat embarrassed, having the attention directed toward her.

"Now, are you all ready for a bit of news?" Elizabeth asked.

"And what's that?" Cain asked.

"Vick, I hope you feel like a party. The town is giving you a welcome home celebration Saturday night. So … what do you think? You feel like being the center of attention?"

Vick smiled, and then thought, *"what the heck, I'm asking her."*

"They're not wasting any time are they? But I have one problem. I'll need someone with a car to join me." Vick looked at Elizabeth. "Your automobile has got me spoiled," Vick said.

Elizabeth's face turned from stoic into a radiant smile.

"I do declare, you certainly have a way of asking a girl out. Is it because of me or my automobile?"

Cain smiled and looked at his Pa. "He's a smooth devil to have been locked away in prison for the last twenty years."

His mother was the happiest he had ever seen, which surprised him, knowing both of their backgrounds.

Lucy saw only what another woman would notice. Elizabeth's face was glowing. When Saturday night rolled around, Vick was impeccably dressed, waiting for Elizabeth to join him. He had used the wad of cash the warden had given him to purchase a new wardrobe, something he took great pride in doing, since he was making up for lost time.

"Being locked up for twenty years didn't hurt him one bit, he looks damn good," Cain thought.

Elizabeth was equally impressed when she saw Vick standing at the end of the stairs, looking as handsome as the day they met.

And, when he saw Elizabeth walking toward him, he realized he could easily fall in love with this woman. She was beautiful in her long colorful taffeta dress, accented with a large chartreuse and crimson velveteen bow that fit tightly around her small waist. Her long auburn hair was pulled back and adorned with a perfect white magnolia, her favorite flower. Elizabeth was thrilled to notice the sparkle in Vick's eye.

"*She is stunning,*" he thought as he reached for her hand.

Cain couldn't believe what a striking couple his mother and father made. "Look at you two. Vick, you look like a Philadelphia lawyer. And I feel slightly underdressed. Do you mind giving a straggler a ride to the dance?" Cain asked.

"You can chauffeur us."

Elizabeth was thrilled seeing how well Cain and Vick were getting along.

"*This night is going to be perfect,*" Vick thought.

The trio left joking, like one big happy family. Cain sensed something going on between the two, but for some reason he found it extremely difficult to think of Vick and his mother being more than friends anymore than he thought of Vick being his Pa. Perhaps too much time has passed and the chances at fatherhood had vanished along with the years.

Actually, Cain didn't know how he felt about the man he had lived most of his life without.

When they arrived at the party, most of the townsfolk were waiting to welcome Vick. He was like the "Prodigal Son" who finally returned home. It was humbling, as folks began reminiscing about that cold foggy morning, over twenty years ago, when they showed up with mules to clear Vick's land and skin logs. One by one, they walked through the fog with their mules," he remembered.

One recipient of Vick's generosity spoke out to the crowd. "To top it off, if it wasn't for Vick Porter, I wouldn't have my home and land I have today. He saved me and my family!"

Elizabeth was embarrassed to know that underneath the fanfare, her father was responsible for the hardship on the very families who were now celebrating Vick's return. Cain had heard the story many times, but to hear the town express their gratitude was extra special to him.

"Just look at all these folks," Cain said to Vick.

As time passed, young women began swarming Cain, making Lucy very uncomfortable, for she had hoped Cain would be giving her the attention he seem to be showing the other girls.

"*I can't afford to let him know how I feel about him,*" Lucy thought. She was by far the prettiest girl around, but her self-doubts prevented her from showing the confidence she needed to fully enjoy the party. All the finishing schools in Chicago could not have erased the insecurity she felt, now that Cain had directed his attention elsewhere.

She tried to refrain from looking in his direction, but the women were making such a fuss over him, that it became impossible for her to ignore what was going on.

"I'm never going to measure up to the Porters," Lucy thought. Finally, a nice looking man asked Lucy to dance, giving her a boost for her bruised ego.

Lucy remained oblivious to Cain who was looking at her out of the corner of his eye.

Vick and Elizabeth were visiting with their old friends, while the sheriff was nursing the punch bowl. He watched Lucy dance around the floor and wondered if his little girl was having fun. He already suspected how Lucy felt about Cain, who was kidnapped by the young ladies in town who considered him a good catch.

Elizabeth loved sharing Vick's evening, but she gave Vick the space she thought he needed. I want to give him time to discover me," she thought. She was well aware that men liked the chase, and she was not going to succumb to being jealous or possessive of a man, when she had lived her entire life without one.

Vick noticed how independent Elizabeth was and wished she would settle down and stay still long enough for him to talk to her. She continued flitting around all over the place, somewhat as the hostess, as if she had nervous energy. "She's playing games," he thought.

Every now and then Vick would look around the room and catch Elizabeth standing at an angle so she could keep him in her peripheral view. "Funny girl. She has no idea I'm on to her," Vick thought.

Elizabeth saw Felicia, who was known as a woman of ill repute, heading straight for Vick. She became curious to see how he would handle the situation, as she watched. The minute Felicia appeared; Vick sensed something vaguely familiar that disturbed him. Then he remembered. "This is the woman I made love to when I was just a kid." He remembered how exciting and beautiful she was. But time had not treated her well. The beauty she once possessed was no longer there, and all that was left was a shell of a woman who appeared to have suffered her share of disappointments and hardships.

Felicia touched Vick's arm. "I recognized your walk. I don't remember your name, but I met you a long time ago. You used to play cards in the saloon where I worked. You're him, aren't you?"

"I'm sure I would have remembered you. Did I get your name?" Vick asked.

"I'm sorry. You look a lot like him, but you have a beard. I didn't mean to bother you." Felicia was slurring her words as she tried to walk away. As soon as she turned, she ran into Elizabeth.

"Oh, excuse me. I didn't mean to bump into you." Elizabeth smiled at her.

"Whatcha smiling about?" Felicia asked.

"I'm sorry, I should have been looking where I was going," Elizabeth said.

"Vick, I have someone to meet you." Elizabeth lied, hoping Felicia would hear.

Felicia turned around again,

"Did you call this man Vick?" She stopped and looked at Vick, squinting her eyes. "So your name is Vick?"

Vick smiled at her and replied. "Yes, ma'am, that's right."

"I used to know a man named Vick, but you ain't him."

For a moment Vick remembered that magical night with Felicia. But that time had long gone. He knew she was covering for him.

"I thought you might need saving again." Elizabeth said.

Vick looked tenderly at her and said. "And just as you promised."

Elizabeth could hardly contain her "butterflies." She was sure Vick could read what was in her mind, as she quickly walked over to another group of ladies.

Vick walked toward the sheriff, still nursing the punch bowl. "Orson, you could have come to my rescue. Didn't you see Felicia putting the moves on me?"

The sheriff looked soused and whispered in Vick's ear. "My job's to protect ya from the outlaws, not from them women. Don't say it too loud, but I did me a little spikin."

"You spiked the punch or the whiskey?" Vick laughed.

The sheriff poured a big cup and gave it to Vick.

"Jest wet yer whiskers on that! If dis' don't make ya slap ya mama down nothing will," he said, followed by a hearty laugh. "It may even make ya slap that Felissy woman down, if ya need to."

Vick smiled at Orson, then took a big gulp of the spiked punch. It was so strong, it took his breath away. Vick could always handle strong drinks, but this was over the top.

"What did you put in this stuff, kerosene? This is way too strong."

"Did it burn the har' off ya tongue? These town parties ain't no fun less'n I'm here to spike the punch."

"I got to hand it to you, this is strong stuff. How about pouring one for Elizabeth? She's a little uptight."

The sheriff smiled from ear to ear, thinking of Elizabeth's reaction when she took a swig of his concoction.

"Better be careful when you give this to Lizzie, 'cause I hear she carries a pretty wicked punch, and I ain't talking about something to drink."

"I'll let you know if I need your help."

Vick made his way to Elizabeth, who accepted the drink gracefully since Vick brought it to her. Vick smiled when she shivered grabbing at her throat. Clearly the drink was something she had never experienced.

"Oh my! What is this? Did Orson spike the punch?"

"Oh, you've had these drinks before?"

"That's why we never invite him to the parties. Some of these stuffy women refuse to invite Orson because he always spikes the punch."

Vick laughed and tried to take the drink back from Elizabeth, but surprisingly, she gulped it down, then gave one last big shiver."

"Whew, I can't believe you drank that!"

Vick could see the drink was already affecting Elizabeth, when she abruptly led him to the dance floor. "Let's dance!" she said.

Elizabeth took Vick's hand and began to show him how to polka. It was the most fun Vick ever had, as he and Elizabeth danced around the dance floor laughing when finally they stopped, out of breath. Elizabeth led Vick to a corner of the room so they could talk."

"I didn't know I had it in me." Vick said. He looked in Elizabeth's eyes that seem to be inviting him to kiss her but he couldn't bring himself to outwardly show his affection. This is not the time or place, he thought.

By the end of the evening, everyone had dipped into the punch and were whooping and hollering. Orson was still standing, substantially inebriated, beside the punch bowl.

Lucy had only one dance with Cain, the Virginia Reel, a group dance. She was so discouraged, and convinced herself that they would never be anything but friends.

When Elizabeth and Vick arrived home, Cain went straight to bed, leaving Vick and Elizabeth alone to say goodnight.

Feeling the effects of the punch, she was sure Vick would kiss her goodnight, but he did not. All the elements were right, but Vick went straight to his room, without giving her a hint of a kiss. He could tell that she was slightly inebriated, and he chose to say goodnight instead of kissing her. Vick did not want to give the impression he was taking advantage after the drinks they had.

Elizabeth was confused that he had let her go to bed without a kiss, and when she retired to her room, she could barely get into her nightgown. She thought she would go right to sleep, but the punch had the opposite effect on her. All she could do was toss and turn and think about Vick. She longed for him to take her in his arms and smother her with kisses. The same man she had spent years dreaming about was only two rooms down the hall and she was wasting precious time when she could be with him.

"Am I crazy?" She asked herself. She knew she was feeling no pain and she was doing wrong compared to her moral standard, but the alcohol was burning and her body ached with desire. "It must be the sheriff's punch," she thought. Elizabeth tried to convince herself to stay in her room but she couldn't. By the time she put on her robe, she lost all sense of reasoning and walked straight away to Vick's door.

When she stood there poised, she took a deep sigh, then lightly tapped on his door. She was caught off guard when the door suddenly opened and Vick's arm whisked her into his room. She did not have time to catch her breath before he began kissing her. It was intoxicating and blissful as she responded.

They clung to each other, consumed with passion as they enjoyed the feeling of having their bodies touch for the first time. "It was more than the drink," Elizabeth knew, as she slipped out of her nightgown. Vick welcomed her into his bed. There was no turning back now. She had gone too far. She could now put claim on something that for so long, had been an illusion.

"I never knew being with you could be like this," Vick whispered in her ear.

It was magical. She did not fight the hidden sensation that erupted after years of being alone. Their lovemaking was passionate, and when it was over, they talked about a life together. It was everything she had imagined, as she lay by the man she loved.

Vick had never felt love like he did for Elizabeth. Each and every little thing about her excited him, the way she moved, her intelligence, and the sweet sound of her voice. Things were moving fast, but Elizabeth felt like she had waited long enough.

Vick must have read her mind whispering, "I don't want to wait. I've been given a second chance and I don't want to waste a minute. You are everything to me."

"Vick, are you sure? Have you had enough time to know if it's me you want?"

"What about you? You know my past. Are you ready to spend the rest of your life with a man who's been in prison?"

Elizabeth put her hands on both sides of Vick's face and looked deep into his eyes. "My darling Vick, if you only knew." They curled up in each other's arms until it was almost first light. Upon waking, Elizabeth reluctantly went to her room.

That morning she made a special breakfast and Cain knew something was up. Vick and Elizabeth waited for the right moment and then talked to Cain about their decision to marry.

"My, my this is fast, I didn't see this coming ... what can I say except, I'm happy for you, if that's what you want. I usually get the lecture instead of giving one. But I don't want you jumping into marriage without giving it ample thought. Are you both sure this is the right thing to do?"

"Don't worry, we're sure," Vick said and Elizabeth nodded.

Cain gave his mother a quick hug, and Vick a handshake, then walked away toward the barn. She noticed Cain had the holster and gun around his waist again, but even that distraction could not destroy the moment, knowing she would soon be "Mrs. Vick Porter."

Chapter 34

ELIZABETH MADE A BEAUTIFUL BRIDE, ADORNED IN HER GRANDMOTHER'S **white wedding dress that had been tucked away in her cedar chest since her childhood.** The dress was sewn with yards of white taffeta and Chantilly lace, then accented with a beautiful long train that flowed behind her as she descended down the stairwell of the manor.

The sheriff stood on the landing, eager to escort Elizabeth through their seated wedding guests and down the aisle to Vick, who stood entranced by his beautiful bride walking toward him.

Cain marveled at how happy his mother was as she joined Vick before the minister. "This could have been me marrying Eileen. Thank God, Johnson Petty showed his real colors for it would have been impossible to be his son-in-law."

Even though his entire world had been turned upside down, the disappointment he felt for Eileen was beginning to wear off. "What happened between me and her was meant to be," he realized.

It was early spring and time for new beginnings, Cain thought, as he welcomed another young woman into his heart. Although she was not as sophisticated as Eileen, Lucy was a beauty in her own right and quite the businesswoman. He glanced over at her as she stood beside his mother and imagined what a beautiful bride she would make when the time comes.

She moved gracefully, not at all like the tomboy she used to be. He knew that, before the evening was over, he would share his feelings.

Cain saw something very special in Lucy and realized this young woman was much more than a small town girl. "Perhaps mother had been right about her all along, and now I'm free to pursue her without feeling guilty."

After the short ceremony, Vick and Elizabeth mingled throughout the manor as their guests gathered around congratulating them. Sweet jasmine and beautiful white magnolias decorated the stairway and each table in the festive banquet hall. The dining room table held an enormous wedding cake on a round crystal pedestal that was large enough to feed everyone and more.

Orson noticed Cain walking toward Lucy and sensed that he was about to make a move on his little girl. He wanted to intercede, but he couldn't bring himself to embarrass either Lucy or Cain. *"There' ain't a thang' I can do about it. She's old enough to know her own mind. I jest hope he ain't plannin' on leading her on to break her heart,"* he thought. There was a part of Orson that thought Cain might be a ladies' man and he did not want his daughter to have to go through that kind of heartbreak. *"I can't git involved,"* Orson decided.

Elizabeth and Vick were talking with the guests when Orson approached them.

"Vick, I need to steal ya away fer a few minutes." Vick was concerned with the look on his old friend's face.

"Orson, you're much too serious. I hope you're not going to drop bad news on my wedding day."

"Nah! I wanted ta tell ya this earlier, so ya could rest easy. I looked into them charges in Odessa and they been dropped fer years. Some eyewitnesses stepped forward and finally told the truth so they cleared ya'. All them years ain't been worth the worry. Ya were a free man."

"Are you sure?"

"Yep, it's a shut case and yer' jest as free as ole Johnson Petty himself. That's my wedding gift to ya and Lizzie."

"I don't know what to say except, thank you. Elizabeth will be happy to know this. Do you want to tell her or do you want me to?"

"I'll let ya do the honors."

After the wedding, Cain asked Lucy if he could escort her home. She was ecstatic, but Cain had disappointed her before, when he confessed that Elizabeth asked him to pick her up for work. She had never forgotten how crushed she was to know it was not Cain's idea, but Elizabeth's. "Perhaps Elizabeth had put Cain up to escorting her home. I must be careful not make a fool of myself," she thought.

But, the minute Cain took Lucy's hand, the sparks again began to fly. He knew she would be someone special to him. He had planned to stay in town to give the newlyweds their privacy, and asked Elizabeth if he could drive the car, since she and Vick were not going on a honeymoon.

Cain helped Lucy into the Model T, and drove past her home headed for Gully's Dam, an old swimming place that had quite a reputation. After Cain stopped the car, he reached to pull Lucy close to him, which she found rather distasteful, since he had never let on that he was interested.

She immediately pulled back. "Cain, what are you doing?"

"Lucy, I'm sorry: it must be spring, your perfume, or the punch, but something is driving me crazy."

"So this gives you the right to ..."

Before Lucy could say another word, Cain kissed her, leaving her breathless.

"I'm sorry Cain. I know you're well traveled, more than me, but I'm not that kind of girl. You should take me home."

Lucy could not believe she finally had the attention of Cain Porter and had turned him down. She had dreamed of this moment, but all she could hear was her voice asking him to take her home.

"Lucy, I do apologize. It must have been seeing my father and mother so happy and got all wrapped up in the moment. I hope you will excuse my behavior. I'll take you home.'

He was disappointed when Lucy said she wanted to go home, but there was no way he wanted to ruin things with her. "How could I have been so forward," he thought to himself.

Upon arriving at her home, Lucy was out of the car and in the house before Cain could think. "I can't believe I messed this up."

After everyone had left, and the newlyweds were alone, Vick took Elizabeth in his arms and kissed her, a long lustful kiss.

"Finally!" he said, "I couldn't wait for everyone to leave so we could be alone. Are you ready for this?" Before she knew what was happening, Vick swept her off her feet and whisked her up the stairs taking two steps at a time.

"Don't you dare drop me," she laughed. He stopped and pushed open the bedroom door and then closed with his boot.

Their wedding night was every bit as special as Elizabeth had imagined. The first thing she noticed was the curtains open to the balcony. She reached for Vick's hand and led him out doors to breathe in the beautiful lilacs that were all in bloom. The stars were out as if to congratulate the bride and groom.

"Can you believe this night? Elizabeth asked.

"No, and I have never seen such a beautiful bride as you are now."

Elizabeth smiled at him as she stood invitingly in her long silk robe. The mixed fragrances of the outdoors made the night special. She thought only a few months ago her life was empty and now she felt like she was in heaven.

"I could not have ordered a more beautiful night." Elizabeth noticed the moon, as it beamed brighter than any night she could remember.

"You're not so bad yourself." she said, as she snuggled closer to him.

"This has been quite a day, and it isn't over yet ..."

"What are you talking about? Are you keeping secrets?"

"Sort of... Are you prepared for something that is going to make you very happy."

"Vick, I don't know anything that could make me happier than what I am at this moment."

"I do have some good news for you".

"Well let's have it then; don't make me wait."

"Orson told me to tell you that it was his wedding gift to you."

"What is it?" Don't tell me it's some of his special punch." Elizabeth mockingly put her hands over her ears.

"Orson checked into the Odessa incident and told me the charges against me have been dropped, for years. I'm totally free."

"She instantly grabbed Vick kissing him. Oh Vick, this is good news. You know what it makes me want to do?

"Let's see, does it have anything to do with a man named Johnson Petty?"

"Yes. I want to rub his nose in it for causing so much pain."

"I wanted to tell you earlier, but we didn't have a chance to be alone."

"Since we're telling secrets I have a confession, too. I've wanted to tell you this, but it's something I have not shared with anyone."

"Sure, let's have it! No secrets!"

Elizabeth felt she would be embarrassed to tell Vick something so personal, but she was not.

"Vick I hope you understand but when Mattie was living, she talked about you all the time, and that's when I allowed myself to develop feelings for you. I can't believe I'm telling you this, but, I felt so guilty knowing she was carrying your child, and yet, I was wanting you for myself. I suppose you think I'm silly for having felt like that, when Mattie trusted me like a sister. She never knew I loved you. In fact, no one knew. Later, after Mattie died, I felt as though I betrayed her. But I couldn't help being crazy about you."

"That far back, huh?" Vick teased.

"Even further!" Elizabeth confessed. "I don't think you remember but I saw you as a boy helping your brother place bags of feed in your Pa's old wagon. I was with my daddy that day and this is when I saw you. What I remembered were your eyes.

"I think you were the first girl I ever saw. I remember now. I wondered if I would ever see you again," Vick smiled.

"Remember when you were trying to throw me off your property? I knew then, something was happening. I couldn't stop thinking about you. Even when I went to live with Aunt Connie ... I told her about my feelings for you."

And just think, if no one had found me, you would have married Johnson Petty," Vick said, kiddingly.

"Oh, you! You just had to destroy the moment."

"You could have made it easier on me if you would have told me you cared," Vick continued to tease.

"Well, I saved you. Remember? Twice ... so far!" Elizabeth pointed out.

Vick felt inspired. "This may come as a surprise to you but I think Mattie had a plan for the three of us?"

"What, do you mean plan?"

"The reason Mattie asked you to adopt Cain is she knew one day I would come home. I'm sure she hoped I'd find my way back and there you would be with my son. Think about it ... Mattie wanted you to be happy and I'm sure she wanted the same for me."

"I spent so much time feeling guilty that I never thought that this could be what Mattie wanted. Vick I wonder if Mattie planned this?"

"This was only speculation but knowing Mattie she was completely unselfish," Vick stated.

A few days later, Cain stopped by the lumber company just before closing, to apologize to Lucy. When he entered the office, she was sitting at her desk working on records, ignoring Cain standing there, and pretending not to notice.

"Lucy, I wanted to stop by and tell you that I'm deeply sorry about the other night. I didn't plan to come on like I did. It's just that you are so beautiful and I don't think you know what you do to me when I'm around you."

She could not believe what she was hearing. This was Cain Porter telling her this. She eventually got up from her desk and walked over to Cain. All it took was that big smile of his and she forgave him.

"Why don't we get out of here?" Cain asked.

"I'll have to close up, do you think Elizabeth will be upset?"

"Not at all. Take your time. Cain watched as she hurriedly put her work away.

Together, they rode Cain's horse out to the place where he had done his practice shooting.

"What place is this?" Asked Lucy.

"Oh, just a place I come to when I want to be alone. Do you mind?"

"It's pretty out here. Do you want to walk?"

That day, everything about the woods was mystifying and hypnotic, with fragrances from the honeysuckle permeating the air with the intoxication of love.

Once again, Cain made his move on Lucy, and again she stopped him. Being together was the only thing that mattered to both of them, but Cain had the experience of love and he thought if he kept trying he might change her mind.

"Lucy, I'm sorry, it's just that you mean so much to me."

"Cain this seems unreal. I can't believe, I'm here with you. The night of the wedding you never asked me to dance and… other times you seemed to ignore me and now… why now? And there's Eileen, who you have never bothered to tell me about."

"I guess I should have explained, but I thought I needed time to figure things out before I talked to you. If it had been true love between me and Eileen, you wouldn't have been able to get under my skin like you did. I don't mind saying it's taken me a little time to figure this out, but Mother knew all along."

Cain pulled Lucy closer and kissed her gently.

"We probably need to go," Lucy said. "I'm not a prude, but we need to go before we get in trouble."

"Lucy, all I want is to be with you, that's all. So don't worry about me. Besides, there's Orson in the back of my mind, and that's enough to bring me back to my senses."

She laughed and then started to walk away, when Cain stopped her.

"Lucy wait." There is another reason I brought you here."

For a moment she was confused, but suddenly Cain dropped on one knee.

She was startled and thought she was seeing things.

"Cain, what are you doing? She couldn't believe this man who had been elusive to her since childhood was about to propose.

"Lucy, I haven't been able to stop thinking about you. When my parents were married, I knew then, we were meant to be together. He took a deep breath and then asked the question.

Lucy, will you marry me?"

She thought she had misunderstood. "Cain, are you sure you know what you're doing?"

He smiled, "Of course, I know what I'm doing!"

Lucy was ecstatic that Cain Porter was proposing.

"I don't know what to say."

"Just say "yes," and make me a happy man!" Cain said.

Lucy kept killing time instead of answering, inwardly enjoying seeing Cain squirm.

"I'll be happy to marry you, but first you need to ask daddy. He has always told me he expects the man I marry to ask him for my hand."

"I wouldn't want to disappoint Orson," Cain assured her.

When they mounted the horse and headed back to town, Lucy released some of her inhibitions and snuggled up to Cain. "She's worth waiting for," he thought.

Chapter 35

"MISTER, WOULD YOU LIKE TO BUY A PAPER?" A YOUNG BOY ASKED A weary traveler. The man dug deep in the pocket of his heavy coat for change and handed it to the boy. He had little else on his mind other than finding an affordable boarding house and entering another poker game.

Glancing at his paper, the man stopped dead in his tracks when he noticed in bold print a headline of an article congratulating Vick Porter and Elizabeth Barkin on their recent wedding. When he saw Vick's familiar name, sweat beaded up on his brow as his eyes focused on the print. He read over and over that Vick had been released from prison and was now a free man.

"The sonavobitch lives right here in this town," he thought. Not only was he free, but the well-to-do owner of the Porter Lumber Company, which infuriated him. The article explained that Vick had served twenty years for murders, which he did not commit, and was exonerated by the governor of Arkansas. And as he read on it named the real murderer as William Abberly alias Buck Dupree who was from Australia.

"I don't believe this," he said aloud. "The bastard has resurrected himself and all these years, I thought he might be dead."

He stood frozen — insanely angry — thinking about what he should do next. He scanned the street and noticed several posters nailed on posts. Careful not to attract unwanted attention, he walked slowly in their direction feeling overwhelmingly insecure.

As he reached the posters, he saw the tables had finally turned on him. Now, he was a wanted man, accused of killing the family at Panther Holler. Seeing his name plastered everywhere in town sent a shock wave through him, and his head felt like it might blow off.

Obviously someone knew his secret. "How can that be?" he wondered. "Someone must have seen me kill my sorry ass partner and his family."

In bold print the poster read **"BUCK DUPREE: WANTED DEAD OR ALIVE."**

Even though his body was outwardly perspiring, his inner body was cold as ice. For many years he had escaped the law, but now he would be a common household name. Charged with killing a family of four who lived in Panther Holler, the posters referred to him as the "Butcher of Panther Holler."

Years of cunning deceit were finally catching up with Buck, and he was showing signs of paranoia, linked with hate, and possibly self-loathing. These days his time around the poker table was not as prosperous, and his best source of income was running with small gangs, rustling cattle, robbing and pilfering in West Texas towns. After reading the posters, his jealousy for Vick's success was all consuming. He imagined Vick was still playing him like he did when he sat across the poker table, years ago at Panther Holler. Everything to the Con was a game.

During Buck's travels, he yearned for the old days when he was back in Arkansas. He remembered the solitude of the Holler, his best years that reminded him of Australia, his homeland. He longed for the sport of hunting and being free, never having to watch his back and the more he thought of the place the more he wanted to return and escape the law.

Coming back to Arkansas and finding he was a wanted man did not quite fit into his plan. This only made him more unpredictable and dangerous.

The idea of the treasure began to give his purpose in Arkansas a new meaning. "He imagined Vick used his stash to buy his way out of jail and set himself up in business. "They should have hung the bastard."

The more Buck contemplated Vick's success, the greater his resentment grew. He plotted ways to get the treasure back and make Vick pay. "Vick lives around here with a good-looking wife," he said under his breath as he walked. "There's plenty of ways I can get even."

Buck passed by a mercantile store and caught a glimpse of himself in a plate glass window. He looked beat and not the same man who used to be when he was at the top of his game. Pausing long enough to study his appearance, he moved his hand over the two warts that had appeared on his face since he last saw Vick. He hated what he saw. His ruddy complexion, charred by the West Texas wind, had left deep wrinkles, but he figured that, with a little grooming and a new wardrobe, he might be able to settle in town right under Vick's nose.

"This will be my biggest gamble ever, if I can pull it off. The pleasure will be all mine," he thought.

Buck's appearance had changed drastically, but with a little work he thought he might be able to pass himself off as a southern gentleman. "Ain't anything to speaking with a southern drawl if I'm careful. Buck's life had left him in a rather pathetic situation, and his ramblings reflected the paranoia that had taken root during his years of gradual degradation. "I'd better take care of Vick before he figures out I'm in town and has a chance to come after me," he decided.

Vick and Elizabeth were enjoying being married and each day continued to be better than the day before, until they received a telegram from Johnson Petty congratulating them on their recent marriage. It also said, that he and his daughter were coming for a visit to discuss Cain and Eileen's future together.

When Elizabeth read the telegram, she stopped in her tracks. "What future is he talking about? He knows Eileen and Cain broke up before they left San Augustine."

Vick was equally concerned and suspicious.

"Elizabeth, there's something real fishy about this.

"Do you think we should warn Cain?" she asked.

"Of course! He needs to know so he can prepare himself."

"I don't know, maybe we're jumping to conclusions. Remember how Eileen begged Cain to stay and talk it out? Perhaps, that's all it is.

It was apparent Elizabeth was upset and worried after receiving the telegram.

"Surely Cain didn't sleep with her," trying to convince herself.

Her mind carried her back to the morning when both Eileen and Cain slept late, and the more she remembered, the more worked up she got. By the time Cain arrived home, Elizabeth was beside herself.

He walked into the house, thinking all was well, when Elizabeth ambushed him with the questions. The look on her face was a dead giveaway that something was about to go down. "Cain, can you tell me why Johnson Petty would want to talk to you about your future with his daughter, Eileen? He's coming here to talk! What do you have to say about this?"

"Well, I don't know. You're acting like you know more than you're telling me."

"Johnson knows you broke it off with Eileen. Don't you think it's a little strange they would want to come here after all this time unless ..."

Cain broke in before Elizabeth could finish. "Unless she's pregnant?!! Is that what you are driving at? Are you trying to say Eileen might be expecting my baby?"

"Well, yes! What else could it be?"

"First off, it would mean I would have slept with her, so why don't we wait and see what's going on."

Although trying to keep his composure, Cain was suffocating inside, thinking of Lucy and what could become of them if Eileen was pregnant. Vick could see how his son was sweating, and knew he had indeed slept with Eileen. He could read his son's mind, since Cain reminded him so much of himself.

After a few minutes of awkward silence, Cain finally got up enough nerve to come clean about Lucy and what she meant to him. "There's something else you should know. Lucy and I have been seeing each other, and I've asked her to marry me."

Elizabeth and Vick just looked at one another, dumbfounded. Neither had any idea Cain had been seeing Lucy.

"Well, if that doesn't just take the cake! I'm not going to fret over you and Eileen any longer, as I'm sure you will work things out. I just hate the thought of having Johnson Petty tied to this family," Elizabeth chided.

Vick kept studying Cain, then finally asked to see him alone.

Elizabeth left the room as Vick walked over and placed his hand on Cain's shoulder. "Cain, you know you can talk to me about anything. I was watching you when you spoke to your mother. I remember that look. It's the same look I wear when I'm hiding the truth.

The fact is, I figure you have been with Eileen. Now, why don't we talk about what we're going to do about it?"

Cain knew he could not hide the truth from Vick, but he was not ready to talk about it. "I don't know," Cain said. "Let's not jump the gun!"

"Settle down now; I want to help. I'm not real good at this, but if Eileen's going to have your baby, you have got to step up and do right by her and this child. Your mother and I don't particularly care for Johnson, but we can both respect his desire to protect his daughter. You, better than anyone should understand how difficult it can be for a woman to raise a child without his Pa."

Cain looked at Vick like he didn't know what to say.

"I'm going to leave you by yourself for a few minutes so you can think, but we'll both be right here if you need us."

Vick took a moment and then walked out of the room, leaving Cain alone.

"So this is what it's like to have a father." he thought.

Several days passed and Cain still hadn't mustered the courage to talk to Lucy about his plight. Each day that rolled around, Elizabeth would look at him as if to ask what he was going to do about Lucy and Eileen?

Finally, Cain was ready to talk. The two men walked out in the gardens were Cain had played as a child. He asked Vick to sit, and then began pouring his heart out.

"Vick, I have thought about what you said, and the only way I can solve my problem is to marry Eileen. I suspect that's why she and her Pa are on their way."

"What about Lucy?"

"I'm going to ride over and talk to her as soon as I get through here. I know mother is going to be disappointed, but if Eileen is pregnant, then there is nothing I can do. Will you talk to Ma for me?"

"Yeah, sure, I'll tell her after you leave. You know you're going to break Lucy's heart."

Vick walked Cain to his horse, while Elizabeth watched from afar. As soon as Cain rode away she walked out to meet Vick.

"You know, don't you?" Elizabeth said.

"Yeah, I know … Lizzie you're about to witness your son become a man."

Cain thought he was never going to get to Lucy's house. It was the longest ride of his life when he finally arrived. There was no other way, he thought, and he knew he was going to devastate not only Lucy but Orson too.

As soon as he hitched his horse, she came running out to meet him, expecting him to take her in his arms. When he didn't, she saw the look on his face and knew there was something seriously wrong.

"Cain, what are you doing here today? Is something wrong?

"Is there someplace we can talk privately?"

"Sure. Why don't we go over to the swing. I hope nothing is seriously wrong. You've got me worried."

"I don't mean to worry you, but something is going on with Eileen, and she and her Pa are coming here to talk to me."

"I don't understand, why would Eileen want to talk to you now, after you broke up weeks ago?"

"Lucy, I want you to try and put yourself in my place and not judge me too harshly, but when I was with Eileen, well … we were intimate. At the time, I thought I loved her and we both planned to marry. I suspect she may be coming to tell me she is going to have a baby."

"Your baby?"

"Yes, I believe that's how it goes. I had been with her and now I think she's pregnant."

"Cain, I don't know what to say. I can't believe this. Is this something you do with all the girls you are attracted to? She's going to have your baby?"

"Of course not, but Eileen and I were serious about each other, and I thought I loved her. I don't actually know about a baby, but what else would make a girl come with her Pa to talk to me? Especially, when everyone knew I broke it off. Her Pa practically threw us off the place, and now they want to come and talk about our future together?"

Lucy was so stunned she wanted to scream. She wanted to beat on his chest and shake him, but somehow she kept her composure and tried to make some sense out of what he had just sprung on her.

"I must have been a fool, thinking I could have a future with you. This is more than I can accept with you having a baby with another woman. I'm sorry Cain, but I must ask you to leave."

"Lucy, I can't tell you how sorry I am about this."

"Just go! Now!" She tried desperately to keep from screaming.

"Lucy please, try and understand; I really love you and it's going to take me time to realize I can't have you."

Cain tried to hold her but she pushed him away.

"I need you to go. Don't waste your breath telling me you love me, when your life is with Eileen. I should have known it was too good to be true, and that something like this would happen."

Lucy sobbed and ran inside. Cain stood there motionless, knowing he had lost her.

Orson watched his daughter get her heart broke, just like he feared, but there was nothing he could do.

Before dusk the next day, Johnson and Eileen arrived.

Elizabeth was totally unprepared, but being raised a nice southern girl, courtesy was ingrained in her. She opened the door and invited Johnson and Eileen into the parlor, where Vick and Cain were sitting, unaware of their arrival. Johnson took Elizabeth's hand and greeted her rather coldly.

"Hello Elizabeth, I trust you are well. Thank you for having us," Johnson said.

"Likewise, Johnson. I received your telegram and was a little perplexed." Eileen gave Elizabeth a quick hug.

"Thank you for seeing us." Elizabeth smiled but hardly knew what to say. She struggled to gain her composure.

"I must say Johnson, when I got your telegram, it was very mysterious."

"Perhaps we should say serious instead of mysterious," he replied.

"Very well. Serious or mysterious doesn't matter at this point. I'm sure we will know the story soon enough."

Eileen looked at Elizabeth with a sheepish look.

Cain spoke up and made small talk about the long drive, giving the weary pair a chance to settle down and relax.

"Johnson, I think we've all waited long enough. What can we do for you?" Vick asked.

Johnson could not believe Vick was already directing their lives. He didn't like Vick questioning him, but he kept his cool and said "I'm sure Cain must have some idea of why I have brought my daughter here. There's really no good way to say this, but Eileen tells me she is going to have a baby."

"And you're here for our congratulations?" Elizabeth asked.

"I wish it was that simple Elizabeth, but Eileen tells me that Cain is the father."

Cain looked at Eileen like he was surprised to hear the news. There was a long silence and then he responded. "Eileen, I am so sorry, I know this must be terribly embarrassing for you and I apologize for what has happened."

"We're not here for apologies; we're here for you to make this right by Eileen," Johnson remarked.

"Of course, if Eileen says this is my child, then I have no reason to believe otherwise," Cain said.

Vick could see the sadness in Elizabeth's face and it was evident she was about to break down.

"Johnson, I understand the concern you have for your daughter, but I want to make one thing clear: There's no one person to blame here. I don't want you to feel like you can punish Cain for this unfortunate mistake. It takes two, and they're both still our children," Elizabeth reminded him.

"Children? Children my foot! They are adults and should have known better," Johnson scolded.

"Please, Daddy," Eileen cried.

"You're not going to make this easy on any of us, are you Johnson." Vick said.

Cain couldn't believe Vick would stick up for him like that, and Elizabeth couldn't have been more pleased, seeing him act the way a Pa should.

Johnson's sarcasm was scarcely veiled with his response. "Vick, I don't think you've been around long enough to take on the father role. You don't wear the title well, and I find it offensive, knowing where you've lived for the last twenty years for you to try and interfere."

Elizabeth was enraged with Johnson and was not going to allow him to come into her home and disparage Vick or Cain.

"How dare you belittle Vick and Cain, not to mention poor Eileen, when you've done nothing but tell one lie after another. First you lie to Cain when you knew damn well his Pa was in prison. Then you go stirring up trouble regarding a shooting in Odessa trying to discredit Vick to his son."

Elizabeth kept getting closer to Johnson and Vick thought for a second he was going to have to pull her off of him.

"Now that I have your attention, I want to make an important distinction between you and my husband. When Vick was in prison, what he did was for survival and he had no other choice. But you, you had a choice and you chose to lie. And because of your lie you almost got Cain and the sheriff killed. So, I ask you Johnson, who is the better man? You or Vick?"

Johnson stood, looking at Elizabeth with his mouth open. He liked women with a fighting spirit and seeing "her mama bear" instinct suddenly made Elizabeth very attractive. For a moment, he wished he had pursued her more fervently.

Eileen could not stand to see her Pa act so calculating when it was her life that he had in her hands. She began to cry, and Cain felt it was his fault that he got her in this mess.

"Please everyone, this is between Eileen and me. We're not children! We know the right thing to do, so no more of this. If Eileen will have me I want to ask her to marry me. And whether you like it or not, we all need to start being civil to one another." In spite of Cain's willingness to marry Eileen, Johnson was not through making an ass of himself.

"That's mighty gentlemanly of you, Cain. We can have this little Arkansas shotgun wedding right here, but after that, I expect you to come back to San Augustine so my daughter can have a proper wedding, one she has always wanted, among friends in our town.

"I have no problem with a big wedding, if this is what Eileen wants," Cain looked at Eileen and smiled.

"It's all settled then! You all can get married here and then when Eileen gets back to Texas she can mail out the invitations, and all you Porter's have to do is show."

"Eileen, if there is anything I can do? I would love to help you," Elizabeth asked, as she tried to ignore Johnson.

"That won't be necessary," Johnson broke in with his curt short answer. "You can help by getting a minister to marry Cain and Eileen tomorrow with just the four of us, and I will see to Eileen's wedding in San Augustine.

"Very well Johnson, if that's the way you want it. However, I do think you need to consult with Cain, since you can't have a wedding without him," Elizabeth said, refuting Johnson's insensitivity.

"Daddy, can't you let me and Cain work this out between us?" This time Johnson saw fire in his daughter's eyes, and thought it best to keep quiet.

The next morning, Cain stayed in his room a little later than usual. He was thinking about Lucy and what she was going through. "I hope Orson doesn't judge me too harshly," he thought. He felt terrible knowing he was entering a marriage with Eileen when Lucy had his heart.

"I loved Eileen once, perhaps I can learn to love her again." He walked to his window and looked over the large spans of gardens he had loved to play in as a child, and wondered if his child would be able to do the same. "I will miss this place," he thought.

When Cain walked past Eileen's room, he knocked to see if she was still inside. He heard her stirring and realized she must still be in bed.

"Eileen, it's me, can I come in?"

When she opened the door, Cain could see she had been crying. His heart went out to her, with her eyes swollen and red. He admired her beauty and thought, "I can make this work. I have to for the sake of my child."

Cain took Eileen in his arms and held her until she cried her last tear.

"Don't worry Eileen, I came to tell you that we can make this work. You know, you're very important to me and I've always had feelings for you, from the first time we met." They looked into each other's eyes, and she could see he was sincere.

"Cain, I'm so sorry! I was embarrassed in front of your family, telling them that we had been intimate. I never wanted to force you into marriage, but I have to think about our child. You know what people say about babies born out of wedlock. You understand, don't you?"

"Of course I understand. Look, this is going to work. We'll get married today and then you and your father can go back and plan the biggest wedding San Augustine has ever seen. Nothing is more important right now than you and our baby.

He could see her come alive again. She nestled in his arms, and for the first time, she felt he had forgiven her.

"Today, we're starting over. No more secrets between us, so let's forget about what all has happened and move forward. Do you think we can do that?"

Before Cain could react, Eileen threw her arms around his neck and began kissing him. It would take time for him to rekindle the passion he had before, but as she kissed him, he knew it was going to take some time before he could respond, since his heart was still with Lucy.

The day of the wedding, Elizabeth had picked fresh flowers and decorated the entire downstairs, making Eileen's special day as beautiful as possible. When the wedding began, Johnson walked Eileen down the stairs of the manor and onto the front porch where the ceremony took place. The elegant long veil she had borrowed from Elizabeth accented the bride's beauty.

Other than the presiding clergyman, no one was present but the family. In the distance, Vick could see Orson sitting on his horse watching the ceremony from a grove of trees. He knew his old friend wanted to see if Cain actually went through with it and got married.

After the ceremony the sheriff spurred his horse and took off leaving a trail of dust. Cain looked up just in time to get a glimpse of a hawk as it flew away. That's when he saw Orson.

After the wedding, when Vick and Cain were alone, they confided in each other. "Did you see Orson?

"Yeah, I saw him. I hope he doesn't feel too harshly about me."

"Don't worry, Orson is a good man. He'll get over it."

"Vick, did you see that hawk, when Orson rode away? Suddenly I'm plagued with hawks. One tried to knock me off my horse when I was coming home from Little Rock. Scared me to death!"

For a brief moment, Vick remembered the time a hawk had helped him save his brother, Sam, or at least that's what he thought when he was a child.

"Do you mind if I give you a little advice coming from someone who knows what it feels like in hell?"

"No, not at all. You mean the time you spent in prison?"

"Yeah, something like that. Yours would be a different kind of hell — but what I'm trying to say is you need to make the best of your marriage and love your wife — if you can't do that, it's going to be tough for both of you."

Chapter 36

IT WAS EARLY EVENING WHEN JOHNSON DROVE THE MODEL T INTO **town after the brief wedding ceremony.** "Perhaps a game of poker, or a couple of stiff drinks could help heal my woes," Johnson thought. The thought of my daughter marrying Cain Porter is enough to make any man drink," he rationalized.

Once in town, there was only one saloon and that would have to do. "Not impressive, he thought. He parked the Model T directly in front and walked slowly through the swinging doors like he owned the place, displaying a hint of arrogance. At first he saw only a bunch of chiseled-faced, rough hombres who were there drinking and listening to the melodies of a piano player and a middle-aged saloon girl. They were all bellied up to the bar, drinking their whiskey while the woman serenaded the regulars.

A man sitting alongside a young cowboy who was shuffling cards at a table in the middle of the room caught Johnson's eye. He saw the well-dressed gambler and thought, "this is more like it." Johnson wondered what the young cowboy and the sophisticated gambler had in common, sitting there as if they were old friends. The kid looked like he hadn't had a bath in a week and his stringy hair hung unkempt around his face. As soon as Johnson approached the pair, the kid looked directly at Johnson's pocket watch, which made him feel very uncomfortable.

The gambler began shuffling the cards in hopes that the newcomer would join them. He cleared his throat and commenced to speak to the young cowboy in a southern accent as part of his charade. By this time Johnson had made it over to the table.

"Mind if I join in for a couple of hands?" Johnson asked.

"We're happy to oblige anyone who wants to play," the gambler said. "You been in town long?"

"Not long. I came for a wedding."

Johnson was still in the clothing he had worn at the wedding, causing the gambler to assume he had a very wealthy prospect here.

"I plan leaving tomorrow with my daughter, heading back to Texas. By the way, my name's Johnson Petty." The men exchanged cordial handshakes. "Nice to meet you," the gentleman said, "I'm Carl Rhodes; doing business in town and staying at a boarding house up the street. Are you staying there?"

"No, I'm staying outside of town a ways. And who's your friend here," Johnson asked.

"Oh, my name's Johnny James but I ain't here to play. Mr. Rhodes was showing me a thang' or two about poker. You men know what you're doing and I don't," the kid gave a little chuckle.

Johnson laughed, "Why son, didn't you know that's who we like to play with?"

"Guess that leaves you and me," the sharp-eyed gentleman said with a smile, "What's your pleasure Mr. Petty?"

"I'm open to whatever you have in mind."

"Excuse me, I'll leave you men to your game," the kid said. He shook hands with Carl Rhodes and nodded to Johnson, then left through the swinging doors.

"Do you like Faro?"

"Fine with me, but I have to warn you, I'm not that good," Johnson replied.

Carl called to the bartender, "Can we get a Banker and a Dealer over here? Bring us a round of drinks, will you? Just bring us the whole bottle, with two glasses."

When the bartender delivered the drinks, Johnson got the idea that Carl Rhodes was a regular and possibly a heavy drinker, which always made him nervous.

The two men Carl requested came to officiate and brought the Faro board, which was on the large side.

The game started off well until Carl began socking down the drinks. By the middle of the game, he was a loud, obnoxious bore, bragging and making wild bets. "How 'bout making the game a little more interesting?" he slurred. Johnson thought it strange that the man's accent would come and go.

"Carl, I think we better stick with the regular game."

"No, how about you me having a little side bet?" His insistent behavior finally wore Johnson down.

"Okay, what you got on your mind?" Johnson asked.

Carl could see that Johnson was getting anxious and thought he was doing an excellent job of spinning his web of deception. He was engaging him slowly.

"Jest sayin' have your money ready to bet at the end of the game."

Johnson remembered being set up in New Orleans and hoped he was not imagining this man was pulling the same trick on him.

The game had turned in Johnson's favor, which excited him, seeing the money he was raking in. By the end of the game, Johnson had a pile of money and was getting ready to make his last bet when Carl abruptly said, "why don't we make that side bet now."

"It think we better stick to the game. I'm sitting pretty good as I see it.

Carl noticed something about Johnson he didn't like and thought, "this could turn out to be harder than I thought. Finally, he reached in his pocket and pulled out another five hundred dollars, the last money to his name.

"Come on, I'll put another five hundred in the pot and you match it. Carl shoved his cash in the middle of the table.

"You win, if I can't guess the last three cards the Dealer has in his hand".

"No joke! So you are betting me you know the Dealer's last three cards. Well, how about that!"

Johnson began rubbing it in for all it was worth mainly because of the con he recognized and the other was to let off steam for his daughter marrying into the Porter family.

"Yeah, that's what I'm saying." Carl gave Johnson a wicked smile, not feeling as secure as he did when he started the game.

"Just as I suspected," Johnson thought, as he remembered being played for a fool once before, when Vick had set him up with the same scam. He had fallen for it before, and he damn sure wasn't going to be made a fool of a second time. "Now, this drunken fool wants to cheat me by setting me up with the same bet. How ironic."

The Dealer said, "Okay, let's get on with it. We have three cards left."

Carl stopped the Dealer, "How about it Johnson? It's a wild bet, but you got a lot of money, and a chance to win another five hundred."

Johnson could see the desperation in Carl's face and thought, "at least Vick Porter was able to hold it together when he cheated me in New Orleans."

He jumped up from the table and shook his fist at Carl shaming him in front of people Carl had hoped to scam. The men at the bar were looking at him like they were glad he was exposed. Carl felt his charade begin to crumble, making him furious. But even in his intoxicated state, he knew to keep his cool and not become embroiled in an altercation.

"Do you take me for a stupid fool?" asked Johnson, rolling the money he won so he could slip it into his pockets and leave. He did not let up as he continued to embarrass the man, calling him a fraud. This did not go over well for Carl who was in town passing himself off as a businessman.

"Someone should tell you that your con is as old as you are."

Carl thought there was only one other man who knew his card counting scheme, and that was Vick Porter. Suddenly, it was not Johnson who had his money; it was Vick who had outsmarted him again. He wanted to blow this arrogant self-righteous snob's head off, but he didn't have his metal breastplate to protect himself. Besides, he knew there was a bigger prize, and he couldn't afford to expose his cover when the real reason he was there was to kill Vick Porter and get his treasure back.

The last words were from Johnson, taunting him. "You're nothing but a drunken fool. You think I didn't know you were setting me up?"

Johnson walked out of the saloon feeling vindicated, that he had gotten the upper hand on Carl Rhodes.

The next morning, Cain kissed his new bride goodbye, while Vick and Johnson packed the Model T for their trip back to San Augustine. It was still dark but one could tell that a big storm was brewing.

Off in the distance, a streak of jagged lightning lit up the sky, followed by a clap of thunder. Even though, the two families were worlds apart still, Elizabeth and Vick did not want to see them take off in a major storm.

"Johnson do you think you ought to be driving when it looks like rain?" asked Cain.

He ignored his new son-in-law and kept loading the vehicle, too anxious to get away from the Porter clan.

"As soon as I get my business taken care of here, I will be coming to San Augustine," Cain said, hoping to hear any encouragement from Johnson.

"Remember, the wedding is in three weeks," Eileen added cheerfully. She noticed how rude her daddy was to Cain, but tried to leave optimistic.

Cain was coming around to give Eileen one last kiss, when Johnson stepped on the gas and left him with Vick and Elizabeth looking on.

Vick thought what a fool Johnson was.

Chapter 37

Eileen dreaded the long trip home, and the thought of listening to her Pa continuing to criticize her new husband was unbearable. And to make matters worse, it was getting dark, though it was still early in the morning.

Suddenly, an onslaught of rain hit the Model T windshield like a gusher. Neither Johnson nor Eileen could see anything, as the lightning from the storm hit all around them.

Johnson began recognizing his stupidity. "Why didn't I listen to Elizabeth and wait for the storm to pass before launching off for home in the storm?" He began to have second thoughts about himself and his attitude, as he saw how his obstinacy had caused him to make such a poor choices concerning Cain and Eileen.

As the torrential rain hit the dirt road, it created massive ruts that caused the little car to slip and slide. Johnson was concerned that the storm might cause him and Eileen to become stranded miles from the manor.

"Daddy, why don't we stop and wait for the storm to pass?"

"What? I can't hear you. Tell me again."

"I said, why don't we stop and wait for the storm to pass?"

"Maybe you're right, honey, but we'll have to keep driving a little longer, until I find a good place to stop."

"Stopping will give us time to eat an early lunch. There's all kinds of food Elizabeth packed for us, and I'm already hungry."

He knew his daughter was trying to cheer him up, while he continued to fight the wheel, steering the car through the large puddles of rainwater that had accumulated on the dirt road. He could tell the automobile was having difficulty with traction. Finally, he found a clear spot on high ground where they could pull off to wait out the storm.

"Eileen, this will give us a good chance to talk. I think I've waited long enough."

Eileen thought, "Oh no, I hope he is not going to continue to browbeat me about my marriage."

There was no outside visibility with rain coming down in sheets as they sat and ate a delicious sandwich from the basket that had been so carefully prepared by Elizabeth. Johnson didn't know why, but he was feeling better about Eileen and Cain's marriage, and decided to tell Eileen how he felt. Before he had a chance to say anything, she assumed the worse and began to speak her mind.

"Daddy, can't you be happy for me and not dwell on Cain's father?"

Johnson genuinely loved his daughter from the bottom of his heart, and for the first time began to realize how insensitive he had been, finally regretting that he had acted so poorly. He could see how he was hurting her.

"Eileen, I have to say, Elizabeth did a very nice job with your wedding. It might take me a little time to come to terms with you marrying Cain, but I promise you I'm going to make every effort to be okay with this!"

She could hardly believe her father. After all he had done to make her miserable.

Throwing her arms around him, she hugged him tightly.

"Daddy, you don't know how happy you've made me. You'll see everything is going to be perfect when Cain moves to San Augustine and begins practicing law. He's going to make a fine son- in-law, and a good father to our child."

Johnson smiled at Eileen's innocent exuberance.

"Now don't push things, honey. Just let everything happen naturally."

He looked at her and thought what a beautiful young woman she had turned out to be, and how proud he was going to be walking her down the aisle. "She deserves at least that," he thought, remembering how happy he had been the day he married her mother. "Eileen deserves to be that happy, too."

After the stranded duo finished their snack, they decided to wait until the rain stopped before beginning their trip again.

"Life is going to be perfect living in San Augustine," Eileen imagined. She could hardly wait for the day when she and Cain would be mother and father to the new baby she was carrying.

Johnson started the car and had not gone no more than a mile when out of nowhere a horse carrying a man in a bearskin coat stepped out of the woods in front of the automobile. Johnson swerved off the road as the horse screamed in terror and reared up in front of them. The sudden stop threw Eileen into the windshield as the car skidded into a deep ditch to keep from hitting the horse. Water from the ditch had entered the floorboard of the car. Startled at how quickly the accident had occurred, Johnson noticed a gash on his daughter's forehead that was bleeding profusely. Blood was running down her face, while water continued to fill the floorboard.

"Eileen, Eileen, sweetheart! Are you okay?" Seeing Eileen was hurt and fearing that she might lose the baby, he paid no attention to the rider.

"I think so. Probably looks much worse than it is. Just a small cut. I'll be all right."

Little did they realize how well planned the scene was. His opponent from the night before, called Carl, aimed to get his money back, not caring who got hurt or even killed in the process.

Coming up on Eileen's side of the car, the rider opened the door, pulled out a big skinning knife and threatened her with it. When

Johnson saw the knife, it was like his world went into slow motion as he saw the man slide out of the saddle.

"Nooooo," he screamed as the man grabbed Eileen and pulled her up toward him by her hair, expertly slicing her throat from ear to ear before Johnson even knew what was going on.

"Ohhh no, what, have you done to my daughter?" he screamed. Johnson was trying to reach Eileen and take her in his arms. "My daughter, you've killed my daughter, you animal! Why would you do such a thing?"

Seizing the moment, the assailant quickly moved toward Johnson, planning to kill him, too.

"Your smart mouth did this to your daughter, Mate, when you took my money last night."

The accent sounded unfamiliar ... British?

Johnson squinted at the man who had just killed his daughter, and then recognized the two large warts on the man's face.

"I recognize you. You're the man from the saloon." Yeah Mate, name's Buck Dupree. Ye' heard of me before, ain't ye."

The man moved toward Johnson. "Too bad, you ain't going to be around to tell Vick Porter he's going to be next."

"Here, I have your money, please, my daughter needs a doctor. Take the money and go. At the same time, Johnson's left hand wrapped around the pistol under his seat and he pulled it up abruptly, surprising the knife wielder.

Although terrified, he managed to fire a round directly into the man's massive chest at point blank range. As the wounded man's body dropped out of sight beneath the car, presumably dead, Johnson, traumatized and whimpering, crawled over to examine Eileen's body as she continued to lose blood. Johnson knew she was dying as he watched his beautiful daughter gasp for air. She was trying to say something but could not speak.

Hard as he tried, he could not stop the bleeding and began sobbing, paralyzed by his grief.

"Eileen!" he screamed.

There was no longer any sound other than the patter of the rain on the car and through the open door, gradually soaking both of them. Johnson was too numb to even notice, let alone care as time seemed to stand still.

Suddenly a massive arm pulled Johnson's head back, and with little effort, the man sliced Johnson's throat. Though unable to speak, he was still alive and looked up to see his killer standing there, silently watching him bleed to death. With his last ounce of strength, he managed to reach his daughter to hold her. His eyes focused on her lifeless face as he lay beside her, dying. A single tear ran down his cheek. He had been unable to save her or the baby she was carrying. The blood was diluted from the heavy rain as it ran down Johnson's face. Still wondering how his murderer had survived the point blank gunshot to his chest, Johnson drew his last breath.

Blood was everywhere, as their arterial wounds had drenched the interior of the car. The ruthless killer watched until he was sure they were both dead and then wasted no time finding the money Johnson tried to give him. The bills were in the same tight roll as the night before when Johnson had rolled his winnings and placed them in his pocket. He took the rings and jewelry from the bodies, and rummaged through their bags to see what else he could salvage. When he finally departed, the scene depicted a murderous rampage and robbery.

That afternoon, the bodies were discovered, to the horror of a salesman who had delayed his departure until after the storm. There was so much blood, the bodies were unrecognizable until after the undertaker washed them. Left behind was Eileen's certificate showing that she and Cain Porter were legally married.

Orson rode up to the manor near dusk that evening to share the awful news about the murders of Eileen and her Pa. Cain saw the sheriff from the upstairs window and ran down the stairs, thinking he might have some news about Lucy. By the time he got to the door, Vick, Elizabeth, and Orson were waiting for him.

Orson's face had a look that was very alarming. The family knew something dreadful must have happened. Cain thought it might be news about Lucy who he knew was heartbroken over his decision to marry the pregnant Eileen. He could never have imagined what he was about to hear.

"What brings you out this way?" asked Cain reluctantly.

"Son, I don't know how else to tell you this, but I got some bad news. So we better go in, and Lizzie, you might need to sit down."

The sheriff could see the blood drain from Cain's face as Vick and Elizabeth led the way into the living room.

"Cain, I don't know how else to tell ya this, but your new wife and her Pa have been murdered. A man found 'em lyin' dead in that new Model T of theirs late this afternoon."

"What?... Oh my God!" Cain walked over to a chair and sat down, placing his face in his hands, then looked up at Vick and Elizabeth, who just stood silently with their arms around each other. Too shocked to speak.

"Do ya want me to leave ya'll and come back later?"

After what seemed like an eternity of silence, Cain finally spoke. "Orson, what happened? Tell me everything."

"I didn't want to say this part, but since ya asked, they had their throats cut and bled to death. It was a brutal scene, and they were robbed. They were hard to recognize 'til after the blood was washed off."

Cain tried to stand but went weak in the knees again, as he grabbed his mother for support. "Are you sure it was Eileen and Johnson? Who would do such a thing?" Vick asked.

Cain turned to his mother, shouting "the baby!"

The minute he thought of the baby, he lost all control. Elizabeth tried to console him by taking him in her arms, but nothing anyone said or did could reach him.

"Noooo," he screamed as he broke away from her and ran as fast as he could down the path that led into the gardens. Elizabeth followed after him.

"I can't believe it! Who would do such a thing?" she cried. Vick wanted to follow them, but he needed to stay and hear what else Orson had to say.

"Vick, it was definitely a robbery. We did some inquiring in town and it was said Johnson had words with one of them city fellers that's new in town, a man named Carl Rhodes. They was playin' cards 'n things got kinda tense when Johnson thought the man was trying to con 'em. All the man was doing was trying to make a side bet with him."

"What kind of side bet?"

"Something to do with guessing the last three cards in the Dealer's hand. That's when Johnson went kind of crazy."

Vick's face registered recognition at those words. He waited for Orson to continue.

"He got real upset and called the man a cheat and accused him of setting him up. They thought there might be a fight, but Johnson left before things got out of hand."

"You sure about this?"

"Orson, this new man, I think he might be Buck Dupree. In fact, I'm sure he is! There's not another man alive that knows this trick except Buck and me. It just so happens that I was the one that played the same trick on Johnson when we played together at the poker parlor when I was in prison. That's how he knew Buck was counting cards."

"So, Johnson recognized the same con like you did."

"That's right, and whoever this man is was setting him up to rip him off. And I can bet you anything, that man was Buck. Also, the way he killed Johnson and Eileen has Buck's name written all over it."

Orson asked, "What? ... His name written ...

"I mean, Buck Dupree did exactly the same thing to that poor family in Panther Holler. I saw the couple's throats slashed. Orson, somehow, Dupree's found out I'm out of prison and he's here to collect."

"Vick, let me ask ya a question. I'm just curious, but my mind goes way back to another time when you beat Elizabeth's Pa playing poker. Is this how you were able to beat Elizabeth's Pa by setting him up?" "You don't miss a beat, do you Orson? I know you can remember how old man Barkin had a reputation, of swindling people. That's when I made up my mind to beat him at his own game. He was trying to swindle Pa like he did every other man in town ... and, yes, I used the same trick on Barkin that I did on Johnson. Anyway, counting cards was a skill Buck taught me when we lived in Panther Holler. He became my mentor and I trusted him until he ran out on me and accused me of murder. When I got locked up, my only survival was showing the warden I could win playing poker, and the way I won was counting cards. Yeah, Buck taught me all about gambling and how to con people. Then, I got better than him, since he was getting older and not as quick minded. I hate to give him credit, but if it hadn't been for him teaching me how to count cards, I wouldn't be alive today. I would have surely died in prison."

"Yer' wrong Vick ... that man don't deserve no credit, 'cause if it weren't for him lying on ya, ya wouldn't have been in prison in the first place. It sounds to me like he was downright crazy. Ya know, I bet he wanted to git even with ya 'cause ya were a threat to 'em."

"Orson, you're probably right about that. Back then, he was proud when I got as good as him, but he got real jealous when he saw I was faster with a gun, and a better card player. That is when I guess I became a threat, but I was too young and trusting to see what it was doing to him. He left me in the Holler because he was afraid I might end up as his competition."

"So ya thank he's back to do you harm and maybe hurt Lizzie and Cain?"

"I think he's up to no good, but I know Buck well, and you can be sure he won't make a move without a plan. We're part of his game. He's playing us like we're all in a poker game. What we can't do is give him a notion that we're on to him. I don't mind telling you, though, that I'm afraid for Cain and Elizabeth. Killing Eileen and Johnson proves Buck is still as ruthless as ever."

"Ya might be wrong about that city feller 'cause nobody thinks he's the same feller that killed Cain's wife and her Pa. It can't be him, he wears them fine clothes, and he don't talk like them foreigners I heared before."

"Orson, no one knows him like I do. He used to tell me tricking people was as much part of the game as winning. Buck will dress up and do what he needs to, to win. He takes fooling people to the next level."

Vick and the sheriff's minds where entwined. "You know what I'm thinking! I can see it in your face."

"Yep, I know what we got to do is set 'em up like he does everybody else."

"You're right. Buck thinks I have the treasure and he might be staking us out right now. We got to be extra careful and not do anything that's going to let him know when we decide to set him up.

"Ya can count me in."

"I am worried about that boy of mine, though, and what he might do."

"He don't need to know that the man we suspect killed his wife is in town," the sheriff warned.

"You're right. Give me some time to figure out a plan. I might have to fight fire with fire, and get him as far out of town as possible."

"Don't thank too long 'cause a man like Buck Dupree don't take time to thank. He jest' acts."

Vick walked the sheriff out to his horse.

"Orson, you be careful going home."

Elizabeth had followed Cain in the direction of the garden but now he was nowhere to be found. When Vick approached her, she was sobbing uncontrollably.

"Lizzie, I hate to see you this upset," he said, sitting and holding her in his arms. "We're going to have to be strong for Cain."

"I'm worried about him. I looked all over the gardens and he's not here. I think he's taken his horse and ridden off somewhere."

"I was afraid that might happen. Why don't we walk out to the stables and see if his horse is gone?"

While they walked, Vick tried to calm Elizabeth.

"I know you're upset hearing about Eileen and Johnson, but you need to prepare yourself for what I just heard."

"Please, no more bad news," she pleaded.

"I think I know who did this; Buck Dupree killed Johnson and Eileen for their money. The way he killed them is the same exact way he killed his partner and his family over twenty-five years ago. From what the sheriff said, makes me believe it was Buck Dupree, who's here in town going under the name of Carl Rhodes."

"Oh my, are you sure? Do you think he's here for the treasure he thinks we have?"

"Why else would he take the risk? We know he's in town under disguise. I probably wouldn't even recognize him. The way the sheriff described him, he's totally changed his appearance. I suspect he knows he's finally a wanted man."

"Do you think he means harm to you and Cain?"

"The man is insane, and, no telling what he may do next. I've got to get him away from town and then take care of him myself."

"No Vick, what if something happened to you? I couldn't go on," Elizabeth began to tear up.

"You don't worry about me. I need you and Cain safe.

Checking the stables, they found Cain's horse gone, and assumed he had ridden off somewhere to be alone.

"I hope he rode over to Lucy's and not into town."

Vick hated to leave Elizabeth by herself while he went to find Cain, but he was concerned his son might run into Buck.

"Elizabeth, you go in the house and lock the doors behind you. I need to find Cain; I think he might be at Lucy's. You know where my rifle is so don't be afraid to use it. Understand?"

Elizabeth and Vick embraced and then went their separate ways.

Vick was right about Cain. He rode to Lucy's in hopes of having her shoulder to lean on. When he arrived, the sheriff promptly greeted him.

"Orson, I hope you don't mind, but I need to talk to Lucy."

"Cain, Lucy ain't here. She left for Chicargy right after ya told her ya was marryin' Eileen. She's a good girl and I know if she knew what happened she would be here 'fer ya. I'm real sorry 'fer ya loss."

"I appreciate you telling me that, but did she tell you I had to marry Eileen?"

"I knew, without her tellin' me a thang". I know you Cain Porter and it was jest a mistake. Right now, ya got your hands full, taking them bodies back to Texas. I reckon it's jest' not the right time to talk with her anyway. I hope ya go to Chicargy after her, and bring her home.

"Sheriff, I'm sorry about all this, I'll try to get my affairs in order and then go to Chicago and bring her back."

"Ya do that son; the sooner the better. She loves ya." Cain shook hands with the sheriff and rode back toward the manor. On the way, Vick rode up beside him and they stopped to talk.

"Cain you alright? Your mother's worried sick about you."

He looked at Vick like he wanted to cry, but instead, he nodded and rode on like he had nothing to say.

When they arrived home, Elizabeth seemed different. She allowed her son the privacy he needed and knew when he wanted to talk, that he would let her know. Vick thought she was surprisingly calm, as she did whatever she could to help Cain. When it was time for bed, insomnia had set in and no one could sleep. All they could think about was Eileen and Johnson, whose bodies laid in two wooden coffins that needed to be driven to Texas for burial.

The next morning, after the sleepless night, Vick and Elizabeth were sitting in the kitchen drinking coffee when Cain finally came downstairs and opened up about his plan to drive Eileen and her Pa back to Texas.

"I want to thank both of you for giving me time to absorb what's happened. I still can't believe they're gone. I just don't understand why someone would kill an innocent woman carrying a child and her father? It doesn't make sense."

"Cain, you know we're both here for you. All you have to do is tell us what you need and it's done. Are you okay?"

"Thanks, but I don't know if I will ever be okay again. I know there's a funeral to plan, and that I have to take the bodies back to San Augustine for burial."

"Cain, we want to go with you if that's okay?"

"Not this time. I know you want to protect me, but if you don't mind, this is something I need to do by myself. I'll probably get the undertakers to lend me their truck and drive the bodies to San Augustine alone."

"Are you sure? I think I need to go with you and let Vick stay here because he and the sheriff think Buck Dupree killed Johnson and Eileen."

Cain was startled when he heard the name Buck Dupree. "When did you hear this?"

"Cain, we don't know for sure, but we suspect he's in town. I knew you had enough to think about without jumping on your horse and going into town for a showdown with Buck."

"So you really think he's in town?"

"Yes, but now is not the right time to go after him."

"If he's the one that killed Eileen and my baby, he needs to pay; right now before he gets away."

"He ain't going anywhere, because I'm the reason he's here. You need to go about your business and leave Buck to me. This is my fight and I don't want you involved."

"I'm already involved. He killed Eileen and my unborn child."

"I know you think it's payback but you have to listen to me. We can't afford to go into town half cocked; we have to be smart about this. I know this man and we can't blow our chances. Don't you worry. Buck's going to get his, I promise."

"I don't understand the connection between Johnson and Buck Dupree?"

"Remember when Johnson left the house after the wedding? Well, it seems he went into town looking for a card game, and we think this is when he met Buck. The sheriff said Johnson played cards with a man called Carl Rhodes who we think is in town under disguise. Evidently, Johnson and this man Carl had a run in.

"Knowing Buck, he likely found out about Johnson and his daughter leaving the next day and planned to ambush them, which is what he did."

"Who would think a simple card game would turn into something like this. Now I feel I need to stay here and help protect you and mother. Do you think he might be planning on picking us off one at a time?"

"No Cain, nothing is going to happen as long as I have the treasure. You can count on that! You got to understand that I know how this man's mind works. You go on to San Augustine and give Eileen and Johnson a proper burial. We'll make a plan to take care of Buck when you come back. Understand?"

The next morning the men loaded the Model T truck with the coffins of Eileen and Johnson, and then said their goodbyes.

Elizabeth thought about Mattie, who suffered to bring Cain into the world, and how proud she would be to see both Vick and Cain together. They were tall and handsome and the spitting image of one another. For the first time since Mattie's death, she understood that Mattie knew Elizabeth's future was not only with Cain, but with Vick. Now, everything made sense.

The next day, Vick rode his horse by Orson's house, finding him sitting on his front porch, rocking excessively, and whittling away on a board. Vick stopped his horse and just sat there. He took a moment to look at this man that had been his friend for over twenty-five years. He recognized the sheriff was troubled about something. Finally the sheriff began talking without taking his eyes off his whittling.

"Vick, if the new man in town really is Buck Dupree, then you should know that he's staying at the boarding house, and is a regular at the saloon."

"You think so, huh?" Vick said kiddingly.

"Now, don't ya go smartin' off on me, 'cause I may have to pistol whip ya." Vick couldn't help but laugh at the sheriff whittling and never missing a beat.

"Have you ever pistol whipped anyone?" Vick chided.

"Only if ya wait too long to go after this hombre. I'm ready to get my posse together and do some lynching. Damn it! Ya moving too slow for my blood, I say let's go into town and catch 'em when least expected before someone else gets killed. We can drag 'em through town a couple of times on the tail end of a rope and then find a tree. Let 'em swing a day or two till he's good 'n ripe. Then leave 'em in a ditch someplace 'fer the buzzards."

"That could have been my fate if you had brought me in twenty years ago instead of letting me ride on."

"I got a nose that can smell a killer a mile away, and if ya don't have it in ya to go after the man, then let me get to 'em. I know I'm flapping my jaws, but when do ya think ya going after 'em?"

"That's why I'm here. I want to talk to you about a plan that includes Cain.

"Cain? Why, that boy can't shoot a gun, so don't tell me ya thinking 'bout using a kid that ain't never stood up to nobody, especially to the likes of Buck Dupree. Cain ain't ready for nothin like that."

"Listen to me, and don't jump to conclusions. I want to set Buck up and beat him at his own game.

"So ya gonna set Buck up?"

"No Orson; we are going to set Buck up! You, me, and Cain."

"Hallaluyer, I thought we were goin' to kill 'em, and ya jest want to set him up."

"We're going to do better than set him up. We're going to set him up and have him run in circles at the same time."

"Wat's wrong with jest takin' a gun and blowin' the sucker's head off and be done with it."

"What's wrong with you this morning? I've never seen you act so negative and edgy. Why don't you tell me the real reason you're upset? I know you better than you think."

"I'm ready to make a move on Buck, and then I guess I'm missing Lucy."

"She hasn't been gone that long and you know she needs time to get settled in."

"I know, but she don't belong in Chicargy. She belongs here with me. Besides, I miss her cooking."

"That's what I thought. You're in a bad mood cause you're hungry. You want me to feel sorry for you so, I'll take you home and feed you. Come on, let's go see Elizabeth."

"Thought ya would never ask."

When the men got to the manor, Elizabeth had supper ready. She listened as they told her their plan to set Buck up.

When she heard Cain would help in Buck's capture, she about lost it. "You can forget about that plan! I will never agree to having Cain get involved with something that could get him killed."

Chapter 38

THE MODEL T TRUCK FINALLY ENTERED THE NARROW ROAD THAT LED up to the Texas plantation. Cain imagined Eileen was there waiting for him on the veranda. It was all too surreal for him, and now his wife of only a few days and her father, were both dead.

The road was lined with mourners waiting confused and conflicted as to what happened.

Cain was directed to drive the bodies through an open field to a family cemetery in the shadow of several big oaks that hovered over two freshly dug graves that would be the final resting place of his wife, child and Johnson. He stopped the truck short of the burial plots and helped the men unload the coffins. He thought, "If I want to visit my wife and child, I will have to come here."

Eileen had many friends who loved her, and he hoped in some way she was aware of how much she was cherished. Even though Cain and her Pa had their differences, he preferred to remember the man as a father who loved his daughter and did the best he could for her.

Cain saw the graves of Eileen's mother and grandparents and felt comforted that the family was now together. After a brief but moving ceremony, the guests adjourned to the pavilion in the back of the Petty home for a luncheon prepared by friends. The wonderful presentation of food and flowers was a tremendous tribute to Eileen and Johnson. Before the meal was over it began to sprinkle and people began leaving.

Everyone tried to console Cain, who was visibly upset as they accepted him as Eileen's fiancée. Trying to protect her good name and his unborn child, he went along with their assumption that he and Eileen were only engaged when the tragedy occurred.

After the last guest left, Cain walked back into the beautiful plantation home without a clue that his life was about to change forever. Johnson's lawyer greeted him, and asked to speak to him privately in the library.

"Cain, I'm Phillip Bradbury, and I was Johnson's lawyer and confidant. Before I leave, there are a few things I need to go over with you."

"Nice to meet you, Mr. Bradbury."

"You might want to sit down." The lawyer was holding a very large book, which Cain recognized, since he too was a lawyer.

Still unaware of what was to come, Cain sat down.

"I presume you knew of Johnson's wealth?" he asked. "I imagined as much," Cain replied.

"I've called you aside because you are the beneficiary of the Petty Estate.

"I beg your pardon?" Cain asked, quite sure he had misunderstood.

"You heard right. You are the beneficiary of the Petty Estate, which I might add, is quite sizable. Johnson was one of the wealthiest men in Texas."

Cain was shocked as he listened to the attorney read Johnson's Last Will and Testament. There were too many details to comprehend, but one thing that stood out was that Johnson's twin brother, who was estranged, was left only a single five acre parcel of land, while the remainder of the estate was left to the last living heir, Cain being the survivor.

"But, I'm not kin …" Cain started to say.

"We will get to that, Mr. Porter," the attorney said.

The attorney went into details and explained that this land of five acres, which was located only a short distance from the plantation, had belonged to Johnson and his brother's parents, and apparently Johnson had thought that it was the only property that his brother had a right to.

The idea that the Will left virtually the entire estate to Cain, who had just married Eileen, was incomprehensible to him. He questioned the attorney to make sure he understood the wishes of Johnson, for it clearly stated that his twin brother Jonathan Petty was not to inherit any property other than the five acres. It also stated that Jonathan would inherit his brother's fortune only if there were no other surviving heirs.

"Cain, to make it clear, I know you are the only other surviving family member because Johnson confided in me that you and Eileen would be married after you all came back from Arkansas. I was sworn to secrecy, as his confidant to never tell anyone that Eileen was pregnant before you married. This promise I will keep."

"Mr. Bradbury, I appreciate your integrity in this matter. I would not like for anyone to destroy Eileen's reputation because of our having to get married. What about Jonathan? Wouldn't he have reason to contest the Will after he finds out I am the heir?"

"You don't worry about Jonathan. We have plenty on him to keep him quiet. I have a letter here that will put him away for the rest of his life if he tries to cause trouble. I never opened the letter, for if I did, it would possibly incriminate me." Cain thought about what Phillip said about incrimination since both of them were lawyers.

"I suppose the letter would involve me too. I don't know if you know but I practice law in Jonesboro.

"When I talked to Johnson about the letter, all he said was, let Jonathan know I have the information that that could put him in prison. This will keep him quiet. There has been a long history of bad blood and dissension between the two brothers that's better left unsaid."

"Every man has a past, and for me I say, let the Jonathan's past remain private. It's not for me to pass judgment on Johnson's brother.

Phillip, I don't know what to say about all of this. It's quite a surprise. Eileen and I were married in Arkansas, for a very short time. We were going to have a second marriage ceremony here for family and friends. I mean we were legally married and I cared for her and the baby very much, but I had no idea I would be heir to Johnson's Estate."

"You and Eileen would have made a fine couple. And as far as people are concerned, we'll say you purchased the property."

"I don't know what to say except, thank you. I don't feel different than I did when I drove here, so I'm sure it will take time for me to get used to the idea. I'm sure you will want the marriage certificate."

"Tomorrow will be soon enough. You being a lawyer know the procedure. Believe me, this property is very valuable for Johnson has cotton fields throughout Texas and other states. It's all too much for me to remember but it's all in this book. You are indeed a wealthy man. Do you think you can handle it?"

"I think so, I have a supportive family behind me and my mother knows a lot about the cotton business."

"It's a big job, but something tells me you and your family can handle a challenge. Will you be able to stick around so we can go over this again?"

"Sure. I'll stay two more days and then drive back to Arkansas."

"You're coming back, won't you?"

As soon as I close my law practice. That'll take about a month."

"Well, you're a fine young man. I know its bittersweet being the heir to Johnson's fortune, in view of what's happened. If I can help you with anything, please feel free to call on me."

"Thank you, Mr. Bradbury, I really appreciate your time.

Cain stayed in San Augustine a few more days to tie up loose ends regarding his inheritance.

The day before Cain left he examined the house in an effort to feel some connection with the personal property that he inherited.

On the long drive back to Jonesboro, he thought of his mother and Vick and how he was going to break the news about his new fortune. When he arrived and drove through the spruce trees that led up to the stately manor, Cain thought, "Home sweet home."

As he walked up the steps, Elizabeth knew it was Cain.

"Vick!" Elizabeth called out. "Cain's home."

She hugged him as soon as he walked in the door. Please come in and tell us what happened," she said.

"I reckon I'm just tired from the long trip. I need a minute."

Elizabeth hugged her son as she walked him to the library. Vick shook hands with Cain welcoming him home.

Thinking of how he wanted to break the news to his parents his mind was racing a mile a minute.

"How was the funeral?" Vick asked.

"There were a lot of people, really nice folks but it was sad for everyone. I reckon I'm going to be moving to San Augustine."

Elizabeth and Vick looked puzzled.

"Move to San Augustine? What on earth for?!!" Elizabeth asked.

"Why, I'll be at home."

Vick was concerned that Cain's grief was swaying his judgment.

"Do you mind telling us why you want to move to San Augustine when your home is here with your mother and me. I know this has been hard on you, but moving to San Augustine is a bit drastic, don't you think?"

"Well Mother, I reckon you would move too if you knew you were going into the cotton business."

"Now young man, you quit playing games and get on with what you're trying to say" she demanded.

Cain smiled and suggested that Elizabeth and Vick sit down.

"Would you please get to the point?"

"After the funeral I was called aside by Johnson's lawyer, who read Johnson Petty's Will. All of Johnson's Estate was willed to me. Everything: the cotton business, Pecan Plantation, everything."

"No! You mean you were the beneficiary of the Estate because you were married to Eileen?"

417

"Can you believe that?"

"No, I'm speechless. I don't know what to say. Vick, say something!" Elizabeth turned to Vick like she expected him to be as excited as she was."

"Well, it's looks like you're going to have your hands full," was all Vick could say.

"Yeah, I reckon I am. I'm glad you waited until I got back before we take care of Buck."

"The only 'we,' is me and Orson. You're not involved.

Cain thought, "why waste my breath." Two against one ain't going to win the battle. He already knew what his mother thought since there might be guns involved.

"Cain, one other thing you need to do is go see Orson. He said he has something to tell you about Lucy. Vick saw the blood drain from Cain's face, as he turned and ran out. "Do you think we should have told him Orson wanted to see him?"

"Might as well, he'll find out soon enough," Elizabeth replied.

By the time Cain drove the undertaker's truck to the sheriff's place, he was beside himself wondering what had happened to make Lucy want to stay in Chicago. After all, she had assumed he made his choice when he asked Eileen to marry him, so what was he to expect.

As soon as he stopped the truck, he opened the door and ran up the steps to Orson's cabin. The sheriff heard footsteps and opened the door to see the panic stricken Cain.

Before he could speak, Cain began to ramble.

"Jest a minute, ain't that the funeral wagon you're in."

Cain thought, "*Why is he interrupting me?*" then said, "Orson, don't you think Lucy would come home with me, if I went to see her?"

"Cain, boy settle down. I don't know what you're talking about."

"I'm talking about how much I love your daughter, and I want her to come back here and be with me."

All the while, Cain was talking to Orson, Lucy was standing behind Cain.

"Well, I don't know why you're telling me bout' this when the person you ought to be tellin' is standing right behind ya."

Cain could hardly believe what he was hearing. He quickly turned around. They looked at each other for what seemed a full minute, and then she threw her arms around him.

Orson smiled.

"Damn you, you could have told me Lucy was here and spared me."

"Didn't your mama tell you Lucy was home?"

"No! She only told me you had something to tell me about Lucy. I suppose I imagined the worst. I didn't bother to stay and hear what else they had to say. Cain couldn't believe his eyes. He noticed how ravishing Lucy was.

"You came back. And I didn't have to go to Chicago after you."

"Well, you know, I missed working for Elizabeth and felt it was only fair to come back and help her."

"Oh, is that why you came back? Didn't you miss me?" Cain asked.

"Orson, I'm going to kiss our girl. I hope you don't mind."

"Sakes alive, ya mean I'm gonna have to see' this mushy stuff starting all over again."

The next morning Vick was on the porch having breakfast when he saw Cain walk past him with his gun strapped around his waist.

"Cain, where you going? Isn't that a new gun you're toting?"

"Yeah, it's one of Johnson's guns I found at the plantation. Pretty nice, huh?"

"Do you mind if I see it?"

Cain unbuckled his belt, and handed Vick the gun and holster.

He looked the gun over and then strapped it to his hip to get the feel. He did the quick draw testing his skill.

"You're right, this is a nice gun."

Vick twirled the gun a few times and holstered it, with Cain admiring his talent. It brought to mind the day he met the professional gunman in the woods who stopped to give him pointers.

"The professional was fast, but Vick was a lot faster," Cain thought.

About that time Orson rode up. Vick invited him to sit and have breakfast. He took off his hat and sat down like he was a regular around the table, and noticed Vick had a new gun.

"What are ya' planning' on doin' with that gun?"

"It's not mine. This is Cain's new gun."

"Cain's?"

"Orson directed his conversation to Cain. "Boy, I told ya to stay away from guns unless ya mean business!"

"That's why I have a gun. I have unfinished business."

"Don't you know better than git' smart with me. I'll have to pistol whip ya. That's a mighty fine weapon, but you ain't suppose to be awearin' no gun. You know how yo' mama feels bout' you and a gun."

"Orson, I think a dead man who was shot and killed would disagree with her, don't you?"

"Well, I reckon you be right there, but be careful and make sure you know what you're doing."

Cain smiled at the sheriff. Vick unbuckled the belt and gave the gun and holster back to Cain.

"Thanks, I'm not going to be gone long," Cain said.

Elizabeth walked onto the porch just in time to see Cain ride off with his gun.

"Can't anyone talk sense into him? I'm afraid he's going to shoot himself or run into Buck Dupree."

"Elizabeth, have you noticed that Cain's a man and has a mind of his own? You don't talk to another man about his gun," Vick pointed out.

The sheriff was sniffing at the aroma coming from the kitchen and Elizabeth knew he was hungry.

"Orson, you got time for some breakfast?"

"You must be a mind reader, Lizzie."

She laughed and walked into the kitchen to fill Orson's plate. The sheriff suddenly got serious.

"Orson, I think I've seen that look before. What's going on?

"I got some news. I kinda' jumped the gun."

"What are you talking about," Vick asked.

"Well, I been layin' low and watching that Carl Rhodes man. He's been hangin' around with that young cowboy. Remember that young fellar that don't act like he's all there? He and Buck, I mean Carl are everywhere together."

"Orson, tell me you didn't mess up our plan?"

"Well, I got ta' thanking,' I didn't like yer' plan as much as mine."

Vick could tell the sheriff was nervous, trying to explain that he had taken matters into his own hands. He wanted to be angry with Orson but he couldn't.

"Orson, I didn't know you had a plan."

"Well, it jest came ta' me. I told that young cowboy fellar 'bout the treasure and how valuable it was." Vick could feel his temper rising.

"I told him the whole story about ya burying the treasure and all that. He was real interested. I had my bottle of Muskie dime whiskey with me and shared it with him. He thought I was all juiced up and telling thang's' outta' school, when I sprung it on him about the treasure. "I told him you buried it at Panther Holler up around the storm shed, but ya were' having a hard time remembering if it was buried in the shed or next to them graves. He got real interested. Before he got up to leave, I told him ya were going up to Panther Holler and do a lot of digging.

Anyway, after that, I followed him and guess who he went running to? Buck Dupree, the man that goes by Carl Rhodes. When I seen him with ole Carl, I knew he was most likely Buck. I waited and watched 'em plotting. That's when I got my deputies keepin' an eye out, and when Buck moves, I want us to move. I already checked, and Buck's leaving the boarding house in the morning."

Vick was livid that Orson had taken matters into his own hands. Now that his plan had been sidestepped he had no other choice but to go along with Orson's plan. Hearing Elizabeth coming from the kitchen he motioned for them to be quiet. She had a plate full of biscuits, eggs and country ham, just to please their old friend.

"This looks mighty good, Lizzie. Yes sireee."

"You can't fool me. I know you've been talking about capturing Buck. Do whatever you want, but you're not involving Cain."

Chapter 39

Sheriff Orson Cargill was reaching the ripe old age of seventy, and whether he wanted to or not, he had begun to slow down. One would think the prospect of retiring would not be that big of a deal to a man like Orson, who had experienced as many things in life as he had. But he was no ordinary man. It was as though he willed his heart to beat a little stronger, so he could breathe to live another day in order to see the sun come up just one more time, guaranteed or not. He often said, "I ain't ready for the bone yard, 'cause I got plenty else to do."

Buck Dupree had managed to escape the law for over twenty-five years by living mostly in small towns where a man's business was his own. People knew there was a dark side to the Aussie, but as long as they didn't see him murder, rob a bank, or catch him red-handed rustling cows, they left him alone. That's the way it was in small towns.

Buck's past was finally about to catch up with him; as Vick Porter, the man he hated most in the world had made a plan to settle the score. Both Orson and Vick were on edge the night before, knowing they would be leaving for Panther Holler early the next morning. Buck Dupree had done insurmountable damage to the Porter family, not to mention those he had killed, cheated and robbed. And they were hoping to bring him to justice. At last!

The next morning there was only one lamp burning in Sheriff Cargill's cabin as Lucy helped her Pa get ready to meet Vick. She had him packed and ready to go the night before, and all she had to do was make breakfast and send him on his way.

"Pa, please take care of yourself."

"Now, don't go worryin'. You know I'm as fit as Vick. Lucy, ya need to go back to bed. It ain't even daylight."

She ignored her Pa, knowing she could never win an argument. She picked up the dishes and watched him as he wound his pocket watch and gathered his snuff and chewing tobacco.

Elizabeth had never known danger before, but now since the murders, she knew that Vick and Sheriff Cargill had to put a stop to Buck's madness before he had a chance to kill again. "Any one of us could be next," she feared. Despite this realization, she abhorred violence and exhibited an uncharacteristic weariness as she prepared food and supplies for Vick and the sheriff's trip to Panther Holler.

She quickly combed and twisted her hair in a bun high on the back of her head, then hurried about, taking care of the morning chores before Vick awoke. She raked the ash in the fireplace until she caught a flame, rekindling the fire; then went about her business making coffee. These were her new husband's last few hours at home before the showdown with Buck Dupree, and she feared that she might never see him again.

Still before dawn, she had everything packed. Afterwards, she walked out onto the back balcony overlooking the vast gardens of their beautiful manor estate, and said a prayer, asking that Vick and the sheriff be protected on their trip to Panther Holler. She knew they were planning to set a trap for Buck Dupree, in hopes of ending what had become a nightmare for all of them. It was way too early to be up, but knowing that her husband and the sheriff were about to confront a coldblooded killer who would show them no mercy, worried her so much, she couldn't sleep anyway.

Soon after she finished praying, Vick woke up and walked out onto the balcony with his morning cup of coffee. He had not slept well either, and knew that Elizabeth had been awake even longer than he had.

"You're up early," he said. "Couldn't sleep?"

He could see Elizabeth had been crying.

"Lizzie, you know I hate to see you sad."

"Vick, I think you and Orson are making a big mistake going after Buck by yourselves. You need to take a posse with you."

He reached for Elizabeth and pulled her close to him. She was trembling as he tried to comfort her.

"You know we have to do this. It's either him or us!"

"But not by yourselves," she said.

"Buck could be setting a trap of his own."

"You have to listen to me. I know you're worried, but Buck could come after any one of us, and I would hate to know something happened when I could have stopped him, especially if you and Cain got hurt. You have to have faith and trust me."

"I know, and I do, but I can't bear the thought of losing you."

Before they finished their conversation, Orson appeared out of the early morning mist, a man on a mission.

Vick spotted the sheriff, then turned to Elizabeth. He sweetly asked her to come to him.

She walked over to Vick, who wanted to comfort her.

"You save those tears, we'll be fine. Come on; I have to finish packing, Orson's waiting."

"What do you think I've been doing since I couldn't sleep? You're not going to need more than a three day supply of food, are you?"

"Who knows, it could be one day or three. You can count on one thing; we'll be back as soon as we take care of Buck. So please don't fret… Are you sure you're going to be okay?"

Vick slipped his feet into a pair of old boots while he finished talking.

"Don't worry about me. I'll be fine. I'll have Cain here with me."

"I spoke to him last night, and he knows he's not going with us."

"Thank goodness you finally got through to him."

"He's a grown man, but it would not be a bad idea for you to keep an eye on him."

Vick gave Elizabeth a hug and walked out to meet Orson. They talked until Vick walked his horse back from the barn.

Cain was upstairs dressed as he waited for Vick and Orson to leave.

The sheriff could tell Elizabeth was unhappy about the trip to Panther Holler, seeing Vick and him risk their lives for a murderer.

"Now, Lizzie, you don't go worrying over Vick. We'll be back fore ya' know it."

Elizabeth remembered how fearless Orson was when he went through fire to save her. "She smiled at Orson, letting him know she was comforted knowing he was with Vick.

"Ya'll be careful, and don't take any chances. I don't want either of you getting hurt," Elizabeth said.

"This ain't nothing but routine; you and Cain take care of yourselves."

By the time the men rode away, Cain who had his own score to settle with Buck was at the barn with his horse saddled and ready to ride. Neither his mother nor anyone else could have kept him from stealing away to follow Vick and the sheriff.

As the new day broke, Vick and Orson had already made good time. They were moving at a fast pace, not realizing that Cain was out of sight right behind them. As Vick rode on ahead, he thought back to the time he and Sam had run away from home. The road was much wider now and the surface had improved considerably since they were kids, helping them make remarkably good time.

The horses were spry as they made their way toward the place where he and Sam had entered the thicket. Orson kept falling behind until he thought of something he wanted to say and then he would ride up beside Vick to talk.

"It's been a long time. Do ya thank ya can find yer' way back there?"

"I have the map etched in my brain. Don't worry, I know where I'm going," Vick replied.

"Panther Holler, that's a strange name for a place. Wher'd it come from?"

"I don't rightly know. There was a sign on the cabin that said Panther Holler. At least that's what Buck told me. When I was a boy living alone in the cabin, I heard screams at night that sounded like a panther. Buck said, it was the panther that chased him and almost killed him. After that, he said he saw shadows from time to time that looked like a panther following him."

"That man's full a tales. He's lying 'cause there ain't no panthers I ever heard about around these parts."

"Orson, I think you're wrong! When Sam and I were young I shot and wounded a panther with a .45 pistol."

"I betcha anything he wasn't a panther."

"Did you ever hear tell of a young Indian kid by the name of Hawk?"

"Not that I can recall. If you're talking about one of them Indians that use to live on the Indian Reservation, it's been too many years."

"When I was a boy Hawk used to come by and we would play in the woods. He had an old .45 pistol, and that's when I learned to shoot. One day we ventured a little too far away from home and that's when we had the run in with the panther. I had no choice but to shoot the cat. Didn't kill em', but wounded him enough to let him know I meant business. I always wondered if that cat wandered off and died somewhere."

"After that, the Indians became like family."

"I heard something about you and them Indians. So that's your connection with 'em huh? When you saved Hawk?"

"I suppose, but it's more than that. I respect their culture. After I saved Hawk, that's when he promised to be my protector. Kind of funny, huh? When you're a boy you believe anything. All the time I was in jail I used to laugh and say, okay Hawk, when you planning on protecting me?"

"Well, ya still alive, ain't ya? Maybe he's been protecting ya all along," said the sheriff. Vick smiled, thinking Orson had an answer for everything. The tribe was fine people and I for one, hated to hear they moved the village. Do you remember when the Indian Village moved?"

"Yeah, I reckon I remember that. Did ya ever find out why them Indians decided to pull up stakes and leave?"

"I heard a rumor that it was because ole man Barkin buying up and swindling people out of their land."

When they rode through the last town, Vick began to recognize where he was. There was only a short distance to go before they would rest for the night.

At daybreak the next day, Vick knew he was getting close to entering the thicket. Surprisingly, there were little changes to the landscape as they rode the last few miles. The trees were taller, more overgrown brush. "It looks exactly as I remember when Sam and I entered the woods," Vick thought. Then he saw the fresh horse tracks near the entrance, indicating that someone was ahead of them. They dismounted and looked around to see if it was one or possibly two horses that had passed into the thicket ahead.

"Looks like ol' Buck is already here. Thank we oughta' follow this trail?"

"Yeah, I've been away from that sonavobitch for over twenty years, and I can still read him like a book. He's here all right. Look, see how fresh these tracks are? I bet he's not but a few hours ahead of us."

"Best we keep going if we plan to gain on him ... or them," Vick said. The duo mounted their horses and took off. They rode for half a day until they saw the military campsite.

"See that shell of a building? Let's check it out before we unload our gear." They rode around the skeleton of the old cabin before they stopped.

"Orson, why don't you find a good place to hitch our horses, while I fetch a little wood to make a fire?"

Vick walked off to gather enough kindling to start a fire, and a couple of bigger pieces for fuel. As he came back with an armload, he was studying the movements of his old friend. He could see some signs of aging, as Orson seemed to move a bit slower than before. "I owe that man my life," Vick thought. "He could have arrested me when I had a bounty on my head, but instead of taking me in, he let me ride on as a free man. Orson had saved Elizabeth in the fire. Both of us would have been dead if it hadn't been for Orson. He is like family to us."

Right then, a beautiful gray hawk squealed and swooped down in front of him, causing Vick to drop the load of wood.

"What the heck?" he said aloud, as he watched the hawk fly to the top of a tall tree, opening his wingspan as though he wanted Vick to know he was there.

The sheriff was busy scouring up grub, and never paid attention to the hawk or Vick shouting. "Hey Orson, did you see that hawk? He almost knocked me down. The darn thing flew right in front of me and liked to have scared me to death!"

"That's the way them hawks do when they got a nest of babies nearby. I ain't heard of no hawk acting up like that though, except the one that buzzed Cain the other day."

As night fell, they hunkered down around the fire in the shell of the cabin that was now minus a roof. Both men were thinking of Buck, and what tomorrow might bring. The next morning, they awoke to the early morning sun filtering through the trees, plus the sweet scent of lilacs. Vick felt inner peace and rejuvenation knowing he was on Buck's tail, and was finally going to end his nightmare.

"That murderer deserves no mercy when I kill him. Buck owes me and he's going to pay," Vick reflected.

As he and the sheriff began to saddle up, they noticed the area around their horses had been stomped down. "Orson, take a look at this underbrush."

"Well I'll be. If I didn't know better, I'd say we had a visitor last night."

"Something has definitely caused the ground-cover to be beaten down like this."

"It's probably just a varmint or perhaps Buck. How much further will we have to go before we get to the next stop?"

"We'll make it before dark if we don't tarry."

"Shut the sissy talk. Who in the heck tarries?"

Vick spurred his horse and left the sheriff eating his dust.

"You ... som'..."

The sheriff finally caught up with Vick and shook his fist at him. "Thanks for the dust breakfast!"

As they rode, they kept slowing down whenever they saw evidence of horses ahead of them. Vick was sure they were right behind Buck and he wanted to be extra careful.

When they came to the lake, it was smaller than he remembered. But one thing was exactly the same: the sound of the water from the waterfall, as it fed the lake from a spring off in the distance. It had been a day and a half since they had seen a watering hole, and the horses were ready for a good drink.

"How about making camp here?" The sheriff asked.

"Looks good to me. Funny how you see things different when you're young, 'cause when I was here with Sam, I remember this lake being huge. I didn't tell you, but Sam almost drowned here."

"You and your brother had a hard time, didn't ya?"

The sheriff's horse was standing there drinking from the lake when Orson's eyes narrowed as he spotted something up ahead.

"Vick, ya see what I see in the lake over ther' hung up on a limb? Yer' eyes are better than mine, but from here that looks like a body."

Vick walked up closer to the water.

"I think you're right. Let's walk up-stream and check it out."

"I imagine ole Buck did that. Guess he ain't gonna give up till he kills everybody in his path."

"Yeah, but who would be out here with him?"

Orson found a stick and Vick freed the body. It drifted over close to where they were standing. "

Vick, I reckon I know this man." The sheriff stood over the corpse with his hat in his hand.

"You know him?"

"Yeah, he's that young cowboy I fed the story to about the treasure. I reckon Buck did this to 'em."

Vick and the sheriff took the body out of the shallow water and then checked out the surrounding area to see if they were alone. After they made sure they were safe they went to were the body was resting.

"We got to give the boy a proper burial," Vick said, as they dug a shallow grave. "I wonder why Buck thought he had to kill 'em?"

"He's jest a kid, but knowing Buck, he used him for information and then killed him, thinking he might have to share the treasure. He was no threat whatsoever."

"Do you know his next of kin?"

"I think he has two brothers whose name is Dudley and Lonnie Peck." All them boys and their ole pappy ain't worth killing. They're in trouble all the time. We need to mark the grave good, in case his brother wants to see the grave."

That night, it took quite a while before Vick could sleep. He kept feeling as though someone was watching them, but the sound of the spring was magical, soothing and relaxing enough to finally put Vick and the sheriff to sleep.

Just before daybreak, Vick awoke to the sound of brush moving behind him. He quickly rolled over and grabbed his gun, but he did not want to shoot for fear of alerting Buck, should he be camping nearby. He imagined *it could be a varmint, but then it might be Buck.* He quietly got up and slowly moved in the direction of the sound. When he got there he looked down and saw another body in a bedroll. His gun ready, he had it carefully aimed at the back of man's head when he rolled over. Vick immediately recognized their visitor as Cain.

"Cain! What in the heck are you doing here?" he whispered. Vick was so upset he threw his hands up in the air, waiting for Cain's explanation. "It better be good," he thought, for at that moment he wanted to pistol whip him.

Cain wasted no time defending himself.

"Just wait a minute. I know how you feel about Buck costing you twenty years in prison and cheating you from knowing you had a son, but I've lost more. The man killed my wife, her father and my unborn child, so deal with it!"

"Well, do you want to be next, cause you damn sure ain't no gunfighter." You can't go up against a man like Buck. I know you been practicing your shooting, but believe me; Buck could take you out with his eyes closed. He's that fast, understand? I wouldn't tell you this, but I'm thinking about your mother. She's all alone and needs you at home. Why don't you let me and the sheriff handle this."

Cain had no intention of backing down.

"You don't know what a man is capable of when his wife and child have been murdered."

Convinced that he was unable to stop Cain, the only thing left was to compromise with him. "If you're not going to listen to me, you can stay on one condition:"

"And what's that?"

"You stay out of sight till I get the drop on 'em. Promise me you won't interfere?"

"But, if I get a chance I'm killing him." Cain challenged.

The sheriff began to stir and when he finally awoke and heard voices, he jumped to his feet and began stumbling around trying to determine where the voices were coming from. Vick and Cain walked back into camp to see a gun barrel pointed at them.

"Orson, put your gun away. You could have killed us the way you were flailin' that thing around."

"Is that Cain there with ya?!" Cain stood smiling at the sheriff, like all was right with the world.

"Wha' the ... Cain, ya ain't supposed to be here!"

"Orson, I've already been through this with Vick. I'm here so that's that. Y'all go on ahead and I'll follow close behind."

"Just don't be gittin' antsy and try shooten' that thang'.' Having a gun don't make ya a gunfighter."

"So I've been told."

Since they were already awake, they mounted their horses and continued their journey. Vick, leading, was concerned about allowing Cain to follow them through the most treacherous part of the route to Panther Holler, but he had no choice, as it would be too dangerous for him to return home by himself.

They had been riding for a couple of hours when, without warning, Buck's horse stepped out of the brush behind the sheriff. He rode up right beside Orson, pushed his gun into his back and whispered, "Mate, give me that gun and don't say a word if you don't want your head blown off."

The sheriff had no choice but hand over his gun. Buck took it and tossed it over a ledge into a holler.

Cain saw what was happening but could not do anything for fear of missing his shot and hitting the sheriff or Vick. He chose to stay out of sight and off the trail, watching for an opening. As he did, the two men walked their horses up close to Vick.

"Hello, Mate," said Buck in his natural Australian accent. "Long time no see!"

The sheriff froze as Vick turned sharply, drawing his gun, but Buck had the drop on him and fired, hitting him seriously in the shoulder. The sting and heat of the bullet caused Vick to drop his gun. It bounced over the ledge.

Instinctively, and thinking of Cain, he leaned off to the side of his horse where Buck could not get another clean shot and spurred his horse heading toward the trees. He figured Cain would know something was going on and stay out of sight. As he reached the woods he kicked his feet out of the stirrups and hit the ground rolling behind a large tree. The fall almost cost him consciousness.

They had arrived at Panther Holler and the cabin was still intact after all the years that Vick had been away.

He knew Buck needed him alive and felt sure he would not kill him until he found the treasure. *"This will give me a minute or two to plan my next move,"* he thought. He could see there were plenty of trees surrounding the cabin where his son could safely stay out of sight.

Cain inched closer, moving slowly, careful not to give his position away. His eyes tried to focus on Buck. Even though he was still too far out of range to really see him clearly, he thought the man looked familiar. Seeing both his Pa and the sheriff in the predicament they were in, Cain knew it was going to be up to him to save them.

As Buck walked him up closer at gunpoint, the sheriff could see from the way he was leaning against the tree, that his friend was badly hurt. Vick was trying to stay conscious, but it was doubtful he could for very long, by the look on his face. His only thought was keeping Cain and the sheriff alive. He knew he could not get away.

Buck finally was face to face with Vick seeing he was badly injured.

"Well, Mate, it's been a long time. You think that tree's going to save you?"

"Yeah, it has been a long time," Vick said, in a voice riddled with pain.

"I thought you were a dead man until you resurrected yourself."

"I've already lost a lot of years because of you and your murderous rampage. Might as well have been dead as locked up in a prison paying for the murders you committed."

"You look right nice with that beard covering that ugly scar of yours. I wasn't sure it was you."

"I'd like to say the same thing about you, but with those two lovely warts you have on your nose ..."

Buck broke in: "We all change Mate, but one thing that has never changed is my hatred and desire to make you pay. You shouldn't have lied to me about the treasure. You set me up with a sack full of junk and now I find you've had it all the time. Just so you know, I've come to reclaim what's mine and then I'm going to do what I should have done twenty-five years ago."

"Well Buck, you've never proved me wrong. You're still the same "no good" you were when I met you." Vick was grimacing in pain as he tried to speak. "The reason I never told you about the treasure was I never trusted you. I always knew you were a liar.

"You've had your say, now where is my treasure? Unless you want me to put this bloke here out of his misery."

"I'd like to help you but twenty years in a prison can tend to make a man forgetful. I may have to dig up this whole place before I find the treasure."

"In your condition? I doubt it, so it's best you start remembering. And don't count on your partner. He looks like he's on his last leg." Vick knew his gunshot was more serious than a shoulder wound and he would never be able to dig.

The sheriff grimaced when Buck said he was on his last leg. Orson had proved a many a man wrong and started to speak, but Vick gave him the eye to keep quiet. The last thing Vick wanted was Buck's attention focused on the sheriff, knowing their lives were as immaterial as the young cowboy they found with his throat cut.

Vick was weak, and concerned he wasn't going to make it. All he wanted now was for Cain to turn around and get as far away as possible, and not do something stupid, since Vick felt he was dying and the sheriff was disarmed. Vick struggled to stand, then came out from behind the tree distracting Buck further.

Cain watched what was happening but could not make out how badly his Pa was hurt. He knew he had to save Vick and the sheriff, but he was unsure of his aim. "Somehow, I have to get closer," he thought.

When Buck saw how pale Vick was, he decided to help him to the cabin. As they reached the door, he admonished,

"Don't you die on me before you find where the treasure is, you hear?"

Just hearing the words shook up the sheriff. Let me use that shovel ya got there and I'll show ya I kin' out dig anybody."

It was now in the heat of the day, and Vick was unable to stand without help. It was apparent he was about to either die or lose consciousness. "Well, Mate, has your memory been jarred yet?"

Vick was exhausted and could only whisper, "I told you I didn't remember, but it seems I might have buried it in back of the shed. Yeah, I think it was there." Although Vick was weakening, he hoped he would stay alive long enough to see his son and the sheriff safe. "If only I can hang on long enough to keep Buck occupied so Cain can make his move."

He pointed to random places that were as good as any, since the treasure was safe back at the manor.

"Well, let's go then," Buck said as he motioned for them to start moving toward the place Vick pointed out to dig.

"Can't ya see the man ain't able to walk?" the sheriff pleaded.

"Well, how about helping him. Get a move on before he dies," Buck shouted.

The sheriff could see Vick struggle to stand and knew he might not make it to the back of the shed. Orson put his arm around him to help as best he could, while Buck pushed him along with his gun stuck in his back. Cain watched from a distance as his Pa struggled to walk the distance from the cabin to the shed. By the time the men got to where Buck thought the treasure was hidden, Vick was reeling on his feet, and ready to collapse. Finally, his legs could no longer support him and he fell to the ground.

Buck straddled the inert body and prodded Vick in the gut with his boot, saying "You better not die on me. I need you to remember where you hid my treasure."

The sheriff did not know what to do, for his friend was dying or already dead. He looked around to see Cain inching closer.

As Vick lay in pain from the gunshot wound, he felt his life slipping away. He could feel his body shutting down, and the pain seemed far less intense than before. As soon as he felt death upon him, he saw his lifeless body crumpled on the ground. He no longer felt fear or anxiety, as he began his journey down a long narrow road toward a very bright light. Vick knew he was dying.

"When I get to the end of the road, I'll be able to rest," he thought.

Suddenly, a magnificent grey hawk appeared before Vick, to lead him.

As he got close to the end of his journey, the scenery changed to a beautiful green meadow, filled with radiant flowers. It was a blissful day, more brilliant than he had ever seen.

He didn't question how he got there, for he somehow knew this was where he was supposed to be. He was at peace; no pain or worry, just the feeling of completeness. "How restful this place is," he thought. He had never before seen such an abundance of beauty, nor smelled such sweetness. Rainbows of colored flowers covered the open field, as far as he could see. Vick looked around and saw an apple tree, loaded with luscious fruit. A young girl sat beneath the tree reading a book when Vick had a sudden desire to pick an apple.

"Do you want an apple?" The little girl asked.

"Yes, I do, but are you here to guard this tree?" Asked Vick.

"No, I knew you were coming and I wanted to thank you."

"Thank me for what?"

"For keeping my book," the young girl said.

Puzzled by her comment, Vick asked. "What book are you talking about?"

"The book you kept with the treasure. You remember my diary, don't you?"

"Yes, I remember now, but I couldn't read it.

The young girl, whom he now assumed was Janie, walked over to a young boy. "That must be her brother, who was also killed by Buck," he thought. Vick continued to watch, as the two seemed to be discussing something of importance, when he saw the mighty hawk flying near another young boy.

This boy was walking toward him through an expansive field of flowers. He looked familiar, and as he got closer, he recognized his brother Sam, who had died much too young. Vick, who was happier than he remembered, began to cry as he tried to reach out to touch him, but he couldn't. Vick cried, but they were tears of joy for he never thought he would see Sam again.

"Sam, you came back," Vick said, grateful to see him.

He wanted to stay, but Sam began to explain why he could not. "Vick, you have to go back, it's not your time. I asked to see you, for you have never forgiven yourself for my death. You've always felt responsible, but you were not."

"But Sam, I'm the one who told you we should run away. You would still be alive if it wasn't for me."

"No, it's not your fault. You go and be happy! Live your life. I know you want to stay, but Hawk is here to take you back."

"Hawk is here too?" Just as Vick asked the question, the majestic grey hawk magically transformed into Chaytan, his Indian friend"

"I can't believe it's you, Hawk!" Seeing him was like it was yesterday. There was no need to speak, for their thoughts were entwined. He knew Hawk would lead him back.

Vick could not comprehend what his eyes were telling him, but in his heart, he knew it truly was his good friend. He tried to appear brave, but was overcome when he was embraced by the radiant aura that encircled "Hawk."

"I can't believe it's you."

He felt himself falling into limitless depths, as secrets were passed to him that only the wisest of men would know. Chaytan turned and held Vick's gaze. Vick wanted to reach out and touch his friend. "Was this real?" He wondered in amazement as the Indian began ushering thoughts into Vick's mind, recounting all the times he was there to protect him. Vick was privileged to see the many events were he narrowly escaped death, and slowly realized that Hawk had fulfilled his word, when he promised him that he would always be his protector.

As he watched in fascination, Chaytan metamorphosed into the hawk whose feathers changed from grey into white shimmering feathers; and just as magically, kept the eyes of Chaytan.

Vick watched as Sam turned and walked away. "I don't want to leave my brother," Vick thought, but he immediately knew that it was time to leave and follow the hawk back to the end of the long narrow road. When they got to the place where Vick had entered and before he could say goodbye, he suddenly gasped for air as he opened his eyes to see Buck standing over him.

"Is he dead?" Buck asked.

As soon as Vick came to, the sheriff sprang into action, like a man who was twenty years younger.

"Look again, he ain't dead," the sheriff screamed, lunging himself viciously upon Buck, before the Australian could even blink an eye.

Vick had never seen such a fight as the sheriff put up, wrestling with Buck, but the outlaw eventually freed himself and recovered his weapon. Just as he did so, Cain came running out of the bushes with his gun drawn, screaming "Buck, drop your gun," never considering that he was in Buck's line of fire.

"Buck, drop your gun," Cain shouted again.

"What is this?" Buck blurted.

And, the miracles continued!

As Vick watched, a hawk flew in front of Cain as if to protect him. Buck kicked the sheriff in the stomach and started shooting at Cain, while the hawk flew around and through the bullets, flapping his wings to confuse Buck. Despite the gunshots, he was unable to stop Cain from continuing toward him, as the sheriff trapped Buck's left foot in a deadlock.

"Why ain't that man dead yet," Buck wondered.

The sheriff was relentless and wouldn't let go, as he grappled with Buck who kept firing into the squawking hawk. The hawk continued to flap his wings to protect the young lawyer, who was running through bullets coming right at him. Buck was sure his bullets had hit the hawk, and he had only one more shot left to take care of Cain, who somehow continued to escape death.

"Why haven't I hit that sonavobitch?" he thought. He then fired his last bullet, but an aggressive and well-timed jerk from the sheriff made him miss.

Buck knew if he didn't think fast he was a dead man, so he dropped his empty gun. Now, with both hands, he was able to free himself from the sheriff's grasp. He raised both arms and stepped forward to confront Cain, who looked very familiar.

"Wait! Who are you? I ain't got no quarrel with you."

Cain stood with the courage of David who slew Goliath, keeping his gun pointed at Buck. For the first time Cain now recognized Buck as the stranger who had instructed him on how to use a gun. "So this is Buck Dupree," Cain thought.

Cain stood frozen, undaunted, and exhilarated to finally have the man his Pa had sought for so long, at the tip of his muzzle.

"Hey, I do know you! You're that clumsy bloke I tried to show how to use a gun. Yes, I remember now. You were trying to learn the quick draw and I helped you. Yeah, you're him all right. Listen, we can work this out, I got a proposition for you. I got a treasure out back. All I have to do is dig it up and I'll split it with you. What you say?"

Vick looked at Cain's face but did not say anything for fear of distracting him. He had no idea that Cain had met Buck before.

Buck extended his open hands, and began to walk toward Cain, saying, "Look, I have no weapon, you're not going to kill an unarmed man?" He kept inching closer, betting his life, certain the young man would not shoot.

Cain's eyes were darting around, as if he was not sure what he would do. He had never killed a man and he knew it would be something he would have to live with the rest of his life. *"Bad thing to do, but this is Buck Dupree,"* he thought, then shouted, "Stop! Don't come any closer."

There was something in Cain's voice that resonated with Buck. He instantly stopped in his tracks.

"No closer, you hear, no closer!"

For the first time in his life, Buck felt remarkably insecure. His voice softened ... "Who are you?" and took another step as he spoke.

Overcome with the fact that his Pa was lying at his feet dying, along with the pain and emptiness of the loss of his wife and child, Cain had endured more than he could stand. With great passion and rage, Cain whispered, "Vick Porter is my Pa, and I'm my Pa's son!"

Buck's eyes fell and he looked like a whipped puppy as Cain shot him in the chest at point blank range. The force of the bullet knocked him down, but Buck's breastplate prevented him from being killed. Now horrified, he was looking up at Cain. The barrel of his gun looked huge.

Buck's voice cracked, "You're Vick's son?" He looked toward Vick, who was watching him squirm as Cain towered over him. Vick nodded to let Buck know Cain was indeed his son. Cain, then shot Buck in the left leg.

"That's for the twenty years you took from my Pa."

Buck howled in excruciating pain, "Have mercy on me; if you're going to kill me do it now, don't drag it out."

Ignoring his plea, Cain now hit him in the right leg, leaving the man wailing and writhing in agony. He looked down at Buck, who was now horrified at the possibility he was going to get another bullet.

Cain stood over Buck.

"You remember the little girl that lived here? The one you killed with a knife?

Buck shook his head wildly, afraid to tell the truth.

"She identified you in her diary. I want you to die remembering the ten-year-old girl named Janie, is the one who brought you to justice."

Buck tried to slither away like the snake he was but, Cain had him. "I don't know what you're talking about. I don't know a Janie."

"My next bullet's going to freshen your mind, for it was Janie and her family you killed right here at Panther Holler, the family you accused my Pa of killing. Remember? She identified you as the man who slaughtered her family."

"Nooo!" Buck screamed in terror as Cain lifted his gun. He put another bullet in his right arm and then another in his left.

Buck's body writhed in complete agony. Cain had two bullets left.

"You killed Janie and her family. And you killed my wife … her Pa and my unborn child. May they rest in peace, and may you burn in hell! This next bullet will send you there."

"No please! Don't kill me, I'm sorry," begged Buck.

Cain had his gun cocked and ready to shoot when the hawk let out a searing screech that echoed deep into the hollers.

Suddenly a brisk, whisking sound grabbed their attention. The sound was of something moving lightning fast through the brush as if on cue. Out of nowhere, there stood a large panther snarling and growling at them.

Buck was beyond terrified and began trying to scoot away as he remembered years before when he was chased by a panther that looked much like this one.

Not only was Buck frightened, but the men were as well, for the large cat was not only looking at Buck, but each of them who were within striking distance. The sheriff had his hand on his gun as he paused for the right moment to shoot the cat.

The panther scanned each person menacingly until his eyes locked on Vick. "Could this be the same cat I shot as a boy," Vick wondered. "Can a panther really live more than twenty years?" as he followed the lines of the panther until he saw hair missing around what appeared to be an old bullet wound near the cat's shoulder.

In a split second he remembered saving Sam and Hawk from the ravaging teeth of this panther when he was a boy. Vick was perfectly calm as the animal actually seemed to recognize him as the boy who had shot him all those years ago. The panther moved toward Vick. but refocused his attention to Buck when the hawk screeched again.

The sheriff thought, "it's almost as though the hawk and the panther are working together."

Cain had his gun on the panther but lowered it when he saw the animal's focus was on Buck.

"Let the panther have his kill," Cain thought. "He's not worth my last two bullets. The panther sent Buck's breastplate flying in the air as he sprang forward clutching Buck's neck in his jaws." Everyone was horrified seeing the beast attack his prey in such a vicious way, but after all it was Buck, a man who had inflicted unbelievable cruelty to his family and many others.

Buck screamed as the cat shook him like a rag doll, while his sharp fangs ravaged through his body. Still Buck was not dead as the large cat dragged him through the thicket and into the holler.

There were ferocious sounds of a hungry beast — then nothing but silence.

Vick did not say a word. He laid his head back with a profound sense of satisfaction knowing that Buck finally got what was coming to him.

The sheriff glanced up at the tree and saw the hawk watching over them and wondered if he had just witnessed a bit of a miracle.

When the reality of what just happened soaked in, Cain ran to Vick.

Pa, are you all right. This was the first time Vick had heard Cain call him "Pa."

"Son," Vick said softly, "What you say we head home."

~

Some say the land heals itself.

The Spirit of the Earth will eventually cleanse whatever stain, evil, or infection man can bring in time. And the places, with the strongest Force of Nature, the forest, the hollers, and all the deep and running bodies of water always renew themselves the fastest.

The Earth waited a long time to cleanse itself of Buck Dupree.

There's a legend recounted in the hills of Arkansas, that many years ago, The Great Ancestors of the Original People, with a magic reserved only for great deeds, turned a young boy into a hawk so that he would protect the white man from himself.

Some say it was the hawk that brought Vick Porter back to life that day.

And there are those who say that the evil spirit that was vanquished on Buck's day of reckoning still lurks in the hollers of the Ozarks, held prisoner by the lonely hawk that circles daily over the place called Panther Holler.

THE END

Thanks to each of you for being there, listening to my insights and challenging my thinking.

Coming Attractions

The sweeping saga of **Ghost of Panther Holler**, a sequel and continuation of **Legend of Panther Holler**, is well underway with its own set of twists and turns, as Annie pieces together more of the story of Vick Porter and his son Cain.

Their journey and conflict will continue as they fight to survive unimaginable odds placed before them in this new tale of adventure, sabotage and revenge.

Please join their journey in **Ghost of Panther Holler**, and expect to meet many new characters who will take you to places you've never imagined.

Check for updates on my website **Annieclarkcole.com**

47290999R00277

Made in the USA
Charleston, SC
06 October 2015